The
SILENT
WOODSMAN

D1596337

The
SILENT
WOODSMAN

The Olympic Peninsula series #1

Cat Treadgold

The Silent Woodsman
ISBN: 979-8-9877363-0-2 (Trade Paperback)
ISBN: 979-8-9877363-1-9 (Audiobook)
Library of Congress Control Number: 2023908225

Any references to historical events, real people, or real places are used fictitiously. Names of restaurants and companies central to the plot (except when indicated in the Author's Note) are products of the author's imagination.

Cover and interior design by Cat Treadgold
Seattle, Washington
cat.tread@yahoo.com
www.CatTreadgold.com

Printed in the United States of America

For my husband, Jeff,

My JJ and my eternal flame.

CONTENTS

PART I

CHAPTER 1

———•———

FOR A CELEBRATED COUNTRY SINGER known for his sunny personality and shit-eating grin, Joe Bob Blade was feeling mighty down in the dumps.

No, strike that, he thought. Considering that his real name was Joe O'Connell, and his true identity was "privileged Irish-Catholic man with a degree from a top music conservatory," one could more accurately call his state of mind a full-blown existential crisis.

Joe paced the plank floor of the log cabin, a space the size of the bathroom in his family's Seattle mansion. His agent Linc's cozy one-room refuge—built deep in the Hoh Rain Forest back in the '60s—might as well be a kennel, and he a dog who had barked himself hoarse. That image was all too apt. Normally he would be outside, blowing off steam. Hiking, climbing trees, fishing, chopping wood, and chasing rabbits … but not hunting them. All the men in his family qualified as expert shots, but he hated the idea of killing anything other than vermin. He would rather dance with the rabbits, like Snoopy.

The woodpile was becoming a hazard. He'd ask Linc or Tom to pack in a roll of wire so he could build a cage around the damn thing. Otherwise, one day soon, he was going to be crushed beneath the giant wall of firewood he had erected. The woodpile to end all woodpiles. *Quick, notify Guinness.*

He'd been about to head out into the sea of moss when the sky opened up and dumped its contents all at once, like a faulty stage effect. Thunder boomed almost immediately after the lightning flashed. A half hour later, rain still clattered against the roof like fervent applause, enough that he started to worry that the river would overflow, and the shingle roof, which he'd just bolstered with clay and thatch, would start leaking again. Thank God the cabin was equipped with a lightning rod. He scrutinized the primitively beamed ceiling. So far, against all odds, his repairs were holding.

He fought an ongoing battle with the devil on his shoulder who urged him to test his voice, see if it had improved one iota since the operation a week ago. If he attempted so much as a squeak, they'd told him, he might never sing again. He couldn't even laugh, not that he felt like it. Or cry. *That* he definitely wanted to do.

He reached for his guitar, which leaned against the wall like a baleful entity. *You could be composing*, it seemed to say.

I couldn't be less inspired, he thought. *Maybe I need a muse, one who can do all the talking.*

He sat on one of the two wooden stumps that served as chairs and strummed, then launched into an ironic dirge version of Simon & Garfunkel's "The Sound of Silence." The guitar was a Martin D-18 1940, beat up but worth something like thirteen thousand dollars. It was his favorite, despite being the least expensive instrument he owned.

His fingers froze, and he stared at the guitar. *What the ...?* He was definitely going nuts. Had it said hello? He held the sound hole to his ear as if it were a conch shell.

"Hello, hello!"

A woman's voice, coming from outside. *Damn.* How had one of his groupies found him? In this deluge, the silly woman could be electrocuted.

He opened the door. The woman was drenched and muddy, her long black hair plastered against pale-gold cheeks, eyes huge in a classic-oval face, her slender body protected from the elements by nothing but a sodden parka and clinging hiking pants. Though wet enough to have been coughed out of a whale, she was undeniably beautiful. He nixed his groupie theory. Groupies dressed to lure, regardless of circumstances. This girl had no mascara streaming down her cheeks. Judging from her quivering and cowering, longing for warmth and shelter was winning the internal battle over fear of what he might do to her.

He invited her in with a sweep of his arm, and she approached with the wariness of a lost dog, taking a step back for every two steps forward. The cold was making her quake like a Chihuahua, whippet, no ... greyhound. She was tall, maybe five feet nine. He gave her a broad smile of encouragement, his usual expression when caught in the glare of a spotlight or the flash of a camera. Mr. Friendly.

* * *

AN HOUR EARLIER ....

Ali paused next to a waterfall at least sixty feet high, dazzled by the way it caught the sunlight as it cascaded over a cliff of smooth rock. The sun glistened on the dripping moss, lichen, and liverwort clinging to the gnarly tree limbs, snags, rocks, and nurse logs. Some of it was soft as green fur. Other types sprouted upward like coarse hair or dangled like yards of thick, yellow-brown rope. Fern fronds reached out from mossy rocks, waving indolently in the breeze. The oldest of old-growth trees, mostly Sitka spruce, western Hemlock, western red cedar, and Douglas fir, had trunks thicker than wine barrels. The misshapen branches of bigleaf maples were bent at odd angles as if poised to grab at passersby. Aside from the benign ferns, Ali was hacking her way through nettles and other defensive plants, on a trail forged not only by deer and elk, but also black bears, coyotes, and cougars—predators usually shy of humans, she reassured herself.

Her twin brother Liam and she had both fallen hard for the magic of the Hoh Rain Forest, which is why she'd come all this way to commune with his spirit. He'd wanted his ashes scattered here, but—supposedly—the explosion had left nothing of him to cremate ... or identify. Just fragments of his motorcycle jacket, part of his passport, and a battered wallet.

Funny that they'd even discussed death. Her only sibling had certainly not expected to die at the tender age of twenty-four. Eyes closed, Ali let the spray of the waterfall baptize her face. *No, he can't be dead.* Denial or justified optimism? That was the sixty-four-thousand-dollar question. She clasped the Navajo medicine bag he'd always worn around his neck. Why had he left it behind? It was supposed to keep him safe.

Ali sometimes *knew* stuff before it happened. It wasn't exactly a voice in her head, more like a random thought stream. A rare message from a spotty psychic network. An hour before she received the terrible phone call, the message had been this: *I'm not dead, but they think I am.* She'd shaken it off as natural anxiety for the safety of her brother on his first trip abroad. When the phone rang at midnight, her heart stuttered like a needle on a scratched record. As she rushed to answer, the coils of the phone cord defied her, and she'd wrangled it like a poisonous snake before finally getting the receiver to her ear.

She believed the reassurance had come from Liam himself. In times of stress, they were on the same wavelength, even with oceans between them.

Gazing upward through the dense canopy of moss-coated tree branches,

Ali realized that the light had changed. She could see no patches of blue sky. The cloud cover rendered the rich palette of greens, browns, and yellows even more vivid.

Easily disoriented, she was still confident of finding her way back. With the brush axe Liam had left behind, she'd bushwhacked a clear path that should make it easy enough to backtrack as long as she didn't venture too far into the wilderness. A machete would have been more effective but way trickier to use without maiming herself. At intervals, to serve as beacons, she'd tacked small squares of foil to snags. When all twenty were in place, she'd know it was time to turn back.

The forest was eerily quiet, save for the rushing of water in the distance. Like a thick blanket of snow, the mosses muffled sound and contributed to the heady fragrance permeating the humid air, also tinged with the scents of fir needles and decomposing wood.

A drop of moisture hit her cheek. *It couldn't be.* There had been no rain in the forecast. Another drop, then nothing. Condensation from the trees? She'd tacked up her last piece of foil. She should head back now—should have done so already. Her watch read three o'clock, and darkness fell early in the forest.

In another ten minutes, she reached a rushing stream. *Good enough.* This was the place where, if he were truly dead, Liam would let her know.

Ali heard only the rubber-band twang of frogs along with the shrill calls of varied thrushes. "Liam," she whispered, "are you there?" She sat down on a rock, next to a nurse log populated by a thicket of saplings. Louder, she said, "You guided me here, I know it." Nothing. She shook her head, disgusted at herself. She'd never been able to summon the voices. She turned the talisman over in her hands, fingering the worn leather lanyard and small suede pouch containing herbs and an arrowhead. How old was it? Who else had worn it? It was a gift from Liam's drama teacher, one of the father-figures he had sought out in high school and the only one who hadn't disappointed him.

A stream of sunlight illuminated the pouch. Could that be a sign? She kept on scolding Liam, "This is all your fault, Bro. Couldn't you confirm that you're alive somehow, pick up the phone, send me a letter? Are you in a coma? Lost your memory like in some soap opera?" Exhausted and dispirited, she slid off the rock and lay on a bed of moss next to a stream. Its babbling was almost like speech. Perhaps it would tell her the answer if she listened long enough.

A large black beetle ambled by, and a bright-yellow, black-spotted banana slug pushed alongside a rotting log. Her eyes fixed on a clump of yellow mushrooms. Fungi of every shape and size abounded in the rain forest. Maybe she needed "magic" mushrooms to commune with Liam. Not that she could tell a psychedelic mushroom from a poisonous one.

A sob escaped. It sounded so ridiculous that she laughed. For weeks now she'd been fighting the need to disassociate, to stand outside herself and observe this melodrama she'd been so unfairly cast in. Her new sad planet had too much gravity. Every time she sat on the overstuffed couch in her apartment, she ran the risk of never getting up. She thought of the supposed witches in Salem who were crushed to death by stones. This had to be the psychological equivalent.

Self-pity was not her way. She dragged herself to her feet and brushed off the seat of her pants. She'd have to hustle to return to the car before dark. If only she'd brought Liam's tent. One of his roommates had taken it camping the day she stopped by to pick up his things or she'd have retrieved it by now.

Her hiking pants were damp, and the flannel shirt over a thin T-shirt was no match for the wind. Ali put on her parka and zipped it all the way up. Where was the baseball cap? Dropped somewhere, along with the scrunchie securing her long braid.

A drop of water splattered on her head, another on her bare hand. A moment later, she was being pelted by the kind of heavy, driving rain rarely seen in these parts. A flash of lightning, clap of thunder …. Why was her shirt damp? The parka was old, and replacing it would be expensive. Between her scant barista earnings and student loans, she had to stretch every dollar to the ripping point. Did waterproofness wear off? Was that even a word? She was a fair-weather hiker. She lowered her head, slicking back her long hair. Without the bill of the cap to shield her face from the rain, the hood was an annoyance. Her hiking boots squelched in the muddy ground.

Could she make it back to the car in this weather? Her extra clothing would be useless without a waterproof coat. Would hypothermia claim her if she stayed the night? Would she be struck by lightning? No one would report her missing. Winter quarter had ended March eighteenth, and spring quarter didn't begin until April fourth. Normally she'd check in with Becca after a hike, but her friend, enrolled in the same master's program in Communication, had used the break to go to Europe with her family. When she'd last heard from her foster parents, they had been in Botswana with the Peace Corps. Liam and she had been so lucky to be taken in by serious, educated people and given so many opportunities. But they had never bonded. After Ali and Liam moved out at age eighteen, they'd nearly lost contact.

Her next shift at the barista job was in four days. How long before someone concluded that the ancient Honda Civic hatchback parked next to Highway 101 had been abandoned? What if it were stolen or impounded?

As she trudged toward the opening she'd forged in the dense foliage, Ali skidded on a mossy rock. Then, as if encountering a foot extended with malicious intent, she tripped on a root and fell.

She rolled and lay still, face up. "Liam, a little help here?" she said aloud, her voice tremulous. She was shivering. The rain had soaked through the useless parka. At least her shirt was wool, the warmest fabric when wet.

Overcome by a weird lethargy, she lay there, limp, the boggy ground sucking at her limbs. She should have sought shelter right away beneath the nearest tree—before she'd turned into a popsicle. Her hands were numb, and her teeth were chattering. Really, it was okay if this was the end. Becca would be fine—she had a large family and lots of friends. And Ali was drowsy. If she fell asleep and never woke, that would be a fairly painless way to go.

The words "Soldier on" echoed in her head, something Liam used to say if she dared rail against a pitiless universe. She was ever the good little soldier … or tried to be.

"Not this time, Bro," she whispered.

Soldier on. The words were louder this time.

She blinked away the drops of water on her eyelids and shielded her face with her arm. Then she smelled it: *smoke.* Was there a campsite nearby? She rolled onto her side, clambered to her feet, and wiped the dirt from her hands on her hiking pants. What if the keeper of the fire were a survivalist or a serial killer? What if he was the Green River Killer? Could she fight him off? A few years had passed since her self-defense class.

Close to hysteria, she let loose a crazy giggle. She was picturing Bigfoot warming his hairy hands at a firepit. If Bigfoot did exist, was he more human or ape? Could he even build a fire? Why did no one ever observe Bigfoot couples? *Come on, pull yourself together*, she told herself.

More lightning, thunder. Shining her flashlight on the column of smoke, she drew nearer.

Hallelujah, a cabin. It was made of logs, with a shingle roof, and rested on a platform amid the trees—a wraparound porch of sorts. Minus the snow on the roof, it might have been the model for the label of Log Cabin syrup. Only a lot funkier. Rustic. Not from a kit. The logs were imperfectly matched and glazed with moss.

"Hello?" she called out. She waited. If she kept just a bit of distance, she might have a chance of escaping if the occupant turned out to be a monster. Although human monsters didn't usually reveal their true natures right away.

They could appear normal and harmless. Even cute. Like Ted Bundy. It seemed like only yesterday they'd executed him. Six years ago, in 1989.

Escape where? Whoever the occupant was, she had no choice but to throw herself at their mercy.

She just stood there, unsteady on her feet, the trembling and chattering threatening to fell her like a rotten snag. The rain was back to the light pitter-patter more typical of the rain forest. It was so quiet she could hear … guitar music.

She took a few more steps, then shouted, "Hello, hello?"

A door opened and a man stepped out.

CHAPTER 2

———·———

NOT BIGFOOT OR A VAGRANT, despite the shaggy beard. Not a lumberjack. Imposing as he was in height and solidity, the man was graced with the heart-melting handsomeness of a teen idol. One of those men you'd still be able to picture as a boy, even at seventy years old. Wide, soulful brown eyes. Soft, shiny, chestnut-brown curls.

Ali hung back, more intimidated by his glossy presence than worried about being poisoned or sliced and diced. Although … he could be the type of guy Becca referred to as a "slow loris"—a sweet-looking primate with a venomous bite. He beckoned her in with an oddly tentative grin, as if just as wary of her as she was of him.

Relax, she told herself. *What are the odds of two Ted Bundys? A man on the prowl for vulnerable co-eds doesn't reside in the wilderness.*

She had almost reached the porch, her boots sucking at the mud. Her stiff limbs might have been made of butter brickle. One wrong step and they'd shatter. She couldn't feel her fingers. The closer she got, the better the man looked. She could detect gold flecks in his clear brown eyes. With a gulp, she let him help her up the steps to the platform. She was further unbalanced by a heady whiff of his woodsy, masculine scent—like a fir tree transformed into a man. A very sexy tree. His image started to shift and blur. Were those branches protruding from his head? She blinked, knowing her eyes were playing tricks on her. But the image didn't right itself; it rippled and expanded. Ah, he wasn't real after all. A mirage.

She was vaguely aware of falling backward, of strong arms catching her and propping her gently against the lumpy logs that formed the walls. Deft fingers removed her muddy boots and soggy jacket.

Then everything winked out.

* * *

JOE CRADLED HIS UNINVITED GUEST in his arms. She was not much heavier than his guitar and trembling all over. Either on the verge of hypothermia or already there.

Heaving a frustrated sigh, he carried her over to the air mattress, kicked away the sleeping bag, and laid her gently on her back. He had to get the sodden clothing off her. As he unbuttoned her flannel shirt, he noted the blue tinge of her skin and lips. In peeling off the white tee and pulling it over her head, he couldn't help but savor the fragrance of forest-fresh woman and wet wool. Next came the pants, equally obstinate. The bra and bikini panties he kept in place, damp as they were. Her body was just so ... so *sweet*. Long, sooty lashes batted against high cheekbones, though her eyes remained closed.

Adjusting his jeans to ease the pressure of his shamefully raging hard-on, he unzipped the sleeping bag to convert it into a comforter, flung it over her, and through the barrier of quilted nylon, attempted to rub circulation back into her limbs. After several minutes of frantic rubbing, she was still vibrating like an overtaxed engine. Body heat was his only option, but Lord, that was going to be awkward when she woke up. Stripping down to his boxer briefs, he crawled beneath the comforter and spooned against her slender back and round bottom. At first it felt like embracing a marble statue after an ice storm. Despite the trembling, her breathing was slow and shallow. The chill suffused his skin too until they were both shivering. Gradually, as heat crept back into their limbs and torsos, his cock stirred again and grew painfully hard. She was breathing more naturally now, a soft, purring snore that made him want to stroke her like a kitten. With a silent oath, he rolled away and made a nest of blankets on the floor.

Exhausted by the ordeal, Joe didn't wake until the first light of dawn. When he finally managed to unglue his eyelids, he took stock of the situation. One long female leg protruded from the comforter. Who was she, and how the hell had she stumbled upon Linc's cabin? What was she doing in this uncharted part of the forest? Unlike his annoyed brain, his cock reacted to her presence with wholehearted enthusiasm. She stirred and sighed but didn't wake. *God*, he'd been a monk for too long, ever since parting ways with Rina after being forced to drop out of the tour. Rina was on the opposite spectrum of female beauty from this wood nymph. She had the kind of obvious assets that appealed to the horny boy in him, the one raised on fantasies of Brigitte Bardot. His fantasy definitely had it over Rina when it came to temperament. Dealing with her shifting moods required too much energy, sapped as he was by their grueling concert schedule. In bed, she was spectacular enough to drown out his doubts whenever he reeled from an encounter with her screaming-banshee side.

Then came his vocal crisis.

Duly noting the chink in his shiny armor—another singer had to step in—Rina had not even bothered with a phone call. Instead, she'd sent him a rambling letter, saying that she needed "space" but implying they could get back together once he was "back to normal." Her callousness should have been a given. What else would you expect from a stunning, self-absorbed twenty-four-year-old? Shrewd business sense and precocious talent were rare traits in a beautiful woman. That she also be mature and compassionate might be too much to ask.

Gingerly, so as not to disturb his guest, he covered the exposed leg. He had to get his physical response to her under control. If she noticed his straining cock, she might scream herself hoarse, and then where would they be? She rolled onto her back, eyes still shut. The move caused the sleeping bag to fall away, leaving her fully exposed and prompting him to grab his jeans and T-shirt and put them on in record time. As if a wrong move might set off a bomb, he drew the makeshift comforter back up ever so slowly, watching for signs of consciousness. With the racket he was making, he was amazed she didn't wake.

He had to stop bouncing around the cabin like Ricochet Rabbit and calm the hell down. *Think.* What could she wear while he washed and dried her clothes? They lay in a soggy heap in the corner, almost muddy enough to stand up on their own. He'd have to offer her his long johns. He almost laughed, imagining Rina in this situation. She'd rather die than wear anything so unflattering. Somehow he didn't think it would be an issue for this woman.

Tiptoeing about the cabin, he boiled water and poured it into an old metal feed tub for a cowboy bath. He arranged a washcloth, bar of soap, and bath towel beside the long johns at the foot of the mattress. Then he draped a clean towel over one shoulder and grabbed the washing powder, his own soap, and the bundle of muddy clothing. Shutting the door behind him, he sighed in relief then pounded heavily on the door to wake her before the water cooled.

* * *

ALI AND LIAM ARE HIKING in an alpine meadow dotted with tiny red flowers. He urges her to hurry, keep pace with him. Only he can't talk. His lips move but nothing comes out. A bear clad in motorcycle leathers rises on its hind legs before them. Liam leaps in front, and with a roar, the bear lashes out with its huge paw. The swipe sends him flying sideways, and he keeps on flying until he's out of sight. Ali tries to scream but the sound dies in her throat.

In the darkness, a man clasps her from behind, smoothing her hair back from her forehead. She can feel the rapid beating of his heart. The nightmare has given way to a delightfully tactile dream. She snuggles closer. He is firm and smooth and smells like wood chips.

Surfacing from a profound sleep, she lingers in a semi-awake haze. Her eyes flicker open just long enough to register a sunbeam shining through a small, mesh-covered window. She squeezes them shut again. The light hurts, and her head aches.

A man looms over her—different from the other one. Frightening. His face is a blank mask of smooth skin. She raises her arms to fend him off, but then Liam appears and pulls him off her so quickly it's as if he were whirled away by a tornado or sucked into a void.

She must still be asleep—or at least hovering at the hallucinatory edge of consciousness.

Liam is sitting at a table in a café, smiling and waving for her to join him. As she approaches, he fades out.

Giant wolves covered in moss bar her way, along with banana slugs that morph into Twinkies then loaves of bread. She slams the door of the café behind her, but the wolves keep pounding.

Pounding. Wolves? With what, their soft paws and delicate muzzles?

ALI OPENED HER EYES TO a room filled with sunlight and redolent of woodsmoke. She was alone. Head still aching, she rolled to a sitting position, where it dawned on her that her clothing was missing. Naked might have been less embarrassing than the frayed, pink-lace bra and panties. The man must have undressed her. What was that clichéd bit of advice mothers typically dispensed? Wear clean underwear in case of an accident. Her foster mother wasn't given to providing words of wisdom, and she had few memories of her birth mother. Her underwear was clean enough, just ratty. She'd bet this man wore Calvin Kleins or went commando. Her face flamed as she recalled his warm body pressed against hers. How was she going to face him again?

Her gaze lit upon a metal tub filled with steaming water. The pounding had been his fist, alerting her to the bath. On the mattress lay two towels, a bar of soap, and upon closer examination, a folded pair of men's long johns bottoms and a plain white T-shirt. The labels read BPO—Big Paul's Outfitters, a high-end competitor of REI. No sign of her own clothes, which had to be filthy. Stripping off her underwear, she stepped into the tepid water and soaped her hair and body. How was she supposed to rinse off? She wrung out the smaller towel and attempted to wipe away the soap, then rinsed her hair as best she could with the remaining water on the stove and soaked her underwear in the soapy water. Washing in the river in March would be painful but a lot more efficient.

Without a brush, she had no hope of detangling her long straight hair. Hers was in her overnight bag in the car. Where was his? She couldn't start rooting around in his stuff like a pig after truffles. Anyway, using another person's hairbrush was gross, like borrowing their toothbrush. For her teeth, she found his toothpaste and made do with her finger. Her hair was too matted for finger-combing. It was just as well there was no mirror.

The pants were too large to stay up on their own. One hand clutching the waistband, she used the other to hold her own underwear up to the woodstove to dry and observed her surroundings. The interior of the cozy one-room log cabin reminded her of the troll house she'd played with as a child—a birthday present from Liam, who knew it was high on her wish list. He must have spent a few months' worth of his meager allowance. Or, more likely, stolen it. A fleece blanket and a down sleeping bag lay heaped on the air mattress, more blankets piled in the corner. A backpack stood against the wall—brand-new. She checked the label: BPO again. He *really* liked that brand. The man wasn't hurting for money.

Insistent knocking on the door, followed by silence. "Come in!" she called out in an absurdly perky voice to mask her embarrassment over her rat's-nest hair and baggy clothing. She tried not to cringe when he took in her appearance, eyes sparkling with amusement and shoulders shaking with laughter. The sound he made—a weird little huff-huff-huff, like Muttley the cartoon dog—caused him to touch his throat and wince, as if the effort cost him.

Heat suffused her cheeks and neck. He looked so … polished, in contrast to her bedraggled form. What were those dogs with the loose skin called? Shar-peis. She resembled a Shar-pei with dreadlocks.

"Um, would you happen to have a belt?" she asked him. "Or a safety pin?" She paused. "How about a diaper pin?" *Don't be a clown*, she told herself. *Just because he laughed at your silly getup doesn't mean he has a sense of humor. He could be mocking you.*

Okay, maybe he had a sense of humor. He did seem to appreciate her joke. He huffed some more, covering his mouth as if to stifle the laugh.

In vain, she tried pulling the fabric out enough to make a knot in the side of the long johns.

Having composed himself, he began to contemplate her as if solving a thorny problem. The sparkle in his eyes had been replaced with what she could swear was a smolder. *Ridiculous*, she told herself.

All business now, the man opened a metal chest that stood in the corner and located a roll of twine. Measuring out a length, he cut it with a knife and handed it over.

But her hands shook, and she dropped it. Nerves? Why not? When had she ever been alone with a man so drop-dead gorgeous? She couldn't have tied her shoelaces in her current state. She picked it up and continued to fumble with it until her grip on the long johns slipped and they slid to the floor. Though she immediately pulled down the T-shirt to cover herself, there was no doubt that she'd flashed him, and he hadn't looked away.

"Oh my God," she whispered under her breath when she noted the crimson blush stealing over his tanned face. "Cover your eyes!" She pulled up the long johns again and resumed her inept attempts to tie them up, swearing under her breath. Even if she'd had three hands, at least two of them would need to work. They refused to obey her.

He was at her side now, enveloping her in his warm, woodsy scent, sweet breath, and calm presence—evoking the delicious memory of his body pressed against hers in the night. He gently assumed control of the rope and circled it around her waist to cinch the long johns in place with a simple bow. Then he stepped back, holding up his hands as if to assure her he was harmless.

He must have read the mortification in her eyes because he shook his head and waved his hands, conveying the message that it didn't matter, everything was fine, no need to worry. And just like that, she began to relax, as if he'd cast a spell to calm her nerves. He indicated one of the stumps, bowed, and mimed pulling out a real chair, like a waiter seating a patron.

He still hadn't spoken, and no one worked that hard to do without words unless they had to. For a time he busied himself at the stove. Bacon sizzled and coffee perked, and the welcome smells filled her nostrils. When he finally turned to check on her, she asked, "You can't speak?"

He nodded, pretending to zip his lip.

"Can you hear?" He might be lip-reading.

He cupped his ear briefly in her direction as if hard of hearing, then grinned to show it was a joke. He waggled his eyebrows, as if to say, *of course*.

He pointed to the carafe on the woodstove.

"Is it drinkable?" She gave it a dubious glance.

He opened his eyes comically wide as if receiving a jolt of energy. That meant that, drinkable or not, it was strong. Weirdest game of Charades she'd ever played. As though it were a prize on a game show, he displayed the pan of bacon.

She gave him a thumbs up, hoping for something sweet and carb-heavy to go with that. She could eat a horse, at least one made of marzipan. A glazed donut would be nice. She doubted his supplies included anything so frivolous.

He poured the coffee into a mug and handed it to her, then he pulled a loaf of bread from a metal box next to the stove and cut off two thick chunks.

She slowly savored the coffee. "It's wonderful. If there's one thing I know, it's good coffee."

Acknowledging the compliment with a slight bow, he went back to busying himself at the stove. With his attention elsewhere, she was free to observe him with naked admiration. A lot of work went into sculpting a body like that. This man had done serious gym time. Did that make him a narcissist or just someone who needed to blow off steam? Was he an actor?

He wore fitted Levi's and a short-sleeved body-hugging black T-shirt, no logo. Thick socks, no protruding toes. BPO, no doubt. Suspiciously elegant and graceful. Was he a professional dancer? He could be a musician …. She'd heard guitar music as she approached the cabin, and a scuffed-up guitar leaned against the wall. It looked as if it had been bandied about by a long string of indifferent owners. Wouldn't a working musician have a spiffier instrument?

The full, unkempt beard concealing the man's lower face was his only primitive feature. His wavy hair just fell into place. There were some enviable people whose hair did that. Unlike hers, straight and slick and resistant to updos and curling irons. His smooth skin was tanned a warm, toasty shade. The slightly hooked nose kept the luminous eyes from appearing too feminine.

Though he could be a hermit who'd taken a vow of silence, she concluded he had a medical reason for not speaking.

He knew she was watching, for he did a sudden about-face, as if to catch her in the act. She couldn't stop the guilty flush. She'd been imagining his jawline beneath facial hair fit for a Sikh as well as his naked body under the fitted clothing. She should have sneaked a peek last night, while she had the chance. Tonight, life-saving body heat would not be required.

Ali sighed. If he couldn't talk, they wouldn't be discussing what happened last night, or anything else for that matter.

He reached out, and she recoiled instinctively. But it was only to touch her hair. After digging around in his pack, he produced a hairbrush and handed it over like a precious gift. But these were serious snarls. Seeing her struggle, he produced a comb. She reached out, but he snatched it back as if playing a game of keep away. He meant to comb it for her. Who would say no to that? She lifted the hair off her neck so that it fell in tangled ropes down her back.

He proceeded with agonizing slowness, working gently at the snarls. The delightful tingling in her scalp unbalanced her, and she spread her legs and planted her feet to keep from falling off the stool. As he continued to work out the kinks and snarls, she closed her eyes and surrendered. Having switched to the brush, he was sweeping it through her hair in long, luxuriant strokes, tugging it back with a gentle force that sent shoots of pleasure down her body. Whenever his fingers accidentally grazed her cheeks and neck, she shivered. All too soon he patted her on the shoulder and stepped away. When she touched her hair, she found it plaited into a sleek French braid. This guy was awfully good with women's hair. Like Liam, a man who knew his way around a woman's body. Which meant trouble. Too bad she was already putty in his hands.

"Thanks," she said, inanely, turning to face him and encountering his back.

* * *

WHAT CRAZY IMPULSE HAD PROMPTED Joe to make like an amorous chimp and *groom* his guest? Not that he was alone in this. With all the blushing and covert glances, she clearly wanted him, too. That didn't mean he could go for it. That excruciatingly hot incident with the clown pants had confirmed his suspicions. Her body was exquisite. However, no woman with any miles on her got the shakes in the presence of a man.

He took his time with the scrambled eggs to give his cock a chance to stand down. Offering his most harmless smile, he handed her the plate of bacon and eggs. Thank God she wasn't a vegetarian. Delivered a few days ago by Linc, the bacon and eggs had to be consumed before they spoiled. Though the river was cold enough for refrigeration, unattended food—no matter how well wrapped—would attract bears. In real life it was gourmet this and organic that. Here he made do with cowboy fare. Rice, black beans, canned corn, dried or canned meat, a few oranges. Nothing suitable for the discerning palate. This delicate girl looked as if she survived on nutrients gleaned from the atmosphere—like an air fern—or perhaps she followed his sister Teresa's spartan regime, making a meal of two stalks of celery, a skinless chicken breast, and half a fruit cup for dessert.

Not that she was scrawny. She was a streamlined type who rarely crossed his path, and if she did, had no interest in his gaudy life. Polite to a fault. Her beauty—evident even in men's long johns—gave her a power she'd clearly never tapped. He banished the image of her semi-naked, silky body.

What now? She'd need time to recuperate. Even if he hadn't been involved with someone else, this woman was the furthest thing from a groupie. She didn't recognize him, and besides, he'd never believed casual sex was worth the fallout. Hard experience had taught him that revealing his identity was a flagrant misuse of power. He'd seen the most sensible, principled women easily abandon their scruples when tempted by a popular singer, even one who wasn't known for his boyish good looks. He didn't want to be *that* guy.

Though the Rina situation was far from certain. Her letter had mentioned taking a "break." Did that mean she felt free to mess around? He didn't.

My God, those eyes. It was hard to believe their color was natural. Like a few shades of mountain lake with darker rings around the iris. Wide, clear, and bright, the eyes of a manga heroine. She was trying not to stare at him, savoring every morsel of her eggs and bacon, sipping her coffee with obvious pleasure. Was she even aware how he'd strained against her, in danger of spontaneous combustion?

He shook off the internal battle as he tidied up. He disliked chatterboxes, but this woman wasn't volunteering *anything*. Just the one clue: she knew good coffee. What did that mean? Was she a roaster? Executive at Sully's? No, too young.

Immediate problem: how to communicate. In writing, of course, but he couldn't pull out his journal because it was plastered with photos of Rina— pouting for her headshot, posing in a teeny bikini, breasts thrust forward like a '40s pin-up girl, strutting on the red carpet in a risqué Valentino creation. It was also half filled with potential song lyrics. The photos would open the door to questions. The less shared, the better.

What else could he write on? He rummaged around in his pack until he found a rumpled pad of notepaper with the logo of the Four Seasons Olympic in Seattle. From his mother's last fundraiser. She'd written the name and phone number of a therapist on it and he'd stashed the whole pad in his pack to appease her.

Like *he* would ever see a therapist. His problems weren't psychological. Anyone in his place would be depressed.

CHAPTER 3

———•———

FROM HIS BACKPACK, THE MAN pulled out a notepad and waved it aloft as if it were Willy Wonka's golden ticket. When he laid it on the stump table, Ali sat and took a closer look. It bore the logo of the Four Seasons Olympic—a five-star hotel. Next he pulled out a pen—not some cheap Bic, though she wasn't an expert on fancy writing implements. He might not be Bill Gates, but he wasn't a pauper, either.

Ali's one long-term boyfriend—was six months long-term?—had come from a "good" Seattle family. He was a senior, she, a freshman. They'd dated for months before having sex. She thought that meant they were serious. Sex wasn't a casual step for her after all of Liam's protectiveness. The experience had been painful, and she wasn't eager to repeat it.

Liam, busy with finishing the work for his associate degree and applying for jobs, knew only the barest details about Ali's relationship with Trip. And yet, out of the blue, he called her that day to see if she was okay. "I'm here for you," he said. "If someone needs to be set straight, you'll tell me, right?"

"Yes, I know" was all she'd said.

Nevertheless, she'd continued to see Trip. The sex was mildly pleasurable, and it had stopped being painful. *What's all the fuss about?* she thought. She was flattered that he wanted her, and he was such an impressive person—so intelligent, outgoing, and well-liked—she felt honored to be chosen as his girlfriend and believed she was in love.

Then Trip had taken her home to meet his family. His father was a patent attorney and a muckamuck in the Episcopalian Church. When they were introduced, Ali was filled with dread. The man was pale and pasty as the moon, with a combover and lips as thin and taut as rubber bands. He wore the kind of quality, stuffy clothing she associated with country clubs. Trip's mother was her husband's perfect match, slender and devoid of makeup, her shirtwaist dress exquisitely tailored. The moment their gazes locked, Ali could read her thoughts: *Who are her people? She has suspiciously dark coloring. Wrong for my boy.*

Trip dispelled her doubts, insisting that she'd imagined his parents' cool reception. After Trip graduated, she never heard from him again.

In short, she did *not* trust men who came from money. *However* … just because this guy was unusually good-looking, had once stayed in a pricey hotel, and owned nice things, that didn't make him rich, or even an entitled snob. He didn't act like one. So far he'd been nothing but kind.

The man joined her at the table. Feeling like a child dressed in her father's PJs, she longed for the dignity of her own clothes.

Leaning across the table, he wrote, "MUST not speak." She waited. "Complicated."

She was glad for her keen eyesight because his letters were teensy-weensy. Nice handwriting. Very precise, almost artistic.

"Name?" he wrote.

"Um … Ali."

"Like Ali MacGraw," he wrote. "Resemblance. Irish?"

Oddly tongue-tied, she couldn't answer immediately.

He wrote, "It's OK. Talk to me." Seeing her hesitate, he added, "In dire need of distraction."

She shrugged. "I don't know. Could be anything. We're foster children—my brother and I." It felt like an interview for a job she wanted too much. "Your turn," she said.

Thumping his chest like Tarzan, he wrote, "JJ." He kept writing, "You're lost. Why here?"

She shook her head. "I'm not lost." *God,* she was going to have to try to explain what she was doing here. "My brother and I both loved the rain forest. He's, uh … missing. My twin brother, Liam." She held up the little bag that hung around her neck. "This is his medicine bag. I thought I might be able to use it to … communicate with him." She wiped away a tear with the back of her hand.

In capital letters, he wrote, "MEDICINE BAG?"

"He was blown up in an explosion. Supposedly. I don't believe he's dead." The intensity of his gaze made her look away. "I don't know why he didn't take it with him. It was supposed to keep him safe. He got it from his drama teacher—he had Navajo blood."

The man tapped her arm to bring her attention back to him, then laid a hand on his chest and patted it, his face full of concern. "How old?" he wrote.

"Twenty-four."

"So sorry," he wrote. "Want to talk about it?"

Her whole face twitched in the effort to hold back tears. Nothing like a little sympathy to open the floodgates. After what must have been a full minute, she still didn't trust herself to speak. Observing her struggle, he held up a finger—*be right back*—and went outside. He was giving her a moment to compose herself. She tried to follow, but he was already out of sight when she stepped out on the porch. She picked up her boots and slammed them together to loosen the dried mud, pulled them on, then wandered a short way down the path, where she found him examining her clothes. They hung on a rack made of branches.

"Still wet?" she asked.

He nodded, apologetic.

She shivered, and he clasped her shoulders in a light but firm grip, turned her around, and led her back inside. For her, the gesture meant more than it should. *He isn't looking for excuses to touch you*, she told herself. *He's treating you like a child with no common sense.*

She narrowed her eyes at him. "You don't need to fuss over me. I can take care of myself."

I doubt it, his look said.

At the door, he knelt to help her remove her boots and damp socks. Then he chafed her bare feet to warm them up.

* * *

JOE HAD TO GET A grip. Tapping Ali's arm, touching her shoulders, holding her bare feet as if he had a foot fetish. Was he losing his mind? They were pretty feet, long and nicely shaped, with clear, unadorned nails. Had she believed he worried about her cold toes? Weirdly, yes. Her fawn-colored skin glowed like mobile art lit by candles.

Twenty-four years old. Somehow she seemed younger. She was back to sitting at the table, hands folded, obedient. Now that he knew about her dead brother, he recognized a kindred spirit, one brought low by misfortune. Vulnerable. He wished he could tell her not to be so trusting. She was lucky she'd landed here. She was also lucky that thoughts didn't equal actions, because his were the wolfish kind and did not match his polite exterior.

"How long have you been here?" she asked.

He sat down next to her to write, "Not long. Don't live here full-time."

She raised her eyebrows. "Vacation?"

"Sort of," he wrote.

"Can you tell me?"

"Worried about writer's cramp." He gave his fingers an exaggerated shake. "Not important. Tell me about you. Want to talk about your brother?"

This time she spoke without emotion. "Terrorist attack. Hamas. Jerusalem."

Now she was speaking in fragments too, as if following his lead. He wished she'd just out with the whole story. He was dying of curiosity. He wrote, "No TV. You're my entertainment. Don't make me beg. Hard on the fingers. It's not even lunchtime. Too early for bed." She blushed, and damned if he didn't blush too.

He lifted the sheet of paper, filled on one side, and elaborately turned it over, earning a lovely, shy smile. At the top, he wrote, "Talk away. Like listening to you. Want whole life story." Seeing her consternation, he drew a smiley face and added, "Kidding. Talk. You'll feel better. Working on Charades technique."

She blew out a shaky breath and sat, cross-legged, on the bearskin rug, wrapping a blanket around her shoulders.

"I like the rug," she said, petting it in a way that sent a dart of desire straight to his loins. "There was a bearskin rug in the troll house I had as a kid. Molded plastic, like the rest of the cabin. This place is great. It's yours?" He shook his head. "Your family's?"

He made a "sort of" gesture. He did *not* want to tell her the story of the illegal cabin, built by his manager Linc's family. It might lead to questions about his identity. He pointed to the rug. "Bear died of old age," he wrote. He slashed a finger across his throat and let his tongue loll out. Her laughter made him absurdly happy.

"Will you ever speak again?"

I'll speak again, he thought, *but will I sing?* He didn't write it down. Instead he nodded and smiled, then gestured for her to continue.

She blew out a puff of air. "All righty then. If you insist …. My brother was traveling in Israel with his friend Caleb. When the explosion happened, they were in Jerusalem, sitting at a café. That's all I know. I got a phone call from Caleb's family … then the American embassy …." She stopped.

He reached out then thought better of it. She had actually *flinched*. He had to resist this constant urge to touch her.

"We have the same coloring—eyes, hair. He's a lot taller. Your height, maybe. Six two?"

If her brother had Ali's startling blue eyes, shiny black hair, and honey-colored skin, he had to be some lady killer.

She was rubbing her temples now as if easing a headache. "I don't know what to do with his motorcycle. I don't have the keys. I can't leave it at his roommates' place in Renton forever. If I could convince someone to haul it over to my apartment, I can't park it on the street. I live in the Shoreline area, just north of Seattle. A lot of crime."

He didn't like hearing that she was surrounded by criminals. Now he had Liam pegged as a reckless, *Easy-Rider* counterculture type. Not that every motorcycle enthusiast fit that bill. Still, they weren't called donor-cycles for nothing.

"You were"—he crossed out "were"—"*are* close?" He underlined "are," wanting to appear supportive.

A frown creased her smooth brow. "I just pray he's not lying injured in some hospital. I can't imagine why he doesn't contact me."

Because he's dead? he thought. He hoped she wouldn't also confess to believing in wishing wells and fairies.

"He has this beautiful, mischievous smile," she went on.

You too, he thought, *though yours is guileless*.

"As a child, he was always up to something. Our foster parents kept us scheduled down to the minute. Getting into trouble required an escape artist. That was Liam, not me."

Joe wrote, "Your birth mother?"

Was he being too nosy? If so, she didn't let on.

"She lost custody when we were five. Thanks to her drug habit. Never saw her again." She paused, smiled ruefully, and touched his knee, oblivious as to how it affected him. "Don't look so sad. We were okay. After a few semi-rocky years—I've blocked most of the memories—we were placed with decent foster parents. We were eight years old by then. They meant well. Took us to plays—they ushered and got free tickets to the dress rehearsals. Encouraged us to read the classics. Dickens, Jane Austen, Kurt Vonnegut, John Irving …."

He gave her a broad smile, impressed by the list. A roll of his fingers urged her on.

"Taught us French they'd learned in the Peace Corps, so the accent wouldn't pass muster in Paris." He raised his eyebrows. She added, "Not that I'd know. I haven't traveled outside Washington state." A rueful smile.

"We were the lucky ones: we got to stay together. When we aged out of the system, we still had each other. George and Emily rejoined the Peace Corps. They send occasional letters—the last one came from Botswana, months before Liam disappeared. We didn't expect them to stay in touch. We weren't the easiest …. Anyway, we both went to college, Liam for two years. Got his associate degree." She paused, and her uncannily blue eyes pierced right through him. "You don't want to hear this."

"I do, I DO," he wrote. He put his hands together in prayer.

She screwed up her nose. "You must be *really* bored. I think you must be one of those great listeners. I bet everyone you talk to thinks they're the most fascinating person in the world."

He was surprised she'd seen through him so easily. Though his interest in other people's stories was genuine. Now that he was famous, he rarely had the chance to draw out strangers. He'd rather recite the catechism than talk about himself. "Not true," he wrote. "And I doubt anything you say would bore me."

Joe saw her weighing his answer for bullshit. He drummed his fingers on the table, aiming for playful rather than impatient.

She continued, "I got a degree in Comparative Religion …. Completely impractical. Waste of an education."

He wrote, "Religious?"

She seemed to ponder the question. "Is it a cliché to say I'm spiritual, not religious?" He smiled. He wasn't religious or spiritual, though he'd been raised a Catholic and sometimes went through the motions for his mother's sake. Not that he believed his mother was particularly devout when no one was looking.

"We know our birth mother was Catholic. There's no evidence she meant for us to be raised that way—no baptism certificates. I chose that major because I thought religion and philosophy might provide answers. I could use some now." Her eyes glistened, and though she sniffed back tears, her voice remained steady. "But no, I don't believe in a specific entity. I *do* believe there is *something* out there. Something that created us. We are too complex to be the result of a cosmic accident. The more I studied religion, the more ridiculous it all seemed. The stories are so similar and too implausible. Virgin birth. A messiah. Death and rebirth. Spontaneous healing. Religion has always been a tool of control for those in power. The opiate of the people. You know, according to Karl Marx." She paused, then added in a smaller voice, as if admitting something shameful, "Only … I've had some weird experiences. Sometimes I just know what's going to happen. Usually it's a voice in my head or a random thought stream. This time the voice belonged to Liam himself." Deepening her timbre, she said, " 'I'm not dead, but they think I am.' " She looked up at him and gave a rueful laugh. "From your face, you'd think I just claimed to channel Ramtha. Listen, disregard all that. You pushed my religion button and I overshared. You? I mean, do you believe in God?"

He grinned, amused rather than irritated by her rant. He hadn't realized his skepticism was so obvious. He shrugged, not wanting to appear judgmental. "I believe in soul mates," he wrote. "You know, Aristophanes. The missing half. Your brother?"

"Yes," she said with fierce conviction.

He wrote, "I'm a twin too."

She lit up. "Then you understand. A brother?"

He nodded. Needing to veer away from yet another road that might lead to his identity, he wrote, "If you know anything, it's good coffee???" Three question marks.

She gave him a quizzical look. "Oh, the comment I made earlier. I'm working as a barista while I get my master's in Communication."

He grinned, appreciating the irony, and she laughed.

"What does Liam do?" he wrote.

"He's the practical one. A machinist at Boeing. He was always resourceful, even in high school. Could fix anything. Sold some pot."

"They believe he's dead," he wrote. "With no body, how can they be sure?"

"It happened in early January. That was months ago. No one matching his description lay in the morgue or was checked into the hospital. But … wouldn't there be *something* left other than pieces of his motorcycle jacket, passport, and wallet?" She avoided his eyes, staring out the window. "As far as I know, he had no reason to disappear. If he was escaping the law or a pregnant girlfriend, wouldn't that have come to light by now? Perhaps he joined the CIA and couldn't tell me."

She wasn't kidding. Her look dared him to roll his eyes. He didn't. It took some effort, but he kept his expression sympathetic and open. He didn't want her to start censoring herself.

"He could be in a coma, too altered to identify." She gulped back tears and stared into space, as if seeing him lying in a hospital bed, face disfigured. Shaken, she whispered, "Believe me, I've mulled over the possibilities to the point of absurdity."

A silence stretched between them. He wrote, "Communication, huh?" He stifled a laugh, then added, "Barista. At Sully's?"

"No, not a chain. An independent coffee shop. I can do wonders with foam."

He wrote, "Do you like working there?"

She gave him a reproving look. "It's hardly my dream job."

He raised his eyebrows as if to say, *Then what?*

"People from my walk of life don't get to have dream jobs, do they?"

He shrugged. *Why not?*

"What do you do?"

"Dream job," he wrote. He pursed his lips. "At least I did. We'll see."

"You're not going to tell me, are you?"

He wanted to smack himself for indulging in self-pity and revealing too much. He shook his head and wrote, "Way too complicated." As a diversion, he added, "I travel a lot."

"Are you a salesman?"

Jeez, she was as relentless as any investigative reporter. Isn't that what you did with a degree in Communication? He wrote, "In a sense."

He gestured throwing the ball into her court, needing to get the attention back on her. He even mouthed the words, "Dream job?" and cocked his head.

She laughed. "You're putting me on the spot."

Such a melodic, merry sound, her laughter. Not like Rina's, which seemed calculated to make her the center of attention. *So what?* he argued with himself. *She likes being a celebrity. What's wrong with that? Just because you hate it ....*

"Okay," Ali went on, "something involving travel—like you, maybe. Something creative. Foam designs on coffee are too ephemeral." He grinned. "I like to draw, and I think I have a good eye for design. Not sure it's enough. Creative professions are hard, and I have school loans—I can't afford to 'follow my bliss.' Liam's drama teacher tried to interest him in pursuing a stage career. When he told me, he treated it like a joke. He said, 'No money in that,'—she lowered her voice in a humorous imitation of her brash brother—" 'You and me, Alf, we gotta be practical, keep our eyes on the prize. No bowl-of-cherries life for us.' " In a normal voice, she added, "You know, he'd have killed it as an actor. I don't know about the talent, but he had the charisma. And the looks."

"You too," he wrote and smiled, aiming for harmless.

Then he thought, *Alf?* Like the short, furry alien with the long snout? He supposed his sister had endured some crazy shit from her four older brothers.

No cruel nicknames, though. The one incident that came to mind was David trying to stuff Teresa down the laundry chute.

Shit, here he was, hamstrung by the limits of the written word and nonverbal communication .... No way to grab the moment. He thought of how great it would be to simply chat about everything and nothing with her in the days before his voice became a limited resource.

And let loose a long sigh.

CHAPTER 4

ALI COULDN'T BELIEVE SHE'D SPILLED her guts like that. She didn't want to wear out her welcome. JJ didn't seem in a hurry to send her home, and she certainly wouldn't be the one to bring this magical interlude to a close.

He'd thrown together a stew of dried beef, beans, and rice for lunch, surprisingly good. When he returned from washing dishes, he also had her dry, clean clothing tucked under his arm.

"Thanks!" she called out after him, but he was already out the door, carrying soap and a towel.

After dressing in her own clothes, Ali visited the curiously neutral-smelling outhouse. Finally she sat, fully dressed, on the bed. Seeing a book lying atop his pack, she went over to pick it up. Ken Kesey's novel, *Sometimes a Great Notion*. The bookmark was an unused postcard with a drawing of a guitar, its caption, "Nashville. Music City USA." Was he into country music?

The waiting brought back a memory of Tim, a friend of her brother's she was crushing on. She'd lied to Emily and George, saying she was going to a movie with Becca, but her date had been with Tim. He never arrived. Later Liam casually mentioned that he had "warned Tim off." The guy never spoke to her again, and Liam told her a year later that Tim had gotten a girl pregnant and nearly OD'd on crystal meth. He'd wanted a medal for saving her from that creep, but she just stormed out, yelling, "You're not my father!"

Fortunately Liam had retired as her protector when they both started college. After the fiasco with Trip, she almost wished her brother was still in the chaperone business. He might have saved her a lot of grief. Yet he always seemed to sense when she needed him. She hadn't dated much after Trip.

Almost all the guys made their move after just one date. She was disgusted by their impatience and didn't see what was in it for her. When, during her sophomore year, she'd finally felt chemistry with a guy in her Introduction to Philosophy class, she'd given sex one more shot. Luis was from Puerto Rico, and like her, he had olive skin and vivid eyes, only his were green. He hadn't changed her mind about sex, but he had made her swear off casual sex. Told that she didn't want to keep seeing him, Luis had refused to let her go. So she'd turned to Liam, who delivered the message more forcefully by paying him a visit. Whatever he said—or did—worked. She decided that Liam was companion enough in the scant free time she enjoyed when not working or studying. After her best friend Becca returned to Seattle from Princeton and her various summer internships, Ali was truly content. Then … no more Liam.

Would sex be different with this man? Her body seemed to think so.

Ali put the book back where she'd found it and sat down at the table with the pen and notepad, doodling a woman with the body of a guitar. Suddenly bone weary, she laid her head on the table.

Hearing JJ on the porch removing his boots worked like a shot of adrenaline. When he saw her, he brightened, shoulders a little straighter. His defenses were back up in a flash. Had she imagined his response? He came over and picked up the sketch.

His eyes widened. He mouthed the word, *Wow.*

Though pleased, she shook off the compliment. "That's nice of you, but it's just doodling. I was passing the time, that's all."

His hair was wet and slicked back, revealing a broad forehead with a widow's peak, and his tanned cheeks were ruddy from bathing in unheated water. From the faint lines on his forehead and the beginnings of crow's feet at the corners of his eyes, she guessed his age at something like thirty. Along with being far more than six years ahead of her in experience, he outclassed her by a mile. Even if he was attracted to her, it was only because she was Eve to his Adam—his only option.

A yawn escaped. "Sorry! I shouldn't be so tired. I must have slept nine hours last night. I did dream more than usual. My brother, a leather-bear, and giant banana slugs." No need to mention the recurring dream that had been with her for as long as she could remember.

"Leather-bear?" he wrote.

She took the pad and drew a tiny bear in motorcycle leathers, its claws prominent and teeth protruding.

With a snort of silent laughter, he wrote, "I love it. A stand-in for what?"

Pretending to concentrate on the drawing, she filled in a few blades of grass at the bear's feet.

He wrote, "A guy who made a pass at you?"

She nodded. "That was the last time Liam let me visit when his motorcycle club was meeting."

She couldn't quite read the way he was looking at her. Speculative. Clinical, almost.

"Take a walk?" he wrote. "You'll do the talking." Noting her panic, he added, "Silence is OK too."

* * *

JOE LED THE WAY ALONG the river. Did one of the "voices" Ali mentioned guide her to Linc's cabin? Linc and his brothers had forged the narrow path they followed now. The few trails in the area of the cabin had to be cleared constantly to prevent nature from reclaiming them. Linc had been his manager since the beginning—eight years back, when Joe was twenty-two and fresh out of music school.

Whenever Joe was troubled, the rain forest had soothed him. Not this time, with his voice missing in action. Then Ali had arrived, injecting a glimmer of hope into his pity party. With her in it, the spartan cabin seemed like a cozy refuge. And now, as they followed his favorite trail, he couldn't imagine another woman so in tune with these surroundings. In her calming presence, he was rediscovering this magical place, catching little details like a pungent whiff of skunk cabbage among the robust aromas of earth and rotting wood. Before Ali, he'd almost stopped noticing the burbling of the streams and the rushing water of the river, the discordant whistles of varied thrushes, and the elaborate chirping of song sparrows.

As a child, Joe learned to identify the trees from their larger-than-life father, a handsome giant of a man with a megawatt personality to match. "Da" had been self-made, an engineer turned businessman. From the time his children could walk, he'd instilled in them a bone-deep love of nature. The monstrous bigleaf maples with their gnarled arms fired up Joe's imagination the most, but Da had also taught them to differentiate between the evergreens, beginning with their bark—thinking they were too small to observe the rest at close range. As he grew older, Joe realized how much the bark altered with age. Needles and cones were more reliable identifiers.

When Brian O'Connell died of lung cancer at fifty-two, the family had lost its "mother" tree—"father" tree not being a thing. The family unit splintered and never fully recovered. Joe and his twin Jake had been nineteen.

Edward, the oldest, used the priesthood as an excuse to shun secular life, which included his worldly family. David's journey led him to practicing medicine in the hot spots of Africa. Teresa and Jake felt compelled to walk in their parents' shoes, even though, Joe suspected, those shoes were a bad fit. Teresa was a socialite, if that could be called a profession, and Jake took over the reins of the family business. As CEO of Big Paul's Outfitters, Jake was successful, respected, and … ill at ease. Or so Teresa told him. Jake had played guitar in high school but had rejected music as a frivolous pastime—a view their mother shared. So, pursuing a career in popular music made Joe a black sheep. Even after his songs shot to the top of the charts, Carrie O'Connell continued to monitor the progress of her son's life in reluctant glimpses, like a kid at a horror show. The scandal sheets gave her plenty of fodder. As for Jake, the giant chip on his shoulder plus a tangle over a woman had left the brothers with nothing to say long before Joe's vocal cords crapped out.

If only Joe could talk …. No doubt he and Ali could discuss trees, ferns, and mushrooms for hours on end. Rina and the word "nature" did not belong in the same sentence. What did he and his girlfriend talk about, anyway? Their careers, mostly, or *her* career. Music. Other musicians. Face it: with Rina, talk wasn't really the point.

Which brought him back to Ali. With her long hair in a braid, he could better appreciate the elegant contours of her bone structure. Did she have Native American blood? Unlike any other beautiful woman he'd met, she didn't seem to realize her power. She was shy and unassuming, reluctant to presume upon his hospitality. In this situation, Rina would be climbing the walls, whining for a hot bath, her curling iron …. Hell, her eyelash curler.

What was the matter with him? He hadn't felt this negative about Rina before Ali arrived. The contrast between the women didn't work in his girlfriend's favor. Which wasn't fair. He was assuming an awful lot when it came to this newcomer. Putting her on a pedestal. Yes, Rina had disappointed him. That didn't mean he didn't still love her.

Waiting for Ali to catch up, Joe almost followed an impulse to reach for her hand. Instead, he pointed to the fallen log that spanned the stream to form a bridge. She crossed with no fear.

On the other side was a grove of bigleaf maples. "They're dancing," she said, eyes shining with delight. The trees' limbs were angled as if they were doing a traditional native dance around a campfire, like in the old Hollywood movies.

A large drop of rain pelted his nose. *Shit*. He hadn't thought to bring their jackets or even hats. By the time they reached the cabin, they were both soaked to the skin.

As Joe stoked the fire in the stove, Ali took off her flannel shirt and held it near the heat to dry, unaware that her white T-shirt had turned transparent. With a frustrated sigh, Joe removed his own wool shirt and draped it over the food storage box. Then he hung her flannel shirt on a hook. Having offered one of his T-shirts, he reluctantly turned his back while she slipped it on.

While Ali sat at the table, sketching, Joe mixed up another stir fry, with corn and canned chicken this time, tortillas on the side. Before bringing the food to the table, he stopped to admire the sketch she'd drawn of the dancing trees. Simple as the lines were, she'd captured the essence of the magical scene. There was even a small campfire at the center.

As darkness descended, they ate in silence. Unless prompted, Ali wasn't inclined to talk. Too bad. He loved the sound of her voice.

Having no other nightcap to offer, he brought out the Scotch, though she'd probably prefer Port or sherry. He couldn't drink himself—might as well pour battery acid on his vocal cords. It was a Glenlivet, eighteen years old. She accepted a cupful and sipped, making a small grimace.

"You're not drinking?" she asked.

He nodded, pretending to grab his throat and struggle for air.

"Alcohol makes you asthmatic?"

Argh, he thought. He shook his head again. He tried making an X in the air in front of the bottle and an X in front of his throat.

"You're an alcoholic but you keep it around to show how strong you are."

He shook his head with an amused, though silent, snort of air. That sounded like a plot point in a cheesy novel. He waggled his finger at the bottle, then at himself.

"Um, you can't drink"—he circled a finger in the air in a "you're on the right track" gesture—"right now," she added.

Bingo. Relieved, he gave her a thumbs-up, and she sipped some more. Hmm ... he didn't want her to get drunk, just relax a little. *God*, he hated not being able to clarify. Making yourself understood through speech was complicated enough.

In the loaded silence that followed, he cast about for a diversion. His guitar, of course. After giving it a quick tuning, he began to play. Slow Spanish music, starting with a solo from Rodrigo's *Concierto di Aranjuez*. She leaned back against the wall, listening with rapt attention and sweetly parted lips. When it was over, she laid a hand on his arm, and said, "You play so beautifully. Please go on." That one light touch flipped the switch back to full readiness. *Jeez*, how could this artless woman have such a powerful effect on him?

It was dark in the cabin and quiet, other than an occasional crackle from the dying fire in the woodstove.

He played on, enjoying her blissful languor as much as the buoying effect the music had on his own flattened spirits. She appeared lost in thought, unaware of his hungry eyes raking over her as he played, imagining her enjoying every wicked thing he wanted to do to her. After the final chords from Granados' *Andaluza* died out, the soft purr of her breathing told him she was asleep.

Then it hit him. He would have to put her to bed. *Again*. He almost groaned aloud. He suspected she wanted him every bit as much as he wanted her. Ergo, *he* had to be the strong one. If he'd had sleeping pills, he would have taken two. But his doctor didn't trust him with knockout drugs, depressed as he was and all alone in the woods. He might sleep through a visit from a hungry bear or a psychotic backwoodsman. For that, he had the shotgun. It had occurred to Linc that Joe might use the weapon on himself, but Joe argued that he could hardly stay out here alone with no protection. Not wanting to scare Ali, he kept the gun hidden. Shooting at targets might pass the time, but he never fired guns here. The cabin had been built illegally, but once discovered by the park service had been allowed to stand under a strict lease agreement that probably didn't permit the use of firearms. Even if it did, the distinctive noise would carry a lot farther than smoke. God forbid another visitor—one who recognized him—should show up.

He thought about leaving Ali where she was, dressed and covered with a blanket. But then she'd be sure to wake up, disoriented, and stumble into him. He lifted her easily into his arms. In her sleep, she snuggled against his chest, making him ache for her. *Lord, give me strength*, he thought as he laid her on the bed, removed only her hiking pants, and tucked her in. He almost fled to the tent Linc had erected in a secure enclosure nearby, but Ali might panic if she woke to find herself alone. In the cabin, there was only one sleeping bag but lots of extra blankets, and he slept hot anyway. He ground his teeth at the prospect of one more restless night on the floor.

CHAPTER 5

———•———

ALI SLEPT FITFULLY, AWARE OF the steady patter of rain on the roof. When she finally reached full consciousness, it was dawn. JJ was sitting on one of the stump stools, absorbed in his novel. He wiped a finger under his eyes and sniffed. Was he crying? She'd seen the movie of *Sometimes a Great Notion*. All she recalled was Paul Newman with his severed arm propped up in a boat, giving the world the finger. She didn't remember crying, and she cried at movies all the time.

What was up with his voice? Was his condition life-threatening? Did he have throat cancer? With his clear, bright eyes, shiny hair, and impressive muscles, he appeared to be at the peak of health. He clearly wasn't looking for sympathy, but her heart went out to him.

After last night, she was ready to conclude JJ was a classical guitarist, despite the battered old guitar. She was sick of the sound of her own voice. When it came to self-revelation, the man was sealed up tighter than an oyster. He might as well be a superspy or a criminal on the lam. What was this dream job of his? What did his voice normally sound like, and what was wrong with it now? What was he doing in the middle of nowhere? What did he look like without the beard? She might never know the answers to these burning questions.

"Good morning," she said when she was fairly sure his eyes were dry. He started, seemed to shake himself out of a reverie. "What are you reading?" She didn't want to admit she had snooped.

He held up the book for her to see.

"Good?"

An emphatic nod.

Silence. She hated that she was the only one who could break it. Finally she said, "Do you play classical guitar professionally?"

Amused, he shook his head. She wanted to scream.

"I feel as if I'm stuck in a *Twilight Zone* episode of *What's My Line*. Are you a mime?" He cocked his head and wrinkled his nose—*Really?* "A Broadway dancer." He snorted. "A comedian." His chest was heaving with silent laughter. "An air traffic controller. A sword swallower. A maître d' at a really fancy restaurant. A voiceover guy. I know, you're the one who says, 'In a world …' in the movie previews." Now he was just shaking his head, not in denial, more like she was a hopeless case. She scooted off the air mattress and, too late, realized she was wearing nothing but the T-shirt he'd loaned her and her bikini panties. She grabbed a blanket to cover herself. He had the grace to look sheepish. She cast about in desperate confusion, seeing her hiking pants folded on the mattress. "No peeking!" she demanded, and he covered his eyes, though his lips twitched so noticeably that she worried he'd break his silence, no matter what it cost him. "Okay, you can look now. Not that you need to look. Sheesh."

She threw up her hands and went over to the stove to help herself to coffee. It was brewed strong enough to wake Sleeping Beauty, no kiss required. But she could swear the coffee beans were top of the line.

* * *

SHE'S ADORABLE, JOE THOUGHT. THOSE Cupid's-bow lips looked even more tempting in a mulish pout. He itched to pull her into his lap.

What was he going to do with her? He'd expected her to lose patience with his vague replies before this. In her place, he would have insisted she put her cards on the table that first night. He should escort her back to the road this very morning. Eliminate the temptation in order to avoid disastrous consequences to his health and her well-being. But he was too entertained. He seriously considered lying about his identity just to get past that roadblock. She'd presented some helpful suggestions. Sword swallower. *Ugh*. Air traffic controller. *Hmm*. Big dead end conversationally. A lot of science he didn't have the faintest notion about. Of course, he could easily deflect technical questions, having no room to elaborate in writing. Airline pilot? He'd need a voice for that too. They were expected to chat up passengers, talk to air traffic controllers. What if she was into aeronautics or aerodynamics? Unlikely. Her brother Liam, maybe … not her. Stupid idea anyway. Joe was too honest.

34

He'd rather swallow a sword than lie. He would just have to keep changing the subject.

"What next?" he wrote. Weirdly, she appeared to panic. *Oh.* She thought he was talking about sex. Cursing his instant physical response, he quickly elaborated, "What were your plans, after you finished"—his pen hovered as he searched for the word—"communing with Liam?"

She breathed easier. "I was going to stay in Port Angeles and hike. There's a loop that starts at the Heart of the Hills campground on Hurricane Ridge. I'll save that for another trip."

He'd hiked that trail. It was far too challenging for a lone hiker. What if she were injured? "Tough one," he wrote, "twelve miles. Steep. Alone?" He waggled a finger at her.

"I always carry pepper spray," she said, defensive.

He wrote, "Wouldn't stop a bear or a man. The real danger: a sprained ankle or a broken leg."

"I've hiked it before, twice. Never alone. With Liam, in fact. Have you? Hiked it, I mean?"

He wrote, "More than once. Not recently. Not for a long time. Too long." He wished he could still appear in public without having to don a disguise to avoid overzealous fans. He could see her imagination was back in overdrive. Had he revealed too much? *Jeez*, now she was going to ask him why he didn't hike his favorite trails anymore.

Instead she said, "After Liam and I moved out of our foster parents' house, we started hiking together, mostly just east of Seattle on the I-90 Corridor. One three-day weekend, he took me camping at Lake Quinault. That summer, we went to Kalaloch and Lake Crescent, where we stayed in the cabins. God, I love all those places!" Her arms flailed enthusiastically. "The Cascades, the Pacific Coast, the Peninsula …." A flush rose in her cheeks, and she averted her eyes. Her excitement was totally endearing. Too bad it embarrassed her. How great it would be to show someone so unspoiled the rest of the world. But maybe, like him, no matter where she went, she'd pine for gray sands, craggy cliffs, and moss-covered forests.

A frown creased Ali's brow. "Our foster parents … we never took vacations. Do you know Tokeland? There's the coolest turn-of-the-century hotel there, next to Willapa Bay. My best friend Becca took me there for my birthday." She stopped, bit her lip. "You don't want to hear all this."

He wrote, "I do! I'm listening" and raised his eyebrows expectantly.

She blinked. "You can't be serious."

"Lake Quinault Lodge?" he wrote.

She smiled. "I would love to stay there someday. Liam and I ate dinner in the Roosevelt Room."

"Boyfriend?" he wrote, studiously casual.

She blew out a breath, as if the suggestion were preposterous. "No," she said, for once maddeningly uninformative.

"Too busy?" he wrote.

Her voice was strained. "I don't want to talk about this."

Now he was worried. Had she been abused, raped?

"My life so far has been work and education. My freshman year, I had my first steady boyfriend. It didn't end well." She hesitated. "But I was young. Few early relationships do."

He wrote, "Liam?"

She shook her head. "No. He was super protective when I was in high school, but he made it clear that once I graduated, I was free to make my own mistakes. I think Trip qualifies as one of those."

"Trip?" he wrote.

"It seemed serious. After I met his parents, everything changed. I don't think I was the type of girl they had in mind for their son. Not white enough, maybe. Soon after, Trip graduated. Not only from the UW, but also from our relationship."

"Liam worried about you dating in high school?" Joe wrote.

"He wasn't great at relationships himself," Ali said. "He was the first to admit that, when it came to women, he was a rake."

It was a comical mental image: Liam gracing the cover of a historical romance—leering seductively, manly chest bared in an open pirate shirt—but Joe managed to keep his amusement under wraps.

"Women couldn't resist him. Like lemmings over a cliff. When I was a kid, he saw every man who so much as glanced my way as an existential threat. And now … well, it's Seattle, you know. It's okay. I've got other fish to fry. I'm almost done with my master's degree. I need to concentrate on getting a job—a job with a future."

Ah … he understood. Her first boyfriend had been an entitled jerk. And now, she was too beautiful. Men needed encouragement to approach someone so intimidating.

She was watching him now, shyly, those amazing blue eyes glassy with desire. "You?" she said. "Wife, girlfriend, boyfriend, uh, partner?"

Great, now what was he going to tell her? He'd started it. He could tell her he was gay and end the story right there. But did he really want to end the story? *End the story, damn you,* he admonished himself. He didn't care who thought he was gay, but lying didn't come easily to him. *Tell her about Rina.* Rina. Was there still a Joe and Rina? Should he really remain committed to a woman who scampered away like a startled mouse at the first sign of weakness? Scratch that. Mink, not mouse. Nothing plain about her and really nasty when the mood struck her. If Rina hadn't been a goddess in the flesh— more jealous Juno than he was comfortable with—would he have even *liked* her? Of course. They had music and fame in common, which was huge. She could be sweet and funny too. Before Ali had appeared, he'd ached for Rina every single night. Ali's presence had, temporarily at least, snuffed that fire out. For Joe, it was usually "out of sight, out of mind." Seeing Rina again would be the test. Whatever he felt for Ali, Rina was unfinished business. With their common manager being Linc and the duets they'd written together, their lives were hopelessly enmeshed. Everyone's fantasy couple.

He could see that his hesitation was fraying Ali's nerves.

He wrote, "I am *not* free." Underlined "not." When he looked up, he saw distress in the swimming surface of her extraordinary eyes. He'd meant, *My life is a prison, my relationships all strained by the pressure to stay on top, my daily existence plagued by the relentless tabloids and the need to navigate the shifting loyalties of my fickle fans.* She'd heard, *I don't want you.*

He went over to the stove to prepare lunch. It was one thirty, and she had to be as hungry as he was. She didn't attempt conversation while he cooked because she was fully absorbed in sketching—or "doodling," as she too modestly called it. While serving the plate of rice, beans, and dried beef, he recognized himself in the sketch, bowed over his guitar, his face in profile. Only she'd left off the beard. The sketch was good enough to grace an album cover—except that she'd gotten the jawline all wrong.

CHAPTER 6

———·———

HE WAS *NOT* FREE. WHAT did that mean? If he were married, engaged, or even just seeing someone, why not say so? *God*, how she wanted him. Not only was he kind and sympathetic, but unless a jaw like Jay Leno's was hidden under that beard, he looked like a classical Greek statue come to life. Who knew such a man existed? From her experiences with Trip and Luis—and listening to Becca and observing Liam and Becca's brother Nathan—she'd concluded all handsome young men were self-absorbed, vain, and on the prowl. The only way to interest them was to play hard to get, and once you gave in, they moved on. This man seemed down to earth, immune to male vanity. She thought of her brother, his fierce love for her versus his indifference toward the women he pursued, all of whom seemed interchangeable and silly. If she didn't ask to be introduced to a particular girlfriend, he didn't bother. JJ didn't seem like that.

If he was part of a couple, what was he doing here alone? On the other hand, lots of men camped or hunted on their own because their significant others had no interest in roughing it.

The silence had thickened until it felt like a wall. Should she ask point-blank for clarification? No, she had to let it go. If he had feelings for her, he'd find a way to let her know.

He wrote, "So quiet. Are you thinking of Liam?"

"Yes," she lied. But then her thoughts did go to her brother. She put a fist to her mouth, and her eyes stung. "I keep trying to rewind the clock. What if I'd traveled with him? He invited me, offered to pay my way. So we could have an adventure together. But I didn't like his friend Caleb—the way he looked at me—and he planned to stay with the guy's family. I know the facts all point to his being dead."

She thought she'd been holding it together remarkably well, but now, the dam burst. Tears coursed down her cheeks. In an instant, JJ was at her side, holding her while she cried. After she calmed down, he found a clean bandana and handed it over. His strong arms had felt so wonderful. Had they tightened in a way that was the slightest bit sexual? She hadn't imagined the frantic thumping of his heart.

"Change the subject?" he wrote after a retreat to the stump.

She joined him at the table, leaning over to read his note. She cast about for a neutral topic. "Tell me what kind of music you like."

"You first," he wrote.

"Okay, I'll start, but you have to say the first name that comes to mind." Seeing his brow furrow, she explained, "I mean, something in the same ballpark." He appeared game. "Carole King," she began.

He scratched his head. "Gordon Lightfoot," he wrote.

"Really?"

He wrote, "Singer/songwriter. Everybody does his stuff."

"Okay, close enough. Ravel."

He wrote, "Debussy."

"Very close!" Their common ground delighted her. "Madonna."

He grimaced and wrote, "Dolly Parton."

"Really? She's a songwriter. Madonna isn't. But they're both strong ladies. Hmm … James Taylor."

"Yes," he wrote, "and Johnny Cash. Hank Williams."

His aspect darkened. The awkward pause caused her to babble, "Becca introduced me to popular music. Foster children don't collect CDs. While we did our homework, my foster parents played King FM classical radio and a lot of Beatles—no other pop music. Liam and I had to discover it on our own." He didn't move to pick up the pen. He was waiting for her to continue, his expression receptive. "I met Becca at the private high school we both attended. In the library. She asked me if I liked the book I was reading, and we got to talking. I'd noticed her in some of my classes, but I was shy and I didn't have many friends. She was a social butterfly. Liam and I were scholarship kids, of course."

She paused, thinking he must be feigning interest. "Uh, I'm going to use the, uh, facilities." When she returned, he was putting food away, the dirty dishes sitting in a plastic tub. "How do you keep the outhouse so …

neutral?" He opened the bottom of the stove and pointed to the ashes. "You use woodstove ashes?" He nodded, smiling.

She pointed at the dishes. "Can I help?"

He wrote, "Only if you want to watch me bathe too."

"Is that an offer?"

At his startled look, she wanted to take it back.

"I'd like to take a dip too," she said, as if offended by his correct assumption. "I still feel the soapy residue of that tub bath. It's a beautiful day."

He mimed shivering.

"I know it will be cold. I'll probably just wade in and splash water on myself. You can let me do the dishes."

He shrugged as if to say, suit yourself.

* * *

How had he let her talk him into this? He watched, riveted, while she stripped down to her bra and panties and waded in until the water reached her knees. Her hair, freed from its braid, rippled enticingly about her shoulders. She had to know he wouldn't look away. Was *she* trying to seduce *him*?

Before his body could protest, he plunged in, a bar of biodegradable soap in hand. Gasping, like the coddled rich guy he was. Might as well dive into a bowl of ice. Not wanting to send the wrong message, he kept his boxer briefs in place as he washed himself, his clothing, and the dishes. Damned if she wasn't tracking his every move, and he could prove it. He tossed her the soap. Though she might have caught it squarely if it were dry, it was too slick. A moment's juggling, and she trapped it against her flat stomach, grinning in triumph. He shook his head in amusement.

She slipped on a mossy rock and fell forward, sputtering as her head emerged from the river. The water was shallow, but those rocks and broken branches could be treacherous. The current grabbed you and yanked you downstream. By the time he reached her, she was already steadying herself, and he'd gained too much momentum. This time they both toppled together in a clumsy embrace. Cursing himself for causing this situation, he grasped her by the armpits, lifted her up, and draped her over his shoulder. The trip to shore was slow and awkward as he stepped carefully to avoid sharp rocks and more slippery footholds. Which meant plenty of time to endure the sweet agony of prolonged contact with her velvety skin.

Once they were on dry land, she slid down his body until they faced each other, startled and shivering. That was when she kissed him. It was a tentative kiss, but it did the trick. She let him press against her as he coaxed her mouth into increasing boldness. Finally, gasping, he held her at arm's length until they both breathed more normally.

She didn't speak, but regret and humiliation were writ large on her face. Even if he could speak, he couldn't think of a simple way to reassure her that there was no need for either. He had enough regrets for both of them. He didn't want to regret taking advantage of her vulnerability as well.

He tossed her a towel then rubbed himself dry as he tried to think clearly. *Damn it, too late to lead her back to the road today.* In an hour, the forest would be too dark to navigate, and the hike would take an hour and a half. In the dark, even he would lose his way. *Another* night together, tortured by lust. Maybe they'd just mess around. Could she handle that? Could he? Wouldn't that be worse than keeping his hands to himself? Like eating one salted nut. On the other hand, sometimes a taste of pie was enough. Pie, for God's sake. Salty nuts. Sex had hijacked his brain. Okay, mind made up. *Keep it neutral. Lie to her if necessary. Get through the night. First thing in the morning, she's gone.*

* * *

ALI WISHED THE GROUND WOULD open up and swallow her. She'd thrown herself at him, making it clear exactly how inept she was and ruining everything. As he pushed her away, she'd seen the resistance in his eyes and suddenly felt like Pollyanna Gone Wild.

Back at the cabin, JJ pretended the incident at the river had never happened, and she had no choice but to follow his lead. She was back to wearing his long johns, at least until her own clothing dried. This time he didn't offer to help comb her hair. She was so mortified, she considered skulking back to the car like a dog with its tail between its legs, but that wouldn't restore her dignity and, at this late hour, might prove fatal.

She was back at the table, idly sketching to pass the time, her subject the banana slug monster from her dream. It was rearing up on the back of its foot—the body part's actual name. She tried to make it look menacing, but she had to admit, it was really cute … for a slug. Thanks to the big eyes on the end of its tentacles. Teeth would have helped, but this slug had such a small mouth, there was only room for three jagged-looking protuberances that looked more like toothpicks. On its way to building a small, sluggy campfire. She lost herself enough in the process that she didn't notice JJ until he stood over her.

41

"Real slugs don't have teeth," she explained. "It's hard to make something look fierce if it has no teeth or claws."

"Big enough, it could slime you to death," he wrote.

She gave a little huff of laughter. "Slime isn't really slimy. It looks gross, but it's kind of a cool substance that can be used as a salve. It even disinfects."

He raised his eyebrows in a "you learn something new every day" expression.

"And they're great for the soil. At least banana slugs are." She could tell he was looking for context. "Encyclopedia Britannica, at the library," she answered. "After seeing our first banana slug, Liam and I were curious. We didn't have a lot of entertainment. No TV, for instance. Sometimes, on weekends, we watched TV at Becca's house. In general, my foster parents disapproved of anyone with money, and Becca's family is loaded. They moved here from New York when Becca was entering tenth grade."

Knowing she was babbling again, she lapsed into silence. Weirdly, he seemed to hang on her every word. Then his expression blanked again as he returned to his place by the woodstove.

He gestured to the iron skillet.

"Looks good," she said. Though skeptical, he gave her a large helping. She tasted it. "Spam? You're good with spices. The potatoes and onions help." She forced a smile. "It might be my new favorite dish."

He gave her a stiff bow. Was it her imagination, or was he on edge?

"Look," she said, "I'm sorry for what happened. I won't … it won't happen again. I'll be out of your hair first thing tomorrow."

The sun had burnished his nose and cheeks, and for a moment she was lost in appreciation of his male beauty. She shook it off and tried to concentrate on eating. He did the same.

Clearing the food, he brought out the whiskey again. For a man intent on keeping things G rated, that seemed like a reckless move. She picked up the bottle and read the label. "Would you say this is a good whiskey?" His smile at the doubt in her voice annoyed her. "I'll take that as a yes."

He kissed her hand and held it to his hot cheek. She almost swooned. He placed a deck of cards on the table and began shuffling them with daunting expertise. Was he a professional gambler, like Omar Sharif? Other than the beard, the resemblance was striking. That irresistible combination of boyish charm, convincing empathy, and wicked intent. A person might not want to admit to being a gambler. Didn't they travel a lot, from tournament to tournament?

"Do you gamble for a living?"

His mock-stern look said, *Not that again.*

"I'm sorry," she said in a tight voice. "I know you're determined not to tell me. Maybe you're an escaped convict."

He clicked his tongue. Obviously not. He was a gentleman who drank expensive Scotch—or at least kept the good stuff on hand for visitors—and played guitar like Segovia. He probably played billiards too. And polo. On the other hand, lots of guys were famously self-reliant despite being educated and well mannered. Just look at Henry David Thoreau. Obviously, JJ had no problem fending for himself in the deep, deep woods.

"Are you a CEO?"

He slashed a finger across his throat then held his palms together and bowed as if in apology. Okay, no more speculation. She got it. He handed her the deck of cards, waiting for her to name the game.

"Gin rummy?"

He gave a slight nod of approval, and, while she cut the cards, lit the kerosene lantern so they could see their hands. She won the first game, or he let her win, because after that he beat her relentlessly. The silence grew textured. Every time she focused on her cards, she would look up to see him watching her, his expression unreadable in the dim light of the lantern. Fatigue weighed her down like an invisible blanket. After the fourth game, he put the cards aside. The animation he'd shown during the games drained away, but the weariness she observed wasn't physical. He extinguished the lantern, leaving only the flickering fire in the stove to relieve the darkness.

A realization snapped her back to full alertness. Whenever they discussed music, he either perked up or deflated entirely. Both extremes. He denied being a classical musician, but he might aspire to be one. Or he could be a musical performer in another genre, possibly a singer/songwriter like Gordon Lightfoot. Was that why he was so devastated by the loss of his voice? If he had a day job, a high-level white-collar position, he still might wish to pursue the creative life fulltime. After the mention of Johnny Cash and Hank Williams, she'd caught a flash of intense pain, quickly squelched. She thought of Rod Stewart—having a rough voice never stopped him. Could JJ be an opera singer? She couldn't name one current star in that profession.

Surprising even herself, she bent over and wrapped him in her arms, intending to comfort him rather than start anything. He stiffened, and she realized her mistake. She was pulling away when his arms stole around her and he pressed his mouth to hers. His soft lips and searching tongue tasted sweet and hot as he devoured her mouth, turning her body to liquid fire. Kissing Trip had *never* felt like this. Too quickly he broke away, gasping. Along with the burning desire in his eyes, she saw determination—determination to nip this in the bud. Wearing him down would only turn their sweet idyll into something sordid. He had his reasons, and she had to accept that they were valid.

He still held her at arm's length, breathing ragged, eyes pleading for understanding. She pulled away and wobbled to her feet. No wind, no rain, just silence. JJ opened the door to the cabin and stepped out onto the creaky porch. He beckoned, and she joined him. Again, the kiss might never have happened.

Suddenly she was desperate to leave. She couldn't bear this—whatever *this* was—any longer.

The silence, punctuated by the soft croaking of frogs and the hooting of an owl, grew more comfortable as they gazed at the half-moon and dense mat of stars. She pointed. "Is that the North Star?" He indicated another one. It was, surprisingly, not the brightest star in the night sky. If only he could talk. *If only* …. Everything would be different. Or would it? Sometimes words just muddled things further.

Sensing him weakening again, she decided to meet his gaze at the precise moment he turned on his heel and went back into the cabin. The narrow window of opportunity had closed. Her sigh echoed in the stillness.

When she came back in, he was wearing his barn coat. He pointed to the bed, caressed her cheek, and left the cabin. She wanted to call him back, tell him *he* could have the bed. But what choice did he have, really? If he stayed, they both knew what would happen. He must have somewhere else to rest his head.

She lay awake for a long time, listening for his returning footsteps.

CHAPTER 7

———٠———

THE NEXT MORNING, ALI AWOKE with the sun, serenaded by a deafening chorus of birds and lured by the smell of coffee and the sizzle of frying meat. She lay still, eyes closed, thinking. If only she understood why he kept blowing hot and cold. All of this was as outside her experience as winning the lottery or surviving a shark attack. If they had sex, who would find out? *No, no*, that was wrong thinking. Even though he had fired her up in a way she hadn't known was possible, what made her think it wouldn't fizzle the way it always did? *Because it won't*, a voice in her head said. *This man is different.*

She flashed to the angel in *The Bishop's Wife*. When Cary Grant's angel left them at the end of the movie, he erased Loretta Young's memory of him. How else could the woman have had any chance of future happiness with David Niven's wimpy bishop? If JJ let her go, how could she love again, knowing that such a man existed?

Oh God, she had to get out of here. JJ was not going to marry her and rescue her from her sad little life. She would have to rescue herself. If life had taught her anything, it was that. Or was it *Pretty Woman*? *Ah*, the wit and wisdom of a movie about a prostitute who finds true love with a ruthless CEO.

Pull yourself together! What if JJ left his wife or girlfriend for you? Would you be okay with that? Nice as he seems, irresistible as he is, he's a complete wildcard. If he's willing to cheat on her, he'd cheat on you, too, in time. You're not that much of a naïve idiot. Or are you?

Ali opened her eyes to find JJ watching her, waves of conflicting emotions passing over his face in that brief moment. He quickly returned his

45

attention to the frying meat. Then he held up a mug of coffee, enticing her to come and get it.

She wriggled into her hiking pants and crawled out of bed to accept the coffee. With a tight, closed-mouthed smile, he handed her a plate of meat and potatoes. He also set a bowl of warm water draped with a washcloth on the ground next to her. Then he pointed outside, made a step toward the door, and counted to ten on his fingers.

"Back in ten?" she asked.

With a nod and a brisk salute, he left the cabin.

After she drank the coffee and ate as much of her breakfast as she could stomach—what, he couldn't bear to be alone with her anymore?—she washed her face and put on her flannel shirt and socks. Finally she shrugged into the nasty old parka and her backpack and reluctantly ventured outside to pull on her boots, recalling how gently he had helped her with her footwear that first afternoon. There it was again—the universe grinding her down with its heel.

Soldier on.

Was that Liam's voice? Or had Ali merely absorbed her twin into her consciousness? Who knew anymore? She could have sworn JJ returned her feelings. Wishful thinking had usurped her usual common sense.

Outside, the ravens were having a screeching contest. The dripping moss sparkled in the sunlight. JJ was chopping wood over by a western red cedar three times as wide as his broad shoulders. She looked up, unable to tell where the tree ended. It seemed to pierce the sky.

JJ drove the ax into a stump and unrolled his sleeves, depriving her of the sight of his glistening biceps. She gave the woodpile a doubtful glance. How long was he planning to stay in the cabin? This pile could keep Burning Man in business. Catching her look, he broke into that sheepish grin that made her stupid with lust.

He was breathing hard from the exertion, but she thought she saw a sigh escape. Reaching into his pocket, he withdrew a scrap of notepaper and handed it to her. It was a four-line poem:

> The Fates, it seems, have played us both for laughs
> They stole my voice and snatched your other half
> But, darlin' girl, your courage is profound
> Whatever's lost can turn up safe and sound.

He took her in his arms and rocked her. Tears spilled down her cheeks. This was goodbye, then.

An impulse made her slip the lanyard with the medicine bag off her own neck and loop it around his. At first he resisted, but she was determined that he keep it. "You need this now. I hope it gives you comfort, keeps you safe, and helps you heal. You're grieving too. Right now, it seems like your voice will never come back. Obviously, everything rests on that. 'Whatever's lost can turn up safe and sound.' That includes your voice." She kissed him on the cheek and turned to go. He started to follow.

"There's no need," she said over her shoulder. "I told you I wasn't lost. I left a trail of breadcrumbs … well, something like that. Nothing edible. I can find my way back to the road." But his mouth was set in a hard line. He was going to ensure she made it back safely.

When they reached the first piece of tinfoil, he grinned at her and just shook his head.

"Primitive, I know," she said. "The foil was a backup plan in case I lost track of the trail I cleared with the brush axe."

He took down the foil and shook it at her. Though tempted to plead ignorance, she knew what he was asking. *How many sheets?*

"Twenty. That's how I knew when to stop … when they ran out."

He blew out an exasperated puff of air. Now he knew how many to retrieve. He wasn't going to leave her markers in place so that she, or anyone else, could find him again.

She kept silent as she navigated her way out of the forest, systematically removing the foil squares and handing them to JJ, who followed close behind. No point in speaking when he couldn't answer. As if to mock her dark mood, the day was gloriously sunny, and when they passed the majestic waterfall cascading down the smooth rock ledge, it was crowned by a rainbow. After the flood, God sent a rainbow as a sign to Noah that his ordeal was over. Or so the Book of Genesis said. There would be no metaphorical rainbows in Ali's future unless she made them happen. The days to come were going to be grim, but she'd survive. She always did.

Soldier on. The words were so loud in her head that she stopped and looked around for Liam. Noticing her hesitation, JJ waited for an explanation. She waved her hand to indicate it was nothing and continued on.

When they finally arrived at her Honda Civic, JJ gave it a dubious glance.

"I know it's not much to look at, but it runs fine," Ali insisted.

JJ blew her a kiss as he backed away. When he collided with a tree, he turned around to face his destination. Without embarrassment. She wanted to believe he was memorizing her face, that he was as reluctant to leave her as she was him. More wishful thinking.

When she started up the car, she caught one final glimpse of his red flannel shirt. He had waited to make sure it would start. If only it hadn't.

* * *

As JOE TRUDGED BACK TOWARD the cabin via his usual route, he pictured a cloud over his head with little thunderbolts, like that Al Capp cartoon character. He didn't do noble gestures, and this one didn't sit well. For one thing, he hadn't helped Ali in her hour of need, just made things worse. And his own situation now seemed even more oppressive. The foil scheme had been kind of brilliant, though it might have spelled disaster for him. Might as well string fairy lights along her route and hang a sign, THIS WAY TO THE CABIN. Along with the beat-up Honda that looked ready for the wrecking yard. If it had been towed, what would he have done? Taken her back with him? He'd have been forced to confess. Would that have been so bad? Yes, yes, *yes*. Outside of fantasy fiction, such unions did not thrive. This way she would find a nice, normal guy who could give her children. *Gorgeous* children. He could see them now, black haired and blue-eyed …. *Stop it*.

Once he reached the cabin, he fell backward onto the air mattress. He was wiped out. Last night he'd tossed and turned in the tent where Linc slept during his brief visits. Linc wouldn't appreciate him using his sleeping bag, not that he needed to know about Ali. His manager was due to arrive with supplies tomorrow. Joe didn't need to explain where the extra food had gone, and anyway, Ali didn't eat much. Linc's only concern was with Joe's welfare. No one approved of him being here alone. But Joe was a stubborn cuss, and they knew better than to push.

Who would have believed a woman so sweet and trusting still walked this earth? A literal babe in the woods. A wood nymph with a sense of humor, sweet like fresh fruit and surprisingly gifted, with her whimsical doodles. Had she left the drawings behind? He picked up the notepad, flipped through the one-sided conversation. There was the comically menacing leather-bear, the banana slug—had a slug ever looked so adorable?—and the dancing trees. You had a rain-forest children's book right there. Other than that, the woman/guitar hybrid remained. The picture of him playing the guitar was gone. *Damn*. He wished he'd hidden the notepad. Although really, he was lucky she hadn't taken the entire thing as a souvenir. He fingered the medicine pouch, thinking she'd regret the gift when Liam came back. Maybe it *would* help Joe recover his voice. *Jeez*. Now she had *him* believing in her magical thinking.

All those guesses about his profession—what a trip. The hours flew by in her company, a true vacation from himself. Now the time he'd sworn to remain secluded yawned before him like a prison sentence. *It's only ten days*, he told himself, *not the rest of your life*. He wasn't being forced to read Dickens aloud till he kicked the bucket like that poor devil lost in the Amazon in *A Handful of Dust*. Not that he didn't like Dickens—most of it, anyway. Reading *Barnaby Rudge* aloud might be up there—or down there— with singing "MacArthur Park" in concert every night. *Damn*, now he had a really bad earworm. Why had someone as talented as Glen Campbell decided to record it?

Being able to read any book aloud or sing "MacArthur Park" sounded like an unobtainable fantasy now. Being able to do *anything* aloud. Laugh, for instance. He'd never met a woman who made him want to laugh as much as Ali. Her upbringing had been almost as pitiful as Oliver Twist's, especially in contrast to his own silk-lined coming of age. He couldn't imagine being callously passed around to one person after another who barely tolerated you. And yet, the end result of all that hardship was *her*. God help him, he didn't even know her full name. There had to be thousands of Ali's in King County alone.

And she had no way of finding him. No one but his family called him JJ. *Well done, you idiot.*

Lyrics started coming into his head to preface the stanza he'd written for Ali. Reaching for his guitar, he sat back down on the stump, idly picking and strumming.

CHAPTER 8

———

A WEEK AFTER ALI'S RETURN to civilization, she received a small package in the mail. Her heart was in her throat when she saw the return address: a post office box in Jerusalem. No name, and the handwriting wasn't Liam's. She tore it open to find wadded pages from the *Jerusalem Post*. Buried within was a plastic toy soldier.

Relief flooded her. *Soldier on.* Liam was alive! With trembling fingers, Ali carefully shook out each of the newspaper pages. No note. Was he injured, held captive? Whatever his situation, clearly all he could manage right now was to send her this sign—or ask someone else to send it. He wanted her to stop grieving, to know that he'd contact her when he could. Until then, she'd have to pretend he'd died in that explosion. It was not as if this proof would satisfy anyone but her. She had not been pressed to finalize anything. In the absence of a body, Washington State didn't let you declare a person dead for seven years. Liam's suitcase had finally arrived. Without checking its contents, Ali set it atop the tower of boxes containing his other possessions. The little soldier stood squarely in the middle, waiting for his master to come home. Stacked in the corner, the primitive shrine took up too much space in the studio apartment, as if Ali had begun to pack for her own journey. She hoped a new beginning did lie ahead. Right now she felt boxed into a corner.

Liam, please don't wait that long to come home.

BECCA CALLED AT TEN SUNDAY morning, the day before third quarter was to begin. "Hey, Ali. What's going on?" Though Becca had lost most of her New York accent, she still tended to drop her Rs. Which was odd because her

French Rs, at least to Ali's untalented ears, sounded completely authentic.

"Hey, Becca," Ali said in a normal voice, as if her life had not undergone a sea change since their last conversation, "how was the trip?"

"Oh, you know, Paris is still Paris. A little less romantic when you're with your family. But more interesting now that we are all older and acting less like doofuses. The looks on the faces of Parisians when we speak French is priceless. They are so confused by cultivated Americans. You up for brunch?"

"Sure. Yanni's, I presume?"

It was their usual haunt, a Greek coffee shop across from the historic Fremont Bridge. Seattle's Fremont neighborhood—the self-declared "Center of the Universe"—featured a giant troll made of steel and concrete that clutched an actual Volkswagen Beetle, a sixteen-foot statue of Lenin, and several other oddities. Once affordable, the neighborhood was being overrun by wealthy California transplants. Most of the quirky apartment buildings and modest houses had been replaced by ritzy condos and townhomes.

Ali parked on the hill near the charming old Carnegie Library with its stucco exterior and red tile roof, pulled up the hood on the new parka she couldn't afford, and stopped for a moment on the corner to watch a sailboat with a tall mast pass under the drawbridge on its way along the canal. Seemed like poor weather for sailing, but you could wait a long time for a clear day this time of year.

Through the window of the café, Ali locked eyes with her friend, a coffee mug raised to her lips, and gave her a cheery wave before coming in.

After they hugged, Becca observed Ali with concern. "Jeez Louise! You look exhausted."

"Gee, thanks," Ali said as she sat down and removed her jacket. Becca never minced words. Ali found her straight speaking refreshing. Normally.

Becca jabbed a thumb at the raindrops rolling down the window. "I didn't miss the wet stuff."

"April in Paris," Ali said. "Must have been nice! I'd love to see Paris in any season. Here we just get April showers."

"Name a month in Seattle without showers," Becca said as she scanned the huge menu, even though they always split a feta cheese and spinach omelet with whole-wheat toast. "It was March in Paris, technically. The chestnuts weren't in blossom." She tossed the menu aside. "Spill."

"Huh?" Ali checked the tablecloth. "Did I spill some coffee?"

Becca gave her head an impatient shake. "Don't play dumb. You seem different, jazzed. What happened? Did you hear anything more about Liam?"

At Ali's smile, Becca's eyes widened. "Is he alive?" she whispered.

The toy soldier story elicited a skeptical grunt. "*Hmph.* I know you don't believe he died in that explosion, but Ali, that is so farfetched. There is no rational explanation for his not contacting you by phone, letter, *something.* What if you still haven't heard from him in seven years?"

Ali sighed. "I'll cross that bridge when I come to it. No one knows about the 'Soldier on' thing but you. Can't the little soldier give me one slim ray of hope?"

Becca picked up the menu again as if noticing a new item. Time to change the subject.

"I like your outfit," Ali told her. Not that it needed to be said. She always liked Becca's outfits. Becca came from old money, and her parents were generous. Today she was wearing a short, flowing, multi-colored skirt, '50s-style cashmere button-down pink sweater, and high-heeled knee-high brown suede boots. In contrast to Ali's usual Levis, T-shirt, and tennis shoes. While Ali could probably pass for a boy if she cut her hair, Becca was all woman and flaunting it, with her curly brown locks piled high on her head, Grecian-goddess style, her large eyes rimmed with liner, her full lips a vivid red. Not believing she could carry off anything more elaborate, Ali limited herself to mascara and lip gloss. But in Seattle and vicinity, it was common to scorn cosmetics of any kind. Standing, the two women appeared to be close in height, thanks to Becca's big hair and heels. Becca was actually five-foot-five, four inches shorter.

"Hey," Becca said, raising her coffee cup, "a toast to our last quarter of school. Working world, here we come!"

They clicked coffee cups. "I'll miss school," Ali said, "but not the debt."

Becca made a face. "God, I hope this degree pays off. If only we'd chosen more practical undergrad majors. I can't believe I was lazy enough to major in French Literature. And you, Comparative Religion." Touching Ali's arm, she said in a gentler voice, "I wish I could help you out financially. You've always had to struggle. If only you could have come to Princeton with me."

It was a sore point for Ali. Princeton had accepted her, and the scholarship offer had been generous. Not generous enough. The University of Washington was infinitely more affordable, but even though a scholarship covered her tuition, Ali had to take out loans to pay for her dorm room, meals, and car expenses. During grad school, Becca stayed in her parents' Windemere mansion while Ali found the cheapest apartment available—in Shoreline.

Ali reached across the table to squeeze her hand. "I don't blame your parents for forcing you to move in with them during our program—or you, for accepting their help. In your place, I'd totally have gone for it. If they were going to pay your tuition, they didn't want to shell out for living expenses too. You're a wonderful friend. Don't feel sorry for me. I'll get by. I always do."

Becca's parents were funny that way. They could have bought their youngest daughter a condo in Seattle or let her live in one of the rentals they owned. What they gave and held back had never been consistent, and it drove her friend nuts. Becca hated being so dependent on them.

Bursting with her news, Ali couldn't hold back any longer. "Something else happened while you were gone."

Becca leaned forward, rubbing her hands together in anticipation. "Go on."

"I met someone."

Becca's eyes widened. "And …?"

"I wanted to stage a little ceremony—to commune with Liam somehow. To find closure. I thought, where else but the Olympic Peninsula? We both loved the Hoh Rain Forest. I took the Edmonds Ferry and drove to Port Angeles, past Lake Crescent and Sol Duc Hot Springs, and parked along 101."

Becca's head was cocked, her expression one of obvious skepticism.

"Listen, I know how you feel about this kind of thing. Don't worry, this is about a flesh-and-blood man."

Becca leaned in, cradling her chin on her hands. "Continue."

After Ali had finished speaking, her friend remained uncharacteristically silent. Finally she said, "Ali, you took some crazy chances there. That is one weird-ass story. You're basically telling me you met the"—she made air quotes—" 'man of your dreams' and narrowly escaped being seduced by a man who might have infected you with an STD or kept you captive as his sex slave."

Ali gave a little bark of laughter. "Way to take all the romance out of it."

"Way to tell it like it is, you mean." Becca waved her hand around. "Okay, okay, we'll give him the benefit of the doubt. Let's say he wasn't just too embarrassed to explain the herpes to you. Or didn't have a condom. You think he's got another woman, is that it?"

"The herpes and condom thing would also explain it. But I do think he's committed to someone else."

"What if he was just being a gentleman? Nah. That would make him one in a million. I don't know any man who would turn down a roll in the hay— uh, moss—with a woman who looks like you. It does make a great story, but sweetie, you're going to have to move on quickly. For whatever reason, Mr. Man in the Woods passed on you. If he wanted to see you again—was even toying with the idea—he would have given you his contact information along with that sweet little poem. Or at least asked for yours."

Ali nodded, thoroughly deflated. Out of the side pocket of her purse, she withdrew the drawing of JJ and passed it to Becca.

"Cute," her friend pronounced after a long moment. "Very cute." She slid the sketch back to Ali. "Someday you're gonna make that mad talent work for you."

"That would be great," Ali said. *Not the way my life is going*, she thought. Becca would freak out if she knew how many times Ali had sketched JJ from memory.

ANOTHER REALITY CHECK AWAITED HER. A letter telling her that George and Emily had been killed in a motorcycle accident in Botswana. In the back of her mind, she'd always wondered if she and Liam might revisit that relationship as adults. That she might finally be able to express her appreciation for everything her foster parents had done for her.

"Oh, Ali, I'm so sorry," Becca said when she called to tell her the news. "I know you hoped that someday they'd be proud of you."

"I suppose. There's been plenty to be proud of in the past several years, if only they'd paid attention. I do wish I had a chance to tell them thank you."

Becca was silent. Ali knew how little she cared for Emily and George and their parenting style. "Do you want to come stay with us for a while? You know my parents always love having you as their guest."

"You're all so great. No, I'll be fine."

LATER, ALI STOOD ON THE tiny balcony of her apartment, watching a particularly vivid sunset gray out. What would be the next shoe to drop? One made of cement, probably. Right on her head. She had taken for granted that Liam would always be there for her. But he'd been cruelly snatched away. Then she had met JJ, who under other circumstances might have turned out to be her "eternal love," the ideal romantic soul mate Birkin described in the closing of D.H. Lawrence's *Women in Love*.

Even the most amazing sunset fades quickly, she thought. *Why would anyone with a track record like mine dare believe happiness as mind-blowing as that could ever be within reach?* Liam would never brood over a girl he hardly knew, no matter how strong the attraction. It was time to put away childish things, find strength in what remained behind. *Great*. Was she quoting the Bible or the William Wordsworth poem Natalie Wood recites in the most depressing great-love-thwarted movie of all time, *Splendor in the Grass*? Besides, what did remain behind? Precious little.

Ali had to throw off this maudlin mood. *Cheer up*, she told herself. *Get a job, look to the future, stop expecting some man to come along, swoop you up, and take you over the rainbow, where we all know, thanks to Dorothy, happiness is also an illusion.*

SOON AFTER THE START OF spring quarter, Ali quit her barista job for the more flexible hours of freelance caterwaitering. Those gigs didn't include health insurance, so when Ali and Becca finished their program with top grades and stellar recommendations, the pressure was on to find a position with good benefits.

As of July, no prospects. Ali was desperate enough to consider applying for another barista job, this time with Sully's, a large chain that offered health insurance.

"You can't do that," Becca insisted. "What's the point of taking on more debt if you're just going to go back to food service?"

They were hanging out on the couch at Becca's parents' house—a colonial-style mansion in the snooty community of Windermere, in easy walking distance of Lake Washington.

"I have something to confess," her friend said, avoiding her eyes. "I got a job. My parents, you know. It's with a private PR firm in Issaquah."

Ah, Ali thought. *Those Princeton and family connections sure do come in handy.* Then was ashamed. If an opportunity like that fell into her lap, she wouldn't hesitate to seize it. Aloud, she said, "That's great, Becca!" Then she quoted, "Issaquah … when the wind blows, you can smell the cows."

"Not anymore," Becca laughed. "Issaquah's all grown up. They have a theater and a cool little outdoor shopping mall called Gilman Village— my parents were early investors. Made up of renovated mining and farm buildings." She assumed a comically hangdog expression. "I'm sorry, I wish I could have finagled a job for you, too."

Ali's laugh was a little forced. "Don't be sorry. Something will come along."

Becca laid a hand on hers. "Of course it will. In the meantime, there's good news for you too."

Ali waited, trying to appear open and receptive.

"My parents own a rental house in North Bend that was just vacated. They said we could live there, both of us. No need to pay rent, just utilities."

"That's too generous," Ali protested.

"You know they can afford it," Becca countered.

Of course they could. That wasn't the point, but Ali wasn't in a position to turn down such kind offers. "North Bend," she repeated, picturing in her head all the towering trees and snowcapped mountains, a friendly town tucked between two rushing rivers. "It's beautiful out there—but isolated. Unless I can find a job in Issaquah too, I might face a tough commute."

"So … your car is reliable and doesn't use much gas. The bus would take you most places. Think positively. Why don't you temp? I've heard of people getting jobs that way. You're still working for the caterer, right? Most temp jobs are covering for someone while they're on pregnancy leave or sick leave or jury duty. But sometimes they're looking to fill a position. You're the fastest typist I know."

Ugh, Ali thought. She'd learned to type in high school, and after six years of higher education, it was still her most marketable skill.

A cozy house in North Bend would sure beat her dingy apartment in Shoreline. Why not? Except that, what if she did get a job? Few companies were located anywhere near there.

CHAPTER 9

———•———

MERE DAYS AFTER ALI'S DEPARTURE, Joe was too restless to remain in the woods. Every inch of the cabin seemed haunted by her presence. Why had he been in such a hurry to send her home? Why hadn't he simply told her who he was? How would he find her now? She'd only divulged her nickname. Ali was short for what—Alicia, Alessandra, Alice? She was a barista in an independent coffee shop. The name Ali was fairly common, but given the combo of Ali and independent coffee shop, he should be able to locate her in a matter of days or weeks. He could have a police sketch made and show it around. But hold on …. Say that he did find her during those few weeks he'd be in Seattle recording the album. What then? He wasn't fool enough to believe that the impressions of a few days were reliable, especially with dazzling beauty scrambling the brain.

Rina was his reality, a flesh and blood beauty—flawed, but who wasn't, when it really came down to it? Joe tried to think back to the beginning. His doubts about Rina hadn't set in for months. Was he really willing to chuck their relationship, maybe compromise their professional standing, to take a chance on a woman he barely knew?

One thing was certain: he was going stir crazy. He had to get back to civilization, away from this stifling pocket of memories of Ali, and get his head clear.

As agreed in advance, Linc had arranged for Joe to spend the following seven weeks in a rental house on a large, wooded property near Four Corners Road, just outside of Port Townsend. Basically a luxurious cabin in the woods. It had been chosen for its proximity to an excellent voice therapist who Linc had convinced to come out of retirement for Joe's sake. Joe would coax his voice back into use under Bill Sweeney's supervision a little longer each day. As far as his recovery timeline went, he was erring on the side of caution. Rather than the recommended week of total vocal rest, he'd committed to two. During the seven weeks in Port Townsend, Joe's only contact would be Bill's therapy sessions and checkups with an otolaryngologist in Sequim. If all went well, Joe would return to Seattle on May seventh to record his next album. He already had ten solid songs under his belt. If the new song, "Babe in the Woods," passed muster, that would make eleven. Rina and he had written two duets together. That came to thirteen. Hmm. Should he add another song? In some cultures thirteen was considered lucky. He'd booked the studio for five weeks. If they followed through with their plans to include the duets on this album, Rina would join him in Seattle in June to record her part.

He had trouble picturing Rina in the Emerald City. Talk about a fish out of water. That is, a colorful, warm-water tropical fish in frigid Puget Sound. He'd often wondered if Rina was just too exotic for him.

For the trip to Port Townsend, Linc had brought along a small chalkboard and chalk for Joe to communicate with, but he hadn't had much occasion to use it, not that Linc could read the chalkboard in the car without taking his eyes off the road.

"Okay," Linc said, "last time we communicated, we agreed that from now on you will tour for no longer than two months, with Larry Wales sticking around to keep your set manageable. After you leave the tour, Rina and Larry will continue on in smaller venues." Linc paused, and Joe could swear his manager was sizing him up to see how much he could handle. "There are rumors about Larry and Rina hooking up. Rina denied it six ways to Sunday. I might have believed her had it not been for the photo that's been making the rounds in the tabloids. Larry's like a younger you, only slighter and a tad shorter, and he's got blond highlights in his hair. Looks a little like Brad Pitt. He can't hold a candle to you, but I wouldn't have signed him if I hadn't seen his appeal." Joe didn't like the pitying glance his manager shot his way. "You all right?"

Joe shrugged off the question and kept staring straight ahead at the road. Was he jealous or relieved? Both, he guessed, not to mention pissed off. Rina was a hard habit to break, and he was powerfully conflicted. However, if she'd really dropped him that quickly, that meant one sexy headliner was as good as another to her, giving any self-respecting man second and third thoughts about keeping what they had going. Larry was a few years behind Joe in stardom status, with only one well-reviewed album under his belt and just a few hit songs. Joe was twenty-nine, on a par with Rina fame-wise. Unlike Rina, Joe would be over the moon if he never had to sign an autograph or see his photo in a tabloid again. Larry was the same age as Rina, twenty-four, and fame was still novel and exciting. Rina was more famous than Larry, and that power dynamic would appeal to Rina.

There were no traffic lights, meaning that Joe couldn't weigh in, so Linc continued, "I really like the lyrics to that new song. Can't wait to hear how you set 'em. It's gonna be months till Rina comes to Seattle to join you. You don't have to confront her now. That kiss might have been one-sided. You couldn't tell from the photo. If that's the only evidence, best to keep an open mind."

When they pulled up in front of the Port Townsend rental and Joe opened the door to get out, Linc said, "Hang on a second. I've got something for you. I know the tour's gonna be a bitch if Larry and Rina really are an item. Maybe this will give you a clue." He handed Joe a sealed envelope. The message inside was scented with Rina's perfume, fancy card stock like you'd use for a wedding announcement. In her messy scrawl, Rina had written, "Hope you're feeling better, darlin'. Miss you! See you in two shakes of a lamb's tail!" No "love" or "fondly" or even "best wishes." Just a heart. Though it looked more like a tomato. He thought of Ali's brilliant doodles and sighed.

"Bad news?" Linc asked. "Did she mention Larry?"

Joe handed him the card.

"Well … shit," Linc said, handing it back to Joe as if it smelled bad. Maybe he didn't like Rina's perfume. At the moment it smelled pretty cloying to Joe too. This whole matter stank to high heaven. "Joe, I can't tell you what to do, but I've got a bad feeling about this. Rina and Larry are my clients too, and I want to keep them happy. Rina's never been hotter, and she has talent to burn. But as a person"—he shook his head—"she has a lot of growing up to do. You're an old soul, and she's a flighty little girl."

Joe threw up his hands in a gesture of helplessness. He wrote on the blackboard, "We'll see." At the moment he couldn't think too far ahead. He couldn't picture himself with Rina, but not with Ali, either, and he couldn't foresee a time when he wouldn't be worried about his vocal stamina.

"Listen, Joe," Linc went on. "I'm worried about you. Want to see a therapist? Maybe get some Prozac?"

"I'll be OK," Joe wrote. "I'm going to put my feet up and think about nothing but music for the album and getting my voice back." He pasted on a grin and shook his hands in the air as if in celebration.

"Nice try," Linc said. "Just keep this one basic truth in mind: If anything, you're more talented than Rina. And you're prettier."

Joe touched a finger to the dimple in his cheek and batted his eyes, earning a bellow of laughter from Linc.

"You're gonna get your voice back good as new, and this 'Babe in the Woods' song is going to take you up to the highest rung of the fame ladder. Mark my words."

Joe gave a half-hearted nod. It was going to be a long seven weeks.

* * *

ALI AND BECCA WERE DRIVING her Honda Accord around their new stomping grounds, the logging-town-in-transition and I-90 truck stop, North Bend. North Bend wasn't far from Seattle, only about thirty miles, but traffic made it seem farther. Keep traveling East, and the next real city, Cle Elum, was another fifty-five miles. Twenty-five miles of wilderness separated North Bend from the Snoqualmie Pass ski area.

You could hike in your own backyard. Mount Si's multiple trails were accessible year-round.

They drove past the ranger station and a museum called The Puget Sound Railway Historical Association. In town they passed coffee shops and fast-food joints. "Wait, isn't that the diner from *Twin Peaks*?" Ali asked as they cruised down West North Bend Way. "The one with the great cherry pie."

"Twede's Café ... I think so."

Becca turned on the windshield wipers. "Uh-oh. More rain."

"The Seattle forecast was for partly cloudy," Ali remarked as Becca turned up the speed on the wipers.

Becca shot her an apologetic look. "Yeah. Almost twice as much rain here as in Seattle, and in the winter it's often snow. Also hotter in the summer."

"*That* I don't mind," Ali said. "Hey, look! A movie theater."

The pelting rain had reduced visibility to the point that Becca had to pull over next to the boxy building that housed the North Bend Theatre. "Want to see a movie? They're playing *Water World*," she remarked, giving them both a fit of the giggles.

Once the downpour let up, Becca started heading down random streets until they reached what looked like a corporate campus. The Frank Lloyd Wright-type main building seemed to rise out of the forest as if grown from a seed. The side buildings were incorporated into the whole as organically as shoots.

"What a cool place," Ali said, her voice almost reverent.

A sign identified it as the corporate headquarters of Big Paul's Outfitters. Ali flashed on all the BPO clothing and gear in the cabin in the woods. She and Becca hadn't discussed JJ or Liam since that brunch in Fremont.

"What is it? You look like you've seen a ghost."

"It's nothing," Ali replied in a hushed voice. "There was an awful lot of BPO gear in JJ's cabin. Weird coincidence, that's all."

"I would suggest you apply for a job there," Becca said, "but there are no openings. I already checked." Ali heard the sympathy in her voice as she added, "I know you still think about him. It's not like the subject is verboten."

Ali just shook her head. "I do think about him, a lot. But talking about him isn't going to help me get past this. Everywhere I look I see him … or Liam. I suppose that's only natural."

They drove on in silence until Becca pointed out another impressive building. "Ever seen a Viking longhouse?" she asked. "They look a little like that."

To Ali, the building looked like an upside-down Viking ship held up by multiple beams.

"That's La Fête Sauvage," Becca said, "a crazy expensive restaurant. My parents love that place."

"Why is it called 'The Wild Feast'?" Ali asked.

"It features wild game. You know, wild boar, quail, venison, stuff like that—cooked by a chef trained at Le Cordon Bleu in Paris. French Canadian, I think he is. Forty-dollar main courses, twenty-dollar appetizers, ten-dollar glasses of wine." Her full lips curved into a mischievous smile. "Your birthday's right around the corner. I'll get my parents to take us there."

Ali's birthday was September twelfth, a few weeks away. "Come on, Becca, that's too much."

Her friend wagged a finger at her. "Nuh-uh-uh! Don't you do that. Don't deny them their little pleasures." She checked her watch. "They adore you. I think they wish you'd marry Nathan and make a man of him, even if you aren't Jewish. You might be part-Jewish, even though the name Ryan is Irish. It's not like you know your heritage." She gave her a playful nudge. "Speaking of little pleasures, there's still time to go to the outlet stores. Then we'll rent a video. Now that I'm doing the eight-to-five thing, I have to take full advantage of my weekends."

CHAPTER 10

———·———

HAVING ONLY VIEWED LA FêTE Sauvage's rustic exterior, Ali and Becca weren't prepared for the sheer grandeur of the place. Becca's parents, Noam and Leah Himmel, were to meet them at seven.

Awestruck, Ali whispered, "Neuschwanstein, right? Was King Ludwig of Bavaria a hunter?"

"Can't recall," Becca said. "Didn't all the aristocracy hunt?"

"Whatever. He'd be right at home in this place. I'd expected something a bit less … rococo. Look at all the gilded scrollwork."

Even the antler light fixtures were gilded. The kitsch was so over the top, the excess had to be intentional. Fairy lights glittered on the walls and rimmed the gold frames of oil paintings that depicted terrifying wild beasts. Elk locking horns, grizzly bears on their hind legs, wolves devouring prey. Taxidermied animals, some whole but most represented solely by their heads, were everywhere. A moose head, its expression less ferocious than surprised. A wild boar with freakishly long tusks, malevolence glittering in its glass eyes. A stuffed wolf with teeth bared.

"I hope these guys don't come alive at night," Ali whispered to Becca. "They look really pissed off."

"You'd be pissed off too if they mounted your head on a gold-plated plaque."

"What's with all the gilding?" Ali jabbed a thumb at the antler light fixtures. "The décor seems to be inspired by Salvador Dali and Eugene Delacroix."

"Not to mention Marie Antoinette." Becca giggled. "I like it. It's so *not* WASPy old Seattle."

Looking around her, Ali wished she'd let Becca lend her a dress. Her Laura Ashley poufy-sleeved floral number seemed even more out of date in these surroundings.

Seeing her parents, Becca waved, and the two women went over to join them.

Becca's father rose to kiss her hand. A sweet, calm man, he stood around five feet seven and had a stocky build, a bald pate, and Becca's eyes. On him, those preternaturally large brown eyes called to mind a kindly sea lion. "Happy birthday, darling. You look lovely."

They all exchanged hugs. Compared to Ali's cold-as-ice foster parents, Becca's dad and mom could have sprung from *Mr. Rogers' Neighborhood.* They made her call them by their first names.

"Oh my God, Ali, you are skin and bones," Leah clucked. "We'll get you something really fattening for dinner." After hugging her own daughter, she said, "Becca, you're putting on weight. I think you should order the salmon."

Ali had no idea what Leah was talking about. Becca was voluptuous, yes, but in all the right places. No one but her mother would call her overweight or even *zaftig*. Leah was still a pretty woman in her fifties, but she'd left *zaftig* behind about twenty pounds ago. She wore that weight well, but it should disqualify her from pointing fingers at her stunningly beautiful daughter.

"Stop sending us those boxes of chocolate chip cookies, then," Becca complained.

Leah was cut to the quick. "No one said you had to eat them all at once!"

Of course Ali's birthday gift was a box of Leah's famous homemade chocolate chip cookies: the size of dessert plates and so packed with chocolate chips that they were more chocolate pie than cookie. Leah made Ali dig deeper to find the Nordstrom gift card for two hundred dollars. "You can buy yourself a nice dress. That one looks more appropriate for a tea party at a rest home."

"Ma!" Becca groaned.

"What?" Leah gave an elaborate shrug. "It's for her own good. How's she gonna meet the right man in that dress? Even a *Shayna Maidel* like this one has to make the right impression." Which immediately made Ali think of how JJ seemed to think she looked great even in oversized men's underwear. When was she going to stop flashing back to JJ and the cabin in the woods at every turn? She shook it off.

"It's okay, Becca," Ali told her. "You tried to lend me something. I should have let you. I just haven't had an occasion to dress up in … forever."

"I think she looks lovely," Noam repeated in all sincerity, making Ali want to hug him all over again.

"I didn't say she looked *bad*," Leah said, as if grievously misunderstood, "just that her wardrobe needs updating. Becca, you have to make her your project."

Becca let out a little huff of laughter. Ali knew what that meant, *Like I haven't tried.* "Ali's got her own style," she said.

Thankfully, Leah moved on. "So, *shefele*, how goes the career?"

Becca had already confessed to Ali that the private PR firm where she worked was run by a chauvinistic jerk who gave her the heebie-jeebies and might possibly have the hots for her. Ali gave the job another two weeks before Becca ran her mouth off and got the boot. She was amazed her friend had lasted this long.

"Okay," was all her friend said, her tone implying otherwise.

"That doesn't sound like a ringing endorsement," mild-mannered Noam said.

"To be honest, it's not so great. I'm sending out résumés again."

Noam's bushy brows flew together. "What's the problem? There's no funny business, is there?"

"Pop, why would you ask that? I just think another job might be a better fit. I don't like the way they run things there."

"All right, then," he said. "You can do better. You know we're behind you one hundred percent. Can we help you find another position?"

"No, Pop, you big sweetie. I can stand on my own two feet. Don't worry."

What a great guy. He always gave Becca the benefit of the doubt. It was so nice to see a father who was on his daughter's side no matter what.

"We can't help but worry!" Leah was practically wringing her hands. "That's what parents do."

Fortunately the waiter chose that moment to reappear. Ali ordered Venison Bourguignon. When Becca chose the salmon, Ali whispered, "Are you sure that's what you want?"

Her friend grinned. "Actually, I love Jean-Louis's wild salmon with raspberry ginger glaze. It's not virtuous at all."

"We *adore* this place," Leah said, popping a wild-mushroom crostini into her mouth. Though her husband was softspoken, Leah had a set of lungs on her, and whenever she spoke, she drew covertly disapproving glances from other diners. "Unfortunately," Leah continued, "we don't get to come here very often. It's a long way to drive, usually in the rain, and we can't bring our friends who keep kosher."

"The atmosphere *is* magical," Ali agreed. "And the food looks delicious." She watched as the waiter passed by with a full platter.

"Chef Jean-Louis is such a find!" Leah went on. "And so handsome and charming. What a *Mensch*."

Noam folded his hands on the table and cleared his throat. "So, Ali dear, how goes the job search?"

"Not so great," she confessed, "although I did sign up at two temp agencies."

"What, you're gonna do secretarial work?" Leah said as if describing cleaning toilets in a sports stadium. "Noam, we need to make some phone calls. I'm sure one of your friends—"

"No, no, really," Ali protested, afraid of what the Himmels might come up with. "I want to take my time, find the *right* job."

Noam frowned. "Can you afford to do that? We could help you out."

"I'm okay, really," Ali said. A falsehood, but the only way to deflect him.

She adored the Himmels, but they could be exhausting. Leah was famous for forcing food on Becca then telling her she was too fat. She had strong opinions on every man her daughter dated, every outfit she wore, and everything she put into her mouth. It was a vicious cycle. Becca might be a truth teller, but she was careful not to wound. Leah said whatever came into her head. Still, she meant well, and she clearly doted on her youngest daughter.

The conversation wandered to the Himmels' travel plans—they were about to depart on a world cruise. Then they argued with Becca that if she was going to quit her job anyway, she should come with them. Ali stifled a yawn, which was more about discomfort than tiredness.

After a cake so rich Ali could only eat a few bites, the Himmels spotted a group of their friends and went over to say hello. Despite the drizzle, it was a mild night, and Ali and Becca said they'd wait for her parents outside.

"Phew!" Becca said when they were finally alone on the covered porch. "I hope you had fun. My parents are like that cake: a little goes a long way."

"What about the job," Ali asked, "any improvement?"

"Oy! I don't know what's going on with my boss. He asks me inappropriate questions, like who am I dating. I made the mistake of admitting I'm single. He's *forty-five*, Ali. Could he really be coming on to me? He's married."

"*Tabarnak!*" a gruff voice exclaimed. It was obviously a curse word.

Their attention was drawn to a burly man in chef's whites who held a lit cigar in his hand. He carefully extinguished it in the ashtray before giving them a little bow and a grin that revealed an endearing gap between his large white teeth. "I am Chef Jean-Louis," he said, mostly to Becca. "You can call me Jean-Louis. This is my restaurant."

Jean-Louis was on the short side—close to Ali's height of five feet nine—and handsome in an approachable, barrel-chested way. Ali imagined his forebears as French-Canadian fur traders. He had dark skin and hair, as if part indigenous—didn't they call it "First Nations" in Canada? His beard was close cropped, the nicely groomed stubble fashionable now. Straight, longish hair, with curly bangs that framed thick eyebrows and large, bovine brown eyes. Cuddly, like a teddy bear. Older, maybe pushing forty.

Ali batted her eyes. "Shouldn't you be in the kitchen?"

He folded his arms across his chest, hands tucked beneath his armpits, eyes twinkling with amusement. "I'm assuming you aren't just here to distract my customers."

"We just enjoyed one of your fabulous dinners," Becca said, instantly going into what Ali thought of as her Eartha Kitt mode, a kind of purring flirtatiousness. Very disconcerting in a woman normally so forthright.

"Oh, you are going to be regulars now?" he said, responding in kind. He gave them both appreciative once-overs—nothing too lascivious—but his gaze lingered on Becca. "We are booked through the holidays, but I can find a way to work you in."

"Um, don't bother," Ali said. "For us, the fare is a bit"—she rubbed her thumb across her fingertips, searching her vocabulary for something other than "expensive" but only coming up with—"we don't have deep pockets." Weird, but listening to Jean-Louis had her thinking in her limited French, which produced the idiom *poches profonde*.

The chef's accent was not like a Parisian's—tight and fluid. It was broader, singsong, and a bit nasal.

"I hear you're from Quebec," Becca purred. "I like your accent."

"*Ouais*, I am Québécois. And where are you from?"

"New York City, originally," she said. "I attended the Lycée Français de New York through ninth grade."

"*Là là*," Jean-Louis said and uttered something that flew over Ali's head.

"*Monsieur*, you have to slow down," Becca said in her sultry voice. In French, she added, "*Je ne parle pas de votre français.*" Which meant, *I'm not referring to your French.*

He laughed—a rich *heh, heh, heh.*

"I have a proposal for you," he said in English. "Quit your job and become my hostess."

"You've got to be kidding," Becca said. "I have a master's degree in Communication."

His face fell, though comically. "*C'est de valeur*. Too bad. It might be a fun break for a month or two. You could eat better than you ever have in your life."

"Just what I need," Becca said. "My mother already thinks I'm a cow."

"*Ben voyons donc*!" Jean-Louis said, his eyes caressing her curves. "You are perfection itself."

Ali gave Becca a pointed look. Best not to encourage Jean-Louis.

He handed Becca his card. "I am serious as a pope. This is a business proposal. There is no need to worry that I will treat you disrespectfully."

They shook hands in a kind of slow motion that seemed to seal another kind of deal. Becca dropped the card into her pocketbook. "*À bientôt, monsieur*."

After he went inside, Ali said, "Seriously? And what did he say to you in that rapid-fire French?"

She giggled like a teenager—so unlike the Becca Ali knew. "Beats me. But I'm fairly sure my response was appropriate."

CHAPTER 11

———•———

LIAM'S HARLEY WAS NOW PARKED in back of the rental. Ali and Becca had transported it by truck from his former digs in Renton, having no way to locate the keys or title. Surely *he* knew where to find them. He wouldn't have taken them with him to Israel.

Ali still believed he was alive, though her working theory—that he was injured and didn't want to burden her—provided cold comfort.

The shrine that had sat in the corner of her apartment, built of the boxes containing Liam's scant possessions—hiking gear, Swiss army knife, favorite Mount Rainier coffee mug—and the suitcase he'd carried on his trip to Jerusalem, was now buried in the basement of Becca's parents' house.

THE SMALL, PREFABRICATED HOUSE ALI and Becca shared in North Bend was located a few blocks off North Main Street. Elegant it wasn't, but it did have a front porch and two bedrooms. Only one bathroom. They were two Felixes, no Oscar, which meant the place was immaculate. If anything, Becca was a hair neater and the greater germophobe. Ali was more concerned about dirt she could see rather than invisible threats to health and well-being.

Becca had been right about the constant precipitation. Fortunately Ali loved to listen to the sound of pattering rain on the roof, even driving rain as long as she didn't have to be out in it.

Crouching before the open refrigerator, Becca picked up the bag of sprouting onions and said, "So much for home cooking." She tossed them in the garbage and pulled a pizza out of the freezer. "Hope you're not too hungry. Dinner's going to be a while." Ali's culinary skills were solid but basic—dinner with George and Emily had been an uninspiring affair—and although Becca had enjoyed helping her mother whip up her legendary feasts since childhood, lately she couldn't be bothered. Her job with The Creep had cratered a week earlier, and she could have experimented in the kitchen all day; instead she seemed to have lost her joy in cooking and her appetite.

After they kicked off their heels and changed into sweatpants and T-shirts, Becca helped herself to a beer and poured Ali a glass of jug wine. Ali opened the damper in the fireplace and lit the little tent of logs and kindling. In no time they were lounging on the threadbare, dark-blue velveteen couch in front of a merry blaze.

Becca groused for a while about the latest antics of her brother Nathan—a ladies' man who had survived on his savings ever since the tech startup he worked for went belly up. He spent countless hours at bars and the gym and precious little time figuring out his future. Recently he'd beaten a DUI, with the help of an expensive attorney paid for by their parents, and Becca was lamenting that he didn't make better use of his excellent brains and education.

Ali's distracted comment that maybe he was just going through a phase alerted Becca to the fact that her mind was elsewhere.

"You're quiet tonight."

"Oh, you know, the future seems a little bleak. Although I did—finally—get a job interview. It would be in the PR department of Redmond Institute of Technology. An entry-level position, but hey, it's a start. I think the title is 'coordinator.' Sounds like an elevated secretary to me. Fortunately the job doesn't start until January—the start of winter quarter. The final catering gig I committed to is New Year's Eve."

It was late November, the start of the holiday party season, and Ali could pick up a lot of extra money working for the small catering company she'd hooked up with, where she both waited tables and helped with food prep and cleanup. If she didn't get the PR job, she wouldn't have to go begging to Becca's parents.

Becca was practically bouncing on the couch. "Seriously?! And you're only telling me now?"

"Don't want to count my chickens."

"You know, the French say, 'Don't sell the skin of the bear before you've killed it.' Guess that's the difference between a culture dependent on agriculture and one based on fur trapping."

Ali waggled her brows at Becca. "Speaking of fur-trapping cultures, are you going to follow up with *Le Gourmet Gallopant*?"

Becca wrinkled her nose. "The whosit? What year *is* this? I assume you mean *Le Gourmet Farfelu*. That's what the French called him. 'Wacky,' not 'galloping.' Anyhow, *The Galloping Gourmet* went off the air in the seventies." She narrowed her eyes at Ali. "You know he was famous for sampling the cooking wine on his show." She snorted. "You couldn't get away with that nowadays. I assume you don't mean to imply Jean-Louis is a tippler."

It was Ali's turn to roll her eyes. "How would you know? Forget I said anything." Interesting how Becca had successfully sidestepped the question with her little rant. "Listen, it's none of my business, but let the record state that I am pro Chef Jean-Louis."

Becca chuckled. "Okay, I admit it: I called him. I'm going to try hostessing a few times. As a lark. I don't think much corporate hiring happens during the holiday season anyway." She touched Ali's arm. "You're still brooding over JJ, right? You can tell me."

"I dunno. I suppose it's like a death. The memory will fade with time, but truly forgetting won't be easy. I hate unsolved mysteries. It drives me nuts that I'll never know why he needed to hide out while he healed. His playing was skilled enough that he could have made a living as a classical guitarist, but for that, he wouldn't need a voice. And he could do better than that beat-up old instrument."

Becca tapped her chin with one long red nail. "The sound was good, right?"

Ali shrugged. "As far as I could tell."

"The way a guitar looks isn't the point. It could still be worth a fortune."

Ali frowned. "He offered me expensive Scotch, though for some reason he didn't drink any himself. The coffee too was top of the line—I know the good stuff when I taste it. BPO is a pricey brand. Just about everything he owned came from there."

"A rich guy recovering from vocal cord surgery."

"Well, obviously. I imagine it would be depressing for any of us to cope with chronic hoarseness. For him, the stakes were higher."

"You think the verse he gave you was a song lyric?"

"Yeah, I think he's a singer who also plays guitar. I even looked through a bunch of magazines at the grocery store, just in case he was featured. I had no idea there are so many tabloids. I came up empty, no surprise. It wasn't the first time I'd looked for his photo there. Anyway, odds are against him being that famous."

Becca cocked her head. "Why didn't you try harder to find him after you returned from the woods? At least the trail was hot then."

"I called the ranger station in Forks asking if they knew about any rustic log cabins between Forks and the turnoff to Sol Duc. They asked me what had prompted the phone call because anything like that would be illegal. I said, never mind." She blew out an exasperated puff of air.

Becca's mouth quirked. "You do know that solving that mystery, even locating him, doesn't mean he's going to kneel at your feet with a flashy diamond ring. Especially if, as you say, he's taken."

Ali knew Becca was just trying to help, but she still reacted defensively. "Look, I don't kid myself that I meant anything to him. We did give each other comfort—I'm fairly sure of that. He must have been attracted to me, only, not enough to act on it. I put some effort into convincing him too. When I think of my awkward attempts to, well, get him to notice me as a woman, I just cringe." She shuddered.

"He kissed you back, didn't he?"

"Most people will pet a Labrador puppy if it slobbers all over them."

"You're hardly the dog-faced woman at the freak show. Stop beating yourself up. Hey, you gave it a shot. I admire your chutzpah. Pizza smells ready." She stood up.

Becca set the pizza on the coffee table trivet, handed Ali a plate, and sat back down on the couch. Each consumed only one small slice before they put down their plates, appetites gone.

A crack of lightning left them both waiting for the thunder, which arrived soon after. The rain drummed on the roof with renewed fervor. They shared a look of wide-eyed wonder.

"Dramatic," Becca said.

"I like it," Ali admitted.

A laugh in her voice, Becca said, "Me too." Serious again, she went on, "Ali, you've got to make a serious effort to put JJ out of your mind. He's not your soul mate, your 'eternal love,' or whatever you want to call it." She heaved a long-suffering sigh. "Look, I totally get it. I wish you could see him again, too, because then you'd have to accept the fact that he's a pipe dream. You need to rejoin the real world and find some nice, average Joe to date. Not a fancy-pants Tom, Dick, or Harry. Whoever that guy was, he came out of the woods and returned to his expensive, complicated life."

Becca was right, of course. There was no point in arguing.

Her friend walked over to the window and stared outside. Unless a raccoon was scampering about out there, there was nothing to see through the rain-streaked glass but the illuminated porch. "In an ideal world," she said, "I'd be working in the press room at Nordstrom. But Jean-Louis seems nice.

It might be fun to step outside my comfort zone and experience the night life." She looked over at Ali. "I know you're not ready to give up on Woody the Woodsman, and I respect that. It hasn't been long since Liam's, um, disappearance, and you have a right to mourn him and, uh, Willy Woodsman. Whatever his name is. JJ the Magnificent. Listen, we are living close to nature, away from traffic. We have each other. Life isn't so bad."

Ali blinked away sudden tears. "You still think Liam is dead."

Becca was silent for a long moment. "I don't know what to think. I know you've been in touch with the American Embassy in Jerusalem. Are you making any headway?"

Ali shook her head. "They insist they're looking into it. I wish I could hire a detective. I know it sounds crazy, but I still sense his presence in the world."

Becca handed her a tissue.

"It's a twin thing," Ali insisted, blowing her nose. "Not woo-woo at all."

Becca took a long sip of her beer. "Okay, Ali. Time will tell, right? If he's alive, he'll turn up. I'm on your side, remember? You are so gorgeous. There have got to be oodles of men out there who would love to help you forget JJ. You never meet any cute guys at those catering gigs?"

Ali couldn't help but laugh. Becca had never waited tables, or she'd know the answer. "Put on a monkey suit and poof! You're invisible. Although … there is a married waiter who's indicated he's up for something. He's not bad looking."

Becca got up in her face. "Seriously?!"

Ali pushed her away, laughing. "Well, *he's* serious. I'm just saying it's not a good way to meet guys."

"Maybe in the new job," Becca said with a decisive nod of her head.

"I do love your optimism," Ali replied as she stacked their plates and took them and the remaining pizza into the kitchen. She didn't bother to remind her friend how Trip and Luis had soured her on sex. And now, no one could compete with JJ.

What Ali wouldn't give for just one more meeting with JJ …. She'd see the real guy, warts and all. Personality warts. Physically, he was definitely wart-free. If he'd regained his voice by now, he might reveal himself right away as a jerk—a charming, wounded guy who'd had her company thrust upon him and made the best of it. No one could be as amazing as the man who starred in all her fantasies.

But the chances of another encounter were nil. She knew only his first initials. Forget needles, this was a sliver in a haystack.

* * *

LINC HAD OFFERED TO PICK up Rina at the airport. Joe hadn't heard a peep out of her since the weird note with the tomato-like heart, but the tabloids had filled him in to his satisfaction. He was a professional, after all, and they were going to record those damn duets and introduce them during the tour—unless, that is, she proposed that she sing them with good 'ol Larry instead. Joe was more of a bass baritone, Larry a high baritone—some called that voice type a "baritenor." Joe would have liked to give him a swift kick in the balls that would make him sing soprano. But no, he wasn't *that* guy. He'd made his peace with Rina moving on.

Which is why he was so surprised when she jumped into his arms, screaming like a little girl. He braced himself just in time or she would have thrown his back out. Her thick blonde curls fanned about her shoulders, and the firm thighs that locked around his waist were naked under her short skirt. Lowcut blouse, bejeweled cowboy boots, classic Rina.

"Rina, for God's sake," he said in her ear. "What are you up to? You're making a spectacle of us both."

"Okay, daddy," she pouted. It wasn't a term of endearment. "Can't I get excited when I greet the love of my life?"

He put her firmly at arm's length. "I thought Larry had that title."

"Larry? We're just friends, always were. Hammed it up for the camera sometimes. He's like the little brother I never had."

"A little brother who's your age exactly," Joe said, careful to remain cool and detached.

"Well, he sure acts young," said the grown woman who was doing a dandy impression of a sixteen-year-old. "I could never take him seriously. We just like to joke around."

"Of course you missed me," Joe said. "I have all those letters to prove it."

Rina was staring up at him through her lashes in a way he used to find irresistible. "I would have written … if you'd written me first. You never replied to my note. I couldn't ring you up. I didn't want to hurt your voice while it was healing."

He didn't bother to pretend he wasn't irritated. "Linc must have told you when I was cleared to talk. A short conversation would have been nice."

"Here I am all excited to see you again, and you're just determined to burst my bubble." She stepped back, full, red lower lip still protruding.

"Joe?" Rina was gazing up at him, her blue eyes doe-like and innocent.

He shook himself back to the present. "Do we still have a chance?"

He didn't have time to answer because the fans had landed like a swarm of locusts. The next half hour was filled with autographs and the friendly or flirty banter the public expected. As usual, Joe couldn't help but admire how effortlessly Rina pulled it all off. He would do well to take a page out of her book.

On the limo ride back to Teresa's townhome where he was staying, he thought of his fruitless search for Ali.

In between recording sessions, Joe had phoned damn near every independent coffee shop in Seattle. If the manager wanted to know what he wanted with this Ali person, he said he was a detective who had been hired to find her because of money she was owed. Most just admitted outright that no one named Ali had been in their employ prior to April. He hadn't needed the police sketch, but he was glad of it because it kept her fresh in his mind.

Then, finally, came the phone call where a woman said, "Ali?" as if the name rang a bell. "I don't give out information about employees, past or present." So he showed up in person, this being the only lead so far, dressed in a cheap suit, signature curls cut short, a weird little pencil mustache completing the effect of underpaid PI. As a five o'clock shadow guy, it was easy to add facial hair to his disguises.

The manager, who introduced herself as Faye, eyed his altered self the way strangers usually did, as if he were someone they knew out of context. "*You're* a detective?" Faye asked with obvious skepticism. Her guessed her age at thirty-five, the no-nonsense, no-artifice type. Solid. The kind of woman who could probably order construction workers around. He felt ashamed of the subterfuge but wasn't willing to come clean. "Why are you looking for Ali?"

After giving her his usual spiel, he showed her the police sketch.

"Why would you have a *police* sketch?" Faye asked. "Is she a suspect in some crime?"

Okay, he hadn't thought that through. "No, no, definitely not. This drawing approximates what she would look like now—you know, ten years later." God, he was horrible at this. "My client last saw her at age fourteen."

"Well, that explains it. It's not a good likeness. Don't get me wrong, Ali's a knockout, and guys were always hitting on her. But she's a cool one, told me she didn't have time for men. This girl looks like she's posing for a shampoo ad. Or a Match-dot-com profile shot."

Match.com had just launched. Joe experienced a pang of jealousy imagining Ali posting there.

"You said, 'were.' Does that mean she's moved on?"

Faye nodded. "Yep. She left in April. Apologized profusely for leaving. Said she wanted to try something new."

"Did she leave a forwarding address?"

Faye cocked her head. "I'm sorry, but I'm confused. Was she living under an assumed identity? Are you from the IRS? The business suit …." She gave it a dismissive sweep of the hand.

He cursed his inept disguise. "No, it's all good. I understand if you don't feel comfortable sharing her address. Was she a good employee?"

"The best. Efficient, polite. A closed book, though. She didn't reveal anything about her past. I can tell you one thing, though."

He waited.

"If she were a criminal, and you put out this sketch, no one would recognize her." That drove home how much he'd enhanced her in his imagination.

With a little more prodding, the woman did, eventually, share Ali's address in Shoreline and her last name, Ryan.

His joy was short-lived. The apartment was occupied by a new tenant.

The name Ali Ryan was almost as common as Jane Smith. No surprise that it turned out to be a dead end. She'd basically erased the two clues she'd given him, other than her master's program, and the UW wasn't giving out *anything*. Apparently Ali didn't want him to find her.

OVER THE NEXT WEEK, RINA was the consummate professional. She even congratulated him for "Babe in the Woods"—not that anyone but Linc knew the story behind it. He'd be curious to see how she reacted when its origins inevitably came out in interviews. Singing harmony with Rina was just as satisfying as he remembered it. No denying things could be great between the two of them, as long as Rina got her way.

He even took her to meet his mother. Carrie was on her guard, though polite enough, and her prickly moments were quickly offset by his sister Teresa, who was never anything but kind. Their reactions to Rina were wholly predictable.

"Do you really think she's marriage material, Joe? She doesn't have much conversation. Did she go to college? Does she even know who's president?"

Yes, she could name the president, but Joe doubted she could pass a civics test. He'd never seen her read anything heavier than the occasional Harlequin romance.

"Mom, she's crazy talented, and some of her song lyrics are surprisingly wise and clever. She's not stupid."

His mother made a wry face. "I didn't say she was stupid. And it's clear that she has many ... positive qualities."

Oh well, it wasn't as if he saw his mother all that much these days. She'd deal with whoever he settled down with. She certainly wouldn't have welcomed Ali, even though his pipe-dream-girl was educated, curious about the world, concerned about others .... The list went on and on. He smiled to himself. In his head, anyway. He was convinced that if he ever saw Ali again, she'd be a tremendous disappointment.

"I like her," Teresa said carefully. Every time he saw his sister, she looked a little more like their pretty, reed-thin, platinum blonde mother. Or maybe it was the opposite: that his mother looked more and more like Teresa. His mother was certainly on the cutting edge when it came to cosmetic procedures. "I'm not sure she's the one for you, though," Teresa went on, choosing her words carefully. He always winced a little when Teresa spoke, hearing the tendency toward huskiness they'd both inherited. On her it sounded sexy. "You're not even thirty. Why the rush to settle down? Your backgrounds are so different. You're so much more, uh, serious than she is. I doubt anything bad has ever happened to her."

"I hear you," Joe replied, "but these days it's less common to find someone who's experienced the death of a parent or brother or sister. Her innocence is refreshing. We can talk music till the cows come home. We don't need to have everything in common. What is it they say? *Vive la différence.* I think she's good for me. She's certainly far better at handling all the attention that goes along with this life. Yes, she's a little spoiled, but she was an only child."

Teresa was stuck on one word. "Innocence," she repeated. His sister was convinced Rina had cheated with Larry during Joe's recovery period.

Three weeks into the tour, Joe surrendered to Rina's charms and they had sex, which was just as addictive as Joe remembered it. Like eating a banana split with cherries on top. Indulgent and vaguely guilt-inducing. A quality of being done by a professional rather than a mutual coming together. Soon everyone knew they were seeing each other again, and yet Larry had been cordial, not jealous at all. Joe wanted to believe that nothing sexual had happened between him and Rina, so he ignored the small voice that kept insisting he couldn't trust her.

One Sunday evening in August after the matinee that closed a successful weekend in Portland, Oregon, they disguised themselves in Sunday-go-to-meeting clothing—a conservative suit for Joe and a relatively modest gingham dress for Rina—and snuck away to a small bistro. He didn't particularly like going to restaurants with Rina. She flirted with the waiters and gave the waitresses a hard time, asking for numerous substitutions, salad dressing on the side, etcetera. Not that she wasn't nice, just difficult. She was used to getting her way.

Rina ordered a bottle of wine and two glasses, indifferent as usual to his strict, vocal-cord-friendly need to abstain from alcohol. While happy to drink most of it herself, she complained about his need to be so careful, saying that "surely one li'l glass wouldn't hurt."

Leaving the restaurant, they discovered that word had gotten out, as it inevitably did—was Rina the source?—and the evening ended with them getting mobbed by adoring fans in the alley.

Later that night in their hotel room, he'd wanted to read for a bit—Saul Bellow's *Humboldt's Gift*. The author didn't have the most positive view of women, and these days Joe found himself agreeing with him more often than not. Sure enough, Rina plunked down beside him on the bed and turned on the TV. He wouldn't have minded an episode of *JAG* or even *Xena, Warrior Princess*, but she wanted to watch old episodes of *Green Acres*. In the interest of peace, he closed his book. He could finish it after leaving the tour to Rina and Larry.

"Babe in the Woods" had been rising in the charts ever since Linc had sent the demo to the DJ in Philadelphia. It was succeeding beyond his wildest dreams. Why had he written it, to find Ali or memorialize her? Unless she never looked at a tabloid, he couldn't believe she didn't know about that song. The longing he felt clearly hadn't been mutual.

CHAPTER 12

————•————

THE HIMMELS' MANSION WAS FESTOONED like a Christmas bazaar. This year, the eighth and final day of Hanukkah coincided with Christmas Day, but it was clear which holiday appealed more to the Himmels, who were secular Jews. The fully lighted *menorah stood on a side table, dwarfed by the magnificent grand-fir Christmas tree whose crowning angel with her ivory-silk gown and porcelain face touched the twelve-foot ceiling.*

Becca was the youngest of four children, Nathan the oldest and only boy. Against all odds, everyone had managed to make it home this year. Myra was doing her residency to become an ER surgeon at Lenox Hill Hospital in New York City after getting her medical degree from Johns Hopkins, and Hannah was working long hours in the Federal Public Defender office in Boston after graduating with a JD *summa cum laude* from Harvard Law. Becca had warned Ali not to ask anyone about how they were doing because Nathan's current situation was a sore point for her parents. The other daughters' success seemed to make her thirty-three-year-old brother's fall from grace even more glaring. Leah's mother, who Ali knew as only "Bubbe" or Mrs. Feldstein, was visiting from her retirement home in downtown Seattle, and although she was only seventy-seven, she seemed to be failing mentally. Becca insisted she'd always been eccentric.

Ali loved the way the Himmels accepted her as family, despite their willingness to air their dirty laundry in front of her.

At the door she was hugged too tightly on all sides, especially by Nathan, who was already under the influence—if her nose didn't deceive her. The women all returned to the kitchen for the final preparations, while Nathan and

Noam continued to work on the Yellowstone Park puzzle in the living room.

"Don't give your brother any more drinks," Leah told Hannah, who was mixing gin and tonics.

"He's already *ferschnicket*!" Bubbe cried out.

"Ma, Bubbe, it's not like he's driving. It's the holidays. What, I'm going to bring Pop a drink and tell Nathan he's cut off?"

"Mix it light, then."

She measured out the same amount of gin for both drinks and told her mother, "Oy. He's thirty. If he passes out before dinner, it's on him."

"No one listens to me," Leah lamented.

At dinner—a sumptuous feast of beef brisket, potato kugel, challah, rainbow slaw, and beet salad—the no-holds-barred conversation continued.

"*Oy veh'z mir,*" Leah said with a despairing gesture that was partly theater. "None of my children are married. What have I done to deserve this? I want grandchildren!" She zeroed in on her son. "Nathan, why don't you marry Ali? So what if she's not Jewish?"

"All right," Nathan said, his eyes glazed but his speech normal. "Marry me, Ali. We'd have beautiful children."

Nathan closely resembled Becca with his curly dark hair, olive skin, and the large eyes they'd both inherited from their father. With all the gym time he'd put in lately, he was almost too muscular for Ali's taste. And she knew from Becca's stories that he wasn't too picky about the women he consorted with. Most of them were married, which he thought was safer.

"Oh, Nathan, my first marriage proposal," Ali joked. "I'm so touched. Ask me again next Christmas. I might even say yes."

"You shouldn't make light of such a serious matter," Leah said with a pout. "This boy needs a good woman to straighten him out. At least, unlike the rest of you, he has years left to have children. You know that fertility drops off significantly after age forty?"

"Good to know," Myra said in a flat voice. "They didn't teach us that in medical school." She finished off her wine and reached for the bottle.

Hannah had a way of rolling her eyes and fluttering her lashes that made her annoyance hard to miss. This time she added a little, "Pfft" of disgust.

Neither sister could hold a candle to Becca, but her best friend's beauty was hard to beat. Myra was tall and long-legged, her short brown hair streaked with blonde highlights. She wore brown cords, loafers, and a Christmas sweater knitted by Leah of two demented-looking reindeer who looked like they were about to kiss. Becca had told Ali she believed her sister was in a relationship with a woman, because the one time she'd visited, she'd had to sleep on the couch—there being only one full-sized bed in the apartment she shared with her "roommate," Cynthia.

Hannah wore her black hair in a chin-length bob and had layered on so much makeup that her true appearance was hard to gauge. With her round, heavily lined eyes and dark brows, she reminded Ali of Clara Bow, the "It" Girl from the silent film era. Her tailored red pantsuit seemed designed to conceal her curves, probably a smart move for a woman in a male-dominated profession. According to Becca, Hannah did date, mostly lawyers, and she usually dumped them after a few months of hearing them complain about their hatred for their chosen profession.

"Where's your mother?" Noam asked Leah in his usual bland tone.

"Not again!" Leah slapped herself on her forehead and promptly left the room.

"She's locked herself in the bathroom," Hannah explained to Ali. "Attention must be paid."

Not that she required an explanation. Bubbe had pulled this stunt during other family meals Ali had attended.

Loud knocking from the hallway. "Mother! You need to come out, *now*. That's enough. We can't serve dessert without you."

"No one cares whether I live or die!" Bubbe could be heard to moan.

Nathan joined Leah in the hallway, noticeably unsteady but not bumping into anything. "I love you, Bubbe," he said through the door. "Come out so I can give you a big hug."

Another ten minutes of urging from various family members lured Bubbe from the bathroom in time for cinnamon apple cake.

Ali cherished every minute of it. Compared to the Himmels, her foster parents had celebrated Christmas as if holding a wake for a particularly dull relative.

* * *

"*BLESS*, O LORD, THIS *FOOD to our use and ourselves to Thy service*. In Jesus's name, Amen," Carrie O'Connell said as the group bowed over their classic turkey-and-all-the-fixings dinner, courtesy of Rostand and a maid hired for the evening. They were gathered together on Seattle's Capitol Hill at Carrie O'Connell's twentieth-century Tudor revival mansion, half-timbered with a twelve-foot-tall privacy hedge.

"Amen," Joe said and placed his white cloth napkin on his lap. Speaking was harder on the vocal cords than singing, and he'd taken to conserving his voice like a miser. Not that he had much to contribute in any conversation initiated by his mother or evil twin. Absent were Edward the priest—never present on religious holidays and generally missing in action—and David, who couldn't zip in for a weekend while he remained in Africa. Somehow his mother had convinced Joe to tolerate Jake for the evening, a sacrifice made only for Teresa's sake. He'd return to Nashville in a few days. Besides being booked for gigs at the Grand Ole Opry and the Station Inn, there would be "impromptu" performances at bars, clubs, and hotel lobbies. Interviews. The occasional out-of-town trip for guest appearances at charity events ….. All carefully orchestrated to build interest in his new album while providing for downtime. As usual, Joe's Nashville-based assistant would find him an unassuming rental house that would allow him to keep a low profile. There were lots of cities with better weather in chilly January and February, but Nashville was the center of Joe's world. The tour for *The Woodsman* album wouldn't begin until mid-April, the final stop being the Country Stampede Music Festival in Manhattan, Kansas, at the end of June. Joe had spent the weekend hanging out quietly with his mother and Teresa, knowing he wouldn't be seeing them again for months. Their low-key activities included puzzles and a few games of Monopoly.

Tonight Teresa had invited Paul Andrews, her mother-sanctioned boyfriend and presumed fiancé, though nothing had been declared. Joe instinctively disliked the guy—why, he wasn't sure. He was pleasant enough looking in a grown-up Dennis-the-Menace way and had all the social graces. Though the fictional Dennis wasn't a redhead like Paul, a classic carrot top with tilted green eyes and freckles. Joe and Paul had been in the same class at Seattle Prep, the top choice of all wealthy Seattle Catholics—though Jake had pushed hard for Lakeside, Seattle's closest equivalent to an Eastern prep school, and got his way. Paul had been student body president at Seattle Prep, where everyone assumed he was headed for a political career. At Princeton, he attended the Woodrow Wilson School with such a future in mind, but now he was CEO of a startup here in Seattle. During high school, Joe had invited Paul over to the house exactly once, when they were seniors. That was where Paul had first met Teresa. She'd been only twelve at the time, but Joe could see that Paul was attracted. *Ew, ick.* Teresa could have anyone. So, why Paul? Joe had also noticed that the guy drank like a fish, though he seemed to be able to hold his liquor.

Joe's wandering thoughts were interrupted by a question. In the silence, he realized it had been directed at him. "Uh, what?"

"Joe," his mother said tartly, "this is a family meal. We request your presence—not just as a seat warmer."

"Fair enough," Joe said, suppressing his annoyance. "What was the question?"

"Are you still planning to marry Rina?" his mother asked. He knew she was not in Rina's fan club. For starters, although Rina wasn't religious, she came from a Seventh Day Adventist family. Though her parents were wealthy, she was trashy by Carrie's standards. Big hair, Tammy-Faye makeup, Jessica Rabbit body. No proper Catholic mother was ever going to appreciate Rina.

"Looks like it," Joe said, holding his water glass out to Teresa to fill. *God*, how he longed for a stiff drink.

"Where is she then?" Jake asked, malevolent mischief in his eyes.

"With her own parents," Joe said. "She's an only child and has never spent Christmas away from them. I decided to leave her to it."

"Huh," Jake said. "What about your 'Babe in the Woods'? Still searching for her?" The question dripped with disdain.

"I guess I dreamed her," Joe said in a deadpan voice. Almost to himself, he added, "Rina is probably more my speed." *Jeez*, had he said that aloud? His mother already took a dim view of Rina.

"Only the best for my brother," Jake ground out.

"Joe didn't mean it as a compliment," his sister said in his defense. "Not that I dislike her. The few times we've met, she was nice. And she's certainly gorgeous and ubertalented. The day Joe marries Rina, millions of adolescent hearts will break."

"Yeah, but most of us move on from that stage of development," Jake quipped.

Ba-dum-bum-CHING, Joe thought. *The perfect setup, Sis.* He let out a weary sigh. "Listen, Rina and I make a good team. A woman like Ali would hate my life." I *hate my life*, he added silently.

Teresa laid a gentle hand on his arm. "Joe, what's the rush to get married? You've only just turned thirty."

"If I want to marry Rina," he explained, "I have to do it sooner rather than later. She's told me her patience is running out. My search for Ali seems like a Quixotic quest at this point, but if by some miracle I did find her, she'd probably be a disappointment. I knew her for only a few days, and nothing really happened between us."

"You mean no sex," Jake said with satisfaction.

"Thank God for that," Carrie declared.

Joe simply stared at them. Why had he bothered to come home for the holidays? His stick-up-the-ass family never failed to disappoint. And his dead father's outsized presence haunted everything. His eyes cut to the tasteful

Christmas tree, with its perfect symmetry and austere sprinkling of white lights and silver balls. No wonder he'd gravitated toward Rina. She was a flocked tree with colored lights, tinsel, strings of popcorn, and ornaments from around the globe.

What would Christmas with Ali look like? The Cratchit family celebration might appear grand in comparison. He'd love to spoil her—treat her to the kind of splashy blowout she'd never experienced.

Oh, Ali, he thought. *Why the hell did I let you go?*

Dessert was pumpkin pie with whipped cream. His mother gave Teresa the tiniest sliver with no crust.

"How come the rest of us get pie and Teresa has to eat a worm?" Joe asked with a grimace. "That's what it looks like." *Or a finger*, he thought, *one belonging to a child.*

Teresa laughed. "It is rather stingy, Mom. It's not like I pigged out at dinner."

"Help yourself then," Carrie said with a tight moue of disapproval.

So Teresa did. The slice was still small, but it did include crust. A minor act of defiance. *Brava, Teresa*, Joe told her silently, longing for the day when his sister would finally stand up to their mother and dare to live her own life.

CHAPTER 13

———·———

IT BEING FEBRUARY, A FEW inches of snow had fallen the night before, already melting. Ali never tired of the mountainous, evergreen-dense, and snowmelt-fed terrain that was their home. At least many of the trees here stayed green. Too bad the skies were always gray, and this time of year, the precipitation seemed to never let up.

She was on the bus, headed for home on a Friday evening, having completed the first month of her new job in the PR department of Redmond Institute of Technology, a two-year vocational college. She was little more than a secretary/receptionist, clinging to the promise of one day being assigned press releases and newsletter stories. At present, her work consisted of answering phones and organizational tasks such as filing and correspondence. Bor-ing. *It's work*, she told herself, *it's not meant to be fun. Everybody has to start somewhere.* Only, she wasn't convinced she was on an upward trajectory. Already she had an awful feeling that the only reason this position had been open was because her boss, Mabel—a doughy woman in her fifties with a head of iron-gray helmet hair—was impossible to please. For one thing, she was creepy. She had a Queen of Hearts off-with-her-head attitude with underlings and a Frog Footman-like subservience with superiors. She feared she'd soon be waxing poetic about the good ole days of cater-waitering. *Could PR ever be my dream job?* she wondered, remembering the conversation with Joe in the cabin.

"ON THE PLUS SIDE, IT'S unlikely my boss will make a pass at me," Ali told Becca, who was bustling about the North Bend house when Ali got home at the end of the first week. Becca was loving every minute of her new role as hostess at a top-rated Zagat restaurant. Now that Becca was a night owl, the roommates rarely crossed paths.

"Uh-oh," Becca said, her eyes huge. "That doesn't sound promising."

"And the atmosphere is gray, gray, grayer. Iron gray, like Mabel's hair. Like a mental institution. After this, I might need one."

"I'm so sorry," her friend said. "And here we are at the grayest time of the year."

Becca fairly glowed with happiness. She was wearing red high-top sneakers, pale-yellow overalls, and a cherry-red T-shirt. Not a lounging outfit.

"You're not wearing that to hostess at the restaurant, are you?" Ali checked her watch. "Come to think of it, why aren't you at work?"

"Not tonight," Becca said with a cat-that-ate-the-cream smile. "Frida is on duty. But I do have a sleepover planned. Jean-Louis gave me a key to his house. He gets home around midnight."

"Are you in love?" Ali asked in a hushed voice.

"Maybe," Becca said. "I'll let you know. Don't want to jinx it."

Ali moved aside the curtain to look outside. "I worry about you driving in all this slush and icy rain."

"It's a short distance to the restaurant," Becca assured her. "And Jean-Louis's place isn't much farther." She gave Ali a hug. "Listen, sweetie, you aren't stuck. Hang in there for a few months if you can. If you decide to throw in the towel, no one makes milk-foam designs like my best friend. And Sully's pays benefits. There's one in North Bend now. You could walk there. I know we once said we weren't going to waste our graduate degrees, but if a job's just 'killing time,' it's not worth it. Life's too short."

ALI "SOLDIERED ON" UNTIL THE end of winter quarter, giving two weeks' notice to help the transition. Mabel accepted her resignation with no surprise or apologies. Julia in Human Resources wore an air of regret but declined to speak frankly. Clearly, for PR minions, this department was a revolving door. For some reason, Mabel was bulletproof. Another unsolved mystery. Was Mabel blackmailing the college? Had her father endowed a chair? Ali might never know. As befit her good-girl upbringing, she trained her successor, feeling terrible that she couldn't warn her in advance of the ordeal to come.

Back at the house that night, Ali found Jean-Louis sitting in their favorite thrift-store Naugahyde easy chair, feet up on the ottoman. He looked right at home. Becca perched on the arm of the chair. Was he the man of the house now? Sure looked like it.

"Um, hi, Jean-Louis. This is … unexpected. But welcome." Ali looked from one to the other and back again. "Are you guys serious?"

He answered quickly, "*I* am. I don't speak for Becca."

"Then I am too," Becca said, and sat down on the arm of the chair again, taking his hand. "Ali, are you okay?"

"I quit my nightmare job," she admitted. "I'm footloose and fancy free." She sounded anything but.

"*C'est plate*," Jean-Louis said. *That sucks*, his expression translated.

Ali waved them away. "No need for condolences. Moving right along …. The two of you look awfully cozy. Are we acquiring a new roommate?"

"Jean-Louis wouldn't live so modestly. He has a beautiful house in the Valley."

Jean-Louis tapped his cheek as if considering the matter. "*Pantoute*. You girls are remarkably neat and tidy. That's more important than luxury. You know, Ali, I could use more help at the restaurant. Would you like to be a substitute hostess?"

Ali shrugged, thinking it would be a step back in the world. "I'm an awfully good waitress."

Jean-Louis bowed his head, apologetic. "*Désolé*, my waiters are all men. That's how it is in the best establishments."

Women had sued catering companies in New York to right that particular wrong, but Ali wasn't going to call Jean-Louis out for his patriarchal notions. Not now, anyway.

"Actually, I've applied to work as a barista at the North Bend Sully's." Thank God she had an excuse. Hostessing paid next to nothing. Not an issue for Becca.

Jean-Louis brightened. "*Heille*, we'd like to photograph some publicity shots. Becca thinks you could be our model. You are game?"

Becca blushed, which, unlike Ali, she never did. "I've been handling PR for Jean-Louis," she admitted.

Ah, that explained it. Maybe Leah and Noam would take her off the *schlimazel* list now. The family fuckups. If Becca was being straight with them about Jean-Louis. Ali doubted that.

She wrinkled her nose. "I'm no one's idea of a model."

"Told ya," Becca said to Jean-Louis. "Way too modest."

"We'll pay you, of course," he said.

Ali shrugged again, though secretly pleased. After her soul-destroying winter, all new adventures were welcome.

Jean-Louis kissed the palm of Becca's hand. *"Allons-y,"* he said, which meant, *Let's go.*

After they left, Ali poured herself a large glass of water, changed into her fleece robe, and flopped back down on the overstuffed couch. She had a lot to mull over. Jean-Louis was a type once described by *Cosmopolitan* magazine as a "warm fuzzy." He and Becca seemed so right together, despite the age difference. He had a grace that didn't match his burliness. Maybe that was just the difference between being a French Canadian and an American.

Ali dreamed that night of JJ. He was leading her out of the forest. But when he turned to confirm that she was still there, his face had no features. By now she had a whole sketchbook of drawings, but she no longer had a clear picture of him in her head.

THE MODELING GIG TURNED OUT to be a hoot once Ali got past her discomfort with being the center of attention.

While the photographers labored to get the lighting and backdrops just right, Ali asked Becca how the relationship with Jean-Louis had developed so quickly.

"You saw what he was like at that first meeting. Getting him to slow down was the hard part. When it comes to sex, that man knows what he's doing. And we have more in common than you'd think. We're both from, uh, exuberant families, though his father passed away a few years ago. You know my sisters and brother are mostly attracted to non-Jews. I have never fallen hard for a Jewish man, either. Too attached to their mothers."

Jean-Louis appeared then, putting that subject to rest. *"Bon ben,* you ladies seem to be enjoying yourselves," he said, breaking into his charming, gap-toothed grin. "I hope you don't mind me monopolizing Becca so much. I know she misses you."

"It's all right," Ali said. "I understand. I've never seen her so, um, happy."

If possible, Jean-Louis grinned wider. *"Faque là,* they are ready for you." He inclined his head in the direction of the small round table, where a generically handsome blond man sat waiting, hands folded. "I thought maybe I could introduce you to him—you would make a good-looking couple—but I'm afraid he is more interested in me." He laughed his low *heh, heh, heh.*

"I saw you flirting with him earlier," Becca said, amused rather than jealous.

"Peu importe," Jean-Louis said with a broad Gallic shrug. "It's always nice to be admired, *hein?* I still have that certain *je ne sais quoi.*"

"Like there was ever any doubt," Becca said, brushing her hand along the immaculate chef's whites that covered his broad chest. Jean-Louis would be posing for publicity shots as well.

"It was a super idea to use Ali for the brochure," Jean-Louis commented later as they viewed the final mockup. "Maybe your famous woodsman will stop by La Fête Sauvage, hein?" Seeing Ali's surprise, he added, "Becca and I, we have no secrets. And yours is safe with me."

CHAPTER 14

———•———

ONCE ALI BEGAN WORKING AS a barista at the North Bend Sully's, she continued to send out résumés, though with less frequency and almost no optimism. She told herself she needed time to recover from her disastrous PR job, but really, it was just that a profound malaise had settled over her. JJ and Liam retreated further and further out of the realm of the possible, becoming hazy, dreamlike figures.

By summer, Becca was living with Jean-Louis at his house in the Valley and deeply involved in promoting the restaurant. Now that Ali worked odd hours, they found time to hike, which was the only activity that lifted her spirits. She read a lot of bulky escapist novels, none of them romances, and was watching way too much cable TV, a bill Becca still covered despite Ali's protests.

Becca still hadn't told her parents that she and Jean-Louis were a couple, though Leah and Noam now knew she was working for him in various capacities. She wouldn't hear of Ali paying rent. Ali was racked with guilt over her loss of ambition, but it wasn't as if there was anyone but her own conscience to berate her for her poor life choices. Leah and Noam saved the guilt trips for their own children, even though they had practically adopted her.

Late in August, Becca asked Ali if she wanted to help her out at the hospitality table during a special event at La Fête Sauvage. Ali could see no reason to say no. Especially when Becca insisted on buying her an appropriate dress. September thirtieth fell on a Monday, a day the restaurant was normally closed and one that Ali wasn't scheduled to work her barista job.

* * *

JOE HAD JUST COMPLETED HIS final set at the Country Stampede Music Festival, a three-day weekend event taking place in the charming college town of Manhattan, "The Little Apple," Kansas. The day had been hot and muggy, and Joe was looking forward to visiting Teresa in Seattle where it was a lot cooler. As a kid, he hadn't been allowed to attend outdoor music festivals, and the Tuttle Creek State Park provided a lush and leafy backdrop. He'd love to stay on to fish or hike, but he was too conspicuous here to indulge in tourist activities. Through the end of October, Rina and Larry would continue the tour in smaller venues. She'd actually agreed to skip Christmas with her parents to join him in Seattle for the holidays. That meant she'd be expecting a proposal.

The roadies were setting up for the next band. Grabbing a bottle of water from one of the coolers, Joe wandered deeper into the shade of the trees in the roped-off backstage area. He needed a moment of alone time and a breath of fresh air. Instead he found cigarette smoke—with Larry Wales as its source.

"I can't believe you smoke, man," Joe said, clearing his throat reflexively.

"Not all of us have to baby our voices," Larry quipped. "I've got range to spare. Gives me a little of that sexy roughness you have in spades."

Joe counted to ten, then turned to go back to the trailer he shared with Rina. What Larry said next stopped him in his tracks. "Dude, you sure are trusting. I envy that." A long silence, then, "You really believe nothing happened between me and Rina while you were curled up in a fetal position? Or are you just gunning for sainthood?"

Joe's hand balled up into a fist. Then he willed his fingers to relax. No, he was not going to punch this piece of shit. He'd known about Larry and Rina all along, he guessed. Joe and Larry had always been cordial. Now he realized what an act that had been. Obviously the younger singer hated his guts. Or was it simply envy? He was surprised the guy had waited this long to drop his bombshell.

Larry couldn't resist rubbing salt in the wound. "She's hot as a pistol, right? But a little high maintenance. Wants to settle down, at least she did with me. I'm not ready for that. When I get to be your age, maybe."

Joe turned to face him, lips curved into a warning smile. "What's the matter, Larry, jealous? I see you with all those groupies. Guess you have a lot to prove."

Larry stomped out his cigarette and held up his hands defensively. "Hey, man, just thought you deserved the truth. Since we're winding things up here. I figured no one really wants sloppy seconds."

Surrendering to some atavistic instinct, Joe strode forward and gave Larry a shove that planted his ass firmly in the muddy ground. No harm done, except to his fancy jeans. "Oops," he said, as he took off for the trailer to pack this stuff.

Not trusting himself to confront Rina, he left her a letter. "Hey, Rina. I had to leave suddenly. Sorry not to say goodbye. I know you and Larry will have a blast on the next leg of the tour. But, under the circumstances, we may need to rethink our holiday plans. I'll be in touch."

No "love" or "fondly" or even "best wishes." Just a heart that looked a little like a tomato. She'd figure it out.

Later that night, Rina left him a phone message pleading for understanding. He'd call her back … eventually.

* * *

BECCA AND ALI, IN PARTY dresses and full makeup, stood next to the tents in the shade of a bigleaf maple in its peak of fall color, a blazing yellow. Ali's stomach did a flipflop when Becca confessed that Big Paul's Outfitters was sponsoring the event. Whenever she dared recall those few precious days and nights, the one clue to JJ's identity seemed to be all the BPO clothing and gear.

La Fête Sauvage had obtained permits from the city for outside tents, but the weather on this late September day had made them unnecessary. Even at five in the afternoon it was still a clear, breezy, seventy degrees.

Becca and Ali had nothing to do at this point but stay out of the way of the waiters and busboys. Becca picked up a perfect yellow leaf and held it in a beam of sunlight. "Have you heard of Lowen Cellular?" she asked.

Ali shook her head.

"Their stock price is sky high, and it's produced quite a few instant millionaires in the company. A lot of them are avid hunters, and once a year, Tom Lowen, the CEO, invites them all to attend a hunting camp at his estate in Eastern Washington. He's a huge fan of BPO and buys all the gear and clothing for the camp there. He also subsidizes a substantial discount as a perk for employees year-round. So the CEO of BPO decided to thank him with this dinner." She paused, watching the progress of the yellow leaf as it floated to the ground. Looking at Ali, she said, "Why would I mention this? Jean-Louis is worried about us. No wives or girlfriends were invited, and none of these hunting enthusiasts are women. In other words, no women but us. There's going to be some heavy drinking."

Ali couldn't see the danger. "What does he think they're going to do, get drunk and drag us behind the laurel hedges?"

"Just don't let anyone get you alone," Becca said, "no matter how harmless he seems."

"Maybe Jean-Louis needs to assign us a bodyguard, or a eunuch, like you used to do in the harems."

They shared a hearty laugh.

Jean-Louis appeared out of nowhere and gave Becca a tender kiss on the lips. Until that moment, Ali hadn't realized their relationship was common knowledge.

"You both look tense," he remarked, rubbing Becca's shoulders. "*Comme toé*. I mean, relax. Chef Jean-Louis has everything under control."

"Shouldn't you be in the kitchen?" Ali asked.

Jean-Louis gave her the stink-eye. "This is not the first time you've told me that my place is in the kitchen. I am well supported by my staff. But it is time for you to take over the hospitality table. You will keep filling the flutes of champagne until dinner starts. If you notice anyone imbibing more than two bottles, let me know."

"Is that a joke?" Ali asked.

"I wish it was. I can't stop anyone from drinking themselves into a coma, but I don't want to run out. At dinner, you'll keep topping off their glasses with either cabernet or chardonnay. Let them see the labels if they like, but if their hands wander, step back. No slapping. Or you can report the *tas de marde* to me. I will endeavor not to commit assault, but I will not hesitate to deliver a quiet tongue lashing."

Jean-Louis looked positively fierce in that moment. His ensemble— orange socks with oxblood loafers, a fitted lilac silk shirt, and black linen trousers—was going to make him stand out from this crowd of he-men like a peacock among herons.

"Jean-Louis," Ali ventured, "don't take this wrong, but aren't you worried that your outfit is a little, uh, outré, for this crowd?"

Jean-Louis broke into his signature low laugh, the rumbling *Heh-heh-heh*. "Once I'm wearing my chef's whites and toque, they won't know. Not that I care. *À bientöt, ma blonde.*" He kissed Becca again and ambled off, still chuckling to himself.

"Why is he calling you '*ma blonde*'?" Ali asked. "Private joke?"

Becca shook her head. "All girlfriends are '*ma blonde.*' It has nothing to do with hair color. Québécois French has some significant differences from Parisian French. It's an education."

Once they were inside, Ali pointed at a long table covered with a gold cloth decorated with royal-blue fleurs-de-lis. "Is that the hospitality table? Should we start opening champagne?"

Becca picked up a bottle from one of the buckets of ice hidden under the table and handed it to Ali. "Be sure to cover the cork with a napkin so you don't put an eye out."

"I know how to open champagne. I'm the food service expert, remember?"

"Don't let it go to your head," Becca said with an extra dose of sarcasm.

As they filled the glasses and the room began to buzz with activity, Ali said, "Your dress is perfect." Becca was wearing a shimmering gold sheath fit for a Greek goddess. Or rather, a Greek goddess in a Hollywood movie.

"Yeah, we look as if we called the table to find out what it was wearing first," Becca said, referring to the royal-blue silk dress she'd given Ali, the color a match for the fleurs-de-lis. "And don't think it's intentional. I didn't choose the tablecloth." Becca touched Ali's necklace. "Nice pearls."

"You know they're fake."

Becca gave her a conspiratorial wink. "I won't tell."

The guests began to trickle in. A short, balding young man at least one size too pudgy for his suit made a beeline for the table, where he picked up a flute of champagne and guzzled it down. Then he held it in Becca's face, impatient for a refill. "How are you *girls*?" he asked as she obliged.

"Easy, *boy*," Becca said. "Don't you think you better pace yourself?"

Rather than taking issue with her impertinence, he grinned and held his glass up for Ali to refill. Taking one of the open bottles, he raised it to Becca, as if toasting her. "This way I can keep better track of my consumption."

"*Oy*," Becca muttered, "it's gonna be a long night."

Ali put a hand on her shoulder. "Don't let them rattle you. Better not to react at all. You don't want to get Jean-Louis in trouble."

Becca drew in a long breath and let it out. "Thanks. I'm lucky that guy didn't get his knickers in a twist."

Ali laughed. "I think that phrase is reserved for women. Men never get their knickers in a twist because all their underwear is comfortable."

Becca grinned. "What about the dancers at Chippendales?"

The next man to approach was fiftyish and also paunchy but with a combover. Leaning across the table, he took a glass of champagne and asked, "Got a joke to share?" He waggled his brows. "You girls look like you're enjoying yourselves."

"We're just so happy to be here," Becca said with a treacly smile.

"Really." The man scowled and walked away.

"Becca …" Ali warned.

"I know, I know. Take it easy. These guys are nothing like our usual clientele. Don't worry, I'll adjust."

A scrawny young man with pomaded hair and a horse face wanted to educate them on the difference between champagne and sparkling wine. This time, after politely hearing him out, Becca said, "Good to know. This happens to be genuine champagne from the province of *Champagne*." She pronounced it in a French accent. Fluttering her lashes, she added, "It was selected by Tom Lowen himself."

He sputtered something under his breath, and like their first customer, took a bottle with him.

Ali sighed. "I don't think we're making any new friends."

"Fine," Becca said. "I know I'm bad at this. You're much better at tolerating jerks."

"You would be too if you'd ever waitressed or had to reproduce ridiculous coffee concoctions for cheeky strangers."

Becca put a hand on her shoulder. "You've got to get back in the PR workforce. I can't stand thinking of you in this situation day in and day out."

Ali shrugged. "I'm used to it. Just keep your cool. I don't want Jean-Louis to have to demonstrate his pugilistic skills before the night is out"—she paused—"or lose Big Paul's as a client."

The rest of cocktail hour passed with no more ripostes from Becca. They received unexpected aid from one glad hander who took to randomly refilling glasses as a means of chatting everyone up. Anyone with a glass had no more reason to bother Ali and Becca.

They moved on to opening bottles of red and white wine.

At seven, Becca said, "I have to visit the powder room. Can you hold down the fort? Let's open another ten bottles of red then hold off until we know the demand."

"Sure," Ali said. "I'll keep opening wine. As for champagne, Mr. Hospitality there has got us covered." The glad hander kept on with his self-appointed task filling flutes. He had never bothered to acknowledge Ali or Becca, who might as well have been invisible. Just like at Ali's catering jobs.

Alone, Ali opened bottles on automatic as she gazed around the room at the various animal heads, thinking that she'd like to bring her sketchpad over and try her hand at them. She smiled to herself. They wouldn't look so fierce once she was done with them.

A man held up a brochure, startling her. She fumbled the bottle, which spilled onto the tablecloth.

"Oh, sorry," he said, putting the bottle upright before it lost more than a few splashes of wine.

Ali marveled at his reflexes.

"That you?" he asked, holding up the brochure again. She looked into his eyes, and the floor began to tilt. "It's a beautiful photo," he went on.

JJ, she thought, reeling. She grabbed the edge of the table for support.

CHAPTER 15

———•———

"ARE YOU ALL RIGHT?" THE JJ lookalike said with genuine concern. "Please, have a seat." He pulled over one of the folding chairs Jean-Louis had set out for them, and she gratefully sat down.

"I'm fine. It's just that—" she hesitated—"you look so much like someone I once knew. You're not … JJ?"

"Well, my name's Jake, but no, my initials are JB." He grinned. "I'm pleased to meet you … uh, miss …?"

"Ali," she said. She couldn't believe anyone could look so much like JJ and not be him. The soulful, gold-flecked brown eyes, the thick chestnut hair—though this man's was cut short and conservatively styled. She'd only guessed at the jawline, of course, but this man appeared shorter. Or was he? A year and a half had passed since JJ led her out of the woods.

"It's lovely to meet you … Ali," Jake said, shaking her hand in a too-firm grip.

"Do you have any brothers?" she asked, resisting the urge to flex her fingers.

He laughed. "A few. They don't look much like me. To start with, they're redheads."

"Are you with Lowen Cellular?"

"No, Big Paul's. I'm the chief executive officer."

Far from sounding all puffed up with his own importance, he treated the title as if it were of little consequence. "I'm sorry if you've had to take a lot of guff from these guys. Give some men a few drinks and take away all the women they stay on their best behavior for, and this is what you get." He made a sweeping gesture that dismissed the entire room as knuckle draggers.

When Becca reappeared, she paled noticeably. "Who *are* you?" she said, unintentionally rude. "Oh God, I'm sorry. It's just that you resemble—"

"I know," he broke in with a stagy laugh, "this JJ fellow. Looks like I have a doppelgänger. And you're …?"

"Becca Himmel."

"Lovely to meet you, Becca." He shook her hand with so much force that her eyes bulged. "I hope you'll both get to enjoy yourselves tonight at some point."

"That's a nice thought," Ali said with the barest hint of sarcasm.

After Jake left, Becca said, "Lord Almighty. That guy looks just like the one in your drawing. But he's kind of stiff. And I think he might have iron digits." She wriggled her fingers. "Not the laidback guy you described. Can't picture *him* roughing it in the woods. But that look he gave you—"

Ali cut her off, "He was just being polite."

"—like he wanted to drag you by the hair back to his cave," Becca said, finishing her thought. "No, let me rethink that … he's the furthest thing from primitive. He looked at you like he wanted to sweep you into his arms and carry you back to his dungeon of love."

Ali clicked her tongue. "You're letting your imagination run away with you. Must be this place. Too much like a castle."

Becca scanned the room. "They're serving entrées. Time to fill wine glasses."

They began to circulate in tandem, Ali with the red wine, Becca with the white. Jake's table came first, and although the man smiled warmly at her, Ali didn't detect the kind of interest Becca claimed to have observed. A few liberties were taken by the other men, though most did little more than brush against them as if by accident, touching their hair or hands as they peered at the wine labels. Nothing worth getting het up about.

That is, until they reached the center table. Only two young men—they couldn't be older than thirty—were currently seated there, either too important or too dangerous to cultivate. Perhaps their tablemates were just circulating. *Too dangerous*, Ali thought with a gulp. From the look of them, they might have clawed their way out of one of the restaurant's oil paintings.

Becca's eyes flashed. Or maybe it was a trick of the light from the gilded chandelier and her gold dress. Regardless of what Ali had seen, she knew she wasn't the only one whose internal warning system had been activated.

One of the men grabbed Becca's wrist and held it while he viewed the label of the bottle she held. He brought to mind a seedy bobcat—dirty blond, scruffy, short, and stocky. The one who zeroed in on Ali had a feral air but reminded her of a wild dog, and not a cute one—a dingo, maybe. Jug ears, slitty eyes, oily manner.

Ali was already thinking of them as Bob and Dink. Did Becca feel as trapped as she did? Like Peter Rabbit confronting Mr. McGregor's cat. Ali placed the bottle on the table, poised to flee.

Dink sat back and said, "What's your hurry? Take a load off. You've got the other tables covered, right?" A quick glance told her every other table was supplied with full glasses and a bottle of red and a bottle of white for refills.

Becca gave an almost imperceptible shake of her head. What did *that* mean? Bob pulled out a chair for her, but she didn't take it. Ali stood back up again. But they didn't flee. They might have been trapped behind an invisible forcefield.

"What's your name, sweetheart?" Dink asked. His breath reeked of alcohol. He must have hit the champagne heavily or brought a flask. If Liam were here, this guy would already be flat out on the floor. When it came to safety, her brother went with his gut, consequences be damned.

"Do you like the food?" Ali asked, not wanting to tell him her name.

Dink took a bite. "I've never had meat like this. I wouldn't venture a guess as to what it is. Good, though." His eyes swept her body. "Tasty. I don't generally like root vegetables, but these beets are good."

"We noticed you when we came in," Bob said. Was that drool at the corner of his mouth? "Most beautiful women we've seen in ages. Hands down."

"Uh, thanks," Becca said in a robotic voice.

"Your dresses match the tablecloth," Bob said. "Intentional?"

"So kind of you to notice," Ali replied.

Then, as luck would have it, Pete, one of the waiters Ali and Becca considered a friend, stood at her side. Pointing to the label, he asked Dink, "How do you like the cabernet?"

"I haven't tried it yet."

"It's a really nice local red," Pete persisted. How could he not pick up on the tension at their table? Ali supposed he was nervous too. Peter was gay, and the testosterone in this room was as thick as the venison steaks.

Pete placed two glasses in front of them. "You've got to taste the cabernet. Chef Jean-Louis won't mind."

He would so *mind*, Ali thought, but Pete had left them little choice. They all dutifully sloshed the wine around in their glasses. Ali went through the motions, although she wouldn't know an award-winning wine if it flashed its medal at her. They sipped; the men guzzled.

"More," Dink said, filling Ali's glass halfway before she could cover it with her hand.

"That's enough, thanks. We're working."

"It *is* nice," Becca said. She took another small sip.

"Are you having a good time?" Pete asked eagerly. He was bored, amusing himself. Maybe she was over-thinking things. Dink and Bob were just being friendly .... They couldn't help it if they came off as sleazy.

"Good eats," Dink said, toasting Pete, "and good company. We're impressed by Big Paul's and The Savage Feast. Its hostesses are smokin' hot."

Pete beamed. "Becca and Ali are the best." With that, he moved on.

Now the men knew their names.

"Ali," Dink purred, "like in the song." He sang, off-key so it was hard to get any sense of the tune, " 'But Ali, for just one more night with you, I'd sell my truck and move to Timbuktu.' "

Not a song she'd heard. She stood up suddenly, and Becca did too, as if released from a spell. In no time they were back at the hospitality table, breathing hard.

Becca blotted her face with a napkin. "What was *that* all about? Those guys are creepy as hell. I can't believe Pete was so dense."

"He's only eighteen," Ali said. She didn't want to get Pete in trouble, much as she'd like to take him to task for volunteering their names.

The restaurant thrummed with activity. A man in front of her stumbled, upsetting a chair. There was a lot of pontificating in loud voices. Several men had reached that stage of drunkenness when you announce everything you have to say in stentorian tones. Some danced alone to the background music, and with classical guitar, you couldn't do much more than sway.

Their final task was to arrange cordial glasses of Drambuie on trays. Like this crowd wasn't drunk enough ....

When the waiters started pouring coffee, Ali and Becca circulated with the trays. They were tempted to skip Bob and Dink, but the two men had been joined by others and no longer seemed interested in ogling them. One of the Lowen Cellular employees stood up with a hand mic. He was making in-jokes about the company and Big Paul's, most of them off-color and sexist. Was his comedy act planned or impromptu? His colleagues loved it, but drunks were easily amused.

Finally the crowd began to thin as men weaved outside to board the limos in the parking lot, Jean-Louis and Jake having anticipated a bacchanal. Ali and Becca had just kicked off their heels when they jumped to their feet, startled by a loud crash. Someone had fallen against one of the tables, pulling off the cloth. Broken china and glass surrounded a man lying on the floor, either dead or out cold. The remaining occupants of the room converged to cluster around the fallen man.

Becca clapped a hand over her mouth. "Shit! I've got to see if this guy is okay. They're going to smother him. Could you find Jean-Louis? He's probably in the kitchen."

Don't go, said an urgent voice in her head that sounded suspiciously like Liam's.

That's nonsense, she told it as she reluctantly slipped back into her heels. *I have to do my part.*

The kitchen was deserted. Hearing voices coming from the direction of the tents, she went to investigate. No one was there. She stepped into the first tent and called out, "Jean-Lou … *oof*."

Suddenly she found herself lying flat against the ground on her stomach, the breath knocked out of her. Her scream was little more than a squeak. She gasped for air as the heavy body of a man pressed her into the canvas floor. The man panted wetly in her ear, as one hand clamped over her mouth and the other ripped the front of her dress and groped her breast. She tried bucking him off the way she'd been shown in self-defense class, but she might as well have been a mouse in a sticky trap. The steely fingers covering her mouth made using her teeth impossible.

Don't give up, Liam's voice commanded. *Fight!*

The hand on her mouth loosened its grip, and she bit into the meat of its palm.

The man cursed a blue streak then slapped her head. Stunned but still conscious, she surrendered, despairing, knowing her best bet for survival was to play dead.

At the same moment she willed her body to go limp, the lead weight of her attacker's body was gone. She heard a series of grunts, curses, and blows. Then, "Ali, can you hear me?" A familiar man's voice.

Eyes still shut, she said, "Yes."

"Ali, it's Jake. Can you move your fingers and toes?"

She'd lost one shoe, but she definitely could move her toes—fingers too.

"Good. I'm going to carry you. Is that okay?" Not waiting for an answer, he lifted her gently into his arms.

She heard Jean-Louis say, "Let's move her to my office. What happened?" Then, "Is he still alive?"

"I didn't beat him up *that* badly," Jake said.

"I don't know," Jean-Louis said. "He's fucked up pretty good."

Ali didn't want to open her eyes. She had a vague sense of being out of danger, but she was still disoriented, and her brain didn't seem to want to focus. When they laid her down on the leather couch, she curled into a ball, silent tears streaming down her cheeks.

"My God!" she heard Becca say. "What happened?"

"A man attacked her," Jean-Louis replied.

"I bet I know who," Becca said.

ALI LOST ALL TRACK OF time. Gradually she felt strong enough to sit up. Someone—Becca, she hoped—had pinned together the front of her dress. She felt sore all over, as if she'd been tackled by a linebacker.

"Ali?"

She opened one eye to find Becca sitting in the chair next to the couch, legs and arms crossed.

"Present." *Jesus*. It wasn't grade school. "I'm awake," she clarified. She opened both eyes and rolled onto her back, experimentally flexing her arms and legs. "I feel like I was run over by a truck."

"Not quite," Becca said, "but you *were* ambushed. By one of those creeps who was giving us a hard time earlier."

"Dink?"

"Huh?"

"Nothing. I thought he looked like a dingo."

Becca continued, "His story is that you were soused and came on to him. Unfortunately, the other guys at the table were too drunk themselves to confirm how little we had to drink. His dad is Tom Lowen. You know, the billionaire?"

"Oh," Ali moaned, "that sounds bad."

"Jake beat him up," Becca continued, "badly. The police want to talk to you."

"Oh shit, of course they do." She moved to a sitting position. "Am I decent?"

"You look quite presentable, considering." Becca patted her knee. "Oh God, Ali, I am so sorry this happened to you. If everyone hadn't been preoccupied with that other guy—"

"How is he?"

"It was a heart attack. He'll live."

"That's good." She noted the raindrops rolling down the window. When had the clouds rolled in? "What time is it?"

Becca pointed to the wall clock. "Closing in on midnight."

A knock on the door. A police officer entered, balding, middle-aged, weary. Ali recounted the sequence of events as best she could. Because she'd kept her eyes squeezed shut, it didn't take long.

After he left, Jean-Louis came in. "*Tabarnak*," he said in an exhausted tone that didn't fit the curse. "What a shitshow. Ali, the police have gone. I've been talking to Tom Lowen, who is a very rich man. He says he won't press charges against Jake if—"

Ali interrupted him. "Jake? Why would he press charges against Jake?"

"He pulled that *ostie de colon* off you and tossed him aside like a sack of flour. Then he picked him up by the shirt and kneed him in the nuts. He might have trouble, uh, siring children."

Ali shuddered. "I guess that's good to hear."

"This is distasteful for me, so know that I am only the messenger. Mr. Lowen says he won't press charges against Jake as long as you don't accuse his son of assault. He wants you to know that he is deeply sorry for his son's actions, and that he is going to get him the help he needs so that nothing like this ever happens again."

"Oh, sure," Ali said, rubbing her neck, "like that's going to happen."

Jean-Louis and Becca were staring at the ground with a general air of defeat.

"What's the point?" Ali went on. "*Attempted* rape. Not actual rape. I can't help but recall that rape case a few years back—guy with rich, famous, connected relatives. His lawyers tried to destroy the victim's reputation. And he was still acquitted. Say that Mr. Lowen and I both press charges. Now we have bad publicity all around: for the restaurant, Big Paul's, and Lowen Cellular. And my reputation is toast. To what end?"

Becca nodded. "I get it. But Ali, you need time to consider. You might not be thinking clearly. What if he does this to someone else? You could put him in prison. Have him branded a sex offender."

Ali gave her a hard stare. "Even if the prosecutors *did* manage to convict him, how long would he serve for attempted rape or assault, do you think? At the very least they'd succeed in reducing the charges. No bad labels for the sons of rich guys."

Becca gave a helpless shrug. "He'd probably get probation for drunk and disorderly."

Ali winced at the sharp pain in her temples. "Do you have any Advil?" Seeing the bottle on the table and the glass of water, she helped herself.

FOR MANY DAYS TO COME, Ali wondered if she'd been right to let the matter drop. Telling her story in court *might* have made her feel less helpless in the long run. But she couldn't shake the idea that Dink's lawyer would have painted an ugly picture of her as just another party girl who put herself in harm's way by drinking too much. On the job, no less. How would *that* help her employment prospects?

Nothing like this had ever happened to her before. Though perhaps it had, and she didn't recall. There had been that period before she turned eight that was remarkably short of memories ….

That night, when Ali finally fell asleep, she was revisited by the old nightmare.

CHAPTER 16

—·—

Part of the horror of the dream was its murkiness. Ali was in bed and convinced in that moment that she was awake. A shadow appeared and started to form a vaguely human shape—just empty eyeholes, a mouth, and hands. It made no sound, though its mouth gaped open and its fingers clawed at a filthy veil. The creature was reaching for her, and each time, it got a little closer. Then Liam appeared and pulled it back down into the ground with a mighty *whoosh*. All the while she lay paralyzed, unable to yell or move. Then she woke up.

Each time the nightmare recurred, she had to turn on the light and read something comforting. Vague as it was, the horror stayed with her. That first night she had the dream twice. In the weeks that followed, the creature showed up almost every night.

Ali took a few days off work, saying she was recovering from a bike accident. No one asked to hear the details. She didn't have that kind of relationship with her co-workers.

On October fourth, the *Seattle Times* published a rave review of La Fête Sauvage, using the picture of Ali and the male model from the brochure. Becca came over with a stash of chardonnay from the Big Paul's event, and they shared a bottle as they sat in front of a crackling fire, the gentle rain on the roof providing a soothing soundtrack. Jean-Louis naturally felt terrible that the event had turned out so badly for Ali and was doing all he could to make it up to her. The review in the *Times* called dining at La Fête Sauvage "the adventure of a lifetime," dubbing the restaurant "North Bend's Tavern on the Green—a fantasy hunting lodge with novel nouvelle cuisine."

"A flat-out rave, *and* it rhymes," Becca marveled. "The perfect quote for when we revise the brochure." She refilled their glasses.

"Or" Ali said, "translated into French, *nouvelle-nouvelle* cuisine. I'm guessing the distinction between 'novel' and 'new' will fly over most people's heads."

Becca gave her a curious look. "Always a danger for writers who are into subtlety. That JJ clone, Jake … have you heard from him?"

Ali wrinkled her nose. "Why would I?"

"Um, because Jean-Louis gave him our number?" From her apologetic expression, Ali gathered that Becca knew her boyfriend had overstepped.

Seeing the tears spring to Ali's eyes, Becca said in a small voice, "I can see you're still hurting. I keep thinking I might have spared you, if only we'd stayed together." She gave Ali's hand a little shake. "I wish you were more open to meeting someone. It must be hard to be so beautiful."

Ali sniffed back tears. "Like you wouldn't know."

"Honey, I'm pretty enough, but not in your league. I'd guess most men are too intimidated to say boo or just want to collect you like in that creepy John Fowles' novel. I'm amazed you made it through the foster-child thing in one piece."

"Thanks to Liam," Ali replied simply. "He was one tough dude." Alarmed at the slip, she corrected herself. "*Is. Is* one tough dude. He was always there. I can't explain it. It's like he had eyes in the back of his head. Or a sixth sense, when it came to me. Even this time, I thought I heard him tell me not to go into the tent."

Becca clearly didn't know what to make of this, so she didn't respond. Instead she said, "Are you going to be okay? Do you need counseling?"

Ali shook her head. "The main consequence seems to be the return of that recurring dream. The one where the man attacks me but is stopped by Liam. At first he was faceless. Now he looks like a cartoon ghoul."

"That's a drag," Becca said. After a pause, she went on, "Even before Liam disappeared, you didn't talk about him much. I detected a subtext that wasn't wholly positive."

"His toughness wasn't always a good thing. He was fierce."

Becca nodded. "I remember. But he didn't hurt anyone physically, right? I figured he just stared them down until they burst into flames. I had little contact with your brother, considering how close you and I have been. Even on those nights he joined us to watch TV, he didn't speak much. I do remember those eyes. Otherworldly blue, like yours, only more deep-set."

She waved a hand as if to cool her hot cheeks. "I had a crush on him. Who wouldn't? Except that he scared me. He flirted, but I didn't get the impression he was really interested."

"He was interested. I told him in no uncertain terms to leave you alone. For him, all women are disposable."

"I wondered. It's just as well. Do you think he'd have grown out of it?"

Ali narrowed her eyes. "Don't you mean, 'Do you think he'll grow out of it?'"

Becca shrugged. "Sure. I'm sorry. I want to believe he's alive too." She paused. "I know Trip and Luis muddied the waters, and now this Dink reprobate, but not all men are cut from that same soiled cloth. What about hiring a matchmaker? My parents would pay. There's Nathan. He's crazy about you. I told you he went through rehab, right? He's even working again. His tech skills are much in demand."

"I like Nathan well enough, but it would feel incestuous. He's like a brother."

Becca stood up and stretched. "Oh well, I tried! But Ali?"

"Yes?"

"If Jake calls, give him a chance. He seems like a decent guy. He rescued you, for God's sake. He's handsome and rich, and he's your type."

Ali's laugh sounded bitter, even to her. "Trip was handsome and rich, and look where that got me? Anyway … Jake's the furthest thing from a woodsman."

Becca made a face. "You hardly knew JJ. You didn't sleep with him. A kiss is just a kiss, right? Lots of jerks are good kissers. But now he's the ideal. Like the prince in a fairytale. It ends with a kiss, nothing more. None of the messy stuff."

Ali wanted to protest, but Becca had a point. What if JJ had taken her up on her obvious invitation? Supposing the sex had been bad? Nowhere to run. He was right to turn her down. If it had been good … then what? He might have still sent her home without revealing his identity. She wasn't sure what was worse. A fresh wave of humiliation swept over her. If she'd kept her hands and lips to herself, at least she'd still have her pride.

"Some of us have to settle for second best," Becca said.

"Is that what you're doing with Jean-Louis?"

Becca burst into merry laughter. "Are you kidding? Jean-Louis is prime cut. I'm the luckiest girl in the world."

LATER ON, AS SHE LAY in bed listening to the now-driving rain, Ali tried to picture her brother Liam. The image was fading. Was she repressing things? She wished she had letters, something to sharpen the memories. The photos were few and far between. Annual school portraits. A profile view from high school graduation. With no party clothing, she and Liam didn't attend school dances. No blurry Polaroids, no home movies. They hadn't really been a family. Now their foster parents were dead, and there were no photos of them. It was as if they'd never existed.

In high school it had been okay for Liam to date but off-limits for her. She'd witnessed enough tearful scenes to conclude he was none too nice to his girlfriends. A Heathcliff, a tortured soul. Angry. Somehow she'd escaped that legacy of their childhood. Unlike him, she didn't blame everyone else for their troubles—their drug-addled birth mother, their phantom sperm-donor father. Not usually. She seemed to be doing the self-pity thing pretty well this evening.

THE NEXT DAY, A MONDAY, the phone rang around three in the afternoon. Ali had just returned from a run.

"Hello!" she answered, a little out of breath.

"Hello," a familiar man's voice said. "Is this Ali?"

"Yes."

"Ali, this is Jake. I'm sorry if I interrupted something. Is now a good time to talk?"

Ali gulped, stunned into silence. His voice was at once warm and formal, like a voiceover for a pharmaceutical ad.

"Uh, Ali? Are you still there?"

Worried she might faint, she collapsed into the nearest chair. "Yes, I'm here."

"Can we meet? Can I take you to dinner?"

Was he really asking her out?

"Um, are you actually … I mean, there's no need …."

She thought she heard a sigh. "Please. I wish I could take you to La Fête Sauvage"—he had a convincing French accent—"because it's the nicest place in town, but the last thing I want to do is make you return to the scene of the crime." He paused. "Only problem is, to find another restaurant of that caliber, you have to go to Seattle or Bellevue. Do you mind if I take you to Seattle?"

"Jake, uh … I don't have a dress." When he didn't respond, she added, "A *nice* dress, I mean." She paused, not wanting to tell him the dress she wore to the BPO event was a gift. "I only had one nice dress. And it's ruined. That man … ripped it."

"Oh, Ali, I'm so sorry." His tone was heartfelt. "It doesn't matter what you wear."

I'll just bet, she thought. She'd love to see his reaction to her Laura Ashley shepherdess dress. She'd figure out something. Too bad Becca and she weren't the same height or body type.

"Okay," she said cautiously.

Clearing his throat, he said, "Are you free next Friday?"

"Yes."

"Pick you up at seven?"

She gave him their address.

ON THURSDAY, A PACKAGE ARRIVED from the downtown-Seattle Betsey Johnson store. Three satin retro-style A-line dresses, one hot-pink, one a cool, shimmery ice-blue, and one bright red. Vibrating with excitement, Ali tried each of them on, amazed and delighted that they fit perfectly and worked with her coloring. Either Jake was a major player or he knew a really good saleswoman. The card read, "I can't replace what you've lost, but you can't blame a guy for trying. I hope this gives you enough choices." Somehow he also knew her shoe size. Later that afternoon, three pairs of strappy sandals— gold, black, and red—arrived. She didn't recognize the designer, but she knew quality when she saw it. Curious, she searched for the name of the boutique. Nothing. Very discreet of him.

She should probably reject the gifts, at least until she got an inkling of what this man was like. He might turn out to be worse than her attacker.

Or he might just help her forget JJ.

CHAPTER 17

———•———

As Friday night rolled around, Ali agonized over which of the dresses to wear for her date, finally settling on the shimmery ice-blue sheath with a saucy fluted hem and the gold sandals. The only jewelry she owned were the fake pearls and matching earrings. She swore under her breath as she stood staring into the entrance closet, wishing Becca had left behind her sassy red swing coat. Ali would be forced to wear her black wool monstrosity from several seasons back—too long, too heavy, almost as shapeless as a puffy coat. With temperatures in the 40s and more rain threatening, a sweater alone wasn't an option. The effect of the new dress would be ruined by goosebumps and lips as blue as her eyes. Her vintage sparkly black cotton sweater was too funky for the elegantly youthful dress, but it would have to do. She wore her shoulder-length, slippery hair loose. No point in trying to tame it into an updo. Locks of hair would escape the bobby pins until she looked like a hedgehog.

The limo glided into their driveway tentatively, as if finding itself unexpectedly at a monster truck rally. Ali tried not to cower as she approached the door, held open by the grizzled driver, and slid in next to Jake. She almost slid right out again at the daunting sight of her date, male-model handsome in his bespoke suit. This was so *not* her scene. It was like that nightmare where she'd found herself at a Miss America pageant wearing nothing but a worn nightie. What if JJ had been clean-shaven and dressed to the nines when they first met? She'd have never worked up the courage to confide in him. She fundamentally mistrusted Jake's rarified world, believing it to be wasteful, corrupt, cruel, and built on lies—a prejudice bolstered by her experiences as a caterwaiter. George and Emily's self-righteous ravings about the upper class hadn't helped.

Eyes wide, Ali observed her surroundings. The buttery leather of the seats, the clear barrier isolating them from the driver, the minibar, Jake himself. A whiff of his expensive cologne made her rethink her dislike for synthetic fragrances.

So far she'd only heard "Hi, how are you, you look lovely." There was no awkward, too-firm handshake. No touching at all. Had she forgotten to say hello? She had to stop astral-projecting and join the party. As if on automatic pilot, she reached out to accept the flute of champagne he handed her, murmured a thank you, and took a long sip. She relaxed a little as it simultaneously cooled and warmed her insides.

If the black wool coat looked as dowdy as she suspected, Jake didn't let on. He called out to the driver, "Lawrence, let's go. We're already likely to hit some traffic." The smile reappeared. "Are you comfortable?"

"Sure. I love limos. At least so far, this being my only limo experience."

Great. From insentient to snarky. She had to get a grip.

He let it pass. "I know so little about you, other than that you are stunningly beautiful and graceful in the face of adversity."

She felt a goofy smile spread across her face, making her realize she'd probably been goggling at Jake like a cornered mouse. "Y-you exaggerate," she stammered, too shy to meet his gaze.

"Jean-Louis says you were a foster child and that you recently received a master's degree in Communication."

"That's right." She stared straight ahead. "You can see just how well that has paid off so far."

"You're young, talented, and charming. You'll land on your feet."

She finally let her eyes meet his. So like JJ's. *Enough,* she told herself. *JJ isn't free.* Jake's surreptitious glances seemed to imply she hung the moon and stars. And he was undeniably gorgeous in his own right.

Still, she didn't trust this ardent wooing, like something out of a seduction scenario from the 1950s. He could be putting on an act. If so, why? What was feeding her distrust? Her own insecurity or the eternal flame she kept lit for the elusive JJ?

Jake's eyes kept dropping to her coat as if he were itching to see what lay beneath—which of the dresses she was wearing and if it suited her. He'd given her sandals a satisfied glance when she entered the limo.

The silence thickened.

"I'm so glad you agreed to go out with me tonight," he said finally. "Jean-

Louis told me you were born and raised in Seattle. I was too." As if sensing her nervousness, he went on to talk about how much the city had changed since the first and only Starbucks opened in the Pike Place Market. She was grateful for the harmless chitchat, though curious as to why he divulged almost no personal information. From his company bio, she knew that he'd graduated from Lakeside and had gone on to earn a bachelor's degree in economics from Harvard University then an MBA from Stanford Business School. If he'd bragged about that predictable rich-boy journey, she'd have liked him a lot less. Gradually she relaxed enough to tell him her impressions of North Bend, and they began to discuss favorite hiking trails along the I-90 Corridor.

The French bistro was perched high above Dexter Street with a sweeping view of the Seattle skyline. Jake helped Ali remove her coat, and she quickly slipped off the sweater, glad that it was warm in the restaurant. He gratified her with a moment of frank admiration that seemed spontaneous, as opposed to almost everything else he did. "I didn't thank you for the shoes and dresses," she said, calmer now and eager to please. "They're lovely."

His smooth cheeks fairly glowed. "Think nothing of it. Seeing you in that dress is thanks enough."

"I didn't get a chance to ask you," she said, not wanting to broach the topic of her assault but too curious to let it lie. "How is it that you were in the right place at the right time? I mean, how did you know I was in danger?"

He broke into that dazzling smile that reminded her so much of JJ. "I had my eye on you," was all he said.

Her menu had no prices. Did his? It must. The wine steward's smug smile of approval told her the wine Jake chose was top dollar. No expense spared.

Trip had been from a wealthy family, and he always paid, but he'd never treated her to anything like this. The performances they attended were inexpensive plays and concerts on campus and the modest restaurants they frequented catered to poor university students.

JJ was a whiskey snob, she reminded herself. How was appreciating good wine any different? This man was just as great-looking in his own highly polished way. A man who worked out religiously, had always eaten nutritious food, and was blessed with excellent genes. JJ would be all those things too. For all she knew, a dinner date with JJ would be exactly like this. So why couldn't she stop comparing them? Jake wasn't giving her mixed messages, a solid point in his favor.

Jake spoke French to the waiter and was surprised when Ali understood.

She ventured to speak some French too, self-conscious as she was about her accent. If he found her efforts laughable, the waiter didn't let on. She wouldn't have dared speak French with the wine steward even if her accent was flawless. She didn't speak wine.

If anything, Jake was a little too socially adept. A CEO would have to be the consummate salesman. Wasn't his job basically to charm the pants off clients and investors? Funny expression. No doubt many women had allowed him to charm them out of their pants … and panties. After being dumped by Trip and having to sic Liam on Luis, Ali had vowed to steer clear of practiced charmers. And now she had a new ideal—her sincere, unpretentious man in the woods, a guy's guy who was comfortable in his own skin, content to listen.

As good a listener as Jake was, he was intensely aware of the impression he made on others, not just her. Ali rubbed her arms to warm them, wishing she could put her sweater back on but not wanting to appear gauche and inappropriate. She wasn't normally self-conscious. Apparently it was contagious. JJ hadn't cared what she wore.

The dinner conversation did little more than skim the surface, and Jake was vague on the subject of family, only mentioning two tall, redheaded brothers and a sister. His father had founded Big Paul's, whose mascot was the mythical lumberjack, Paul Bunyan. He seemed to be on the "right" side of politics, which for her was the left side. Predictably, he was against gun control, despite all the mass shootings over the years, so they veered away from that subject quickly. After all, Big Paul's sold hunting gear, and hunters tended to believe that liberals would start with automatic weapons and eventually get around to their grandfather's deer rifle.

Ali was on guard in a way she never had been with JJ. When Jake asked about her family, she gave him the sitcom version, a few stories about her hippie foster parents, emphasizing the slightly kooky part and neglecting to mention their emotional distance. They'd volunteered her for babysitting at a women's shelter and dragged Liam along when they worked on projects benefitting the homeless—that was where he learned to build or fix anything. They didn't believe in the Bible, but they did favor quotations such as "Idle hands are the devil's workshop." For some reason she didn't tell him that George and Emily had died.

"Thank goodness for my twin brother Liam. How we longed to kick up our heels. He could be pretty intense, but he was true blue."

True blue. What did that even mean? Jake just gazed at her as if her every word was golden. Although, unlike JJ, he didn't ply her for details. Why not? He was a master of the schooled expression.

"Liam disappeared in January of 1995," she said. "Everyone believes he was blown up in a terrorist attack."

"I'm so sorry," he said with sympathy but an odd lack of hesitation. Wouldn't your average person receive such a revelation with a degree of shock? Wouldn't he question the "everyone believes" part of her description of Liam's fate? His reaction was more appropriate to news of a simpler tragedy—a car accident, an illness. Had Jean-Louis mentioned her brother? Of course. He loved the sound of his own voice. What else had he told Jake?

Jake placed his warm, callus-free hand on hers and gave it a light squeeze. "The odds of that happening must be astronomically high. How terrible for you. Where did it take place?"

She ran through the details of the incident without clarifying her belief that Liam was still alive. She struggled with the urge to pull her hand away because he was actually holding it now, and that felt too intimate on such short acquaintance. It also felt too good, as if she were betraying JJ.

The old sadness engulfed her, despair over a future without her brother or JJ in it. When she took a moment to fight back tears, Jake kindly averted his eyes. She went on, "I wanted to hold a little private memorial service to bid him goodbye. I drove down Highway 101 past Port Angeles and Sol Duc Hot Springs and parked in a random spot by the side of the road. Then I hiked in a short way and buried the medicine bag next to a tree."

Now she was just lying.

"That was brave of you," he said. "You might have gotten lost."

CHAPTER 18

———·———

WHEN JAKE DROPPED ALI OFF at the door to her house, it was just past eleven. She was feeling more relaxed, thanks to two glasses of wine and an after-dinner cordial. When he made his move, she didn't resist. Jake's kiss was soft and firm, teasing and surprisingly pleasant. In spite of herself, she started to respond.

Then the door opened, and they sprang apart as if a gong had sounded.

"Oh!" Becca exclaimed. "Um, Mr. O'Connell. I just … I didn't mean to interrupt anything."

Ali wasn't convinced, and she doubted Jake was either, but she figured Becca had done her a favor. "No problem. Jake, thank you for a lovely evening." She reached for his hand, noting how he automatically went into that too-firm-handshake mode.

"Can I call you?"

"That would be nice. Thanks again!"

After the door closed behind Jake, Becca dragged Ali into the living room, where Jean-Louis sat on the couch, holding a glass of cabernet with such élan that he might be about to introduce a classic film on PBS.

He grinned at her. "I see you have a new *chum*."

"That's the Québécois term for boyfriend, right? I think you're getting ahead of yourself. We've had exactly one date."

Becca gave her an obvious onceover. "New outfit?"

Ali kicked off her heels. "Jake was thoughtful enough to replace the torn dress."

Becca raised her eyebrows. "Suits you perfectly. The sandals too?"

Her sly smile prompted Ali to ask, "It was you, wasn't it? You told him my dress and shoe sizes."

"He did ask," Becca said, "and he can afford to be generous. Did the gifts make you uncomfortable?"

"A little," Ali admitted, "but I do like the dress."

Becca pointed at the sandals. "Those are nice too! He must really like you."

"I guess so," Ali replied. Then she thought, *Is that true?* She did think Jake admired her. But she hadn't felt the kind of connection she'd observed between Becca and Jean-Louis at their first meeting. Jake was totally buttoned-up—the type of man who played his cards close to his chest. Unlike Jean-Louis, who wore his heart on his sleeve. "I hardly know him," Ali went on, "and he already knew quite a bit about me." She gave Jean-Louis a pointed look.

"Guilty as charged," Jean-Louis said with a comic frown. "I do like to talk. But I trust him."

"Why is that?" Becca asked, curious rather than accusatory. "It's not like he's a regular."

"He *is* a regular," Jean-Louis admitted. "Lunch, usually, when you are not there." He twisted sideways to peer at Ali. "You could do worse than Jake O'Connell. He is a little stiff, perhaps. A little too carefully charming. That goes with the territory, I think. I know what he deals with because I must do the same—be kind to everyone, no matter how little they deserve it. Offend no one! They are all potential 'friends' who can make or unmake your business." He finished off his wine and held the glass out to Becca to be filled. "Ali, would you like some?"

She shook her head. "I already drank too much at dinner."

"My experience with the man is limited," he continued, "but I see no reason not to like him. I detected none of the arrogance that often goes with power. Unless he is hiding some moral defect, he is a gentleman." He leaned forward, eyes boring into hers. "*Là là* … dating someone who reminds you of an ideal man from your past seems a little *téméraire*, uh, foolhardy. Like replacing a beloved pet dog with the same breed." He stood, as if preparing to go. "*Pis*, even if JJ were to magically reappear—poof!—it would not be just. *Juste*. Fair, I mean. You have endowed him with many remarkable qualities. Sometimes the mountain gives birth to a mouse."

Ali looked to Becca for an explanation.

"He means, sometimes you're destined to be disappointed."

Jean-Louis slitted his eyes at Becca. "*Heille*, I don't need an interpreter," he said tartly.

She patted him on the shoulder. "Of course not." To Ali, she said, "Jean-Louis has a point. It's hard enough to make a relationship work without all the baggage."

Ali looked from one to the other. "I thought you both wanted me to date him."

Jean-Louis gave a dramatic shrug. "I simply make myself the devil's advocate." He stood. "Did you get what you came for, *ma blonde*?"

After they left, Ali sank back down on the couch to review the date. The memory of JJ was fading, but Ali's impression had been of a man like Jake, only taller, more muscular, and with Jean-Louis's ease, grace, and lack of pretentions. Jake was nice, but he cared about appearances far more than Ali ever could. He was a wine snob, a meticulous dresser. He wore five-thousand-dollar bespoke suits, monogrammed shirts, and un-scuffed Italian shoes. Even his socks looked expensive. Becca had once joked that she couldn't date a particular man because she "didn't have the wardrobe." Her bohemian style seemed perfect for Jean-Louis. Unless Jake supplied Ali with clothes for every occasion, how would she manage? She would be too self-conscious wearing anything except what he had given her.

As she often did when harried, she reached for her sketchpad. The picture she doodled was supposed to be of Jake in his suit. But the end result looked more like JJ—his confident stance, muscular build, and shaggy hair. He glared at her with an air of reproach. With a heavy sigh, she tossed the pad aside and turned out the lights.

Her last thoughts before sleep claimed her were of Liam. She tried again to picture him and wondered how he'd react to Jake. Not well, she thought. He made it a point to never date rich girls.

That night she had The Dream again. It had blessedly left her alone for a few nights. At times the face almost came into focus. She turned on the light and read a magazine until she was calm enough to sleep.

JAKE WAITED ONLY UNTIL MONDAY to call again. Clearly aware of her sartorial predicament, he proposed the one date that wouldn't require her to scramble for appropriate clothing: a hike for the following Saturday. Western Washington was experiencing a beautiful Indian summer with daytime temperatures in the 60s and several clear days in between bouts of rain. Jake asked her if she was up for Melakwa Lake, a high-elevation challenge known for its brilliant fall colors—the yellow, red, and orange leaves of alders, maples, and huckleberry bushes. Her hiking clothes were far inferior to anything you could buy at Big Paul's. She tried not to squirm when he blandly assessed her appearance.

At first she might have been hiking with a stranger. They were cordial, sharing anecdotes from past hikes—the black bear sightings, the sudden shifts in weather. He had summited Mount Rainier, along with other impressive peaks. But he kept his pace slow and steady, and she was never winded on the steep, rocky path.

During a water break, she asked casually, "Do you visit the Olympic Peninsula much? It's one of my favorite places on earth."

"Sure," he said with his uneasy grin. "I love Hurricane Ridge. There's a beautiful twelve-mile loop that begins at Heart of the Hills campground."

"Yes, I know it." She put her water bottle back in her pack. She had discussed that hike with JJ. That was odd. "What about the Hoh Rain Forest?"

"What about it?"

"I've heard there's a log cabin hidden in the thick of the forest about an hour and a half's hike from Highway 101."

"Probably more than one. It would be a good place to go off the grid. An attractive destination for survivalists or people escaping the law."

"Do you know of any cabin in particular?"

"No." He gave her a sidelong glance. "Do you?"

Before she could reply, he took her by the shoulders and gazed into her eyes. She couldn't feel the heat. In fact, he might have been a doctor making a diagnosis. "I'm almost afraid of you," he said.

Her laughter sounded false in her own ears. "That's ridiculous."

"I wonder." He drew her in for a kiss. She felt her shoulders relax and her lips respond, an unfamiliar stirring …. But then he pulled away and held her in a loose embrace, more like a brother than a lover.

They sat on a flat rock overlooking the lake for lunch, which was nothing fancy: turkey and Muenster-cheese sandwiches, regular potato chips, apple slices. Evidence that not everything had to be gourmet with him.

Jake didn't kiss her again till they stood on her doorstep. As before, his lips lingered, seemed to carry a question. Again, just as she began to melt into him, he released her.

He checked his watch. "Will you look at the time? Sorry, I have to run."

She thought, *What just happened?* The word *calculated* came to mind. Did this man ever let passion carry him away? What was his game? What made her suspect there was one?

He smiled and tweaked her nose as if she were a young Shirley Temple.

She suppressed the urge to say, "Gee Willikers!" How old was he? Somewhere around thirty. Somehow he acted a lot older.

"You're quite a hiker," he said. "I'm impressed. Maybe someday we'll climb a mountain together." Nothing sounded less appealing—she balked at the prospect of crampons and crevasses—but she smiled in response. "I'm sorry we can't keep this going and have dinner tonight. I have a business thing."

"That's okay. I had a really fun time." *Ugh, so Shirley Temple.*

"Good! I'll see you soon." She half expected a pat on the head.

The house was unoccupied. Becca rarely stopped by anymore. To debrief, Ali would have to make an appointment. She wasn't feeling particularly dreamy as she boiled water for tea.

After she warmed up a plate of roast chicken and potatoes and steamed a handful of green beans, Ali sat in front of the TV and turned the station to Turner Classic Movies, where she found a fun black and white film starring Ray Milland. *The Uninvited.* Scary for its time, no doubt. Nothing to lose sleep over now. She wondered if Jake liked classic films. She wished he was more like Ray Milland. Dapper but grounded. Brave, confident, not hyper-masculine but no dandy either. Wait, that *did* describe Jake. He was handsome, in fantastic shape, rich, and a good kisser—pretty much everything a girl could ask for.

Only, he wasn't JJ.

Ali groaned aloud and beat her fists against the couch. JJ was off the table. Did Jake want her or not? Was she the one giving mixed messages now? Had she indulged in so much fantasy that no real man was going to fit the bill?

PART II

CHAPTER 19

———•———

AT EIGHT SUNDAY MORNING, ALI was foaming milk at her job at Sully's. The steady stream of customers allowed her to go on automatic so that the time passed quickly. The coffee chain sold soundtrack compilations, and they'd just put out a new one, *Country Crossover Faves*. She was just thinking that country music was pretty catchy, that she ought to listen to more of it, when a lyric permeated her consciousness, "Ali, for just one more night with you, I'd sell my truck and move to Timbuktu." Ali … Timbuktu. Something Dink had said …. She clutched the counter, reeling against a wave of vertigo.

"Steph," she asked her co-worker, "do you mind if I take a quick break? I have to make a phone call."

Stephanie glanced about in a panic. The place was almost filled to capacity. "Okay, but don't dally."

"I won't, I promise," Ali said, taken aback by the old-fashioned word. Steph, with her Southern accent, candy-pink lips, and big hair, might have stepped out of a country song herself.

Ali fled to the backroom, where the music was still mostly drowned out by customers talking and laughing. She was desperate to understand the lyrics. "Babe in the Woods …." She didn't catch the rest of the chorus. Then she heard, "The Fates" and "laughs"—or did she just think she heard them? She closed her eyes and was able to make out "stole my voice," "courage," and "safe and sound." Could it really be the poem JJ had written for her?

Her heart was pounding. Stomach queasy, she sat on a box and put her head between her legs.

"Ali?" It was Stephanie. "Ralph and I have our hands full. Are you off the phone? Ali, are you okay?"

She thought she heard, "Ali, if you ever hear this song ...." *Oh God. It can't be*. It was addressed to *her*.

"Steph, the song that's playing, do you know it?"

Steph nodded. "Sure. It's Joe Bob Blade's big hit, 'Babe in the Woods.' Everyone knows that song. Crossed over from the Country charts. Ali?"

The song had finished. With a mighty effort, Ali produced a reassuring smile. "I'm fine."

The rush of customers continued, and somehow she made it to the end of the shift without incident. From work, she headed straight for the grocery store. If the song was such a huge hit, she might find answers on the periodicals rack. Her car was currently in the shop, so a trip to a record store would require a bus ride to Bellevue.

She scanned the covers of the many tabloids and fanzines. Then she caught sight of a familiar face. Similar to Jake's, but more sensual, the lips parted. A cleft chin like Robert Plant's. The magazine was called *Spurs 'n Sparkin'*.

The headline read COUNTRY MUSIC IDOL JOE BOB BLADE TELLS ALL.

Her stomach lurched. She quickly paid for the magazine and ran home as fast as her unsteady legs could carry her. Sitting on the couch, she flipped to the article.

On a recent Friday afternoon, our interviewer Anthony Ray Dorian caught up with Joe Bob Blade for a heart-to-heart at his manager's office in Nashville. Far from what you'd expect of a country music star, Joe Bob was born into a prominent Seattle Catholic family and studied to be a classical guitarist. He spent a few years as a session musician before his manager Linc Blaydon discovered him on open mic night at a Nashville bar. The rest is history.

Anthony: Joe, the last year and a half have been life-changing for you. You were already flying high, with two big honors under your belt: the Country Music Association's Horizon Award and the Academy of Country Music's Top New Male Vocalist Award. For a while there, it seemed like you always had a song in the Top 40 on the Hot Country chart. Then you lost your voice and your career almost ended. Just like that. But you surprised everyone: you're hotter than ever.

Joe: Yeah, Anthony, it hasn't been easy. When your whole livelihood rests on the health of your vocal cords, it's like the end of the world when they cut out on you. I was told I might never sing again. I was lucky, though. The surgery worked. I managed to keep my mouth shut and recover enough to record an album. I only recently felt comfortable touring again.

Anthony: Keeping silent was a challenge, I hear. You were holed up in some remote cabin, and a girl appeared out of nowhere.

Joe: My manager Linc and his brother built a log cabin in the rain forest back in the '60s. Don't worry, y'all, it's legal. Linc has a special arrangement with the park service. I chose a place off the grid, so I wouldn't be tempted to speak. But then this gorgeous girl showed up like some wood sprite conjured out of a fever dream. At first I worried that she'd tracked me. Fans can be surprisingly tenacious. But it was soon obvious she had no idea who I was. God, how I wanted to talk! More than that. It was like someone read my mind and made a special delivery. But she was so innocent and sweet and sad. What could I do? I couldn't take advantage. I returned her to civilization."

Anthony: "And she inspired your biggest hit to date, 'Babe in the Woods,' which was Number 1 on Billboard's Country Music Chart and then became a crossover hit as well. Last week it shot up to Number 5 on the Pop Music Chart."

Joe: "Yeah, that was nice. Still, it didn't work, did it? I mean, its original purpose."

Anthony: "To find Ali, you mean. You've always had your choice of women. What made this one different?"

Joe: "To begin with, she'd never heard of me." [Laughter] "She was fresh and sympathetic and oh so trusting. Like a little lost lamb. With these otherworldly blue eyes."

Anthony: "Were they really blue as sapphires?"

Joe: "Originally I wrote 'eyes of azure hue,' but my recording engineer thought I was saying 'eyes of as are you,' which didn't make any sense.

Not that all lyrics need to make sense." [Laughter] "Anyway, 'azure' is one of those words that's rarely used outside of Scrabble. Might as well call them 'cerulean,' like a mountain lake, though sometimes I did think that. Only, too many syllables. Back to my point: I've never seen anything like those eyes. A guy could drown in them."

Anthony: "Careful, you're going to make Rina jealous."

Joe: "For a while there, the pressures of the road and the public scrutiny got to us, and we took a break. I did try to find Ali, I'll admit it. After I got back, I beat myself up for letting her go. I didn't know her last name. I told her I was called JJ, and yes, those are my initials, what my family calls me. She told me she worked in an independent coffee shop in Seattle, but which one?" [Laughter.] "I made phone calls, described her to a police sketch artist. By the time I found the right coffee shop, she was long gone. Learning her last name didn't help; it was too common. What else could I do? Oh yeah, record the song I wrote in the cabin, after I escorted her back to her car. I figured she'd hear it and contact me."

Anthony: "How, through your manager?"

Joe: "I don't know. I guess I should have put my manager's number in the song. What was that song with the phone number in it?"

Anthony: "Tommy Tutone. 867-5309."

Joe: [Laughing] "Yeah, that song 'Jenny.' I'm sure Linc is relieved that I didn't. More than a few did write to Linc, claiming to be Ali. I suppose they thought it might get them a meeting. He forwarded the letters. None was the least bit convincing. Anyway, water under the bridge. A girl like that … I'm sure she's moved on too. And let's get real. It's like I was under a spell. I didn't know her at all. She was a fantasy left over from my teenage years. I don't know."

Anthony: "As opposed to every man's fantasy, young and old, Rina Bakersfield."

Joe: "Yeah. I'm a lucky man, no question. Maybe I dreamed Ali up. It feels that way now." [Laughs] "As a songwriter, you find your inspiration where you can. I'm a red-blooded man, and I didn't invite that girl to visit. Nothing happened, so there's nothing to regret."

Anthony: "When will you and Rina tie the knot?"

Joe: "No date yet. As agreed, I left the tour early to conserve my voice. She's still on the road."

Anthony: "With Larry Wales. There were rumors they'd hooked up. Worried?"

Joe: "When Rina and I were on a break, they had a fling. As I've admitted already, we had our bumps in the road. We're solid now."

Anthony: "Back to Ali. What about that last verse?"

Joe: "She had been through hell. I tried to cheer her up. Lord knows, she helped me."

Anthony: "Who was this 'other half' you refer to in the song, a lover who died?"

Joe: "I wouldn't tell you something like that. I'm a public figure. She's not. She deserves her privacy."

Anthony: "The short time it took that song to succeed must have broken all the records. How did that happen?"

Joe: "I owe it all to Dickie Devero, a DJ at WMQD in Philadelphia. A big shoutout to Dickie! You are the greatest, and I owe you, man. He sent the demo to colleagues in four major cities: Nashville, Los Angeles, Seattle, and Cincinnati. Within days, the album started selling out everywhere."

Anthony: "One last thing. How's the voice? All better?"

Joe: "Good as new."

Anthony: "A relief for fans everywhere."

Ali ran to the bathroom to throw up. An hour later, when she had partially regained her equilibrium, she forced herself to read the lyrics to "Babe in the Woods," printed in a sidebar:

The road was once the thing I liked the most
Till I fell for the spell of moss and rocky coast
The Pacific Northwest alone it calmed my nerves
When the sportin' life threw me a nasty curve.

Babe ...... in the woods
My BABE in the woods
so green and yet so blue
good as gold with eyes of sapphire hue
you colored my world and made me dream of you.

On the night we met I couldn't speak a word
That made me the kindest man you'd ever heard
But I never claimed to be a paragon
And every dream-man fades in the cold gray dawn.

Babe in the woods....

Of all life's gifts, my truck she is the queen
The praise, the girls, the perks all lost their sheen
But Ali, for just one more night with you
I'd sell my truck and move to Timbuktu.

Babe in the woods....

The Fates, it seems, have played us both for laughs
They stole my voice and snatched your other half
But, darlin' girl, your courage is profound
Whatever's lost can turn up safe and sound.

Babe in the Woods....

The road, it is a lonely place to be
And up till now I've found good company
But Ali, if you ever hear this song

Please don't keep me waitin' for too long.

Please don't keep me waitin' for too long … (fade out)

ALI WAS LYING ON THE couch, catatonic, when Becca breezed in unexpectedly at around one in the afternoon. There had never been a more welcome sight.

"Ali? My God, what's wrong with you?"

Ali never took naps. So, of course Becca would panic.

With a great effort, she hefted herself to a sitting position. "The world ended."

Becca sat beside her and gave her a long hug. "Is it Liam?"

"No." Her voice sounded listless, even to her. "A dream died. The dream of JJ." She handed over the magazine, folded open to the interview.

After several minutes, Becca looked up, her expression grave. "Oh, Ali, I'm so sorry. This is so much worse than I ever could have imagined." Then she gasped. "But … oh my God! Joe Bob Blade … that name … he went to the same high school as us. Though he graduated at least five years earlier."

Ali's breath hitched. "*What*?"

"Don't you read our alumni magazine?"

"No. I don't give them money. They must have lost track of me."

Becca rolled her eyes. "They really like to brag about him. You remember the glass case displaying photos of famous alumni? If you and I ever attended those reunion events, we would definitely have seen his picture there." Becca shook her head in wonder. "Talk about a small-world story."

Ali gave an impatient shrug. "Not really. It's the best co-ed Catholic school in Seattle. Where else would a prominent Seattle Catholic family send their son?"

Ali was recalling her time in the woods with JJ. Gordon Lightfoot, Dolly Parton, Johnny Cash. His "dream" job involved a lot of travel. The guitar. The obvious skill. She'd guessed he might be a singer, only, she never would have dreamed he'd turn out to be *this* famous. "This guy wrote a *song* about me."

"Ooh, we have to get the CD," Becca said. Seeing that Ali was incapable of action, she ventured out on her own, returning an hour later. "Found it at Silver Platters in Bellevue." She popped it into the player.

Listening to the song, they began to understand its appeal. The lyrics might be simple, but the music was totally catchy, with interesting modulations, a soaring bridge, and a memorable guitar riff. Joe's mellow baritone had just enough roughness to give it interest. The emotion in that voice was undeniable.

After they'd played the song several times and the rest of the album all the way through, Becca ejected the CD. "Ali, he's an undeniably talented songwriter. You can take comfort in the fact that he was truly into you. In the moment. He's moved on. You gave him fodder for his song, then he found other inspiration."

Ali raised her head, her expression doleful. "How is it that Jake and he look so alike? They've got to be related. But if so, why would Jake lie to me? Don't people usually brag about famous relatives?"

Her friend tapped her chin. "He could be estranged from his family."

"Becca, do you need to be anywhere?"

Becca checked her watch. "It's three thirty. Jean-Louis is treating me to dinner at six, but I can hang out awhile. I'm going to meet him at the restaurant. Want to come along? I'm sure he wouldn't mind. You can console yourself with an excellent meal."

Ali's eyes were downcast. "No, I have no appetite. Thanks for asking. Let's go for a walk in Issaquah. The fall leaves are beautiful. A lot of them blew away in last night's storm, but they're still spectacular."

They parked on Front Street and headed down an alley.

"Are you gonna try to contact JJ—I mean, Joe Bob?"

Ali's laugh might have been squeezed out of her. "How? Through his manager? 'Hey, I'm your babe in the woods! I know you're seeing fellow singer and sex goddess Rina Bakersfield, but you did write that song about me, so maybe you'd like to drop her and see if I really am the very model of innocence and beauty you once conjured up in your imagination? You might not live up to my fantasies, either, but heck, let's give it a shot.' "

"When you put it that way …. Don't you think you're being needlessly pessimistic? Besides, not all those 'relationships' they write about in magazines are real. Keep in mind that he gave that interview knowing he needed to please his fans and placate the woman he tours with."

Ali put a hand on her arm. "I read the interview more than once. He sounds pretty cynical. Here's a pull quote for you: 'Let's get real. It's like I was under a spell. I didn't know her at all. She was a fantasy left over from my teenage years.' "

Becca came to a halt so suddenly, Ali nearly ran into her. "Stop beating yourself up. They call them fanzines for a reason."

"It rings true. Anyway, that's that. I liked the album. I never thought of myself as a country music fan. Nice title: *The Woodsman*. Reminded me a little of John Denver, only the voice is deeper and not quite so pristine. That just makes it more interesting."

"Uh-huh. What about Jake?"

"What about him?"

"Are you going to keep seeing him?"

Ali shrugged helplessly. "Well, you all seem to think he's a nice enough guy, and he certainly *looks* good. Kind of like a TV anchorman. Come to think of it, Brian Williams was never my fantasy. Now that I know the man in the woods has moved on—and, let's face it, is a bit of a jerk—I might as well give Jake a chance."

Becca raised her eyebrows. "A 'chance'? He doesn't ring your bell?"

"I didn't say that," Ali was quick to reply. "I'm attracted to him. He certainly knows how to kiss. A little too well."

"Hmm. Explain."

"Well, it's a little practiced. Like being attended to by a really talented masseur. Or do I mean 'calculated'? I don't get a sense that he's carried away by passion, so it's hard to let myself be carried away. But the skill … that might extend to … other things." She sighed. "Only, he doesn't even try. Nothing beyond a kiss. Okay, a really long kiss. Sometimes two."

"You've had two dates, right? Maybe he's following the three-date rule. There's no rush, is there?"

"I wish JJ had made love to me," Ali moaned. "Everything would have been different."

"You mean, you could have become just another notch in his bedpost. Oh, that's right, no bedposts in a tiny log cabin like that. If I were you, I wouldn't assume he's anything like you fantasized. It was a friend's cabin. He didn't build it. He's no frontiersman. Or backwoodsman … woodsman … whatever he calls himself."

"I saw him chop wood."

"Yeah, that makes him Davy Crockett for sure."

"Point taken."

Ali stared at the brilliantly tricolored Japanese maple next to their bench, thinking she would never get past this devastating moment enough to appreciate simple beauty again. Becca broke the silence. "Not to give Joe too much credit, but I'd take what he says in that interview with a grain of salt. It's the public message—what he's willing to share for the sake of the song. I know he sounds like a jerk, and maybe he is, or maybe it's just the image he cultivates—very devil-may-care. His song obviously resonated with a lot of people, men *and* women, aside from the music. Who wouldn't be envious of a guy who's having a personal crisis and then is comforted by an angel right out of his fantasies? Like in *The Bishop's Wife*. The story is awfully romantic, even if it's heartbreaking for you."

"Funny you should mention it. When I was at the cabin, that movie came to mind. I thought about life after JJ. I almost wished someone would erase my memory of him. Is Jean-Louis your fantasy?"

Becca chuckled. "My fantasy used to be bad boys, tortured souls like Heathcliff. A guy like that would never take you seriously, and that includes treating you decently." She paused. "I have a new fantasy now, and Jean-Louis fits right into that. A man who truly loves me, values me, and treats me like an equal. Makes me laugh. That is what I wish for you too."

Ali gave her a nudge. "So, are you advocating for Jake or JJ, um, Joe Bob?"

Becca nudged her back. "Jury's out. Underneath the slick veneer, Joe Bob might be a decent guy. I still think he's not for you. His life is way too complicated, and you seem to have little in common." She paused. "Though that's not a deal breaker. You know the cliché: opposites attract. Jake, on the other hand, seems on the level."

They lapsed into silence again as the foot traffic increased.

"Are you okay for money?" Becca asked.

"Sure," Ali lied. She was barely squeaking by. "I feel bad about not paying my share of the rent and utilities."

Becca laughed. "No need! I was born into money. My parents have more than they could ever spend in a lifetime. Isn't it right that I should share the bounty?"

Ali shook her head. "You're one in a million, Becca. I feel weird about accepting Jake's gifts. Obviously he doesn't trust my fashion sense."

Becca wrinkled her nose, as good as admitting she agreed with Jake. "Just how many clothes has he sent you?"

Ali feigned interest in her newly varnished fingernails. "Only the three dresses and the three pairs of shoes."

"That's not that big a deal," Becca said. "The guy wears gazillion-dollar suits. What are a few dresses to him? Betsey Johnson dresses. They're nice, but hardly in a stratospheric price range. Two hundred dollars or so. Chump change for Mr. Bespoke. What about the shoes?"

Ali shrugged. "I don't know. They came in a plain brown box, and I didn't recognize the brand. They're Italian."

"Can you recall the name?"

"Carlo Alfonsi."

Becca's jaw dropped. "Maybe he got them at a discount?"

Ali sat up straighter. "How much are we talking?"

Her friend was almost apologetic. "In the five-hundred-dollar range. Could be worse. You wouldn't believe what people will pay for shoes. You've seen *Sex and the City*, right?"

"Where would I see that? Did we get HBO when I wasn't looking?"

"Jean-Louis has HBO," Becca admitted. "That series is really fun. They spend a lot of money on shoes and purses. And have a lot of sex, as the title suggests. I've never seen so much naked flesh on a TV show. The men too." After a long silence, she added, "I just don't want you to be the mouse who walks right into the snap trap because the cheese is a really tasty Stracchino from Italy."

"No one's getting snapped up here. And I'm not picky about cheese."

"Ever tried Stracchino?"

"Nope. Is it good?"

Becca licked her lips. "Sweet, rich, and creamy. Once you've tried it, you might never want to go back to plain old Philadelphia cream cheese."

CHAPTER 20

—·—

THE NEXT DAY, A PACKAGE arrived from Boutique Luigi Zorro, one of the priciest clothing stores in downtown Seattle. So much for "chump change." Another obligation. Maybe if Ali didn't rip the packaging, she could tape it back together and return it. But she had to see what was inside.

She soon abandoned the idea of sending it back. Jake must need her to look a certain way for whatever date he had in mind. If he was willing to spend big to make that happen, who was she to argue?

It was a cashmere sweater dress, a warm shade of rose brown that complemented her gold-toned skin. It skimmed her body without revealing too much. A modest scoop neck. The shoes were a more practical pump than the others he'd sent. Ferragamo .... Even she recognized that brand. Five hundred dollars? The dress ... six hundred, a thousand? It was a perfect fit. Knowing her size was one thing, knowing what cut would work on her body quite another. How did he do that? He must have a knack for such things, like those guys who guess your weight at county fairs and carnivals.

Finally, a dress that worked with her fake pearls. Were they good-enough fakes? She hated having to worry about this stuff. What occasion was he dressing her for this time?

WHEN SHE RETURNED FROM HER shift that evening, her answering machine held a message from Jake: "My mother is hosting a fundraiser in downtown Seattle for Hear Us Roar Rescue, an anti-poaching foundation. Will you be my date? She's convinced me to buy a table, and the other guests won't be from Big Paul's, I promise. I hope you like the dress. I'll call back later."

She put the dress on again and lay down on the couch. She'd never dreamed such an elegant garment could also be comfortable enough to sleep in. In these shoes, you could walk to and from a Seattle parking place with nary a blister. With Jake and his limo, nothing like that would be required. Too bad he hadn't bothered to include lingerie. She'd have to spring for panties that wouldn't show lines. Something she wouldn't be embarrassed to be seen in—if it came to that. Most likely a thong. She hated thongs.

At nine, the phone rang, and she checked the caller ID before answering. "Hi, Jake," she said, brightly, she hoped not too brightly. Just the right degree of brightness.

"Hi, Ali." Just the right degree of warmth. He was much better at this game. It worried her. Still, she was unexpectedly happy to hear from him. She had to admit she enjoyed being wooed. Unless she was being bought.

"You still there?"

"Yes! Sorry. I was in the middle of something." *Of course you're in the middle of something*, she admonished herself. *Unless you were just sitting, waiting for his call. Which you kind of were.*

"Should I call back?"

"No, it's fine."

"How's the dress?"

"The dress. Yes!" *Darn it, a rhyme.* "I like it. I mean, I love it. I'm … I'm wearing it."

He laughed. "Are you taking it out on the town without me?"

She cringed. "Uh, no. It's just that it's really comfortable. More comfortable than my bathrobe." *Hmm, that sounded off.* "I had to make sure it fit. Then I didn't feel like taking it off. But I will, I promise. I won't eat in it." Worse and worse. At least she hadn't admitted to this being the *second* time she'd tried it on. *Please, put me out of my misery.*

"Did you get my message?"

"Yes. But you didn't say when the event is."

"Oh, I guess I didn't. Next Saturday evening."

An unpopular shift. *Darn.* There would be a lot of Halloween parties on the weekend before the holiday. But she couldn't say no. She'd get someone to swap shifts with her, although it would mean owing them bigtime.

"You still there?"

"Yes! Of course. What time?"

"I'll pick you up at five. We need to arrive on the early side, since I'm helping my mother with hosting duties."

"Are you going to leave me to my own devices? At the fundraiser, I mean?" She was terrified of being interrogated by strangers with their noses in the air while he whipped up Seattle's crème de la crème into future business contacts.

"My sister will be at our table. She's a doll. I promise that if I'm distracted by duty, she'll keep you entertained."

An image popped into Ali's head of Jake's sister, a ballerina doll on a music box dancing for her amusement.

"I'm sure I'll be fine. I just don't want to embarrass you."

"I'm not worried. Only that someone will try to steal you away."

"Hah!" Ali exclaimed.

Silence on his part. It had been a stupid reaction. Why was she so ill at ease with this man? She had never felt this way with JJ.

After she hung up, she carefully slipped out of the dress, lamenting that she still didn't have the right coat. Could she borrow one? Becca's swing coat was too short for this dress and funky-nice, more appropriate to a Cyndi Lauper video than an assembly of Seattle's snootiest. Besides, Becca wore it constantly. When she surveyed what remained of Becca's outerwear, she found only a pale-yellow frock coat—not her color. She would try one of those high-end consignment stores, but there was no guarantee she'd find anything that would work.

"Well, darn it," she said aloud. "He'll have to take me as I am. Or keep buying me clothes." If he wanted sophisticated and elegant with a great wardrobe, he should've picked someone from his own crowd.

SATURDAY ROLLED AROUND QUICKLY, AND she ran herself ragged taking extra-early shifts for Ann at Sully's so she'd cover Ali's undesirable one. She'd also convinced Ann to cover for her Sunday morning, in case Saturday turned out to be a really late night. The more time she spent away from Jake, the more she warmed to the idea of him. JJ—she couldn't think of him as Joe Bob— was a fantasy, and Jake was as close to a flesh-and-blood prince as she would ever come. She'd never owned any but the most basic wardrobe items to fit her needs, and for the first time, she had beautiful things.

That week Ali and Becca crossed paths only once. Becca flitted in and out as if she'd sprouted wings. This was the first time Ali had seen her friend in love. Becca had been secretly disdainful of most of the men she'd dated while rooming with Ali, so much so that it wasn't clear why she bothered. Watching Becca then had made Ali even more reluctant to date. Besides, she'd had her hands full with her course work and barista job, and later on, catering gigs.

Ali tried not to be ashamed of her sturdy wool coat as Jake escorted her to the limo. Had he given it a dismayed second glance? Perhaps not.

They were headed for the Chief Joseph Club on Fourth Avenue, one of the oldest private clubs in Seattle, founded in 1903. It was a venerable brick fortress—nothing else like it outside of Pioneer Square—known as the preferred club of conservative businessmen and women. Most rich men were fiscally conservative, she guessed. Jake was against poaching; she knew that much. Did he approve of trophy hunting if no laws were broken? She hoped not.

"Have you ever been to the Chief Joseph Club?" he asked her.

"Uh, no. I rarely get out of North Bend."

He laughed, so she grinned as if she'd been joking. Now that she lived in North Bend, Ali had seen her world shrink to the square mile that included her home, Sully's, the video rental place, and the grocery store.

"Do you like movies?" Ali was following her own train of thought, so to Jake the question must have seemed out of the blue.

"Yes, of course. All kinds. Classic films, blockbusters."

"Westerns?"

"Sure."

"Clint Eastwood or John Wayne?" Ali wasn't sure where she was going with this. She had started with their gay friend Pete the waiter's litmus test, which had everything to do with whether he was attracted to the leading man. So far Jake had been vague when it came to his cultural preferences. She and JJ hadn't discussed movies, just music. Ali wondered if work wasn't pretty much Jake's life, aside from staying fit, eating out, and drinking expensive wine. He might just be pretending to have outside interests. By "outside," Ali meant the classic arts—classical music, foreign films, theater. She wasn't a culture snob. She liked both John Wayne and Clint Eastwood. Arnold Schwarzenegger, even though he was more action star than actor. She watched *Masterpiece Theatre* on PBS but also *The Simpsons* and *Friends*.

As usual, she couldn't read Jake's expression. His normally soft brown eyes seemed to bore into her. "I like them both," he said.

So do you, a little voice reminded her. *Maybe he's eclectic in his tastes, too.*

"*Kagemusha*?" she went on.

"Akira Kurosawa. Who doesn't?"

He'd answered that trivia question correctly. Didn't mean he'd seen it. A lot of people didn't like it, Ali guessed, though few who fancied themselves sophisticated might admit that.

"*The Seven Samurai* was better than *The Magnificent Seven*," he added, much to her surprise.

Further probing would have to wait. They'd arrived at the Chief Joseph Club.

The club seemed a curious spot to hold an anti-poaching event, considering the hyper-masculine décor. No animal heads or hunting scenes, but lots of huge oil paintings depicting grand landscapes. Persian rugs and heavy dark wood, probably mahogany. She wondered how many of the actual members were trophy hunters. Jake had explained you could ask a member to sponsor your event; the host or hostess didn't have to belong.

Ali quickly realized that her outfit was too understated for an evening event, but once the terrible coat had been spirited away, she blended in well enough. A little black dress would have been ideal. She'd give Jake the benefit of the doubt. Perhaps he thought a cashmere sweater dress was a more practical addition to her wardrobe. She could have used a LBD, but really, any of the three cocktail dresses he sent originally would have been more appropriate than this one. What choice had she had? This was the dress provided for the occasion, almost as if he'd set her up to look like a fool. She quickly rejected that theory. What motive could he possibly have for doing that? As his arm candy, she was an accessory. Her appearance reflected on him.

A slender Hollywood blonde with her hair in a tight chignon and wearing an intricately beaded black cocktail dress stood next to the round table in the front. "Teresa!" Jake called out. She swiveled on her stilettos and flashed a brilliant smile. Though sincere, somehow.

The woman gave Jake an enormous hug. "JB!" she said in a breathy voice. Then, surprisingly, she hugged Ali. "Hi there! Any friend of my brother's is a friend of mine."

Ali turned to Jake. "JB?"

He actually blushed. "Jacob Brillard."

It was the first unguarded reaction Ali had observed. She couldn't let it drop. "Brillard?"

"An ancestral surname. Families with pretentions do stuff like that. Give their children grand-sounding names to honor their ancestors. I'm just lucky it's my middle name."

It was nice to hear him poke fun at himself.

Teresa shook her hand with genuine warmth. "Hope I didn't shock you with the hug. We haven't met."

"Meet Mary Alice Ryan," Jake said, holding out his arms as if presenting his protégée or his newest creation.

"Please call me Ali."

"Ali," Teresa repeated, as if the name had triggered something. She recovered quickly. "I'm Teresa." She handed over an elegant calling card with only the name "Teresa O'Connell" and her phone number in gold-embossed letters and numbers. "Sorry for the subterfuge. Jake already told me about you. I've been tasked with keeping the sharks away. Now that I see you, I understand why such precautions were necessary."

"Is Mom around?" Jake asked. From the way he scanned the room, he seemed eager to greet his mother. That was a good sign.

"Here and there." She fluttered her fingers about. "There were some glitches. There always are. But all is well. You go find her. Leave Ali to me."

Jake blew Ali a kiss and took off for the other side of the room. "I'm a little underdressed," Ali said when Jake was out of hearing range.

Teresa took her arm. "Your outfit would be perfect for a business luncheon. But no worries. You look lovely."

She almost admitted the origin of her ensemble, but quickly thought better of it. Teresa might conclude she was a gold digger.

"How did you meet? Forgive me, but—this is a compliment—I'm used to seeing my bro with a different type of woman. Flashier. Um, let's call it like it is—trashier. You Catholic?"

"I know … Mary Alice, right? And Ryan. But nothing, really. I wasn't raised in any religion."

Teresa's eyes grew round. "Huh. We're *quite* Catholic. Though it's mostly cultural at this point. Old Irish family. There are five of us kids. Would have been more, but health issues, you know. Mom and Dad were told to stop. A tragedy."

"Five? Brothers, sisters?"

"I'm the only girl. Four brothers. We used to be close. Everything changed after Dad died eleven years ago. They all talk to Mom. It's just that not all of them talk to each other. One is a priest—the eldest. He lives in Philadelphia. David is second in line. Joe and Jake are fraternal twins."

Joe? Ali thought.

Teresa chattered on, unaware of Ali's inner turmoil. "What about you—siblings?"

Stunned by the suspicions rattling in her head, Ali took too long to reply. "Just one, my twin, Liam. He, um, has been missing since last January. After a terrorist attack."

Teresa froze. "Wow, just wow," she said, deflated. "That is shocking and so … random. Where? Mideast? Army?"

"Jerusalem. Hamas. On vacation. In the wrong place at the wrong time."

"I'm so sorry." She laid a hand on Ali's shoulder, then petted her sleeve. "Nice. Cashmere?"

"I guess so."

Teresa's head tilted. "You don't know?"

A low, quiet voice behind Ali said, "Teresa. Who is …?"

Ali turned, and they just stared at each other. The photos in the magazine hadn't prepared her for the man in person. Now she observed the differences between him and Jake. The cleft chin. Jake's face was leaner. This man was at least as tall as Liam. Jake's silhouette was less muscular, more refined. JJ was wearing all black—button-down shirt, sport coat, and slacks—no tie, and regular, not cowboy boots. Realizing she was blatantly drinking him in, head to toe, as if he were a heavenly vision, she dropped her gaze to the Persian rug, which, surprisingly, had seen better days. But then, as with any heavenly vision, she had to check to make sure it was really there. She saw him gulp.

"Uh …." It was Teresa. "JJ, Ali, do you two know each other? Oh! I get it," she said to Ali. "You're a fan."

"No. I mean, I am. But …." Ali was suddenly far too hot. *Darn this woolen dress*. The room was expanding and contracting. The next thing she knew, she was lying on the floor, staring at the paneled ceiling.

CHAPTER 21

———•———

DAMN. AFTER ALL HIS SEARCHING, Ali had gone and turned up right under his nose. She looked so goddamn beautiful. What the hell was she doing here, talking to Teresa? Joe had only stopped by at his mother's request so she could introduce him to two or three of the major donors who were big fans. She was also trying to finagle a reconciliation with Jake, but that wasn't going to happen. It wasn't up to him. No one held a grudge like Jake. His mother claimed to have warned his twin that he was stopping by—an obvious lie. She wasn't above lying when it suited her purposes. He'd bet Jake didn't know Joe was in town to record an album. His mother had pleaded with him to do just one song, but he'd begged off, saying he didn't want to upstage the featured speaker.

Teresa stared at him as if he'd grown an extra head. No time for explanations or reunions. He might cause a scene and ruin the event. "Later, Sis," he said and fled to the other room, where his mother and the donors were waiting. He turned on the folksy warmth the donors expected of him for only ten minutes before dashing to his rental car. He hoped the visit paid off for his mom, because this evening was going to land him in serious hot water if news got out. Thank God Rina had remained behind in Nashville.

Safe in the car, he breathed a sigh of relief, then another of frustration. Rina versus Ali? No contest. Ali was fresh air and sunlight. Rina was a cloud of perfume. Sweet-smelling, expensive perfume, but stifling in large doses. And even though he understood her fling with Larry Wales on a rational level, he hadn't really gotten over it.

Why hadn't he realized Ali would turn up sooner or later? He shouldn't have reconciled with Rina after she admitted to betraying him. What if Ali had turned up earlier? What would have been the plan? To test the waters and see how things went? His original reasoning was still valid. Who was she, really? Had she even heard the song? Now that she knew his true identity, was she going to pant after him like every other woman? Or would she be furious that during her entire stay in the cabin he'd lied to her by omission? The dead faint pretty much ruled out her moving on.

She was as beautiful as he remembered, spiffed up but no more breathtaking. A class act. Her hair was shoulder-length with bangs, and she wore subtle makeup. That sleek, soft rose-brown dress looked exquisite on her—and really expensive. How could she afford it? Had she landed a great job after completing her degree? None of this made sense.

He called Teresa on his cell phone.

"Okay, JJ, what was that all about? That girl actually swooned. Does that happen to you often?"

"Why is she at the fundraiser?" he asked by way of prevarication.

"Who is she to you?" Teresa countered. He heard a gasp. "*Ali*," she said, answering her own question. "Oh, this is rich. You never found her. Until now."

He didn't bother to deny it. "*Why* is she at the fundraiser?" he repeated with more annoyance.

"She's, uh, Jake's date."

"Fuck," he swore under his breath.

"JJ, are you still there? Are you going to run away like a startled bull, or are you going to face her?"

"Bulls don't run away, they charge. I'm not running away. I will talk to her, just *not here*," he ground out.

"Oh boy, you are going to tell me this story in full detail next time I see you."

He hung up. His hands were shaking.

* * *

HAD ALI HALLUCINATED JJ'S PRESENCE?

Teresa helped her up and led her over to a bench in the corner. "I'll be right back. I'm going to fetch you some water." Ali closed her eyes, still unsteady, grateful for a moment to compose herself.

Teresa returned ten minutes later. "Wow, you must be some kind of super fan." She handed Ali the glass of water.

"I'm sorry. I don't know what's come over me. I was surprised to see JJ, uh, Joe Bob ...."

"Joe O'Connell," Teresa said with a laugh. "Joe Bob Blade is his stage name. A bit much, I'll grant you that. His real middle name starts with a J, but Joe Jamison doesn't fit the persona." Teresa gave her a sly glance. "How do you know him?"

"We met, once, a while ago." Ali scanned the room, worried that she'd called attention to herself, but it was as if no one had noticed.

"Not many of the guests have arrived," Teresa said. "The waiters didn't want to interfere. And Jake's several rooms away, chatting up the guest speaker."

"Oh," Ali said. She smoothed her dress and noticed a run in her stocking. This evening was going downhill fast. After what had happened, she didn't see how she could possibly stay for dinner. "Are Joe and Jake the brothers who don't talk, by any chance?"

"You guessed it," Teresa said. "Joe just stopped by at Mom's request to schmooze some donors. He was really eager to avoid running into Jake, although they managed to tolerate each other at Christmas. Barely. I'm sorry he didn't hang out long enough to greet you properly. He's in town to record an album."

"Uh, Teresa?" Ali whispered. "I have a run in my stocking." She pointed.

Teresa fished around in her purse and pulled out a small envelope. "I always keep a spare."

Her cell phone rang, and she turned her back to answer it before Ali could thank her. Ali fled to the powder room, where she marveled at the fine quality of the "spare" pantyhose.

When she returned, Teresa was putting her phone away. "You won't say anything to Jake? I mean, about my knowing JJ, uh, Joe."

"Ooh, I *am* intrigued!" Teresa pretended to shiver. "Mum's the word. And, speaking of Mum ...."

An older version of Teresa approached—just as slender, her aristocratic face placid and smooth, suspiciously so. Artfully blonde. Calm and serene in a way her daughter most definitely was not.

She extended a long, silky hand that made Ali wish she had sprung for a professional manicure. "Hello." When the woman smiled, her eyes were lightly bracketed by crow's feet. "I'm Carrie O'Connell. You must be Mary Alice."

"Ali," she said, automatically. "I'm very pleased to meet you, ma'am." At least she hadn't said, "*Enchantée*." This ice queen made her want to run for her life. Ali was a conspicuously breathless fish out of water.

"I'm so pleased you could come." Mrs. O'Connell spoke with enough warmth that Ali almost believed her. "Jake has told me so much about you. You and Teresa should help yourselves to cocktails. The guests are starting to arrive." She gripped Ali's hand and gave it a little shake. "Call me Carrie."

"Thanks so much … Carrie," Ali said with a curtsy. If the woman found this strange, she didn't let on.

"She has that effect on people," Teresa said when they were alone again. The heat rose in Ali's cheeks. Teresa laid a hand on her arm. "I meant that she throws people off their game. Don't give it a second thought. I can tell she likes you."

Ali felt as if she were auditioning for a part in a reboot of *Dynasty*. If so, she was blowing it, unless she'd be playing the comic relief or a servant aiming above her station. She was the last person you'd accuse of social climbing.

Dinner itself was uneventful. Chicken, not the rubber kind, in a delicious marinade. An arugula salad with blue cheese and hazelnuts. Asparagus, al dente. A sourdough dinner roll. Teresa picked at her food, but Ali wanted to eat it all, so she did.

Jake appeared halfway into the main course and apologized for making them wait. After being introduced to the other guests at the table, Ali felt as if she'd been relieved of her cloak of invisibility. Fortunately, she didn't have to make much small talk before the speaker came to the podium—a South African activist who told heartwarming stories of daring animal rescues and poachers who met bad ends. The fact that he outstayed his welcome suited Ali just fine. His long speech took up some of the time she might have been expected to mingle.

She wasn't sure why Jake had told Teresa to fend off admirers. There were none she could see. He disappeared again at dessert, which allowed Ali to dig in. The minute he was gone, their tablemates stopped feigning interest in her.

"Where do you put it?" Teresa asked, her curiosity getting the better of her. "You're so tiny."

"No more so than you," Ali said. Although Teresa did have more in the chest department. Pushup bras could only do so much.

"Well, maybe, but I have to starve myself. Unless you're coming off a diet …."

Ali didn't feel like confessing that she basically existed on rotisserie chicken and the salad bar at the local corner market. Becca's cooking had been a lot more tempting. Ever since her friend had hopped aboard the Jean-Louis train, Ali had lost interest in eating.

She covered her mouth. "Am I eating too much?" she whispered. "It's just that I'm enjoying the meal."

"The chef here is rather good," Teresa said. "I'm sorry. It was rude of me to mention it."

The waiter took away Ali's chocolate mousse cake just as she was about to savor the last bite. She shot him a reproachful look.

LATER, IN THE LIMO, JAKE apologized. "Not a very glamorous date, in the end," he said, a little sheepish. "It was a command performance for me, and I wanted a gorgeous woman on my arm. Will you forgive me?"

Ali thought about her awkwardness, how she had fainted at the sight of his famous brother—the one who couldn't get away fast enough. She knew what she had to do now and was working up the courage. "Thanks again for the outfit," she said. *Inappropriate as it was*, she added silently.

As if reading her mind, he said, "About that ... I'm sorry. I bought it thinking this was going to be a luncheon. When I discovered my mistake, I should have sent something else or told you to wear one of the cocktail dresses. But I didn't want you to think ...."

He stopped. This man had a bad habit of not finishing his sentences. *What* didn't he want her to think? That he knew she didn't have the wardrobe to date him? *Really*, she thought with irritation, *rather than this "item of the week club" approach to dressing her, he should just take her to Boutique Luigi Zorro and let them dress her for every possible occasion*, Pretty Woman style.

Moving in closer, Jake slipped his arms around her and drew her to him. She pulled away. "Jake, tell me what's going on."

He appeared taken aback. "Whatever do you mean?"

"Joe showed up tonight. Joe Bob Blade. You didn't see him?"

Jake paled, cleared his throat but didn't speak.

"Your twin," Ali said flatly. "You've known who I am to him all along."

He was still hedging. "I have no idea—"

" 'Babe in the Woods,' " she broke in. "Until yesterday I'd never heard the song, had no idea he'd written it for me. But *you* knew."

Jake didn't confirm or deny. He was staring straight ahead, working his jaw. *Uh-oh.* Was he going to attack her? She was a sitting duck. She recoiled.

"Stop it," he said in a grumpy voice. "I'm angry, yes, but not at you. I'm sorry you got in the middle of this. I should have known better. It's too bad you're so gone on a cad like him. He's all but engaged, you know, and he still has a wandering eye. You're proof of that."

"He didn't—"

"Tell me you would have said no."

Now she was the one to look away.

"That guy …. Fuck him. Well, good luck with that. If you'd given me half a chance, you might have realized I'm the better deal."

The better deal, she thought. Maybe he was. Would she regret confronting Jake before she'd had time to get to know him? She didn't think so. She could never have a serious relationship with the brother of the man she was in love with, no matter how much of a creep Joe proved to be.

"I'm sorry, Jake," she said finally. "I'm not sure what's going on between you two, but it would never work out with us, not now. I'm not sure what you hoped to accomplish." She turned to look him in the eye. "Tell me you really want me. I don't feel it. I won't be a pawn."

Jake didn't deny it. Had she hoped he would? Back to the celibate life …. Maybe she should have slept with Jake. She might have, if Joe hadn't reappeared tonight. The silence seemed to hum with regret for the rest of the trip home.

When the limo drove up to the house, she asked, "Do you want the clothes and shoes back? I can box it all up for you in a few minutes."

He gave a little shudder of distaste as if she'd offered him a nightcap of Kool-Aid. "What would I do with them? You can burn them in a ritual bonfire if you like."

So bitter. Ali felt terrible, as if she had been the one who'd staged this nasty little *East of Eden* scenario.

Once the door had shut behind her, Ali leaned against it and heaved an anguished sigh. *Darn that JJ.* If not for him, she might have fallen hard for Jake. Jake would have been most women's dream come true. And JJ wasn't the soulful, solitary woodsman she had taken him for. He was Joe Bob Blade, the devilishly handsome country singer who broke hearts as easily as he topped the charts. From now on, that's how she must think of him.

No, you can't think of him. You must not think of him at all.

CHAPTER 22

———◦———

THE DESIGNER CLOTHING HUNG IN Ali's closet like a reproach, so, even knowing Jake didn't want it—would probably trash it or donate it to a charity—she packed it all up and mailed it to him at Big Paul's Outfitters.

Becca suggested Prozac. Only, did antidepressants work if your depression had a real cause? Ali was mourning the death of a dream.

On Monday, she worked the five-to-eleven morning shift at Sully's. As she was leaving, a hand shot out, barring her path. The man sitting next to the door looked up from under his baseball cap. Joe wore a disguise on a par with a Groucho Marx mask. Poindexter black-framed glasses, a mustache, and a shaggy beard.

Legs wobbling, Ali thudded gracelessly into the chair opposite him. When she'd recovered enough to speak, she said in a shaky voice, "What are you doing here?" She pointed to his espresso. "I don't remember serving you."

He put aside the newspaper he'd been hiding behind. "You didn't. And you were preoccupied. I think if you *had* served me, you wouldn't have known. You're not one of the friendliest baristas. You do seem efficient." He leaned back. Listening to him speak required an adjustment. A sarcastic undercurrent ran beneath everything he said in his mellow, slightly scratchy baritone, as if he just couldn't get over the absurdity of life. That didn't jibe with the Ben Casey-type, steadfast admirer she'd believed him to be. *Welcome to reality.*

"Nice disguise. You look like a Sikh comic doing a Groucho Marx impression."

"Exactly what I was aiming for," he said with a straight face. "Do you have a moment? I'd like to buy you a coffee."

Ali laughed, as was his intention.

"Okay, no coffee then. Take a walk? It's a beautiful day." He pointed to the Katsura tree outside the window, its glossy red, yellow, and coral leaves glowing in the sunlight.

"Only if you take off the disguise."

His upper lip twitched, making the mustache dance and go askew. "People will recognize me," he whispered.

"In North Bend?" she whispered back. "I don't think so. In Nashville, sure."

"People in North Bend know my music," Joe protested as he adjusted the mustache.

She stood up, legs steadier now. "Okay, let's walk. The beard is more convincing than the mustache. But since you weren't wearing one the other night, I assume that even you aren't studly enough to grow facial hair that bushy in less than a week." She paused, heat climbing up her neck. "I'm sorry. I don't know where that came from. I'm not usually so snarky. I'll meet you outside."

She rushed through the door so quickly, she nearly knocked over a customer. "Sorry!" she called over her shoulder.

Once outside, she speed-walked to the street corner. After confirming that Joe followed, she kept on, slower and in silence, until she was sure they were alone. He kept the cap on but took off the beard, glasses, and mustache, stuffing them into the pockets of his bomber jacket. In his black T-shirt, leather jacket, and worn jeans, he had a James Dean vibe that appealed to the primal in her. His beauty was blinding, like staring into the sun. She cast about, looking anywhere but at him.

"Are you cold?" he asked.

She frowned, then realized she was hugging herself, a defensive gesture, and let her arms fall to her sides. She had layered a polar fleece and down vest over her black Sully's T-shirt. If anything, she was too hot. Especially since heat just seemed to rise off this guy.

"I'm sorry I left so abruptly the other night," he said.

She fixed her eyes on the sidewalk ahead. "I wondered." She wanted to add, *You could have at least made sure I was okay*, but that would have called attention to the humiliating fact of her fainting at all. Then she'd have to make up something about not having eaten to avoid admitting the obvious: that she'd been overcome by his presence.

"I called Teresa, who told me you were okay."

"Oh, good," she said. *Snark city.* She added, "I'm glad she thought it was necessary. Does she know how we met?"

"The name 'Ali' rang a bell."

He touched her arm. She flinched at the contact and stopped walking.

"Why are you avoiding looking at me? I took off the disguise."

"I think I'd have an easier time if you hadn't," she admitted.

"Is it because I'm famous?" No snark in his voice now.

"No." Ali snuck a peek. Still painfully gorgeous. "It's just that …. You wouldn't understand. I assumed you were some normal guy with serious survival skills, escaping from society." She hugged herself again. "Not some rock star waiting out his recovery from vocal cord surgery."

"I'm not a rock star," he said, clearly miffed. "I'm a musician."

At a loss for a reply, she simply stared at him.

"When did you finally figure it out?" he asked.

"A little over a week ago," she admitted unhappily. "I heard the song on a compilation Sully's is selling and recognized the verse you gave me. Then I found the interview in *Spurs 'n Sparkin'*. Did you know we went to the same high school?"

She caught Joe's wide-eyed reaction. "No kidding. Not at the same time, obviously."

Ali frowned. "Becca recognized your name. I don't get the alumni magazine, or I might have figured it out sooner."

After a moment of loaded silence, Ali blurted out, "I listened to the entire CD."

He brightened. "Did you like it?"

"I did." She strived to keep her tone neutral. "I don't listen to much popular music, I confess, especially not current stuff, except when it's forced on me at work." She knew that sounded bad, so she added, "Even if it wasn't about me, I would have liked that song. It's very catchy."

"I would have told you who I was," he said with an undercurrent of emotion, "but it was an unusual situation, to say the least. If you hadn't found the cabin, you might have died. You were upset over your brother." He blew out a frustrated breath. "And I had only one lousy pad of notepaper."

"Right, from the Four Seasons Olympic. That should have been my first clue. Most survivalists don't stay in five-star hotels."

"The doctors warned me not to speak. They told me that if I did, I might never sing again."

"You said as much in the interview."

He cleared his throat. "I might have sounded a little flippant."

Without missing a beat, she quoted in a low drawl, " 'It's like I was under a spell. I didn't know her at all. She was a fantasy left over from my teenage years.' "

He stopped walking and grasped her arm to hold her back. "Sounds like me, word for word. I said a lot more in that interview. How I searched for you."

She looked down at his hand, still holding her arm. He let go. "Yes, you made some phone calls. But after all, you've moved on."

"And you're sleeping with my brother."

"Whoa. *Dating*."

"There's a difference?" He sounded bitter.

"There is for me."

"I'm confused. How did you end up *dating* my brother?"

She realized she was shuffling her feet and forced herself to stand her ground. "This isn't a story I can tell quickly, but ever since those few days in the rain forest, I thought you must have some connection to Big Paul's Outfitters. The clothing and gear were all over the cabin."

"It's the family business. We all have shares in the company and get a lot of free stuff."

"Then, when I met your brother …."

He nodded, unsurprised. He'd guessed the truth already. All he said was "Baristas must get paid pretty well."

She met his gaze and saw the accusation there. "What are you getting at?"

"At the benefit. The dress, the shoes. Not from JCPenney."

"Jake bought them for me. So what? I didn't ask for them. And he obviously needed me to look a certain way."

"You okay with that?"

If they'd been in a claustrophobic room with klieg lights, she couldn't have felt more accused.

"I don't know what I'm *okay* with," she said, sounding like an aggrieved child. "I just don't see how it's any of your concern. You and I had an intense encounter over the course of a few days in really unusual circumstances. Why do I owe you an explanation about anything?"

"I just want to make sure you're not taking my brother for a ride."

"Ah, because you care so much. Brotherly concern, is it?" She was fighting back tears. Why had she allowed herself to hope he might want to explore his feelings for her? "I had as good as given up on men. You seemed so different. I basically offered myself, but you didn't take me up on it. You really listened. You were so sympathetic. Now you sound like my brother."

No longer cocky, he just stood there, arms at his sides, red-faced, stunned.

"Go back to your … girlfriend." There was a catch in her voice. "We're done here. You can tell her you're completely over your babe in the woods. That, in truth, she never existed." She took a step to leave then decided she couldn't let him go still believing *he* was the injured party. "And, for the record, I ended it with Jake. Did you think I could go on seeing him after I understood that you and he were brothers? It's too bad, because if not for him …."

She threw up her hands. *God*, had she really been on the verge of attempting to explain what had gone down at La Fête Sauvage?

She was running now, heading for home, which—thank God—was only a few blocks away. When she slammed the door behind her, she was panting as if chased by the hounds of hell. She threw herself on the bed and surrendered to the tears. After crying herself out, she lay there, too devastated to move, for what seemed like hours. Eventually a pounding headache had her dragging herself to the bathroom to take two ibuprofens. Having no interest in food, she went back to bed and fell into a fitful sleep.

At two in the morning, her eyes popped open, and she didn't sleep again. It was a long, long night.

* * *

JOE WANTED TO CHASE AFTER her. He forced himself to stay put. *Well played, you idiot*, he thought. *What are you, twelve?* Things hadn't gone totally south until the accusations started flying. Damn that Jake … the old rivalry, entirely of his brother's making. Joe had never been jealous of his twin. Until now. Ali had confirmed that they weren't "sleeping" together. That didn't preclude kissing or even first or second base. *That sneaky bastard.* The worst part was that he was certain Jake knew who Ali was to him, though he couldn't say how. Ali wouldn't have told him. Had she really believed Jake to be him? Maybe for a split second, from a distance. He knew Jake had his charms … when he cared to use them. No doubt they were on full display for Ali.

Ali had ended it. Was that true? Did that mean Joe still had a chance? What about Rina? Reason had flown out the window the minute he saw Ali again, and he was still trying to retrieve it. Coming here today had been a mistake. In his efforts to scope things out, he'd confirmed her worst fears that he was nothing but a spoiled celebrity. He had to admit that was truer than it used to be. Initially, all he'd wanted was to make a living playing music, and he had, gradually gaining respect as a session guitarist. Why hadn't he left it at that? When Granny died in 1990, she left every one of the O'Connells set for life. But when opportunity knocked, you answered. And there were all those beautiful women …. With no one special to ground him, he took full advantage.

That brief wild period ended with Rina, more siren than woman. He'd reasoned that a good partnership was what he needed, not some angsty romance that could derail his career. Although she'd cheated on him and lied about it, Rina had begged for a second chance, and he'd foolishly forgiven her. They'd even discussed marriage. The minute he'd seen Ali again, he knew that couldn't happen. In fact, he didn't care if he ever saw Rina again. *Shit*, what could he do? They were scheduled to tour again in January. The sex kept her on best behavior, making their proximity tolerable. If he stopped sleeping with her, he might as well cancel the tour, because she would make his life a living hell. He couldn't do that to Linc, who was like a father to him.

What a mess.

CHAPTER 23

———•———

ALI HADN'T CHECKED HER MESSAGES that evening, and it was just as well. Carrie O'Connell, Joe and Jake's mother, had invited Ali to lunch on Wednesday. *Ugh.* The woman terrified her. Could Ali say no? But then she'd always wonder why Carrie had summoned her. Was she a man or a mouse? Neither, but that was beside the point. She had to man up and see what she was up against. She had nothing to be ashamed of.

HERE SHE WAS AGAIN, FACING another command performance for an O'Connell without a decent costume. The best Ali could come up with was her navy skirt suit and ivory-silk shell. It looked like a uniform you'd wear to check in guests at a moderately priced hotel. The entire outfit, including the low-heeled pumps, had been purchased on sale for less than a hundred dollars. It would scream CHEAP to a woman like Mrs. O'Connell, but there was no helping it.

Ali had promised to call Becca as soon as she got home from lunch. After driving by the O'Connell mansion to confirm the address, Ali parked three blocks away. She did *not* want the lady of the house to see her battered old Honda Civic. Ali could think of only one reason for the summons—to make her go away. She should have told Carrie on the phone that she and Jake were no longer an item. But what if the woman knew about the connection to Joe? Perhaps she'd offer to pay Ali big bucks to spin out of her family's orbit forever. God, she hoped not. That would be too, too humiliating.

The O'Connell residence was located on historic Capitol Hill, a few blocks from the street that went all out on Halloween, which was tomorrow.

No decorations here. Carrie probably turned off the lights so the children would pass her by. Jake had described his childhood home as twentieth-century Tudor revival, half-timbered with a twelve-foot-tall privacy hedge. If Ali were a well-heeled ghost, this behemoth would be her favorite haunt. You could always float over to Volunteer Park to check out the Seattle Asian Art Museum or visit your pioneer buddies in the Lake View Cemetery.

After ringing the doorbell, Ali admired the extensive wraparound porches, their surfaces immaculate, as if no crow or pigeon dared anoint them. She was surprised when Carrie O'Connell herself greeted her. She peered over the elegant woman's shoulder, expecting to see a butler. Then she realized such a gesture might be interpreted as slavering over the luxurious interior. Every item of furniture looked like a museum piece.

"Welcome!" Carrie said with aggressive good cheer. She was wearing a sleek, flared dove-gray-silk pantsuit that would have worked on Katharine Hepburn in *The Philadelphia Story*. Her gleaming, straight-blonde hair fell almost to her shoulders. "I invited Teresa, and she would have loved to come, but it was too last-minute."

Ali followed her into a sunny nook, where a table was set with antique china, sterling silver, and crystal glasses. Did Carrie always pull out all the stops for casual luncheons?

"I'd offer you a cocktail," the woman said with a graceful wave of her long-fingered hand, "but I can't drink at lunch. I'm just no good for the rest of the day." She checked her gold-filigree watch. "Besides, I'm starved. What about you? Let's eat." Carrie finally stopped talking and looked at Ali, who felt as if she were at a podium with no notes.

"Yes," Ali said because a reply was expected, "let's eat. That sounds like a good idea." Carrie continued to eye her quizzically. "Um, thank you so much for this invitation."

The woman laughed, a tinkling sound. "I can just imagine what is going on in your head." She sat down and gestured for Ali to do the same. "Do you like smoked salmon? I didn't know if you had any dietary restrictions."

"I'm fine with anything, really."

"How very low maintenance of you."

An impressive assortment of antique china serving dishes were piled with exotic offerings, almost a buffet's worth. Crackers, runny cheeses, watercress sandwiches, a fruit tray. Carrie might have been expecting the ladies bridge club, not one slender woman. Reading Ali correctly, she said, "Don't overthink it, dear. There was a meeting here yesterday for one of my charities. I just grabbed a bunch of leftovers from the fridge. It's Rostand's day off, but also, privacy is best in this situation. Personally, I like leftovers."

Uh-oh, privacy. Maybe Carrie had hired a hitman.

The woman sat down and helped herself to a watercress sandwich. "I made these, of course. Not much effort required." She popped it into her mouth.

Ali took a dainty bite and swallowed before saying, "Nice."

"I hope you're not going to make me taste everything before you do. Please, help yourself. I promise, nothing is poisoned."

Ali laughed uncomfortably. The O'Connell matriarch was alarmingly eccentric.

She poured Ali a glass of amber liquid. "I thought iced tea might be a nice change from coffee."

"You mean because I work at Sully's." *Cards on the table.*

"For now. I'm assuming your ambitions run higher. There's nothing shameful about it. I hear they offer generous benefits." She took a sip of tea. "I love that you do what it takes to survive." She paused. "That was a lovely dress you were wearing the other evening."

"Courtesy of your son." Too feisty? Ali was trying to keep her tone neutral.

"Oh, I know that." Carrie gave a dismissive wave. She made a lot of sweeping gestures. Maybe she was a former dancer. There was a balletic quality to her movements. "I don't mind," Mrs. O'Connell continued. "He can afford it. And you can't. You could hardly show up at that fundraiser in some little number from Nordstrom Rack." She spread brie on a cracker as she gave Ali's current Nordstrom Rack outfit a onceover. Finally she said, "Please don't misunderstand me. I didn't invite you here to warn you off. You probably think I'm going to declare that if you marry my son, I'll cut him off." She paused. "Like in *Pride and Prejudice?*"

"Now that you mention it—"

She was about to add that there was no need, but Carrie broke in, "I would never. Not that I could … cut him off, I mean. He has his own money. Jake has dubious taste in women. Usually. In your case, I'm quite pleased. I had you investigated, of course."

Ali was stunned into silence.

"You're squeaky clean, my dear. And so industrious and self-motivated. I have only a few concerns."

Here we go.

"One, you seem to have two of my sons on the hook."

Whoa. She *was* well informed. But she was wrong, and Ali opened her mouth to say so.

Carrie persisted, "I know about your brief encounters with Joe, first at the fundraiser and then at your workplace. That was so rude of him to surprise you like that. In that ridiculous disguise. Who was he kidding? I truly doubt anyone would have recognized him. Though he does turn heads. Next to Edward, he's the best looking of my children. Edward's a Catholic priest, you know. What a waste of DNA. I should have grandchildren by now."

Ali couldn't help fixating on the phrase "brief encounter," like the movie, which to her implied a sexual tryst. "I hardly know Joe," she insisted. She took a long sip of iced tea. Her mouth had gone dry.

"I'd say that initial encounter was significant, no?" the woman said. "I'm not referring to the fundraiser."

"You know about 'Babe in the Woods,' " Ali said.

"Yes. Even if I didn't, I'd have figured it out. Your name is Ali, and you fit the description."

"I had no idea who he was," Ali blurted out. "He said his name was JJ. That's all I knew. I don't follow country music, or perhaps I'd have connected the dots months ago. I hoped we'd meet again, but I didn't believe it possible."

"He tried to find you," Mrs. O'Connell said. "Moved heaven and earth to do so." She was leaning forward, elbows on the table, staring Ali down. "Lots of people know that song. If you'd recounted the story to just about anyone, they'd have mentioned it to you."

"I don't have a lot of friends, and I don't confide in strangers."

"And yet you, by some startling coincidence, began to date Jake, Joe's twin, who, though they are not identical, closely resembles his brother. Did you believe Jake was Joe?"

Wow, this woman was good. "JJ owned an awful lot of BPO gear. The logo was everywhere in the cabin. When I finally met Jake, I thought he was JJ. For about a minute. Then I just hoped he'd—" She cut herself off as heat suffused her cheeks.

"Honest. I like that." Carrie leaned back in her chair. "Well, my dear, you *are* in a pickle, aren't you? Jake's smitten with you, but you are gaga over Joe. Joe is deeply involved with a very beautiful and talented singer who could have any man she wanted, maybe in the world. Not that you aren't pretty, quite extraordinarily so. I don't particularly like Rina, by the way. She's terribly self-absorbed. What a shame that men tend to overlook glaring personality defects when they are powerfully attracted." Ali could hardly respond to that, so Mrs. O'Connell went on, "Do you think you could love Jake?"

Ali shook her head. "After the fundraiser, I broke it off."

Carrie's expression was more smug than understanding. "The two of you would never have suited. Jake has some growing up to do. Not that Joe totally knows *his* mind. Obviously he's conflicted or he'd leave you alone. You do need to consider that he's been fantasizing about a lost waif, not a strong survivor like you."

Ali ordered her shoulders to relax. She was sitting on the edge of her chair, her body rigid as if poised to spring to safety. "And I fell for a gentle, sympathetic woodsman—the best listener I ever met. Perhaps we both need a reality check."

Carrie rose to her feet, picking up her iced tea. "Let's move to the living room, shall we? I appreciate your practicality, Ali."

Having migrated to the more formal living room, they now perched on stiff, pristine upholstered chairs. You could hardly call them "easy" chairs. No one would fall asleep in them. Heaven forbid they should drool.

"You have a good head on your shoulders," Carrie continued. "I'm not averse to you getting to know Joe a bit more if he keeps throwing himself in your path. However, fair warning … I'm guessing Joe will try to get you out of his system before he finishes his current album and leaves town in two weeks. That could be dangerous for you."

"Dangerous?"

"You're not terribly experienced, are you? Believe me when I say that you have never come up against a man like Joe. Even women who are used to leading men around by their noses end up putty in his hands, and that can cause a girl to lose all sense of perspective. You're going to have to think long and hard before you do anything that … can't be undone."

Did Carrie think Ali was a virgin? The silence sucked all the air out of the room. Finally she said, "I'm not the whore of Babylon, but I've been around the block a time or two."

Carrie regarded her critically then repeated, "Or two."

Well, that was right on the nose. She'd had precisely two lovers, though "sex partners" was a more appropriate term. In a hurry to move on, she said, "You mentioned a 'few' concerns. Have I heard them all?"

Mrs. O'Connell finished off her iced tea. "I believe so. I know you come from the school of hard knocks, so perhaps being toyed with by Joe Bob Blade won't leave you fit for an asylum. I wish you well, my dear."

* * *

JOE KNEW HIS MOTHER WAS up to something. He'd been staying with Teresa at her townhome in Madison Park but thought he'd stop by the Capitol Hill house for a quick visit before returning to the recording studio. He couldn't help but notice the old Honda Civic parked a few blocks away, thinking how out of place it looked in the neighborhood—like a rat in a hamster's cage. He had pulled over, several cars away, when he caught sight of Ali, dressed in a navy skirt suit that made her look like a hot stewardess. She unlocked the car and got in. *Ah, of course.* This was the junker she'd left parked along Highway 101 when she'd happened upon him in the woods. He checked his watch: one thirty. He could only conclude that she'd been visiting his mother, which had to be at her command. He was *not* happy. He waited until Ali had driven away before parking in his mother's circular driveway.

Not only was he angry at his mother, but he was also ashamed of himself. He'd done some digging and found out Ali's work schedule and address, a house she shared with her mostly absent roommate Becca. Now his mother was harassing her. What a pair they made. If Jake hadn't let Ali go easily, Joe might have feared for her sanity.

Though he had a key, Joe never showed up at his childhood home without calling first. He knocked. It had to be Rostand's day off because his mother answered the door.

"Joe," she said warily, "what a nice surprise."

"Did you have a *pleasant lunch?*" he asked with accusatory emphasis.

"Ah, I am discovered," his mother replied blandly as they seated themselves in the living room, a place he was never tempted to linger. It reminded him of the waiting room of a fancy funeral parlor.

He leaned in, hands on his knees, eyes narrowed. "What are you up to, Mom?"

"I might ask you the same," she said, unruffled.

Joe clicked his tongue in disapproval. "Mom, did you hire an investigator? I should have known."

"Where my boys are concerned, I am a mama bear. I like to know when someone is trying to tag my cubs."

"Ali's not like that."

"You may be right. If so, you two boys are both going to chase her away. Jake's, um, *generosity* and your considerable charms may not be enough for this girl. She doesn't seem the type to let herself be whisked off to become one of Jake's possessions or a member of your entourage."

Joe fell back in his chair, stricken by her words.

"Decide what you really want before you upset her life any further. She was canny enough to see through Jake. Much as I love that boy, he was up to something—pursuing her for all the wrong reasons."

"How could you know that?"

"I am, by nature, suspicious. Ali is not his type."

"She's anyone's type," Joe said, immediately wishing he hadn't.

His mother surprised him by laughing—a tinkly, almost genuine sound. "Now I know how far gone you are."

CHAPTER 24

———•———

STUCK IN TRAFFIC ON I-90, Ali tried not to worry her lip. Why hadn't she sensed that she was being followed? Her blood ran cold. Carrie *really* didn't like her.

She sent a silent message to her brother. *Liam, what should I do?* She was certain there could be no positive outcome with Joe. Either he pursued her and messed with her head or he left her alone and even more devastated than before. No one would choose *her* over Rina.

Why did Liam stay away? After the accident, he might have been in a coma or suffered from amnesia but … wasn't long-term amnesia rare outside of soap operas? Say Liam had chosen to disappear because he wanted to start over … what would be his motivation? He'd had a great job, lots of buddies in his motorcycle club, a pretty, pliant girlfriend who hadn't come forward after his supposed death to say she was having his baby. Come to think of it, the girlfriend hadn't even called to commiserate. Ali guessed Liam had dumped her before leaving for Israel. Two months was about his limit.

She sighed and turned up the music on the radio. "Paranoia, the destroyer" the Kinks sang. She wasn't paranoid, just realistic. Her own brother, kind and generous in so many other ways, had always been a jerk with his girlfriends. What made her think she had ever been anything more than a distraction for Joe?

THE SOUND OF THE DOORBELL was startlingly unfamiliar. It was way too early for trick-or-treaters, Ali and Becca didn't get solicitors, and friends like Pete didn't show up without calling first. Ali had just stepped out of the shower.

Her hair was wet, and she was dressed in comfortable, baggy jeans, a white tee, and an oversized flannel shirt.

She peered through the peephole and felt her heart leap. *Down, girl*, she told it. *This is the Big Bad Wolf, not Prince Charming.*

"Go away!" she shouted through the door.

"Please … give me a chance to explain."

Explain what? Why he'd accused her of shaking down his brother?

To hell with it.

The door flew open—the reverse of a slam—hard enough to break the spring on the door stopper. Ali just stood there, stoop-shouldered and defeated.

"Do you have a moment?" Joe asked, as if selling encyclopedias. "May I come in?"

She moved aside so he could enter.

* * *

THE SIGHT OF ALI TOOK Joe's breath away. She looked much like she had the night they met, wet hair and all. He drank her in: the shimmering blue eyes, the glowing, warm-hued skin, the sweetly curved lips, the fresh, orange-blossom scent.

"I love the jack-o'-lanterns on the porch," he said, referring to the cat-faced pumpkin giving the frightened dog-faced one an evil glare. Their whimsical style was pure Ali.

She shifted uncomfortably. "Have a seat," she said, self-consciously touching her hair and assessing her surroundings with a frown as if observing the place through his eyes. "It's shabby, but clean. Becca and I are both neatniks. Not that I see much of her these days."

"The chef," he said, sitting on the couch.

"Your family knows *way* too much about our business. I need to dry my hair. Can I get you something? Black tea, herbal? No coffee here, sorry. I've gotten so I can hardly stand the smell."

"Water would be nice," he said, rising to his feet. "I can help myself."

She was already backing away. "We drink tap water here. There's ice in the freezer."

While he waited, he paced around the living room. Noticing the sketchpads, he picked one up and flipped through it. The subjects of the sketches all looked like a combination of Jake and him. *Lord*, this woman was talented. They had Jake's jawline but Joe's hair, Joe's laidback demeanor. *Had she meant to sketch him or Jake?* he thought, burning with jealousy.

Had she seen an easygoing, sensual side of Jake his brother only revealed in private? He set the pad aside. *Stop it,* he told himself. *She said she'd broken it off.* But they'd had *three* dates. Jake must have touched her, fondled her, *something.* At the very least, that scheming brother of his had kissed Ali. The thought of Jake touching her in *any* way made Joe want to punch the wall.

He was just reaching for the other sketchpad when Ali returned. He quickly folded his arms across his chest, his posture defensive rather than the relaxed stance he was aiming for. She appeared just as tense, perching on the edge of the easy chair, back ramrod straight like someone called to the principal's office. And Joe looked like a disapproving principal. He unfolded his arms and willed his shoulders to drop.

Sitting across from her, he said, "I think we got off to a bad start."

"Nothing wrong with the start," she said.

He nodded. Where was his legendary charm? Now that he was here, could finally *talk* to her, he might as well be on enforced vocal rest. He'd hoped to get to know her better, to see if his crush held up in the real world. To find out if Ali could possibly be his future.

After a stretch of brittle silence, she spoke again, her voice low and uncertain. "You're the uninvited guest. Ball's in your court."

"What you said before you, uh, left me a few days back, 'if not for him' … what? What didn't you tell me about Jake?"

"I'm amazed you don't know already." Her long look accused him of far more heinous crimes. "Although I assume Carrie didn't sic her investigator on me until Jake and I showed up together at the fundraiser." She clasped her hands in her lap and stared at the floor. Then, voice neutral, she spoke as if recounting the plot of a TV show. "I helped Jean-Louis and Becca out at a special event for Big Paul's at La Fête Sauvage. At the end of the evening, someone had a medical emergency, and Becca and I got separated. There was a man there who had clearly been on the prowl for the perfect victim. Guess that was me. He was the son of Tom Lowen, of Lowen Cellular fame. He followed me into one of the empty tents."

Joe swallowed hard, dreading her next words.

"He pushed me down, tore my dress. Jake showed up at that precise moment and pulled him off me. If not for Jake …." She shrugged, as if the incident were no worse than a bad day at the office.

"Jake *rescued* you?"

"*You* rescued me too," she said, "in the cabin. So you're even. It's a tie. *Ding, ding!*" She pretended to ring a bell.

Her sarcasm was like a slap. "How can you joke about it?"

Flailing her arms, she asked, "How can I *not* joke about it? If not for Jake, I could easily have been raped. How do you think I've survived all these years of setbacks, anyway? I make light of things. It's my defense mechanism."

"Jake rescued you, and you didn't fall for him? Would you still be seeing him if I hadn't showed up?"

Stunned, she said. "*What*? Are you plunking for your brother so you can feel less guilty about Rina?"

He dragged a hand through his hair. "Of course not. Only … what's wrong with him?" He kept his tone light to mask his jealousy.

"Nothing. I don't have the wardrobe. That's a Becca-ism. While we were in grad school, she decided to stop dating a particularly image-conscious guy because he wanted her to dress preppie in order to fit in with his crowd. I don't work in your brother's world. I'm like a … a button mushroom in a patch of chanterelles. I fit into JJ's world just fine. After all, he was just a guy taking a break from society in a cabin he built himself. I figured he worked at Weyerhaeuser, or maybe Boeing, like my brother."

Joe was holding his smile in check, trying not to laugh at the mushroom comparison. He didn't want Ali to think he wasn't taking her seriously. She had no idea how beautiful she was. Or how much Joe longed for normalcy. He drank the last of his water and put down the glass. "Fair enough. Though I never told you I built the place. I can't help your assumptions."

She was avoiding his eyes again. "I knew you were no woodsman," she confessed, unconsciously wringing her hands. "Even before you took me back to the road, I had concluded that you were a singer on vocal rest. If not famous, then, uh, prosperous enough. You weren't roughing it out there."

She fetched a pitcher of water from the kitchen, refilled his glass, and placed the pitcher on the coffee table.

He didn't blame her for being bitter. "It was wrong of me not to come clean," he said, willing her to meet his eyes again. "I have never been a comfortable celebrity. Life was better when I was a working musician." He took a sip of water. "Will you accept my apology? Can we try to have a normal conversation?"

To his relief, Ali relaxed slightly. "I met your mother."

"Did you like her?"

She hesitated before replying, "She's formidable."

Joe smiled. He knew the power of his smile. The O'Connell kids had been raised with all the social graces, learning manipulation from their mother and the art of schmoozing from their father, who had definitely kissed the Blarney

159

Stone. Beneath her disarming demeanor, his mother was a barracuda. Joe was too loyal to say it. "She's intimidating but nicer than most people realize. My dad was pretty great too."

"You're lucky."

Of course his relationship with his parents was way more complicated than that, not quite the *Leave it to Beaver* situation she was no doubt imagining. And yet, he detected no subtext of envy or reproach.

"Yeah. And you weren't. Lucky, I mean. When it comes to family. Your brother being the exception. Your foster parents were cold fish."

Ali looked stricken. "Did I say that? Now that they're dead, I feel even worse about not appreciating them more."

Joe couldn't believe his ears. "They're *dead*?"

She nodded gravely. "They'd rejoined the Peace Corps and were stationed in Botswana. Motorcycle accident."

Joe was momentarily struck dumb.

"The shittiest part is, when I heard the news, I mostly felt bad for my own sake. Because I hoped that someday we might … I don't know, have a grown-up relationship. Now that's impossible. I wish I could mourn them. But I'm afraid there was no"—she paused—"love lost between us."

"I get it," Joe said.

"They were old hippies with the best of intentions," Ali went on. "We were a little wild. Especially Liam. My wildness was more about rebellion … and attitude. I was mouthy. They expected us to be grateful." Her sigh was weighted with guilt. "We didn't deliver."

"You were kids," Joe protested. "You needed time to warm to them. Why didn't they get that?"

Ali made a vague gesture. "They sort of did. It would have helped if they hadn't insisted quite so much on our contribution to society. Between homework, lessons, and volunteering, we didn't get much chance to be children."

"I can't imagine." Joe got the picture. Ali and Liam were supposed to be their legacy, not their progeny. "I don't think you told me anywhere near the whole story about Liam. You were close, but sometimes that closeness was stifling. Care to elaborate now?"

"Hmm. The *whole* story. You never hear the *whole* story from one person. All I can tell you is my perception of Liam. It's shifted over the ten months since his disappearance." From the side table, she picked up the sketchpad Joe hadn't flipped through and found a drawing of a man on a motorcycle, casually insolent, seductive. "I've been trying to capture his essence. I only have school portraits and a few Polaroids."

Joe grinned. "I love it. I kept your sketches from the cabin. You could make a children's book. *The Friendly Rain Forest*, or *Hoh Sweet Home*." That made her smile. "May I?" After a slight hesitation, she handed the sketchpad over.

Once again, he marveled at her talent. The animals had distinct personalities and little human touches. The wolf, grinning and drooling, wore a bib with a picture of a lamb on it.

She peered over his shoulder. "I know. Even when I aim for bloodthirsty, I get cute."

He flipped through the book. Bigfoot wore frayed cutoffs, a Hawaiian shirt, and Birkenstocks. He looked cuddly, like they all did. The black beetle had big round eyes on its tentacles and six red tennis shoes. A horse sat on a stump, human-style, front hooves gesturing, eyes wide and teeth bared as if telling a story.

Her laugh was rueful. "Unless I'm in a bad mood, I don't do 'fierce' well. The *Where the Wild Things Are* monsters are a lot scarier."

"They're adorable," Joe said, gazing up at her. "*You're* adorable."

She blushed with pleasure, and he found he had gravitated toward her till they were almost touching. He forced himself to give her space.

"I'm sorry." *Jesus*—he was blushing too. "That just slipped out." He concentrated on the picture of Liam. "The resemblance is striking." A drawing of them as children showed them both with short hair, standing back-to-back with their arms crossed, trying to look tough.

She rolled her eyes. "I'm starting to forget what he looked like. We really weren't that much alike. I drew that to show the two of us right before Liam's growth spurt. At seven, I was a tomboy and tall for my age."

"Liam had a growth spurt at age seven? Isn't that really early?"

"When hormones kick in early like that, it's called 'central precocious puberty.' That was something we learned later. No underlying medical cause, as far as anyone knows. It was an adjustment, to say the least."

Yikes. Poor Liam, Joe thought. *He really didn't get to be a kid.*

"You told me your birth mother lost custody of you. How did that happen? What was she like?"

"Her name was Nancy Ryan, and she was pretty and had long dark hair. She left us in a hot car. While she was getting a fix. Someone reported it to the police. All I remember is being really hot and thirsty and sleepy ... and scared she wouldn't come back. Things like that had happened before, in the house, not the car. It must have been August. Liam and I did our best to forget the years before George and Emily. We don't know what happened to our mother."

Joe couldn't take his eyes off her. "What else do you recall?"

"Nothing important, other than wondering where she'd gone this time and wondering when we'd eat again. She stumbled around a lot, cursed a blue streak when she fell. When we cursed too, she spanked us." Joe frowned. "Not hard. She wasn't really abusive. Just … absent. Neglectful. Sad. I don't know her drug of choice. She slept a lot. Heroin, probably. It's a wonder Liam and I were so healthy. We ate nothing but junk. Ramen. Sugary off-brand cereals. Saltines. Cheese Whiz or Velveeta, SpaghettiOs. He appointed himself my protector. At first I teased him for chasing my 'friends' away. Most of my friends were boys. When I turned twelve and they started flirting, I lost patience with them. Liam transformed my girlfriends into blithering idiots. When the boys started, um, expressing their interest more openly, Liam became my shadow. It was unnerving. Even our foster parents urged him to give me space."

She'd been speaking as if in a trance of memory. Now she turned her blazing-blue gaze on him. It was like being caught in a tractor beam. "Were you like that with Teresa? She was the youngest and the only sister of four brothers. I bet she was as cloistered as a Saudi princess."

Joe pictured Teresa as a twelve-year-old. Not only was she already a stunner, but she'd also developed early. Of course they'd been protective. Not protective enough.

"We did watch out for her," he said. "She was a beauty from her first breath. We never worried about her, though. She always walked the straight and narrow. Excellent grades, sunny disposition, no adolescent moodiness. Until …. Well, that's not my story to tell."

Joe thought back to her senior year. When Teresa had finally realized her chains were of her own forging, her act of rebellion had been a doozie. Their mother had never gotten over it. It wasn't long before Teresa willingly submitted again to her society shackles. She'd flown too close to the sun. Someday, he hoped, she'd break free again.

Ali was still staring at him expectantly.

Joe asked, "Have you ever thought that Liam had been through something awful himself? Beautiful boys are just as vulnerable, you know."

He knew that firsthand. Fortunately his brushes with pedophiles had been nothing more than that. Though he did mature later than Liam, Joe's ninety-eight-pound weakling stage had been mercifully brief.

Ali looked away again and sighed. "I've always wondered. Liam's a hard nut to crack. He rarely lets down that stony façade. Sometimes I think his weird growth spurt was achieved through sheer force of will. So he could protect not only me, but himself."

Lounging back on the couch, Joe regarded her thoughtfully. For some reason that explanation made perfect sense. "Why not?" he said with an insouciant shrug. "Stranger things have happened."

Ali might not be tense anymore, but she did look thoroughly deflated. *God*, how he wanted to pull her onto his lap, give her comfort.

Get real, he told himself. *What you want from her has nothing to do with comfort.*

CHAPTER 25

———|———

ALI BRISTLED IN A WAY that told Joe his languid body language was spooking her. He tried to put a lid on it, sitting up straighter. "Still think Liam is alive?"

Her answer floored him. "I received a package from a post office box in Jerusalem."

He sat forward again. "What was in the box?"

"A toy soldier. He used to tell me, 'Soldier on.' It's a message."

Joe tapped his chin, considering the possibilities. "No note?"

"No," she said.

"Why not?"

"You already know my crazy theories. He wanted to disappear. He has a brain injury and has lost the ability to write. He's hopelessly disfigured, wears a mask, and is leading some radical group. He's been recruited by the CIA."

Their shared laughter relieved some of the tension. At least now she seemed to be acknowledging that her theories were absurd.

"Do you think I'm in denial?" Ali asked, smiling shyly.

Joe shook his head. "When Jake and I were kids, we were close like that. One time I had a premonition that he was hurt, and I rushed to tell our mom. She gave me a stern lecture about how things like ESP were 'utter nonsense.' Imagine her surprise when it turned out Jake had fallen off his bike and been badly banged up—scrapes, contusions, a concussion." He took a sip of water. "We certainly don't have that kind of connection now." He smiled. "You know, maybe you might be on to something with Liam. From what you've told me, he's just the sort of guy to take on some secret mission."

She chuckled. "It makes more sense than anything else, weirdly."

She tapped his knee, shattering his fragile control over his physical need for her. "Hey," she said, clueless as to the power of her touch, "it's nice to hear you talk about yourself. You'd rather ask questions. Being a great listener is how you guard your privacy."

Resting his arms in his lap to conceal the bulge in his jeans, Joe said, "I don't like to talk about myself. I get quoted in ways that make me sound like an ass. You have no idea how nice it was to have your company in the cabin. I'd been alone for a week, and I was going stir-crazy. I didn't have to be 'Joe Bob Blade' with you. I was *so* sorry to see you go ...." *Behave*, he told himself and changed the subject. "What happened during that time between leaving your birth mother and starting life with George and Emily?" His voice was lower, huskier. What was he doing? He held her hand, his eyes roaming over her, and she hadn't pulled away. He let go when he realized he'd been rubbing her palm with his thumb.

Ali blinked, her eyes an otherworldly blue. "Oh. Isn't that weird? I've blanked on most of it."

He cleared his throat. "That sounds ominous," he said in a more normal voice, straightening up on the couch and struggling for control. He shifted uncomfortably. A haze of sex seemed to have descended over them like the humid, seductively fragrant air of the tropics.

"What is she like?" Ali said softly.

"Who?"

"Rina."

There it was, the ice-water dunking he deserved. Joe took a deep breath and blew it out. He couldn't explain Rina or why he'd forgiven her betrayal. But ... *had* he forgiven her? They were on thin ice and they both knew it.

"Rina doesn't have a lot of patience with weakness, which is how she sees my vocal troubles." He made a derisive sound, his disgust directed at himself. "I'm way out of line here, I know. I shouldn't have come." He scanned the room, needing to talk about something else. "I like this place. It's homey. You guys have good taste. When you hear that old song, 'Over the river and through the woods, to Grandmother's house we go,' you picture something like this. A colorful, comfortable, homey refuge from real life, a holiday type of place."

Ali laughed. "You give us too much credit. It's Goodwill and Value Village all the way."

"Yeah, but how many people could create an atmosphere like this with only those resources?"

"Becca's the creative genius."

"If you say so." She was way too humble. Joe already knew she had artistic talent. Why not a gift for interior design too? "I feel as if I could stay here forever. We could make hot chocolate and do a puzzle. And we could pretend the rest of the world didn't exist."

Ali's eyes glistened. "How is your voice now?"

Her manner toward him had softened. He was ashamed of himself for playing the sympathy card, but it felt so good to have her in his court. "Always a concern. Another reason I prefer listening to talking. Then I can save it for singing. Recording is particularly thorny because every little flaw is set in stone. Part of my legacy, for good or ill."

"Your legacy," she repeated, as if questioning whether a composer of popular songs could have one. Or perhaps his own insecurity was leading him to detect mockery rather than understanding.

"What I meant to say is, it's on the record. If my voice starts to cut out, the engineers wonder if I'm losing it again. When they tell me to take a break, I worry. I've been avoiding alcohol because it's dehydrating. What country singer worth his salt can't go on the occasional bender? Not that I'm a drinker, it's just that … it would be nice not to have to think hard about the wisdom of a single beer or shot of whiskey. Rina likes her wine, and she hates it that I have to be so careful. She loves to dance, go to clubs, stay out all night. I can't keep up with her." *Nor do I want to*, he added silently.

"You'd think another singer would understand," Ali said.

"Well, she doesn't. She has vocal cords of steel. Mine have been problematic for a long time, not just when I met you. I'd like nothing better than to stop worrying and eat and drink and stay up late and shoot the breeze like everyone else." He looked at his watch and jumped to his feet. "Man, I had no idea it was this late. I'm sorry for bumming you out. I'm due at the studio in the U District in an hour. If I'm late, my sound engineer's going to bite my head off."

"Why does your voice need to be perfect? The scratchiness is really minor. To me it just makes everything you sing more interesting."

He took a step toward her then stopped himself. "You're kind," he said, "and to a degree, you're right. My struggle is to keep scratchy from becoming raspy, which feels awful and takes all the fun out of it. Then there's just … gone. I know the majority of my fans would be okay with raspy. But if all that's left is a bark, I'm finished."

"Why are you really here?" she said. "I mean in this house. Did you think we'd make love?"

He was taken aback by her frankness, realizing the truth in her words, a truth he hadn't acknowledged himself. "I, uh …."

"We know so little about each other. You think I'm a bad fit for your world. I agree. But I can't help how I feel. About you, I mean."

Joe hadn't expected straight talk. Ali seemed to be giving him permission to go for it, but that wasn't what he wanted. Surely she wasn't thinking straight. What *did* he want? Not a nooner. He pictured a long weekend in the Bahamas. Candles, Mai Tais, Brazilian jazz, and a slow seduction. But he had no time for indulgences. He had an album to record, another tour to survive. Life had him flailing in a riptide, and he selfishly wished he could place Ali in suspended animation until it released him again. He couldn't ask her to wait, not with the future so murky. For all he knew, he was circling the drain to hell. He couldn't let her chuck her own goals only to be sucked in too.

Logic was no match for the heat of her hand on his chest. He kissed her wrist, then drew her in until no space remained between them. *God*, she smelled wonderful, like an orange grove. Their bodies hummed with mutual need as they rocked together. He planted small kisses along her jaw, hesitating as he reached her mouth. For a moment, their lips barely touched as they breathed each other in. Then, surrendering to the inevitable, he kissed her, the sweet languor of desire claiming them both as their tongues probed and tasted with growing hunger. His hand crept down the small of her back and inside her jeans and panties to massage the soft curves of her naked bottom. He strained against her as her fingers tentatively explored beneath his T-shirt, sliding over his hard nipples and down to his navel.

One last thread of sanity remained. *You can't let this happen!* his conscience screamed. *She deserves better.*

He grabbed her hand to stop it from moving lower and willed his breathing to slow, hating himself for letting things get this far. *God*, how he wanted her naked and writhing beneath him. Just when he thought he'd won the battle, she unzipped her jeans and invited his fingers inside. His willpower dissolved as he found the moist bud of her sex. Tentatively, he strummed her sex in a gentle rhythm, her little moans egging him on. She was clutching his ass now, and he was crazy with desire. He felt her tension mount, knowing she was close. She cried out, and her body shuddered with release.

His jeans had just hit the floor when the phone rang. They both froze.

"Hello there, this is Ali and Becca's answering machine," Becca's sultry voice purred. "You know the drill."

At the beep, Becca said, "I sound like a moose in heat. We have *got* to change that message. Happy Halloween! Listen, I'm at La Fête Sauvage. Call me as soon as you can?" She hung up.

Joe struggled into his jeans, breathing hard. "My God, Ali, you're so … exquisite. I could never get enough of you."

He sat heavily on the couch, put his head in his hands, and groaned. Then he checked his watch again. "Shit! I gotta go. I'll be in town for at least another week. Let's try to … talk again."

And he was gone.

* * *

ALI FELT LIKE SHE'D BEEN saved from drowning then left to freeze to death.

She was draped over the couch, tearful and wrung out. Its cushions still echoed with Joe's elusive aura and taunted her with what might have been. Gradually, she forced herself into an upright position and willed herself to think rationally.

Here were the cold, hard facts: Joe believed his life was no longer his own. That it belonged to the record company, his manager, and Rina. If he weren't so tired and stressed, he might realize he had options. Sure, he should finish the album, but after that, why not take a break? At least until his voice was fully restored. He could even retire. Money clearly wasn't an object. But no, he wasn't ready and might never be. He loved music too much. Perhaps he wasn't done proving himself. Whatever the case, she didn't figure into the equation.

More than ever, she believed she was in love. Whereas he felt nothing more than lust. Still … the way he focused on her, with that amazing intensity …. In the cabin, it had been like that—like she was Scheherazade. The Sultan's wife had captivated her husband with her storytelling skills for one thousand and one nights. Ali had barely managed two. And "captivate" was too strong a word.

If only Joe wasn't quite so handsome. Today his curly chestnut locks were mussed in a devil-may-care way, and the five o'clock shadow made his skin even more luminous. He had all the nice features of his brother, only with a classic cleft chin, and he was so much more at ease that he just wore them better. Both brothers had the same soulful brown eyes, but Joe's shone with an extra degree of warmth. Only Joe radiated the charisma that marked him as a star, and his brother as no more than a nattily dressed disciple of Tony Robbins.

She would bet everyone Joe met felt exceptional. That was his special sauce.

The phone rang again. Though it wasn't a number she recognized, Ali answered.

"Hello?"

"*Âllo, âllo*! Ali, this is Jean-Louis."

Jean-Louis had never phoned Ali, so she was momentarily speechless. That hardly mattered. The chef wasn't one to let a conversational vacuum slow him down.

"I know this is most likely a surprise. I have a visitor here at the restaurant who is eager to meet you. Are you free right now?"

"Jean-Louis, this isn't a good time."

"*Là, là*. Pull yourself together. Unless you were suddenly called to work."

"No—"

He didn't wait for an explanation. "You will want to meet this man, believe me."

"Wait … *this* man?" she echoed.

"Don't worry, he is old enough to be your father. *En effet*, I am fairly certain he *is* your father."

CHAPTER 26

ALI'S FATHER? HOW COULD JEAN-LOUIS possibly know that?

She stopped outside the upended Viking ship and braced herself against a railing, wheezing slightly as she struggled to catch her breath. Several minutes passed before she calmed down enough to enter. Ali *knew* she should have changed into her skirt suit. She was ridiculously underdressed in this lunch crowd of business executives.

She was about to head for the service entrance when Becca appeared at the main door, dressed like a flamenco dancer and grinning from ear to ear. She ran out to give Ali a giant hug.

"What's going on, Becca? I'm about to have a heart attack here."

Becca rubbed her hands together. "This is so exciting!"

Ali balked at Becca's attempt to drag her inside. "I can't go in there. I'm wearing jeans. The customers will be scandalized."

"Don't be silly. There's no dress code. Why should you care as long as Jean-Louis doesn't? Besides, you *always* look beautiful."

She caught sight of Jean-Louis across the room, standing next to a tall man.

Her first thought was "aging rock star." A tiny hoop earring and spiky, bleached-blond hair. Sixtyish, she guessed. Jagged cheekbones and a rangy body. His casual clothing—a rugby shirt with the sleeves pushed up, down vest, khakis, and sneakers—clashed with the hair and earring. His features, height, and stance were familiar. *Ah.* She knew who he resembled. In a daze, she said, "Liam?"

He replied, "Ali?"

Lightheaded, she steadied herself against the smooth mahogany of the booth. "Who are you?" She hadn't meant the question to sound like an accusation. If this was her father, how had he found her?

"Easy, now." He held up his hands. "I'm harmless, I promise. My name is Duncan Walsh." She thought she detected an Irish brogue. "I'm delighted to meet you." They shook hands.

Jean-Louis appeared to regret his surprise-party approach. "Please, Ali, have a seat. There is a simple explanation, I promise."

"When I saw Duncan," Becca broke in, "I knew he had to be your father. He looks so much like Liam. But wow, now we know where you both got those unusual blue eyes."

It was true. Duncan's were faded, but otherwise the same hue as Liam's and her own. Deep-set, like Liam's. Long lashed like hers. Both twins had inherited the slightly crooked nose. His skin was weathered, eye creases more like fishing nets than crow's feet, and his cheeks and chin were faintly pockmarked. "Okay, I can't help but see it," she said, slightly breathless.

His smile faltered. "Who is Liam?"

The question cast a temporary pall over the giddy reunion.

Uh-oh. He didn't know much. In finding a daughter, he'd also lost a son. "Liam was my twin brother."

"*Was*?" His face fell.

"Or *is*. I believe he's alive, although the rest of the world would say I'm nuts. I'll explain in a minute. How did you find out about me? Did you talk to our mother?"

"Nancy and I met exactly once. Apparently that was enough."

Ali wondered if Duncan had paid for her mother's services. "She was an addict. We entered the foster system at age five. No word from her since. What makes you think you're our father, other than the obvious resemblance?"

"Now first of all, I didn't pay to be with her," he said as if she'd voiced the question aloud. "She was a free spirit, not a prostitute. As for how I found you, I saw the photo in the *Seattle Times*—the one accompanying the review of La Fête Sauvage. The resemblance to Nancy was so striking that I had to investigate. I thought you might be her daughter, but until I saw you, I didn't dare hope *I* was your father. Though the timing does fit."

"The timing?"

"I met Nancy at a Christmas Party in 1969. I had just been drafted and was blowing off steam. You would be the right age."

"Liam and I were born on September twelfth, 1970. Nine months later." She sniffed back tears. "I feel as if I'm looking at Liam at sixty."

His laugh was rueful. "Um, fifty-two. I was twenty-five at the time. Irish skin doesn't weather well." In a more subdued voice, he said, "Tell me about Liam."

Becca and Jean-Louis exchanged a look and started to back away.

"Can we bring you lunch?" Jean-Louis asked.

"I'm not sure I can eat much," Ali said, "but a diet Coke would be welcome. Maybe some breadsticks? Duncan?"

"Do you have Guinness?"

"Of course," Jean-Louis said. "I will alert the waitress to bring you drinks and appetizers. *Aweille*, Becca! Ali can bring you up to date later."

"Don't leave without saying goodbye," Becca said with a wink.

Ali and Duncan were finally alone. There was something about this man that made her want to spill her guts. His expression so eager and receptive. She gave him the family-friendly version of Liam's life, emphasizing the high points that would make a father proud. The excellent grades, the respected job, the ability to fix anything, the successes with women.

"He sounds like a bit of an A-hole," Duncan said. "I assume he has some failings that you're not sharing, other than using his good looks to seduce women."

"He has a temper," Ali said, realizing they were both talking as if he were alive.

"That manifests itself how?"

She chose her words carefully. "He was determined to keep men away from me. In high school, anyway."

"As your father, I can't be too upset by that." He tensed, bracing for the worst. "What happened to him?"

"Um, that's a weird one. He disappeared after a terrorist attack. Hamas."

Duncan's eyes widened in shock. "Bus stop? Marketplace?"

"Café. In Jerusalem. The American embassy mailed me his wallet—ID, cash, and credit cards still inside, though partially melted—and passport. They were only salvageable at all because they were buried in the pockets of his motorcycle jacket. The authorities weren't able to identify any … body parts." She cleared her throat to add, "As his twin, I believe I'd know if he were no longer in the world. Also …."

"Yes?" Duncan said eagerly.

The conversation paused as the waitress served them their drinks, along with a basket of Jean-Louis's signature parmesan breadsticks, two crabcakes, and wild turkey wrapped in bacon.

"Do you think the bacon is from wild pigs?" Duncan whispered after the waiter left.

Al laughed. "I'm not sure Jean-Louis is that much of a purist. Feel free to ask."

"No way," he said. "I want to stay on the man's good side. You were about to tell me why you believe Liam is alive?" He filled his plate and started in on a wild turkey roll. "Mmm, that's good! I hope you don't mind me eating while you talk. I didn't know I was hungry until I saw all this deliciousness."

She smiled and reached for a breadstick. "Of course not! Jean-Louis is an excellent chef. I know this is going to sound hokey, but here goes. Liam sent me a toy soldier. Let me rephrase that … I received a toy soldier sent from Jerusalem with no note. He used to tell me, 'Soldier on.' "

Duncan nodded. Neither spoke again for several minutes as they dug in. Ali closed her eyes in pleasure as she savored her last bite of crabcake.

Duncan finally asked, "You have theories?"

"Crazy ones. Your guess is as good as mine. Anyway, time will tell. Or it won't. I'm not giving up hope."

Duncan's eyes searched her face. "You don't *seem* to be a drug addict like your mother."

She smiled. "No."

"I know you are currently a barista. Becca says you could be a professional artist."

"Aw, she tends to exaggerate."

"She also said you are far too modest. Jean-Louis told me you have two men in your life. Brothers who look much alike."

"Jean-Louis!" Ali huffed. "The man does love to talk." She sighed. "They are twin brothers but not at all alike, as it happens. And one of them is already history."

"Jean-Louis says you can do better."

She gave an impatient shake of her head. "Jean-Louis needs to butt out. The problem is, the one I want is taken."

"The country music star."

Ali wondered how the chef would like it if she shared the details of his personal life without his permission. "For pity's sake. How much did Jean-Louis tell you?"

"More than he should've, I suppose. He told me about the event here. How you were attacked." His aspect darkened.

"Jake pulled the guy off me before he got very far."

Duncan's face reddened and his hands balled into fists. "*Bastard.* So … you had a rescuer. He's not good enough for you?"

"I didn't say that. Just that he's not the one that I want."

"What happened to the guy who attacked you?"

"Jake beat him up so badly his billionaire father almost had him arrested. I told him I wouldn't press charges against his son if he'd forget the whole thing. Not that going to court would have been the smartest move. Attempted rape is notoriously hard to prove, especially when the would-be rapist has deep pockets."

Duncan's mask of fury made him look even more like Liam. He closed his eyes and appeared to count to ten. Opening them again, he let out a harsh breath. "Don't mind me. I just wish I could have been there to protect you. I'm not like Liam. I've had my anger management classes. After my second marriage failed."

Ali tilted her head, looking him over. "You remind me of Billy Idol. All snarly, in a good way."

Duncan's laugh was low and rough, a little like Liam's. "That's the thing about not having any children you know of. No incentive to grow up. Too much hard living."

"It suits you. You look good." He seemed pleased by the compliment. "We're heading into the rainy season here. And it rains even more in North Bend than it does in Seattle."

Duncan made a face. "I know. I'm leaving town tomorrow, that's why I had to force the issue. Ever since I saw your picture in the paper, I've been trying to figure out how to meet you. I figured you were a professional model hired by an ad agency, and why would a place like that provide personal information to some guy off the street? I called La Fête Sauvage a week ago, and Becca told me the owner didn't go through an agency—that he'd hired his girl's best friend. She wouldn't reveal your identity over the phone, so I decided to try my luck in person."

Ali gave his lean forearm a squeeze. "Thank God you did!"

Duncan patted her arm then quickly pulled his hand away as if fearing a slap. "I have no idea how to be a father."

"That's okay. I have no experience being a daughter. My foster father was like a less warm and cuddly Captain von Trapp—before Maria got to him." Suddenly remembering that George and Emily were dead, she felt ashamed of disrespecting him. "It's wrong to speak ill of the dead. They were killed recently in a motorcycle accident in Botswana."

Duncan paled. "Oh, Ali, that's terrible."

She sighed. "What's terrible is that it wasn't more devastating. We never really bonded, and I think that's how they wanted it." Shaking off the sadness and guilt, she changed the subject. "Tell me about you. I've been talking about myself far too much lately."

Duncan hesitated, as if reluctant to open up. "Okay. When I got back from Vietnam, I knocked around for a while on the East Coast. I did a lot of diving in 'Nam, so I moved to Miami and became a commercial deep-sea diver. Married twice. Both disasters. I have one more gig; then I may retire."

"Deep-sea diver. That sounds amazing."

"It *can* be. We spend a lot of time in underwater compression chambers and then decompression chambers. Sharks are just as scary as you think."

Ali waggled her brows. "I'll bet. *Jaws* terrified me."

"One time I got hired to look for sunken treasure. That was pretty cool. Not the norm. Usually it's some underwater welding thing."

"Are you seeing anyone now—romantically, I mean?"

Duncan shook his head. "Alone in the world. It's best that way, the job being what it is."

"You mean, dangerous?"

"Yeah." He didn't elaborate, and she was afraid to ask.

"When did you arrive back in the Seattle area?"

"About six months ago, for a job." He grinned, revealing white but crooked teeth that made his smile all the more endearing.

"Do I really look like my mother?" Ali asked.

"In black and white, a dead ringer. But those eyes … I've never seen eyes that color except in the Walsh family." He stared off into the distance, as if remembering. "Nancy was beautiful enough to be an Indian princess."

"East Indian?"

"American Indian blood would be my guess. Sorry, that's not politically correct. Tribes don't have princesses, except in Disney movies. She claimed to be adopted, didn't know who her real parents were."

"Claimed?"

"I have a good bullshit detector. I was pretty sure Nancy was making up her past as she went along. I was"—he grimaced—"a one-night stand, so I can hardly blame her for telling me a fairy story. She said she'd run away from her adopted parents and had been living on a commune on Lopez Island. When was the last time you saw her?"

"That day in August she left us locked in the car."

Duncan's jaw grew rigid.

Ali didn't want his anger or his pity. "It wasn't for long. I think we would have been okay. We were pretty good at taking care of ourselves. For five-year-olds, that is." She paused. "Family services already had a bead on her. The car incident was the last straw. We never saw her again. I always assumed she'd died."

Ali was relieved to see that Duncan had recovered his equilibrium.

"You could probably find out."

Hmm. The idea had occurred to her. "What if she is still alive but a complete mess or a scheming narcissist? Do I really want to know? Would she become my responsibility, just because we share DNA?" She stared into her empty glass. "That sounds cold-blooded. Sorry. Gut reaction."

"Don't apologize. Makes sense to me. Nancy was something else. Willowy, with big eyes and delicate features." He'd been staring into space again, and now his focus returned to Ali, and he sighed. "She could have been a professional dancer. The girl could really move. I'm assuming a lot on the basis of one meeting. It's more likely she was just a party girl. Liked having men spend big on her. Bragged about it, even." He blew out a breath. "We went back to my motel. She insisted she was on birth control, and I believed her. *Eegit* that I am. I didn't have a phone number to give her. I wanted to stay in touch. In those days I liked to rescue women, the more screwed up, the better. She wrote down a number, and when I tried it later, it didn't work. Jeez, you were only five when she lost custody?"

Ali was surprised to find that she was tearing up.

Duncan handed her a tissue. "I didn't mean to upset you. So … this man you like so much, Joe … tell me more."

"Do you follow country music?"

Duncan looked apologetic. "I'm more of a Police fan. Or Neil Young."

"Right. Personally, I like all kinds of pop music, but I know nothing about country music, which is why I didn't realize Joe had written a song about meeting me."

She told Duncan the story of the man in the woods, how he'd comforted her, cared for her, then led her back to safety.

"Wow," he said when she was done. "How did you end up dating his brother?"

Ali told him that part too. "At first I thought he was JJ. Their hair and eyes are the same. Their smiles, though Joe's seems more genuine. Joe had a beard when I met him, so I didn't know what his jawline looked like. But … the way they move, uh, comport themselves is totally different. Jake is a few inches shorter. We only went on three dates. The third one was at his mother's fundraiser, where Joe made a surprise appearance. It was totally humiliating.

I fainted, and Joe disappeared before I regained consciousness. After that I couldn't date Jake anymore. He was only pretending to be into me. I was a weapon in his ongoing rivalry with his brother."

"I'm sure he was attracted," Duncan said. "How could he not be? So … then Joe started sniffin' around, even though he's involved with someone else?"

She nodded, embarrassed.

"Good song?" Duncan asked.

"*I* think so. I have the lyrics memorized. Wanna hear 'em?"

Duncan gave her his full attention as she recited the lyrics. Afterward he cocked his head, skeptical. "It's a big hit, really? Isn't it pretty long?"

"There are longer hit songs, and I'm not doing it justice. The guitar riff is super catchy. Each verse modulates up. Joe's voice is low, mellow, and a little scratchy. Exactly what you'd expect a gorgeous, passionate boy-next-door to sound like."

Duncan gave her his endearingly crooked grin. "He obviously has you captivated. Along with a million or so others, I bet."

Ali didn't want to think about Joe's zillions of fans. "I want to hear more about your … *our* family."

"I hope there will be time for that in the future," Duncan said with a smile. "Big Irish Catholic clan. Most of them are still in Ireland. There were too many of us to feed. I came to Boston in high school to stay with relatives and never went home. After I became a citizen, I promptly got drafted."

"Our mother told us she was Catholic," Ali said, "but I don't remember ever going to Mass. Were you practicing Catholics?"

"Yes, most of them. Me, I attend Mass when I can, but I'm capable of thinking for myself. I get some comfort from it, I admit. According to the Church, I'm still married to my first wife, of course. Divorce isn't recognized. I'd never inflict my beliefs on others or judge them for their personal decisions. I like to think of myself as a reformed Catholic." He paused. "What about your foster parents. You said they weren't warm or fuzzy, but I hope they weren't abusive."

"No, they were decent people." Ali waited for the familiar wave of shame to pass. "We weren't the easiest children to raise. They gave us so much." Her voice was choked with emotion. "What did we give them in return? Attitude. They were do-gooders, joined the Peace Corps out of college and returned to it after we aged out of the system. They died without knowing what happened to Liam. If only they hadn't insisted on quite so much volunteer work."

"*Volunteer* work? How old were you?"

"It started when we were twelve. At first it was just doing odd jobs at a soup kitchen. Eventually we were helping to build houses for the homeless."

Duncan shuddered. "Didn't you deserve a break now and then? Sounds like they treated you like junior Peace Corps volunteers, not children. Even scouting is a lot more fun than that. The scouting world understands that you need entertainment along with your civic lessons or you won't stick with it." He gave her arm a gentle shake. "You were independent souls. If they understood human nature at all, they would have given you space."

"I suppose so. That seems a lot to ask of people who didn't birth you and sacrificed their time and money to raise you."

"The state pays them, you know."

Becca appeared on the sidelines, giving them both a little wave, and Ali gestured for her to come over. "Can you join us for a few minutes?"

Duncan stood to kiss her hand, an unexpected gesture coming as it did from this rangy, punked-out guy. Sitting down again, he said, "Jean-Louis told me about what happened at the restaurant. I'd like to pay that spoiled rich kid a visit," he snarled, giving Ali another glimpse of Liam.

"You wouldn't." Ali tugged at the sleeve of his rugby shirt. "Swear you won't. We just met. I don't want to have to visit you in prison."

He raised his hands. "All right, darlin'. I don't want to go to prison either. And once I got started, I wouldn't stop at one punch."

"No costume this year?" Ali asked Becca. The Spanish-dancer ensemble looked like a costume, but most of Becca's fancier wardrobe pieces were costume-like. Usually she could be counted on to come up with something high concept, inspired by a movie.

"Sorry," Becca said. "I thought about Ace Ventura Pet Detective—you know, the gelled hair, the Hawaiian shirt, the alligator and all. Jean-Louis thought it would be too kitschy for his elegant watering hole. Even though I'm working in the office today, not as a hostess."

"Crocodile," Duncan said.

Becca cocked her head. "Huh?"

"In the Ace Ventura sequel. It's a crocodile. Snout is V-shaped. Alligators' snouts are wide and U-shaped." He turned to Ali. "Are you going to dress up for the children?"

Ali wrinkled her nose. "Not this year. It's only fun when Becca and I do it together."

Becca squirmed a little. "I'm sorry, sweetie. Maybe next year. Mr. Walsh—Duncan—what's next for you?"

"I have an early flight tomorrow to Waco, Texas." To Ali, he said, "Will you stay in touch? You could email me." He patted his pockets in search of something to write on, and Becca fetched a pen from the office. Duncan wrote down his Hotmail address on a Fête Sauvage matchbook. "It may take me a while to answer." He kissed Becca's hand again. "Darlin', it's been a pleasure. I'm glad my daughter has such wonderful friends."

Ali kissed him on the cheek, and they exchanged a heartfelt hug.

After Becca and Ali watched his rental car drive off, Becca said with a sigh, "He's the coolest dad I ever met." She gave Ali a speculative glance. "Do you even have a private email address? I know you don't own a computer."

"I had email at my last job. And Hotmail is free. I can use the computers at the library."

LATER THAT NIGHT, AS ALI watched a marathon of corny Christopher Lee vampire flicks, details from Joe's visit kept coming back to her, along with Carrie's warning that Joe would try to get her out of his system. Is that what had happened? She'd never felt anything like the pleasure he'd given her, and now, when he inevitably disappeared again, she couldn't imagine being able to move on.

Then she thought of her father and smiled. "The Lord giveth and the Lord taketh away," she said aloud. Too bad she wasn't religious.

CHAPTER 27

————·————

THE MESSAGE ON ALI'S ANSWERING machine almost stopped her heart.

"Hi there, Ali. It's Joe. I'm back to Nashville in a few days. Tomorrow night I'm doing a short set at the Baler Tavern in old Ballard. Around ten. Unpublicized, because frankly, it would be mobbed. Somehow we've kept my presence here out of the news. We finished recording the tracks for my new album yesterday. I hope"—he paused—"you can make it." His voice sounded a little scratchy. Emotion, or vocal fatigue?

It was late Thursday afternoon, and Ali and Becca had been clothes shopping at the Loehmann's just off I-90. You could score big in the Back Room where they sold designer stuff. Not today.

Becca sank into the couch as she kicked off her high-heeled boots. "Will you go?"

Kicking her own boots off, Ali flopped down next to Becca. "How can I not? Joe did take the trouble to ask me."

Becca clicked her tongue. "After that, it's back to Rina."

Ali visibly deflated. "I know."

With a determined air, Becca rose to her feet. "If you're going, so am I. You might need to cry in your beer afterward, and I'd like to offer myself as a designated driver."

Ali frowned. "Thanks for the vote of confidence."

Becca rolled her eyes. "*Ça va mal finir*," she said. French for, this will end badly.

Ali didn't argue.

THE NEXT EVENING, ALI AND Becca set out for Seattle's Ballard neighborhood in Jean-Louis's Jeep. Like Pioneer Square, Ballard had retained much of its turn-of-the-century flavor. So much of old Seattle was just gone, the graceful buildings that replaced the devastation from the 1889 Great Seattle Fire torn down in the name of progress. In Ballard, a former fishing village founded by Scandinavian immigrants, you could still shop for Swedish and Norwegian imports, visit the Nordic Museum, drink in dive bars, and admire historic architecture on Ballard Avenue. Many of the residences were built by fishermen or farmers shortly after 1900 or were sweet little Craftsman dwellings from the '20s and '30s. Unlike Shoreline to the north, Ballard had lost almost all its original trees, especially the tall Western red cedars and Douglas firs. Of all the Seattle neighborhoods Ali had visited, it definitely had the most character.

Ali felt like a failed political candidate en route to her concession speech. Would she even get a chance to talk to Joe alone? This might be her last memory of him. And it would leave her with nothing but regret.

They arrived at the Baler Tavern around nine thirty and ordered two glasses of merlot. Becca repeated her promise to keep it to one, though Ali insisted she could drive home. In this situation she didn't trust herself with more than one drink.

The Baler featured all sorts of musical acts, mostly hard rock, but also country, folk, and bluegrass. Bands with small but loyal fan bases. You might consider the atmosphere homey if both your parents were chain smokers. The smoke was so dense, it was difficult to make out the dimly lit stage on the other side of the room. Ali and Becca didn't talk much; the current band was too loud. In a scene of mostly men, they kept their heads down to avoid the supplicating eyes.

As the musicians completed their set and were packing up their equipment, a waiter greeted the lone women and asked, "Are you Ali?" She nodded. "The two of you, follow me." He moved them to a table near the stage marked RESERVED.

Becca took a handkerchief out of her purse and dabbed at her eyes. "I hope he starts soon and keeps it short. I can't wait to get out of here. I'm starting to feel like a trout in a smoker."

Ali sneezed. "I'm pretty sure a canary would die in here." Leaning close to Becca's ear, she added, "Maybe we should look dreamily into each other's eyes. If they think we're a couple, they'll leave us alone."

"Nah. They'd just propose a threesome."

Sensing a presence next to their table, Ali looked up. She couldn't help but gape; the woman had to be Rina Bakersfield. You didn't see many like her in Seattle. Fashion doll features, kohl-rimmed blue eyes, luxuriant streaked-blonde tresses—otherwise known as "big" hair—and chunky turquoise jewelry. Her blue-silk blouse under an embroidered vest gaped to reveal deep cleavage. Her long legs were encased in black jeans, and her teal cowboy boots were studded with gems.

"You girls fans?" she said, sweet as pie.

"Um," Ali said, "of whom?"

"Of Joe, of course." Her rippling laugh seemed designed to draw attention—though all eyes were on this woman already. "When Linc mentioned his plans, he said Joe had invited some others. I assume he was talkin' about you. Since you're sitting at the 'reserved' table. I'm Rina."

"It's an honor!" Ali said, with all the enthusiasm she could muster. Rina reached out to shake her hand and she reluctantly complied. Rina's grip was limp, as if Ali's touch was vaguely distasteful. Her long, blood-red nails looked lethal.

"How do y'all know Joe?" Rina's drawl was getting thicker.

"Um, I'm dating his brother, Jake."

Rina tilted her head, all wide-eyed innocence. "But Jake and he don't talk."

"I'm also friends with his mother and sister." *There*. That should stop the interrogation.

Rina pulled up a stool. "Mind if I join you? I didn't catch your name."

"Mary Alice," Ali said, congratulating herself on her quick thinking. The name "Ali" would have been a dead giveaway. "And this is Becca."

After shooting a panicked glance Ali's way, Becca quickly recovered her cool. They were both fighting the urge to flee. Joe couldn't have been expecting Rina. If so, why invite Ali?

Maybe Ali was already primed to love anything Joe did, but when he came out on stage—greeted by hoots and hollers—she almost forgot their surroundings. He beamed at the audience, his slow smile taking in the room as he waved and blew kisses to a few delighted women who had just arrived in the back. He hadn't spotted Ali yet. His ensemble was skin-tight and all black, his shirt partly unbuttoned to reveal a tantalizing V of lightly furred, muscular chest. Crocodile-skin cowboy boots. Or were they 'gator?

"I know y'all weren't expectin' me, so I hope you don't mind my intrudin' on your evening." The volume increased at the entrance as fans clogged the door. Joe had acquired a twang in the last week. "I've been in town recordin' my new album, and some friends convinced me to offer a li'l preview."

He sat on the chair and started to tune up. "Kinda smoky in here. Maybe y'all could give it a rest?" The smokers stubbed out their cigarettes in the ashtrays. Not that it did much good. You'd need to open the front and back doors and turn on industrial-strength fans. Even then ….

Ironically, Joe began with a melancholy song called, "Red Sun," about the beauty of a sunset during forest fire season. The next number was more upbeat, meant to be fun, she supposed, though the fact that each verse featured a different impossible woman gave her chest pains. It was called "Catch and Release," in that none of the women were keepers.

The chorus began with "All were pretty women, mighty good at sinnin', with a hole where a heart should be."

The supposedly uninvited audience couldn't be keener. Someone yelled, " 'Babe in the Woods'!" and the rest took up the chant.

For the first time, Joe's eyes met Ali's. Then quickly slid over to Rina, whose smile had a flat, fixed quality, as if she were a life-sized cutout. Ali detected a telltale widening of his eyes, though he recovered in an instant. No warm glances or blowing of kisses between them. "Uh, aren't y'all sick of that song?" Joe said, playing an elaborate riff on his guitar.

"No! No way!" voices chimed in from all directions. "Sing it, Joe!"

Was Ali imagining the animal-in-a-trap expression? It was fleeting. Joe was soon smiling as if nothing would give him greater pleasure. He was careful not to sing to Ali. Or Rina, who was tapping her full lower lip, scouring Ali with her eyes. Ali knew her own face was glowing like an electric coil. After the second verse, she heard Joe clear his throat. When he drew out the word "babe," his voice cracked. By the end of the third verse, it was cutting out. Nevertheless, he finished the song, and as if the glitches never happened, stood and bathed the room with his brilliant smile. The audience erupted in fervent applause.

Rina's small scowl was replaced by a toothy smile as she rose to give Joe a full-body hug. When she offered him her lips, he gave her a quick, closed-mouth peck that would have satisfied the code keepers in late-'30s Hollywood. The crowd started calling for a duet.

Joe whispered something to Rina and handed her his guitar. She mounted the stage alone, swinging her hips and waving the guitar in the air. "That Joe," she said in a folksy voice, "he thinks y'all would like to hear a number from li'l ol' me." No one was going to object to a song from Rina Bakersfield. Whistles and hoots of approval ensued.

Becca was tugging at the sleeve of Ali's secondhand motorcycle jacket. Under it, she wore a violet T-shirt, her best jeans, and knee-high boots.

Nothing else she owned would have been vaguely appropriate. Ali was hit by the cold, hard realization that if she didn't belong in Jake's world, she was even more out of place in Joe's. "Ali," Becca said in a low, urgent voice, "let's get out of here, *now*."

As Rina tuned Joe's guitar, keeping up a stream of flirty banter, Ali felt a hand on her shoulder and popped out of her chair like a champagne cork. When Joe kissed her cheek, she almost swooned. "Sorry, girls," he said in a hoarse voice, "I'm not used to smoky bars." She staggered a little, and he caught her. "Whoa there. You okay?"

"Fine," Ali said, face heating up again. She'd only had the one glass of wine, but of course he'd assume she was wasted. "We're on our way out. So great to see you perform. I'm looking forward to the new album."

But Joe was already dragging her along. "I need air, and I think you do too." If Rina noticed them leave, she didn't let on, belting out her song with gusto like the consummate professional she was.

Joe pulled Ali out the back door, next to the Dumpster. "What a fiasco," he rasped. "Listen, Ali, I don't know what to say. Rina wasn't supposed to be here. Linc must have invited her. I sure as hell didn't."

Ali backed away a step, hands raised defensively. "It's fine. Listen, I've loved … it's been great getting to know you. But we don't …. It was just a dream, wasn't it?"

Cupping her cheeks, Joe drew her in and kissed her with the desperation of a man facing banishment to a penal colony. His warm body exuded the cedar scent she recalled along with a hint of expensive cologne. The embrace hurtled her back into the heady world of sensation he had introduced her to at their last meeting. His lips explored hers with all the passion and none of the calculation she'd felt in Jake's. She sagged against him, surprised she didn't just dissolve into a puddle. With one touch, he could turn her entire being to mush, flood her with love, desire, and anguish. When he finally wrenched himself away, his fathomless brown eyes were glistening. "I can't make any promises right now. If you're smart, you won't wait for me to, uh, disentangle myself. I wish things were different, but I don't see …."

How had he meant to finish that sentence?

I don't see how it would work out between us?

I don't see us together?

She might never know. Ali had won the jackpot and then lost everything in the blink of an eye. Still, she couldn't help but take heart at the phrases "right now" and "if you're smart."

They were standing well apart by the time Rina appeared. She assessed the scene with slitted eyes, hands on hips. "What have we here?"

Ali broke in, "I had a message for him from his sister Teresa. Bye, Joe." In her silliest, gushiest voice, she added, "It sure is nice to hear you sing. You too, Rina. I know the tour will be a grand success." She'd been inching toward the door. Now she turned and ran, hoping that Joe wasn't about to get his eyes scratched out.

* * *

"MARY ALICE." THE HONEY IN Rina's voice had turned rancid. "I thought she called herself 'Ali.' "

When it came to Rina's verbal ammo, Joe was bulletproof. He couldn't be more done with this spoiled hothead.

"Rina, darling, how nice of you to show up. You should have let me know."

"I'm so glad I didn't."

Rina was just itching to slap him. She'd done it before. He braced for it, knowing it was what he deserved for all the subterfuge. He'd told her, as nicely as possible, that he couldn't marry her. If she refused to take no for an answer, that was her problem.

But then, she surprised him. Her voice softened, and she took his arm. "Come on, *darlin'*. The show isn't over. Turn that frown upside down." She pasted on a bright smile and waited for him to do the same.

Ali and Becca were long gone, and Rina and Joe spent another fifteen minutes signing autographs and shooting the breeze with their fans. As they left the bar, Rina said, "I'm headed back to my hotel. I was gonna invite you to join me, but I don't go out of my way to be humiliated."

He eyed her warily, knowing she wasn't ready to admit defeat.

"Sleep well," he said.

"That's hardly likely." She stalked away.

When he called her cell the next morning, Rina didn't answer. Their manager Linc told him she was already on her way back to Nashville.

CHAPTER 28

THE FOLLOWING WEEK, ALI PERFORMED her barista duties like an automaton. She couldn't stop obsessing over Joe's last words. How long did he mean by "for now"—until he retired? The tabloids implied Joe and Rina were still an item. He remained tethered to his demanding career and mercurial duet partner by choice. Ali's newfound father Duncan had mentioned his misbegotten attempts to "rescue" women. She couldn't rescue Joe either.

When Ali broached the subject of Joe with Becca, she got all huffy. "Ali, you're asking for trouble. That family is bad news. Why don't you let Jean-Louis fix you up with someone outside their screwy universe?"

"Thanks, Becca, but no thanks."

The memories of the heady encounter with Joe at the house and the desperate kiss at the Baler Tavern were too fresh. Might as well forget being struck by lightning. In retrospect, it seemed like the cruelest act of all, branding her like that then shutting her out of the corral. She was beginning to think like a country music song. Or a cowboy song. There was probably a difference. She still hadn't bothered to learn much about country music. Being obsessed with Joe was bad enough without immersing herself in his world.

In her first email to her father, she described Joe's performance at the Baler, including The Kiss. She ended with, "I know it's ridiculous to carry a torch for Joe. So what if Jake had ulterior motives? Perhaps, underneath it all, he did genuinely care for me. I should have given him a fair shot."

Let's be honest, she told herself after hitting "send," *that is total BS. You were right to reject Jake. You trusted your instincts. He just wasn't that into you.*

Becca and Jean-Louis helped Ali survive the holidays. First, a prix-fixe dinner at La Fête Sauvage the night before Christmas Eve, where they seated her next to a winemaker from Chelan, in Eastern Washington. It wasn't just the resemblance to her preppie boyfriend Trip that made it easy for her to turn him down: he got plastered on his own product and was totally obsessed with his yacht. During Christmas dinner at Becca's, Jean-Louis basically held court, entertaining them all—even Bubbe—with hilarious anecdotes about snooty or unreasonable customers and doling out compliments like party favors. Newly sober Nathan didn't shoot too many longing glances her way. Leah made a point of telling Ali how much she liked the dress Becca had helped her select.

Nathan blurted out, "She could wear the living room curtains and still look like a million bucks."

Whose living room curtains? Ali thought, wishing she could inspire a like devotion in Joe. Tara's curtains had looked spectacular on Scarlett O'Hara. The von Trapp children rocked the play clothes Maria fashioned from old draperies. Curtains from Carrie O'Connell's house would also look good on most people. The dingy-brown plaid curtains in their North Bend house? Not so much.

NEW YEAR'S EVE WAS AN after-hours party for special customers at La Fête Sauvage.

Ali sent multiple emails to her new father describing the holidays, Becca's family, and her longing for Joe, who hadn't contacted her in any way since The Kiss. As she lay alone in bed, idly sketching a skunk in a tux, Ali wondered for the umpteenth time if she had been right to pass on Jake.

She propped herself up in bed to read a chapter from *Great Expectations*. She was revisiting all her favorite Dickens. Young Pip was calling on ancient Miss Havisham and crushing on Estella, the girl the old woman had raised to break men's hearts because she herself had been jilted at the altar. Miss Havisham's money gave her the power to hurt people. Maybe Joe and Jake were two peas in a pod—rich guys callously toying with other people's lives. Ali couldn't help but distrust the upper classes, thanks to the rantings of her late foster parents.

Then, finally, the tide turned in her job search, providing the perfect distraction from her obsession with Joe. She interviewed with an architecture firm in downtown Bellevue. And just like that, she had a new PR job.

ALI'S FATHER WAS SLOW TO reply to her emails. "Dear Ali," Duncan wrote, "I love it when you call me Dad. Please keep it up!" He was finally surfacing for some R&R. The estimated completion date of his job was mid-April.

> I know you worry about dying alone. We all do! You're young, much younger than you realize. And here's food for thought: you don't need a man in your life to be happy.
>
> You've got a good job now (hurrah!). Maybe you can learn to like coffee again.
>
> As for Joe, good riddance. I picked up one of those fan rags, and Joe sounds like quite the alpha male wolf. Being too successful with women can spoil a guy. Being the one who got away gives you an edge.
>
> In your shoes, I'd wipe my feet of that screwed-up family. But don't mind me. You've got a good head on your shoulders. If Joe proves me wrong, then I'll embrace him like a son.

Duncan wasn't sure what came next for him. He had friends in Florida, and he disliked Pacific Northwest winters. Ali didn't blame him. January had been one of the wettest months she could recall, and February was looking like more of the same. Still, things were looking up. The job was challenging enough that she couldn't brood twenty-four/seven.

ON SATURDAY BECCA STOPPED BY with box lunches of pheasant and radicchio salad. She placed the boxes on the coffee table, and Becca sat in the easy chair while Ali resumed her place on the couch, where she'd been sketching an angry rabbit brandishing a carrot like it was a broadsword. Becca was helping Jean-Louis to open a new branch of La Fête Sauvage in Bellevue. As they ate, Ali told her she was learning a website-building software program, and—along with issuing press releases and creating a newsletter—was refreshing the company's website.

Becca wiped her hands on her napkin. "So, you found your dream job."

Ali had to give the statement some thought. She flashed back to the cabin in the woods, to her efforts to guess Joe's profession. He'd admitted only that it was his "dream job." That was why he was determined to keep it, no matter what the cost. She could hardly argue with that. With his entire future as a singer on the line and his touring partner, Rina, a loose cannon, his hands were tied. How could he possibly introduce Ali into the equation? Which brought her back to the present. Was her new PR position really her dream job? Hardly. It could be fun and challenging, but mostly, she was consigned to a cubicle where she was glued to a desk chair and stared at a computer, breathing recycled office air, and looking at a no-frills world illuminated by fluorescent bulbs. Most office jobs were like that, she supposed, but surely not dream jobs.

Becca cocked her head. "Ali? Where did you go? I didn't ask you to solve a complicated mathematical formula."

Ali looked down at the sketchpad lying next to her. "It's a good job. No bosses chasing me around the conference-room table or giving me assignments that are doomed to fail. They're all perfectly pleasant. Is it weird to say that I miss being a barista? The hours passed quickly, and the schedule left time for my drawing. If this is what I'm going to do until I retire …." She didn't finish the thought. It was too depressing. She regarded Becca, who beamed with health and well-being. Why not? Doing full-time PR for Jean-Louis, she got to do her dream job in a dreamy fairytale setting with her dream man.

As if disconcerted by Ali's scrutiny, Becca stared at the floor. "A job is a job, I suppose. If there's satisfaction to be had, then you're one of the lucky ones."

Easy for you to say, Ali thought.

"Have you seen the tabloids lately?" Becca spoke in a soothing voice, as if trying to soften a blow.

Ali put her lunch aside, appetite gone. "Tell me."

"The wedding is planned for June. At Rina's family estate outside of Georgia."

One big, fat tear escaped.

Becca reached out to squeeze her hand. "It's the *tabloids*, Ali. Nothing they report is reliable. *Nothing*. But I thought you should know what they're saying."

Refusing to let herself cry, Ali wiped the tear away with the back of her hand. "I still believe in him, Becca. I believe in the man I met in the woods."

"I know you do, sweetie, and you may be right. I just don't want you to be blindsided." Becca sat beside her on the couch. "But … you don't really know Joe. A few mostly one-sided conversations in an isolated cabin and a few intense encounters don't add up to squat."

Ali's jaw tightened. "That's not how I see it."

"Don't get mad," Becca said. "I'm speaking as your friend. Maybe in the future Joe will make someone a great husband. But things have come to him too easily. You don't want to be one of those things."

"I don't think you get it," Ali insisted. "He's had major vocal issues. He did *not* sound happy when I spoke to him. In fact, I had a sense that his life had taken on too much momentum. He was desperate for the runaway train to stop."

Becca put a hand on Ali's shoulder. "He can pull the cord on that runaway train whenever he likes. Sorry, but if your best friend can't give you straight talk, who can? I wasn't present at those conversations, though I'd wager the real reason he showed up here was to see if you'd fall into his arms. And you did, didn't you? Guys like that don't have to make the first move. If the woman makes it easy, they don't risk being accused of rape. Or, at the very least, of being a vile seducer."

" 'Vile seducer,' " Ali repeated. "That sounds like something out of last century. Or the century before that."

Of course Joe had showed up at the North Bend house hoping for a booty call. If his tight schedule and Becca's phone call hadn't intervened, would she have ever heard from him again?

That final goodbye at the Baler Tavern …. Joe's meaning had been clear, even if his body had other ideas. He needed all his energy to navigate the stormy seas ahead. Ali was a complication he couldn't afford.

She had to let him go.

ALI SPENT A MISERABLE VALENTINE'S Day in front of the TV with only a pepperoni pizza and a bottle of wine for company. Flipping through all the cable channels, she could find nothing but romances. Too weary to go to Blockbuster, she considered the limited library of videos, all watched to death. She started with *Lethal Weapon* then moved on to *Streets of Fire*. With the movies as mostly background noise, she sketched. The results were too nightmarish. The wolf looked lethal, not adorable at all. Even in a '50s housedress, Mrs. Bigfoot appeared capable of boiling pet bunnies. She set the sketchpad aside.

After all that, The Dream. The grasping hands, the blurry face. She awoke on the couch, NPR blaring from the alarm in her bedroom. It was a quarter to six. She had fallen asleep in front of the TV. Her neck hurt, and an ice pick hammered into her right temple. Before she could face reality, she needed at least two cups of coffee. Fortunately she could stand the taste again.

The Dream. Was she supposed to do something about it? Would letting herself be hypnotized bring back the memories of that early foster mother? If so, would that help her get past it or revitalize whatever trauma had prompted the recurring nightmare to begin with?

Between sips of potent brew, she muttered, "Get thee behind me,

Valentine's Day," as if warding off the Prince of Darkness himself. Darkness. She pulled back the curtains. Had the sun even come up? She stepped outside to find that snowflakes were falling. She pulled her fleece robe tighter and shivered.

FEBRUARY SOMEHOW LUMBERED ACROSS THE finish line. The icy winter rains and occasional snowfall made Ali's bus commute a misery. Still and all, the job continued to be more than tolerable.

All was not lost. There was Becca and Jean-Louis's June wedding at La Fête Sauvage to look forward to. Ali knew she was leaning too heavily on the couple, acting like a baby bird afraid of flying. If they weren't so nice, they'd have tossed her out of the nest by now. Now that she'd finished helping them revamp the restaurant's website, she had no further role to play in their business, and they didn't get enough alone time as it was. Jean-Louis was training a new head chef to free up his schedule. The publicity following the *Seattle Times'* rave review made this expansion possible—a mixed blessing, in that work now consumed most of Jean-Louis's waking hours.

"You guys must be getting sick of me." Ali was sitting with Becca and Jean-Louis at a pub near Bellevue Square, across the street from the site of the new location. "Just say the word, and I'll make myself scarce."

Jean-Louis waved her off. "*Comme toé*! Relax. One day, Becca and I are sure to grow tired of each other. Spending more time with you now will push that inevitability out into the distant future."

Ali had trouble seeing past the man's nonchalant air to tell if he was kidding. Much as she liked Jean-Louis, he always seemed to be "on." Oh well, he couldn't help being so charismatic. It didn't seem to bother Becca, even though she was a deeply private person.

Becca punched him playfully in the shoulder. "Watch yourself."

Ali stared into her pear cider, wishing she'd chosen something stronger. "Don't worry about me. I'm resigned to celibacy."

Jean-Louis's raucous laugh quickly made him the center of attention and caused Ali to shrink into her seat. "Never fear," he said as he wiped his eyes, "your prince will come. If you're lucky, he won't be an actual prince, not even the kind of princeling who is the scion of a wealthy family. He'll be a steady, hard-working type with a sense of humor. That is what I wish for you."

"Here, here," Becca toasted.

"I don't care anymore," Ali insisted with an abrupt wave of her hand that was meant to be airy. "I'm enjoying my work. When the weather stops being so cruddy, I might even be happy again."

"Men are pigs," Jean-Louis declared.

"Not you," Becca cooed.

"I've been a pig in my time." He screwed up his nose. "*Groin-groin.*"

Ali was taken aback. "What was *that*?"

Becca snorted with laughter. "That's how French pigs oink."

"I am older and wiser now," Jean-Louis went on, straight-faced and trying to appear sage. "The time for piggishness is past."

Becca narrowed her eyes. "It better be."

Jean-Louis wagged a finger in Ali's direction. "*Franchement,* Joe and Jake are, *au fond*, simply normal guys. Jake has a business to run, a mother to appease, a brother to have the top on. Joe made no promises. Clearly, he was intrigued by you. But he has other cats to whip."

"Um, fish to fry," Becca said. "Idioms, you know. Whipping cats isn't PC. And I think you mean 'a brother to one-up.' "

"You have a bad habit of correcting me," Jean-Louis complained.

Becca kissed his cheek. "Sorry, babe." To Ali, she said, "I know you don't want to hear this, but sweetie, it's time to move on. You've got a good job, and you're still the most beautiful woman I know. Life has so many wonderful things in store for you."

Ali's sigh was so comically loud, she almost laughed at herself. She wanted to tell Becca to mind her own beeswax. But with all Ali's obsessing aloud about Joe, she could hardly blame her friend for speaking her mind.

ON MAY ELEVENTH, ALI NOTICED a small item in the entertainment section of the newspaper reporting that country music star Joe Bob Blade had left his tour due to health issues. Rina Bakersfield was continuing on with Larry Wales, whose latest successes had made him nearly as famous as Joe. Ali knew Rina and Joe were supposed to be married in June, and she wondered how his fiancée could abandon him like that in his hour of need. *The show must go on,* she thought. The article cast her into a funk that lasted all weekend.

On Sunday night, she called her father.

"Lass, what's up? You sound a little down."

Ali told him about the article.

"Aw, more trials and tribulations. Poor sod. And right before his wedding. Shame on his fiancée for pressing on without him. Tells you something about her, doesn't it?"

It certainly did. However, Joe's questionable taste in women was no longer her concern.

"Would it be too forward of me to offer up a reality check?" her father asked.

Ali was sick to death of people telling her things she didn't want to hear, but what she said was, "I'm listening."

"That is one hell of a difficult scene—the world of the rich and famous. If Joe offered you the moon and the stars, you'd jump for joy. But how long would that euphoria last? You'd have to give up your career and follow him around. Watch him be fawned over by one gorgeous gal after another. And as time wore on, the girls would still be young, and you wouldn't be. You'd turn into a jealous harpy."

His words made perfect sense. Ali cried herself to sleep that night.

Only, her despair was premature. On Wednesday night, just after ten, the phone rang.

"Do you love my son?" The clipped female voice sounded like Carrie's. The question was highly disorienting, to say the least. "Mrs. O'Connell?"

"Speaking."

"Do you mean Joe?"

"Of course. Do you love Joe?"

"Yes."

"You love the man in the woods."

"Yes."

"That's Joe," Carrie said. "The real Joe, no matter what the PR people and the press would have you believe. He never wanted … all this."

Ali could imagine the woman's beautiful hands fluttering around. "Okay," she said. "But what—"

"Are you free this weekend, starting Friday?"

"Yes …." Ali's heart was pounding. She'd have to call in sick.

"Are you willing to take a gamble, maybe a big one?"

"What do you mean?"

"I want you to go to Joe. He may turn you away. So you see, a big gamble."

"Can't someone get his permission?" As much as Ali longed to see Joe, she didn't want to burst in with no notice. She couldn't bear it if he rejected her.

"No," Carrie said. "Where he is, he doesn't have a phone. I believe they set up a short-wave radio or satellite phone system in case of emergency—I don't know, I'm not technically minded. And don't ask me how that works anyway, since he can't talk. For all I know they are communicating in Morse Code. Whatever it is, none of those methods is conducive to broaching the delicate subject of a possibly unwelcome visitor."

Ali cleared her throat. "Mrs. O'Connell, if he doesn't want visitors, why would I go? Why not Rina?"

"You've helped him before." Mrs. O'Connell's voice had become even more clipped and impatient. "That time in the woods … he was deeply depressed. You gave him a reason to return to civilization."

Ali swallowed, hard. "Is he deeply depressed now?"

"Yes. He's been absolutely forbidden to talk—not a peep, mind you—so he'll have to communicate in writing again. Talk to him, that's all I ask. You don't have to sleep with him."

Ali was glad Carrie couldn't see her face.

"You know he's a perfect gentleman. If he's determined not to welcome you, that will make for an awkward night, nothing more. Linc will retrieve you the next morning." Silence. "Ali, are you still there?"

"Yes."

"What do you say?"

"Yes."

Carrie's sigh of relief was loud enough to register over the phone. "A car will pick you up Friday morning at six. You will fly in a private plane from Boeing Field to William R. Fairchild International Airport in Port Angeles. Linc will be waiting for you. Wear hiking boots and a warm, waterproof coat."

Ali had stopped breathing. A private plane? Ali had never flown in a *commercial* plane.

"Ali? Are you still there?"

She gasped, and her next question might have been squeezed out of her. "Linc is Joe's manager, right?"

Carrie hesitated before replying as if deciding not to remark on the weird change in her voice. "Also his best friend. I've told him how to recognize you."

She'd love to hear how Carrie had described her. "Where will Linc take me?"

"I believe you know the place."

PART III

CHAPTER 29

———·———

As the limo transported Ali to Boeing Field, she sketched a black bear with puppy-dog eyes standing on its hind legs at the door of a cave, paws flailing, mouth open in a roar—a silent roar. Fierce. Other than the eyes, a far cry from her usual adorable creatures.

Joe might be too preoccupied with his silent roaring to listen to reason. For Carrie to enlist Ali's help, the situation had to be dire. She didn't believe for a moment that a woman like that would welcome a dowdy daughter-in-law of questionable heritage. Clearly, Carrie liked the idea of Rina even less. Besides, Rina would be as out of place in that cabin as a gold-plated toilet seat in an outhouse.

Ali's smile had a bitter edge. The image of Rina in an outhouse was the height of absurdity. Ditto the image of her negotiating the trail in stiletto-heeled cowboy boots. Or bathing in the river. No way in hell.

Ali tried to control her trembling as she took her place behind the pale, rail-thin pilot with a silver buzz cut who introduced himself as Sammy. Registering her trepidation—it was hard to miss—he said, "This Cessna 182 Skylane is practically brand-new. It's safer than drivin', ya know. I flew fighter jets in the Air Force."

"I'm sure it is," Ali said in a high, thin voice she herself didn't recognize. She cleared her throat. "Uh, to be honest, I've never done this before. Flown, I mean. At all." Though her hands were shaking, she managed to take *Nicholas Nickleby* out of her overnight bag and place it on the seat next to her. Though it was unlikely she'd be able to calm down enough to read it. "I'm sure you're an excellent pilot."

"That I am." His squinty-eyed gaze seemed to question whether she was liable to do something crazy like try to bail out while they were rolling down the runway. Zeroing in on her fumbling fingers, he asked, "Need help with the seatbelt?"

She managed to complete the task before he lost all patience with her. Clearly the word "fear" was not in his vocabulary, and he had no use for damsels in distress.

"Just keep breathing," Sammy told her as the plane began to move. "I'd say 'enjoy the view,' but in your case ... keep your eyes shut and try not to get freaked out by the liftoff. Gravity is going to bear down on you for a minute there. You'll get used to the vibrations and the shifting wind currents." He handed her an enforced paper bag. "In case you need to barf."

Fully expecting to die before she could get sick enough to upchuck, Ali shut her eyes and concentrated on breathing. Once the initial sinking sensations of liftoff had passed, she opened her eyes and stayed riveted on the view for the rest of the flight. The shrinking skyscrapers—dominated by a toy Space Needle and the unexpected grandeur of Mount Rainier—the highways snaking between the patchwork of buildings, then the wide expanse of ocean. Finally more green fields and the forested hills and snow-frosted mountains of Hurricane Ridge.

Thirty minutes later, they landed in Port Angeles. The pilot, who hadn't spoken since they started taxiing, said, "See? You're a natural." He took the paper bag and waved it at her. "You didn't even need the barf bag."

Ali could see why he wasn't working for United.

The next leg of the journey was in the company of Joe's manager Linc, a little rough around the edges but a smooth talker compared to Sammy.

As he took her duffel bag, he said, "So, you're the famous 'babe.' "

She peered over her own shoulder as if another candidate had appeared. *God*, this was awkward. "I'm not sure why I agreed to this," she said.

His long, measuring look said he wasn't sure either. He looked like a really tall version of Samuel Clemens, aka Mark Twain, as depicted in the iconic portrait, including the bushy hair, eyebrows, and mustache. At least six feet five and gangly.

He was driving a new black Ford Explorer that, he explained, belonged to his brother Jimmy in Port Angeles. Jimmy still lived in the house where they grew up. Linc and his two brothers had helped their father build the illegal log cabin the summer after the pulp mill where he worked closed. When a park ranger inevitably stumbled across it, drawn by woodsmoke, Linc's family was offered a long-term lease agreement. They had to swear to be responsible stewards of the land—no littering, polluting, or hunting—and to make the cabin available to the forest service on occasion. It helped that Linc donated generously to local conservation projects. As he had the last time, Linc had notified his buddy the chief ranger about Joe's stay.

A few hikers had run across the cabin and told their friends, sparking rumors, but no one had been able to locate it twice, even in the aftermath of the song that made it famous. Linc and his family might have lost track of it themselves if not for their elaborate marking and mapping system.

When that subject was exhausted, Linc stopped beating around the bush. "Joe was in a foul mood when I drove him out here a week ago. I know it's a drag to lose your voice, but that guy has so dang much to live for."

If he could be frank, so could Ali. "Why am I here instead of Rina?" She dreaded his answer.

"That's over, far as I can tell." At her audible sigh of relief, he added, "No worries there. I don't blame Rina. She's ambitious, and Joe … well, I don't know anymore. I told him, 'You can concentrate on songwriting now. That's where all the money will be, with the invention of mp3s. Sooner or later, people won't wanna pay for CDs. They'll just send each other music files through email. Or someone will figure out a way to make it all available for free.' Joe never liked the road much. He's a natural, of course, makes love to the crowd. It's gotta suck having that taken away from you."

Ali couldn't believe her ears. "His performing career is over?"

"Unknown. He had more surgery, against his original laryngologist's advice. There are risks—like scar tissue. He'll have to stay silent as the tomb for another week. After that … well …." He shrugged.

"Isn't it bad for him to be in the woods alone?"

"I've been camping nearby. Joe waves to me at sunrise and sunset. Sometimes we play cards. I try to be sensitive to his moods. He hasn't wanted company much."

His *moods*. Ali would not be confronting the same congenial woodsman she had long fantasized about. This man was at the end of his tether. He might even turn her away. "His mother says he has a satellite phone."

Linc guffawed. "How's he supposed to communicate on that? With clicks and claps and whistles? He doesn't dare make the tiniest sound."

A few minutes passed. Linc asked, "How long can you stay?"

"I'm supposed to be at work on Monday."

Linc whistled. "Darn. This might take some time. He's gonna be real mad at first."

A chill ran through her. She wrote down her work number and stuffed it in the pocket of his jacket. "Can you call in for me and tell them I have a family emergency?"

Linc gave her a sidelong look. "Carrie said you don't have a family."

That stopped her. Everyone at work knew she was a foster child with a missing brother.

Linc scratched his grizzled head. "How about if I tell them a friend has gone missing? And only if it comes to that. If the visit goes sour, I'll get you home, pronto."

Goes sour. She imagined Joe shoving her out on the porch and slamming the door.

Linc's idea of small talk didn't help. "I never thought Rina was good for him. She's something, though. Hoo-boy. Not sure any guy with a pulse would say no to that. Joe and me have been friends for over ten years. Of all my clients, he's the most serious artist." The look he threw her put her on the defensive.

"What?" she asked, trying not to sound irritated. Did Linc think she'd get in the way of that?

"You'd be good for him," he said instead. "His mom told me about your background. You're salt of the earth. He needs that. Not a painted doll, even one as talented as Rina."

The silence stretched between them until Linc said, "No one wanted him to go. The first time—when you wandered in—was his first bout with vocal nodes. He thought the surgery would fix him good as new, give him a bit of a break even. He got a little, um, *escapade* and a good song out of it." His wink made her squirm. Linc definitely assumed they'd had sex. "Anyhow, that's why we're being mother hens, much as it pisses him off. Under normal circumstances, I'd trust him to take care of himself. Now I worry about leaving him alone with a gun."

They both chewed on that for a while.

It was around two in the afternoon when Linc pulled over. "We always park random-like, in case someone notices and marks the spot." He opened the back of the Ford and hefted out two good-sized BPO backpacks, lumpy, as if filled with stones. "Supplies," he told her. He strapped a sleeping bag and air mattress to the bottom of one pack and set it down next to her on the grass. "There's room for a change of clothing. Nothing impractical, mind you. As you may recall, there's a river nearby for bathing, if you can stand the chill, and a camping shower that feeds from a bucket. Me, I do without. You get used to a little stink." He grimaced. "We hope you can convince our boy to come home soon. Real soon."

The few items of clothing she'd chosen barely fit in the pack. At the last minute, she took out one of her T-shirts so she could fit in her sketchpad.

"Sorry it's so heavy," he said as he helped her strap it on. "I'm carrying roughly twice that load. I included canned stuff and more ground coffee."

She felt new sympathy for llamas and mules. With a bungee cord, he attached one last item, a medium-sized whiteboard. "There are pens and erasers inside the pack. Let's hope he's willing to use them."

CHAPTER 30

———•———

DURING THE HIKE TO THE cabin, Ali tried to calm her anxiety by concentrating on their surroundings. Rays of sunlight poured through the foliage, making the droplets that studded the moss and lichen on the trees, stumps, and rocks sparkle like diamonds. How could Joe not find comfort in this lush cocoon of greenery, its soothing soundtrack of rushing water punctuated by distant trilling, chirping, croaking, and whistling?

Joe's case couldn't be hopeless. Of course he would sing again, hollow as such assurances would sound coming from her.

Was Joe really suicidal? Her spirits flattened again.

Ali felt like a turtle with an ill-fitting shell. With every step, her burden seemed to grow heavier, as if, one by one, a troupe of mischievous sprites were hitching rides. The back of her shirt was soon soaked through, despite the chilly air, and hot spots from chafing marked the delicate skin of her back and neck. A good-sized daypack was one thing, but hauling the equipment required for tent camping was about as appealing as a vertical climb up a rockface.

Finally the cabin came into view, looking deceptively cozy. Smoke from the woodstove puffed through the chimney, and the afternoon sun made it appear to glow from within. Stopping dead in her tracks, Ali fell to her knees, breathing hard.

Linc laid a light hand on her shoulder. "Easy now," he said in a soothing voice, as if calming a skittish animal. "Just let Joe know he's not alone. Yeah, he might wanna send you away. But no matter what, all of us—his family also—are mighty grateful you're here." He gave her a moment to collect herself. "You wanna know the real reason that song is such a hit?" She looked up at him. "People respond to the longing in Joe's voice. You made a hell of an impression, girl."

On the porch of the cottage, Ali gratefully shrugged out of the accursed backpack, stretched her arms, and rolled her shoulders. Linc called through the door, "Joe? Are you there? Can I come in?"

The door swung open. At first unnoticed, Ali observed the changes in Joe's appearance. The fashionable stubble that peppered the strong jaw, the luxuriant chestnut-brown curls that fell almost to his broad shoulders. If he'd looked this way at their first meeting, she would have never mistaken him for a woodsman. More like the young, beautiful, and haunted hero of some tragic nineteenth-century saga—Melville's Billy Budd before his unjust execution, devoid of hope and impatient for the end. And yet, gorgeous as he was, the once sparkling eyes were dull and shadowed, and the full lips had a sullen twist.

"Hey, Joe," she said in a small voice. He staggered back, white with shock.

* * *

JOE COULDN'T BELIEVE HIS EYES, which flew to Ali's anxious face before alighting on Linc's grim one. He mouthed a silent curse. Much as he rejoiced at the sight of this elusive woman who'd hovered constantly at the edge of his thoughts, he didn't want her to see the pitiful wreck he'd become.

No one spoke. It was some weird standoff, as if they were waiting to see who would draw their gun first. Joe's heart did a flipflop. Ali looked dead tired. The boulder of a pack Linc had saddled her with now lay at her feet. He moved to haul it in but then hung back instead. He was curious as hell to hear an explanation for this extraordinary visit.

Ali broke the silence. "Don't blame Linc. I wanted to see you. I can't possibly understand what you're going through, but your mother … I mean I … thought you could use a … a friend."

His *mother*? What the hell had she been thinking? If only he'd had some warning. A *friend*? That was rich. He stepped away from the door to let them in.

As Ali took in his recent remodeling efforts, his eyes feasted on her. As he'd once confessed to that interviewer Anthony, a guy could drown in those eerily changeable eyes that ranged from the color of the sky one minute to the most brilliant cobalt blue the next. She was observing the queen-sized bed frame he'd built, complete with bedposts, and the high-quality air mattress they'd carted in. The end table he'd carved from whole logs to match the dining set.

"You *built* all this?" she asked.

He was warming to the idea of her visit. Now that he'd run out of make-work, Ali might be just the distraction he needed. *A distraction. Shit*, he couldn't use her like that. He'd have to keep his grubby hands to himself.

"Do you mind if we h-hang out?" she stammered. "Linc says there's time to get back to the road before dark."

His manager twisted the tip of his mustache the way he did when he was stretching the truth. They both knew it was too late in the day. *Linc isn't okay with any of this*, Joe thought, noting his manager's stiff movements as he set up the whiteboard on the end table and arranged the felt pens and eraser next to it. Neither Linc nor his mom believed he was serious about Ali, and Linc thought Ali didn't deserve to be treated as a single-use container. His mother reasoned that Ali's feelings didn't matter as long as Joe had a shiny new toy to play with, something—anything—to keep him from swallowing the barrel of his gun. The question was, did Ali know what was expected of her?

Linc emptied half the contents of his own backpack and hefted hers inside before giving them a salute of farewell and scurrying away. Finally alone with Ali, Joe flicked his eyes over the bulging backpack, sleeping bag, and air mattress, and raised his eyebrows. She blushed, avoiding his eyes. *Ah.* She obviously assumed she'd share his bed, the sleeping gear she'd brought with her notwithstanding. Once again, *he'd* have to be the strong one.

Sprawled on the floor with the pack between her legs, Ali dug around until she located a bag of ground coffee. "Can't do without this." Item by item, she removed the cans of refried beans, miniature bottle of hot sauce, cans of tuna, and jar of mayo. "No wonder this thing was so heavy."

Reaching down, Joe pulled her to her feet, holding her hand an extra beat.

A brilliant idea, the whiteboard. He wrote, "Let's take a walk. We don't have much time before Linc takes you home." The disappointment in her eyes sent a rush of warmth down his body. Didn't she know a joke when she read one? That was the bitch of communicating in writing. He added a winking smiley face.

Ali recovered quickly. "Can I change my shirt? It's soaked through."

Though it wasn't cold enough to snow in late May, heavy jackets were still necessary after the sun went down. Ali pulled a fresh T-shirt and a parka out of her pack, and Joe reached for his flannel-lined barn jacket. She was right, he did own a shitload of BPO. He missed his brother—all his brothers.

Losing touch with his family had been one of the more heart-wrenching consequences of stardom.

Ali turned her back to change her T-shirt without asking Joe not to look, so he looked, noting the pink spots on her creamy flesh where the pack had dug in. Only by sheer force of will did he keep from reaching for her to massage them away.

Joe grabbed the nearly empty gallon jug and followed Ali onto the creaking porch. While she gazed up into the moss-laden forest canopy, he stood close enough to catch a heady whiff of her sweet orange-blossom scent mingled with the humid, earthy air. Ali took in the leaning tower of firewood and grinned.

At the river, Joe used the water purifier to fill the jug and set it aside. Then he sat on a fallen log, beckoning her to join him. A bald eagle soared high overhead, then a great blue heron nabbed a tiny fish right in front of them. Aware that she was spying on him, Joe assumed a mask of serenity. Perhaps her presence would be the ultimate balm. He was already seeing the forest through new eyes.

The minutes ticked by unnoticed as he debated what to do. Finally he realized the light had changed. The birds were all singing at once in their discordant version of "Taps." Reluctantly, he led the way back to the cabin.

Once inside, Joe lit the kerosine lamp, focused the battery-powered lantern on the whiteboard, and motioned to the bed. *Damn.* Of course she'd take that wrong. On the board, he wrote, "The bed is more comfortable than the stumps. Have a seat." He paused, then added, "Don't get any ideas." He smiled, aiming for harmless.

Her thready laugh showed him just how freaked out she was.

He wrote, "Stir fry is on the menu. Tonight we also have a fresh special." *You,* he thought as his eyes roamed over her. "Salad," he clarified. He brandished an avocado, bag of lettuce, and a package of blue cheese. Putting everything down again, he wrote, "As you said, no roughing it here. Linc brings more than I need. If Mom had her way, Canlis would cater my entire stay." He paused. "I have simple tastes, believe it or not."

She uttered a little *humph.* "I'll have to take your word for it. We're still relative strangers."

He wrote, "Let's start again. Allow me to introduce myself. My name is Joseph Jamison O'Connell." He rolled his eyes.

"You don't like it?" she asked.

He wrote, "Kind of a mouthful." In florid cursive, he signed his full name. He snickered, then winced. He must take more care. Any sound at all could hurt his healing cords. He folded his arms, waiting for her to respond.

"I like it. Jamison is a surname from your family tree?"

With a nod, he wrote, "Jake is Jacob Brillard."

She said, "Beyond the superficial resemblance, no one could confuse the two of you for long. You're smooth; he's all hard edges. I'll say this for Jake: He gave me nice things. He treated me like a princess. He was real ... or at least seemed to be at first. You were a dream ... a dream-man. Of course, it turned out Jake had an agenda."

Joe squeezed his eyes shut, pained to hear his own lyrics quoted back at him. He slowly erased the board.

"What is it with you two?" Ali asked. "Why does he hate you? A woman? Mom loved you best? Dad taught you how to throw a baseball?"

"He doesn't hate me," Joe wrote. "He envies me. There's a difference."

"He only wanted me because he thought you did."

"Maybe at first," Joe wrote. "But you're hard to resist. He wanted you."

"No, he didn't, truly. There was zero chemistry. He wanted you to think he was having sex with me, but he had no interest in actually doing it. Not like ...." She couldn't meet his eyes, and he was gratified by her glowing cheeks. "But to be honest, I'd given up on you. After I stopped seeing Jake, you kept blowing hot and cold. Then ... you didn't ...." She stopped.

What didn't I do? he thought. *Didn't encourage you in any way in the months that followed that shit show at the Baler? Yeah, that.* How could he express in the fewest words possible that he wasn't in a position to make promises?

Erasing the board, he started over at the top. "It started in high school. He was always smaller than me. By quite a bit, until his late growth spurt. You know how it is with siblings." He paused to gauge her reaction, then erased the board again. "Or you don't," he continued, "since you and Liam weren't in competition. Everyone tries to find a niche to claim as their own. For me it was music." He considered his next words as he erased the board. "Jake played guitar in a band for a bit. He wasn't bad. My parents weren't crazy about either of us playing music. They wanted conventional lives for us, 'respectable' professions." Joe made a face, then looked over his shoulder at Ali as he cleaned the slate. Her expression as she gazed at him was uncomfortably close to worshipful. Not a bad idea to bring himself down to earth a notch. The story he was about to tell didn't present him in the best light. He hoped she'd give him some slack, take into account his age and immaturity at the time. "I think Jake joined the band to get girls," he wrote. "To be honest, that's one of the main reasons any kid joins a rock and roll band. His group was playing at our school dance, and by some cruel stroke of fate I hooked up with the girl he had his eye on—someone he'd wanted for a long time."

"Jeez," Ali said, neither surprised nor judgmental. "Poor Jake. The bad stuff that happens in high school is really hard to sluff off. Blows to the ego like that. Did Jake confront you?"

"No," Joe wrote. "Not his style. Sarah and I dated for about a month. Jake had stopped talking to me, but he wouldn't say why. He finally confessed to David, who was quick to pass the information on. I'd already lost interest in Sarah, but the damage was done. She still didn't want Jake. His interest in the band waned pretty quickly after that."

"That happened a long time ago," Ali said. "He hasn't talked to you since high school?"

Joe wrote, "No, that time he got over it. But he stopped being gracious about my good fortune. I won a bunch of awards as a junior and senior and then a scholarship to music college. It's not as if Jake had nothing going for him. He had some stories published in the *Strand* magazine—a real coup for a teenager. He had a real knack for thrillers. Shame on Mom and Dad for their lack of enthusiasm. Talk about 'damning with faint praise.' Da's opinion meant everything to Jake—to all of us." As he started at the top again, he wrote, "That's what we called him—'Da.' It's an Irish thing. We just worshipped the guy. And he was hellbent on Jake taking over for him at Big Paul's someday. When Jake got accepted into Harvard, he really lorded it over me." Joe rolled his eyes as he erased the board. "My college was also located in Boston. By then Jake was only a few inches shorter than me. He was the star of his high school track team and a babe magnet in his own right. We were on good enough terms that we even partied together during our first year in Boston."

He stopped writing and stared at the board before erasing it.

"It happened again, didn't it?" Ali said, dread in her voice. "*Another* woman?"

Joe wrote, "You guessed it. I'll spare you the ugly details. There was no coming back from that one."

Jake had brought a date to the bar where they always met on Fridays for dinner. Wendy had flirted with Joe shamelessly. They'd all gotten shitfaced, and at the last minute, she'd hopped into Joe's cab. She claimed Jake and she was "just friends." The fact that Jake had never scored with her didn't make her rejection in favor of his brother hurt any less. Joe was deeply ashamed of his actions that night, a betrayal that could never be made right. Throwing

Joe's abject apologies back in his face, Jake spoke the dreaded words, "You're dead to me."

Though they steered clear of each other for the remainder of their undergrad education, they pretended to get along at family gatherings for their mother's sake. But Joe knew no real détente would happen without some extraordinary circumstance—either Jake would experience some kind of religious conversion, or more likely, find a way to even the score. Seducing Ali would have served that purpose. So Joe was confused. It seemed that Jake's heart had not been in the game. What had held him back?

Their father's death four months after their nineteenth birthday cemented Jake's future as the heir to BPO. In his will, their father proclaimed the succession to be "his dearest wish." One of the top executives had stepped into the CEO position with the understanding that he would relinquish it to Jake after he finished business school. Having so little contact with his brother, Joe didn't know what had prompted Jake to assume the trappings of the sophisticated man about town. Each family gathering, he noticed that his brother had progressed further in that direction. Joe could just imagine the fortune he spent on clothing, fine wine, and gourmet feasts. All that hard work and decadent play wouldn't leave much time for writing.

He looked over at Ali, still quiet and attentive, waiting for more. She had to be wondering why Joe was standing there lost in thought. He didn't have the energy to explain it all in writing. Lacking the nuances of inflection and tone, his confession would come off even worse than the facts implied.

He wanted to tear his hair out at the futility of it all. Despairing of ever explaining himself to his satisfaction, he left the board to finish preparing dinner. As he assembled and dressed the salad, Ali pulled out her sketchbook. Intrigued, Joe peered over her shoulder. In the soundbox of the guitar she drew was a face he recognized as his own. *Clever.*

"I assumed your guitar was an old beater, but it's not, is it?"

Joe wrote, "It's vintage, the work of a well-known luthier."

"Becca guessed as much. After you, uh, serenaded me, I figured you were a professional musician. You confused me by sticking to classical guitar music. That was the point, wasn't it? To throw me off the track."

She didn't miss much. Joe drew her attention to dinner, which was getting cold. To his relief, she let the subject drop.

"This is great, even better than last time," Ali said after a few bites. "The meal, I mean."

Silence descended again. After they were finished, Ali took his plate and placed it along with hers in the plastic tub half filled with water. Then she turned to him and asked in an almost tearful voice, "Are you going to be all right?"

Joe took a deep breath and blew it out slowly. "Time will tell," he wrote. "The wedding is off?" Her casual tone didn't fool him.

She dragged the bearskin rug into the corner and sat, long legs folded to one side. The perfectly innocent pose was all it took to get him revved up.

As he loomed over Ali, she appeared even more vulnerable. She'd mentioned at least one boyfriend, and he guessed there weren't many more. Though far less experienced than Rina, she'd responded to him in ways that let him know it would be good between them. The memories delivered a new surge of lust.

Noting the crease between the perfect arcs of her brows, he knew he had hesitated too long before answering her question. "No wedding," he wrote. "Rina announced the engagement to force my hand." He kept his gaze directed at the board. "I thought I'd made it clear it wasn't going to happen, but then—God knows why—she told the tabloids the wedding was back on, and I couldn't deny it without calling her a liar. After that Baler Tavern fiasco, she was furious. I tried to calm her down but I"—he stopped writing. The honest answer was, *I couldn't fuck her anymore, and that was the only way to calm her down.* He erased everything and started over. "The tour was an ordeal for us both. We had to pretend to be a happy couple. She must have been relieved when I had to bow out."

"Did you ever love her?"

"I thought so," he wrote.

Joe believed he loved Ali. He almost wrote it on the board. He was desperate to fuck her. Truth to tell, he barely knew her. And she knew even less about him.

"I've had exactly two lovers," she said, her confession a huge relief to Joe. "They were enough to make me swear off men. I told you about Trip. Turns out I wasn't good enough for his family. The second … well, ultimately Liam had to scare him off."

"What happened?!" he wrote.

"He was bad news. When I tried to break up, he wouldn't go away."

If Liam ever resurfaced, Joe would be sure to thank him.

Embarrassed by her admissions, Ali avoided his eyes. "Men don't like to take no for an answer, do they?"

"You're thinking about the man who tried to rape you," he wrote. He closed his eyes, pained by the thought that she was alone in the world and easy prey for men like Tom Lowen's son.

"I *do* feel sorry for *you*," she continued. "Of course you're depressed. Do you think I can't understand what losing your voice means at this point? It's like the world is ending. But there is always hope. My foster mother used to say, 'This too will pass.' She was fond of spouting platitudes like that, and I didn't appreciate them at the time. But some of them help when I'm feeling blue."

With the lantern directed at the whiteboard, Ali's face was illuminated solely by the woodstove and the kerosine lamp. Her doe eyes glittered and her smooth olive skin glowed in the dark. For a moment, Joe just stood there, mesmerized. "Do you think there was a specific incident that turned Liam into your protector?" he wrote.

"I think it has something to do with the three years after we were taken away from our mother. Before George and Emily took us in." She was rocking herself.

He wrote, "You seem upset. Earlier you told me you have no memory of those years."

Ali looked up to read the board before saying, "It's not a complete blank. After our birth mother disappeared, we were placed with our first foster mother, Frida. Frida didn't have a husband or any live-in boyfriend who lasted longer than a month or two." Ali shut her eyes. "In my memory, all faces are blurry, even hers. Like our mother, Frida seemed distracted, although she did feed us regularly. We were little kids and poorly supervised, so I'm surprised we didn't wander out into the road and get killed. *Something* did happen—and it was bad. Ever since I was a child, I've had a recurring nightmare. Up until the incident at La Fête Sauvage, the nightmare had left me alone for over a year." She licked her lips, making it difficult for Joe to concentrate. "You're almost too beautiful to be real," she whispered, echoing his own thoughts. He nearly took her in his arms, but then she returned to the subject of her dream, her voice carefully neutral, "A phantom rises up next to my bed. A big diaphanous gray cloud that looks vaguely human. The features sharpen. Just as I think I'm about to recognize the face, Liam appears out of nowhere and pulls it down with a *whoosh*." She pretended to grab something out of the air with both hands. "Like a vacuum cleaner sucking up a great big dust bunny. Can we change the subject?"

Ali had explained that her defense mechanism was to make light of dark memories, but he couldn't summon a smile. Had one of her foster mother's scumbag boyfriends tried to rape her? He crouched down to drape a blanket over her shoulders. Instead of backing away again, he hovered, willing her to lean against him so he could cradle her in his arms. When she didn't, he went back to the whiteboard, uncertain what to do next. With a frustrated sigh, he changed the angle of the lantern and held up a deck of cards.

Ali greeted this latest diversion with relief. "Good idea. We could play gin rummy. Promise you won't let me win this time? I don't mind losing over and over … and over again."

Grabbing a pillow to sit on, Joe shuffled the cards and let her cut them. She had an adorable way of worrying her full lower lip as she concentrated on her hand. Noting a stray lock of hair, he reached out to tuck it behind her ear.

His touch startled her. A nervous giggle escaped, quickly stifled. "Becca said that if we, uh, slept together, I would just be another notch in your bedpost. And now there are actual bedposts to put notches in."

There it was—the elephant in the room. *You can't go for it*, his conscience warned him, *not with your future so precarious. Damn*, he should have gone out of his way to reassure Linc and his mother that suicide wasn't an option. Why else would they offer up Ali as a sacrificial lamb? Yeah, but … reassure them how? His behavior had spoken louder than words, and it had given them cause for concern.

Still blushing furiously, Ali turned her attention back to the game. "Let's play cards." She frowned, as if hating the hand she'd been dealt. He was distracted enough that even if her cards were bad, she might actually win. Though he longed to take Ali up on her roundabout invitation, he was determined to wait until the timing was right for both of them. In the first depressing days after his second surgery, he'd listened to a radio play of Arthur Miller's *The Crucible* on NPR, and now Elizabeth's words of warning to her husband drifted back to him: "There is a promise made in every bed." John Proctor didn't understand the implications of his affair with Abigail. Like Abigail, Ali was young and relatively inexperienced. She couldn't help but see a promise in one night of sex.

As his hands automatically drew cards, laid down melds, and discarded deadwood, Joe let his mind wander to the immediate challenges ahead. The doctors were still trying to determine the cause of his vocal issues, because his technique wasn't to blame. Allergies were part of it. The second operation was his last chance. Absolute voice rest for another week, then at least two more months of staying as quiet as possible before he joined the last leg of the tour for one month only. He didn't want to go out a complete loser, and he believed in this new album. He couldn't ask Ali to quit her hard-won job and stand by him through his coming ordeal, not on such short acquaintance. Rina would eat her alive. If he gave in to this overwhelming urge to make love to her tonight, no amount of whiteboard reassurance could prevent her from feeling hurt and rejected when they inevitably parted ways.

He won the next two hands; losing would have required greater concentration. Finally he came to a decision: he would keep his mitts to himself. Now that he'd vowed to do the right thing, his turmoil subsided enough that he could let her win a hand.

She raised a triumphant fist in the air. "Hurrah!" With a wry smile, she added, "Thanks, but you didn't need to let me win." She put down her cards, scooted over on the floor next to him, and laid her head on his shoulder.

His resolve shattered.

CHAPTER 31

———•———

As ALI CLOSED THE DISTANCE between them, Joe appeared to recoil. She drew back. In this confined space, you could only retreat so far. She didn't want Joe to act against his conscience. But if he really was done with Rina, his reluctance must stem from a misplaced desire not to hurt Ali. That meant she didn't figure into his future plans. *You regret the things you didn't do, not the things you do* was the conventional wisdom. She wouldn't be the one to call a halt to this. If the opportunity never came again, she'd regret it the rest of her life.

Joe drew in a long, ragged breath and blew it out slowly. After a moment of indecision, he lifted her onto his lap, wrapped her in his arms, and pressed her close. She felt his cock stir, his breathing quicken, and his heart thump frantically against her back.

Then, nothing. For an agonizingly long time.

Finally he stood, pulling her to her feet. Their bodies were still pressed together as if any degree of separation might break the spell. Neither of them moved. Someone had to end the stalemate. Ali unbuttoned her flannel shirt. To take it off, she'd have to pull away. What if he tried to stop her? There would be no clarifications or reassurances.

To hell with it. She wriggled out of her shirt and pulled off her tee, releasing Joe from *his* paralysis. They were in a race to see who could remove their clothing first. She tripped as she stepped out of her hiking pants, and he caught her against him, steadying her briefly before ridding himself of his jeans.

Clothing gone, they came together again, frenzied kissing and fondling slowing their progress toward the bed.

What sweet nothings would Joe whisper if he could, what other sounds would he make in the throes of desire? No, it was better this way. She didn't want misleading declarations or false promises.

* * *

DAMN, THEY WERE REALLY GOING to do this.

Joe pulled away to gaze at the dim outline of Ali's body, barely visible in the dying light of the woodstove. She was so perfect, like Goya's *Naked Maja*. His large hands could easily span that tiny waist. No woman had ever affected him the way this one did. He didn't want to overwhelm her with his need, and he didn't know how much she was ready for. She had gone silent, and *he* couldn't prompt her to tell him what she wanted or didn't want.

Then he realized that his hesitation had sent the wrong message. She thought he was going to put on the brakes. Should he? Could he?

He had to. With a disappointed sigh, he flopped down beside her.

She rolled over to face him. *Thank God*. She wasn't going to let him be noble, and his body's response made it clear he was onboard with her calling the shots. It was a helluva strain to remain passive as she planted tentative kisses along his jaw and down his neck. Seeing her gaze land on the medicine bag, he took it off. He hoped she was pleased that he wore it, but now was not the time to raise the ghost of Liam.

* * *

ALI HAD FIGURED HIS COCK would be large, but it was also quite ... beautiful.

She wasn't new to blow jobs. Trip, in the early days before he decided to take her virginity, had given her specific instructions, but what pleased him might not work for everyone. She licked around the rim, then took it in her mouth, where it seemed to take on a life of its own. It tasted nice—salty and sweet.

All too soon, Joe pulled her back up beside him. *Oh no*, he was having second thoughts again. He shut his eyes as if in pain. When they opened again, the guilty reckoning had passed. With new possessiveness, he moved on top of her and eased himself inside. At her gasp, he hesitated, but she urged him on. She watched his face—the parted lips, the heavy-lidded eyes that roamed her body. She liked the feeling of power. Joe pulled out before shuddering against her.

Her detachment ended abruptly when he brought his fingers back into play. She heard herself whimper, then cry out like an animal, surrendering to a pleasure so intense that she nearly blacked out. Afterward, utterly satiated, she snuggled against him.

Then froze. Why had she pushed so hard for this to happen? She wanted Joe to reassure her, but how could he? Write something on the whiteboard? "Don't worry, you're my girl now." As if …. He hadn't used a condom, though he *had* pulled out. His mother had sent her to comfort him. Was this the kind of comfort she'd anticipated? Ali was afraid so. Joe wasn't in any position to make a commitment. Come to think of it, he hadn't so much as hinted at such a promise. She rolled away, wondering if her receptiveness had just sounded the death knell of their relationship, if you could even call it that.

A steely arm halted her momentum, easing her back toward him. He propped himself up on one elbow. When she dared meet his eyes, he cradled her face and placed a soft kiss on her swollen lips. Then he pulled her into a close embrace and let loose a long sigh of contentment. She snuggled against him.

Lightning flashed. An instant after the room lit up, thunder boomed. Rain slammed against the roof as if the gods were emptying the sky all at once. Or pounding the roof with their fists, a horde of outraged chaperones berating them for their recklessness.

Joe went rigid.

"What is it?" she gasped.

He swung his legs over the side of the bed and struggled into his jeans. Lightning flashed and thunder boomed again in close succession. Grabbing the flashlight, Joe pulled on his boots, flung the door open, and made a mad dash into the darkness.

Ali lay still, bereft, trying to absorb what had just happened. Now that she finally understood what she had been missing, it might never happen again. Not like this. No one else would do. If she couldn't have Joe, she would die.

The rain kept battering the roof, making her question the solidity of this place. Wrapping herself in a blanket, she waited in dread for Joe to return.

After what seemed like an eternity, she heard heavy footsteps on the porch. A fist rapped twice, the door creaked open, and Joe and Linc appeared. "Sorry, Ali," Linc blurted out, his glance speculative as it passed from Ali to Joe. "It's too dicey to be in a tent during a thunderstorm."

Joe stoked the fire in the stove and poured water into the kettle to boil.

"Of course," Ali said in a tremulous voice. "We don't usually have storms like this in the Pacific Northwest."

Linc dropped his hood, shrugged out of his jacket, and dried his face with the sleeve of his flannel shirt. "More rain here than in Seattle, but yeah, it's rare. Usually it's sheet lightning. No problem in the cabin. It has a lightning rod. You all were asleep?"

She stammered, "N-not quite."

A fogbank of silence engulfed them. Joe made a pot of herbal tea, and when they were all calmer, they settled in for the night, fully clothed. Linc had left his sleeping bag in the tent, so he inflated the flimsier air mattress meant for Ali and covered himself with blankets.

Fully clothed, Ali and Joe shared the bed. Turning her face to the wall, she wondered if he slept. It didn't sound like it, not that he snored—much. She listened to the rain assaulting the roof until she finally dozed off. She feared the freak storm had destroyed any chance to square things with Joe.

THE NEXT MORNING, ALI AWOKE to silence. She was alone, and the rain had stopped. Sunlight streamed through the windows.

Finding coffee in the thermos, she filled a mug then stepped outside. Joe and Linc were in view, but too far away to overhear. Though Linc was the only one speaking, Joe's body language made his annoyance clear. Arms folded across his chest, he scowled at the ground. Sensing her presence, they both turned at once and headed back into the cabin.

Joe picked up the felt pen and wrote on the whiteboard, "You're going back."

"Are you sure?" Her eyes stung but she fought back the tears.

He wrote, "We all are. I can see everyone is nervous about me being out here alone." He looked at Linc then wrote, "Give us a minute?"

Joe waited until the stomping on the porch subsided before he erased the board, slowly, as if gathering his thoughts.

"Thank you," he wrote. He took her hand, kissed the palm, then held it to his cheek. "I can't stay here and brood. I have to face the music." A hint of a smile. "So to speak."

Ali couldn't smile back. She was too afraid of what he might write next.

"You shouldn't get pregnant," he continued. "I pulled out in time. Though that isn't 100% reliable." He erased those sentences before writing two more: "I'll be in touch. Please, be patient."

He kissed the top of her head. Taking her by the shoulders, he gazed into her eyes, his expression unreadable. His mouth formed words. *Trust me.* She thought he was moving in for a kiss when Linc appeared.

They hiked back to the road in gloomy silence, emerging at the precise spot where the Ford Explorer was parked. Linc unlocked the doors, and they all piled in. Ali sat alone in the backseat.

For one fleeting moment at the Port Angeles airport, she thought Joe would take her in his arms. Instead he repeated the nebulous farewell from the cabin: a kiss on the forehead and a soulful glance. No "trust me" this time.

After wishing her a "safe flight," Linc handed her his business card. "In case of emergency," he said.

"Emergency." Like if she was pregnant? Not an emergency like a desperate need for reassurance. *Patience. Trust.* Did Joe have any idea how much he was asking of her?

Left to her own devices for over two hours in the waiting area, Ali sketched a crazed ground beetle, a mournful Douglas squirrel, and a hostile deer. At Sammy's approach, she crumpled up all three drawings and tossed them in the wastebin.

CHAPTER 32

———•———

ON MEMORIAL DAY, BECCA AND Jean-Louis met Ali for lunch at their new hangout, the pub across from the construction site for the Bellevue location of La Fête Sauvage. Becca reacted to the news of Ali's second visit to the cabin in the woods with outrage. You'd think she'd taken a leisurely stroll into a warzone. Jean-Louis, less invested in her fate, tried to calm his fiancée.

"Okay," Becca said, her gestures not quite so emphatic, "let me get this straight: You offered yourself up to wounded lover boy after his mother acted like a pimp."

Jean-Louis whistled softly. "You really dislike him."

Ali blew out a frustrated breath. "Come on, Becca. That's not fair. I knew what I was doing."

Becca's smile was more like a sneer. "You had sex with him, didn't you?"

Jean-Louis was shocked, but not by Ali's actions. "Becca, this is none of our business. That is Ali's decision. Who appointed you the morality police?"

Becca appeared chastened. "I just don't want her to get hurt."

Jean-Louis grunted. "*Ben là*, everyone gets hurt. If not, they live too carefully."

Becca took a few Ujjayi breaths, which irritated Ali. Calmer, she asked, "How will he make sure you're not pregnant?"

Ali was fully on the defensive now. She wasn't sure why she'd expected Becca to be in her court. Too late now to shut down the whole debate. "He still can't talk, and we didn't really get to do a postmortem, uh, post coitum— you know what I mean. He, uh, pulled out in time."

Lips still compressed in disapproval, Becca argued, "That's not reliable. I know you don't use birth control. You didn't get a morning-after pill, did you?"

Ali remained silent.

"We'll leave talk of STDs for another time," Becca said, sarcasm still evident. "After you, uh, made love, what then?"

"A storm intervened," Ali said.

"Aha!" Becca brandished a french fry. "A message from on high. Too bad it didn't come sooner. What do you mean, a storm intervened? Lightning struck the cabin?"

"No, there's a lightning rod. What I meant to say is, the rain was coming down so hard that Joe had to go rescue Linc."

"Linc? Who is Linc?" Jean-Louis said as he hailed the waitress to order another round.

"Joe's manager. They didn't dare leave Joe alone because they were worried about the gun."

Becca grew positively bug-eyed. "You wandered into the arms of a man with a gun? A pistol?"

"No!" Ali gestured for her friend to turn down the volume. "A rifle. For protection. You know, there are bears and cougars, and—who knows?—some demented survivalist might show up. Joe was so dead-eyed when I arrived, I was afraid he wouldn't let me stay. His mother had assured me he'd be a total gentleman, and he would have been, I know it, it's just that …." She couldn't finish.

Becca thrummed her fingers on the table. "Nature had its way."

Ali sighed. She shouldn't be so surprised by Becca's negativity. Her friend had never believed in Joe. "He was wearing Liam's medicine bag."

Becca raised a pointed, red-nailed finger in the air. "Ah-ha! Proof positive of his devotion."

"Sarcasm noted. Still, why else would he wear that moth-eaten old thing if not to remind him of me? It obviously wasn't protecting him."

Jean-Louis's exasperated expression told her his role as referee was beginning to pall. "Medicine bag?"

Becca brushed him off. "I'll explain later."

"Back to the storm," Ali said. "Joe was worried about Linc getting struck by lightning or the river rising or something." When neither Becca nor Jean-Louis commented, she went on, "I think Joe will be all right now. And I think I'll see him again."

"You *think*," Becca repeated. "What kind of life do you envision for yourself and him, pray tell? Even if he stops touring, he'll still be a celebrity. And the more reclusive he becomes, the more the fanzines will hound him. What about *your* work? You're enjoying the job, right?"

Becca wasn't about to give her a break.

"I've got a bunch of new skills. I could become a website designer. I could do that from anywhere. I'm a wiz with HTML and style sheets, and I'm learning how to use Dreamweaver."

Becca kept shaking her head as if Ali's behavior defied all logic. "Ooh, freelancing in the tech world is hard. Kids learn that stuff before they lose their baby teeth."

Nothing Ali said could convince Becca that Joe wasn't going to drive her off a cliff. She simply wouldn't let it drop. "What did he say when you left?" she asked.

"Nothing."

Jean-Louis raised an eyebrow. "What do you mean?"

"He couldn't speak. Everything he 'said' "—she used air quotes—"was on the whiteboard."

"Huh. So what were his immortal last words?" Becca asked.

"He wrote, 'I'll be in touch. Please be patient.' "

"Did he kiss you again?"

"On the forehead."

"Like a daughter."

"He could hardly grab me and kiss me senseless with Linc waiting outside. I think he would have if Linc hadn't come in. And he mouthed the words, 'Trust me.' "

Becca made a disgusted sound. "As a rule, men who ask you point-blank to trust them are anything but trustworthy."

Jean-Louis gave her arm a little shake. "*Chérie*, you have seen this man once and have never spoken to him. He is doing his best to communicate without spoken words. How can anyone know what he is really thinking? To me it is clear that he loves Ali. I believe his situation is impossible. He is, excuse my French, *complètement foutu*."

LATER THAT NIGHT, BECCA'S SKEPTICISM hung like a stink in the air as Ali lay prostrate on the couch. She would have felt a whole lot better if Joe had asked for her email address or promised to call by a certain date. You couldn't be vaguer than "in touch."

Sex with Joe, for her, had been nothing short of mind-blowing. But what if his mind wasn't blown? Still, he'd left her no choice. What could she do but wait? Either until he contacted her again or she received a definitive sign he never would. As in, he and Rina tied the knot.

Now that they'd had sex, would Joe decide he'd gotten what he wanted and move on? How could sex with someone as inexperienced as she be anything but a letdown? Yes, but if he didn't truly love her—*love*, not just desire—then all the Happy Hooker's tricks would be for nothing. Didn't beautiful groupies swarm him like butterflies did bright colors? Rina looked built for sex.

As for the remote possibility that she might be pregnant, Ali didn't have long to worry. Her period arrived on time. She should have been relieved.

* * *

JOE WAS LOUNGING ON A deck chair, gazing out at the bay and the snowcapped Cascades. Waldron Island—population, about a hundred—was part of the San Juan Archipelago. No cell service or internet, and the house was powered by a generator. Well water and a septic tank. A large pond that he shared with a river otter. Compared to the cabin in the woods, it was a five-star hotel.

The roomy '70s A-frame was modest—mansions and paved roads were verboten—but the décor was comfortable, if dated, with a library of bestsellers and classics and a music studio. Years ago, Waldron had been mined for sandstone, which meant much of the trees and undergrowth had been cleared. As was common in the San Juans, there were organic farms and apple orchards. Dirt roads cut through areas of dense forest and abundant foliage.

A hermit's paradise. Joe might have enjoyed being a hermit if ninety percent of his brain space—both conscious and unconscious—hadn't been taken up with Ali. Ali naked, Ali sketching, Ali writhing beneath him. Ali's cupid's-bow lips, Ali's brilliant blue eyes …. Ali, Ali, Ali. *Aye-yi-yi*. He was going mad. Even if he'd wanted to contact her, how? The Pony Express had it over the mail service here. The estate belonged to his voice therapist Bill Sweeney, who could no doubt use Joe's infusion of cash to fund his newest getaway. Bill kept all visitors away. There would be no babes in the woods.

A month and a week had passed since Joe had left Ali behind. The second surgery appeared to be a success. With Bill's help, he improved a little every day. At the end of July, gods willing, he'd join the tour for its final month. Rina was the headliner this time. Larry Wales had moved on, replaced by a singer he'd never met, a rising talent named Lester Phillips. As special guest artist, Joe would perform only three solos and join Rina for their two duets. He wasn't sure why she had agreed to the arrangement. True, he was still a major draw—never more so, thanks to the rumors that his public appearances would henceforth be rare—and his segment of the tour was sold out. But he feared the real reason was that she wanted another crack at him. Not that there was any chance she would succeed. It just made things more awkward.

Joe was learning to meditate, reading *The Complete Works of Shakespeare*, and playing the guitar. Activities chosen to crowd out thoughts of Ali, thoughts that came roaring back the minute he was idle again. He spent hours staring through a telescope, on the lookout for rare birds and sea creatures. He roamed the island, drove the tractor. When he wasn't conducting their therapy sessions, Bill stayed out of his way, having moved to the caretaker's cottage to give Joe full run of the estate. The strange little man—he had Asperger's, Joe guessed—claimed to be writing a novel. The pantry offered simple dry and canned supplies, and the vegetable garden provided greens, potatoes, carrots, and strawberries. According to Bill, there were serious marijuana fields nearby. Joe wasn't interested. Edibles made him nauseated, and he avoided smoke of any kind. In retrospect, the woodsmoke in the cabin probably hadn't helped his recovery.

Now, as he nursed a mug of slippery elm tea, he recalled his last exchange with Teresa, who'd turned him on to instant messaging:

JJ, anything serious happen with Ali?

NOYB.

That means yes. I know you can't phone her, but you've got to do something. I know you're serious about her.

I think so.

Ah.

I don't really know her.

You know.

I'll call her after I finish the tour.

Might be too late.

I told her to be patient.

She replied with a sad-face symbol—a closed parenthesis and a colon.

What? he responded.

You're an idiot were her final words.

That amazing night with Ali haunted Joe in the worst way. She had to understand what it meant to him. Of course he wanted her, but in what context? Where would they live? Not in Seattle or Bellevue. The tabloids would hound them. Could Ali be happy living on an island with few amenities? Did she want children? So many things needed to be worked out. Selfishly, he hoped her new job was a bust. He was convinced her future was in illustration, not the corporate world—work she couldn't do as his wife. He didn't want to make her choose between him and her dream job, did he?

Yes, he was taking a chance by staying incommunicado. He wanted Ali to get clear on what she wanted too. Or so he told himself. Maybe he *was* an idiot.

* * *

ALI'S EXCITEMENT OVER BECCA AND Jean-Louis's wedding at La Fête Sauvage was dampened by Joe's radio silence. *Be patient*, he'd written. What did that even mean? He couldn't write her two or three lines? Surely his mother's investigator knew her email address. Whatever. Wedding bells were not in her immediate future.

The week before, Becca's family had treated her bridesmaids to a spa day at the Salish Lodge, with its spectacular view of Snoqualmie Falls. Her oldest sister Hanna was the maid of honor. Ali's fellow bridesmaids were Becca's other sister Myra, a first cousin, and two of her Princeton roommates, one who flew in from Portland, Oregon, and one from New York City. Nice as they all were, Ali was an outsider. Duncan was her guest at the house in North Bend, but she had been so busy that the two of them hadn't had time to exchange more than a few sentences.

At the wedding reception, Becca seated Duncan next to Laurie, an attractive middle-aged woman with pert features and big blue eyes. Medium height, maybe five feet five inches tall. With her blonde pixie cut, long legs, and short skirt, she somewhat resembled Twiggy, the disturbingly slender model from the '60s. Laurie did most of the talking. With Duncan, Ali could see where her own introverted personality came from. Also at her table were the former roomies from Princeton, fully engaged in a private conversation about their high-pressure jobs.

Other than the bridesmaids, Ali knew only Becca's parents, her grandmother, and her brother Nathan—all seated at the family table next to the portable dance floor. Jean-Louis had removed all but eight tables. The family table accommodated twelve but Ali's only six, though the sixth chair was empty. Somehow Becca had convinced her father and mother to invite only the most important of their business associates to keep the occasion intimate. Thus there was no need to set up outside tents—much to Ali's relief. June weather could be tricky, but Sunday the twenty-second had been lovely. In these parts it always cooled off in the evening, so not many ventured outside anyway. Besides, everyone was too enchanted by the fairytale interior.

Becca had clothed her bridesmaids in simple chiffon dresses, nipped in at the waist '50s style, the hem just below the knees. Ali suspected the style and color—robin's-egg blue—had been chosen with Ali in mind. The simple outdoor ceremony in the afternoon had been a secular affair. A string quartet. No Jewish or Christian pageantry. For the dinner and reception, they had changed out of their wedding finery, and Ali was wearing her gift from Becca's parents: a little black dress.

Becca apologized to Ali for not including any bachelors besides Nathan. After asking Ali to dance and holding her too close, Nathan drifted over to chat up a flashy blonde named Cécile, a cousin of Jean-Louis's—the only representative from Jean-Louis's small clan other than an older brother, the brother's wife, and his mother, who was self-conscious about her English and so stayed close to her family members. As far as Ali could tell, Nathan was still sticking to nonalcoholic beverages.

"Dad," Ali said, profiting from Laurie's trip to the powder room, "I don't think I was born in the right century."

"Well, you look good in a little black dress and pearls."

"The pearls are fake, and that's a timeless look."

"Sure is." He grinned.

"What do you think of Laurie?" She indicated the empty chair.

"I like her, though she talks a blue streak. My head might hurt after a while. Not ruling it out. What about Becca's brother?"

"Nathan?" Ali wrinkled her nose. "It's like he's *my* brother."

Duncan chuckled. "Thank goodness. The way he held you wasn't exactly brotherly. He's a nice-enough boy, but he's looking to score. Not for anything permanent … or even lasting." Duncan drained his glass of red wine. "Speaking of which, you haven't caught me up on your soap opera."

"Which one is that?"

"The Saga of Joe Bob Blade."

"Certainly not a rom com," Ali said.

"Ouch. Last I heard, you were being transported back to the rain forest to keep Joe from offing himself, though he hadn't invited you and he still couldn't talk. You never told me what happened."

"It was weird … at first. Then Joe was, uh, glad to see me."

"Does that mean what I think it means?" he asked, giving her a smile of encouragement.

"Yes," she said, trying to summon a smile herself.

"Well, that's good. I think. It was bound to happen sooner or later. Was it good?"

"To put it mildly."

"That's great. You're not Catholic, so there's no need to go to confession. You aren't pregnant, I presume?" He sized up her slim form. "Not unless the baby is the size of Thumbelina."

"No, but … I don't think Liam would approve."

Duncan considered this. "Maybe not. Depends how it turns out. He wants you to be happy, the way we all do."

"Thanks for still using the present tense," Ali said. They both observed a moment of silence.

Ali watched as Nathan whispered something in Cécile's ear, his hand caressing her back. "Liam is too much like Nathan."

Duncan clasped his hands across his firm abs and nodded sagely. "I was like that once. Takes one to know one. When you're young and virile and too handsome, it's especially difficult not to exploit your power." He jutted his chin at Ali. "You're too beautiful, and that's even harder. You have more power than you know, and if you choose not to use it, others will take unfair advantage. All's fair and so on and so forth. Irresistible young men can get too spoiled, too dazzled by the smorgasbord of gorgeous women available to them to recognize quality. Too many tempting desserts to be sampled before you realize what you really want and need is a good steak."

Ali grimaced. "I'm the steak?"

Duncan flashed her his crooked grin. "A *good* steak. The best. Filet mignon. Or asparagus with hollandaise sauce. Guacamole. Anyway, you are a delicious treat, but you are nourishing. You aren't instant gratification. Hard for a guy to look past the sweets." Nathan and Cécile had stopped dancing and were lip-locked in the center of the room. "Speaking of sweets, Nathan's going to have some powerful indigestion with that one."

Indigestion or not, Ali envied them in that moment. "Maybe I *should* go a little wild. If you play the field, I suppose, it's harder to fall for one person. It might hurt less."

Duncan gave her hand a squeeze. "You could look into sex clubs," he joked.

Ali just stared at him. "There are sex clubs?"

Duncan chuckled, choosing not to elaborate. "If you want to be reborn as a 'free' woman, there's oodles of time for that. Let's see how this Joe thing plays out first. Make sure it's in your rearview mirror before you enter the fast lane."

Ali spilled a few drops as she refilled their wine glasses, thinking it might be time to ease up on the vino. "Okay, Mario Andretti. With all my heart, I believe Joe's a nice guy. Being too handsome doesn't automatically make you a jerk who breaks women's hearts just because you can."

"I'll second that," Laurie said, clapping. Ali wondered how long she'd been standing there. "I know plenty of jerky ugly men. No one should be judged by their looks. Sometimes the ugly ones are the jerkiest, especially if they're rich. They want revenge for all the years they couldn't get laid."

Duncan waved his white-cloth napkin in surrender. "All right. I shouldn't project my own issues with women on everyone else. Make that, *former* issues."

He asked Laurie to dance, and they stayed on the floor until the band played "Love Shack." Duncan asked for her number, which she handed him with a delighted smile, and they all went over to say goodbye to Becca and Jean-Louis.

"Did you have a good time?" Becca asked Ali, as if afraid she hadn't. "Where's Nathan?"

"On the terrace, making out with Cécile."

Becca snorted in disgust. "Sorry. I keep hoping my brother will grow on you. Especially now that he's sober."

"He may be sober, but he appears to have some other addiction issues, like with sex," Ali said.

Becca made a face. "Yeah, I know. One addiction at a time, I guess." She gave Ali a huge hug. "Thanks for being my best friend."

"Always. I really enjoyed visiting with my dad."

Becca grinned. "Coolest dad, ever."

ALI SLOGGED THROUGH THE REST of a typically soggy June. Despite Duncan's reservations about the weather in Seattle, he purchased one of the last little bungalows in Fremont, figuring he could always turn it into a rental. Traffic between North Bend and Seattle being what it was, Ali couldn't see him as often as she liked.

On July fourth, they walked to Gasworks Park to view the fireworks. Ali would spend the night in his tiny guest room.

Duncan and Laurie were fast becoming an item, although she was otherwise occupied this evening. "She's calmed down some," he said as they weaved through the crowd. "Now I can get a word in edgewise. And she's fun and cute."

"That's not nothing," Ali said. "How did she end up at Becca's wedding?"

"She volunteers with her mother at the food bank. But her main work is selling real estate."

Ali shot him a sheepish glance. "Looks like I underestimated her."

He shrugged. "First impressions—notoriously unreliable. And speaking of first impressions, any word from Joe?"

"No," Ali blurted out. "It's terrible. Every time I'm in the supermarket, I'm afraid to look at the magazines near the checkout stand. I keep thinking I'm going to see some sensational headline that explains his silence."

"Yeah, I get it. It's probably too late to say, 'Protect your heart.' "

"A bit late."

A young guy in motorcycle leathers walked by, staring Ali down.

"Cheeky bastard, checking you out in front of your father."

She took his arm. "I'm glad you're here to defend my honor."

As they walked along, he said, "Darlin', I know it's hard, but don't go jumping to conclusions."

"What do you mean?"

"Silence is easy to misinterpret. So is the written word. I'd bet my bottom dollar you'll hear from Joe again. Didn't he once tell you he needed time to 'disentangle' himself? I believe that's the word he used. A drowning man can't take a break to send an email."

The thought had occurred to Ali. She and Joe had had so few normal conversations. Maybe Joe was simply tired of the additional barriers. Maybe he wanted to wait until he could see her and talk to her in person.

Or maybe she was grasping at straws.

CHAPTER 33

———•———

ALI LEFT WORK AT NOON on Friday to meet Becca and Jean-Louis for dinner in Bellingham, a college town a couple of hours north of Bellevue and close to the Canadian border. They'd stay in a motel and get an early start the next day on their hike to Lake Ann in the Mount Baker area. Before hitting the road, she stopped at a grocery-store café for a latte and a sandwich.

In the three months that had passed since she'd parted ways with Joe, Ali had done her utmost to shut him and Liam out of her thoughts. Once upon a time, she had treasured silence. Now she was all about distraction. She chased anxiety away by listening to audiobooks and music everywhere but at her workplace—classical, because anything popular reminded her of Joe. On her daily run, she carried her Discman. At her new job, which did not pay for overtime, she toiled until her supervisor herded her out the door.

She lived for the moment, managing to stay upbeat with the help of her cheering section—Becca, Jean-Louis, and Duncan.

All well and good—until she walked into that café and saw the adjacent magazine rack.

The blaring headline read: COUNTRY MUSIC STAR JOE BOB BLADE'S SILENCE SPEAKS VOLUMES. The subheading, WHO IS THE FATHER OF RINA'S BABY?

Rina's *baby*? If Rina were pregnant with Joe's baby, did that mean they'd slept together since Ali had last seen him? *Hold on* … the tabloids *saying* Rina was pregnant didn't make it so. Nor did it follow that Joe was the father.

But it *felt* true. Ali hadn't heard from him. Joe had rejoined the tour, and if he could sing, he could talk, not that he needed a voice to reach out to her. So why the hell not, knowing this awful news was out there? If not Joe, then Linc. Or Carrie. Or Teresa. For all of them to keep Ali out of the loop after everything she'd done .... *No one forced you to go to bed with him,* she reminded herself.

While her latte cooled and her sandwich stayed in its wrapper, she flipped to the story.

Country star Joe Bob Blade is in hot water. His on-again off-again fiancée, Rina Bakersfield, dumped him in February after he lost his voice and left their multi-million-dollar tour. Then Joe disappeared. Rumors flew that he'd retreated to that infamous cabin immortalized in "Babe in the Woods" with his tail between his legs. A few months later, he was on the road again, back in Rina's arms.

"Rina is drawing the curtain on one of her most successful tours, ever," Rina's spokesman Pietro Pardee stated for the record. "She dearly loves Joe, and he loves her. He left the tour for health reasons, not because Rina broke off their relationship. The wedding was postponed, not canceled. They are presently deciding on a date that fits her recording schedule. Possibly September."

That's the official word, folks. Let us remind you that Rina Bakersfield was raised a Seventh Day Adventist, and her family can't approve of putting the baby carriage before the marriage. Maybe that's why she's so closemouthed about Baby Joe or Josephina. Joe hails from a venerable Irish Catholic family. They can't be too thrilled, either.

Stay tuned. Could be they're already married.

The article was set in a large font and illustrated with two pages of photos, both candid and official. In one of them, the couple was clearly arguing. Another showed them kissing, Joe's arm braced against a wall. Having ignored all but the interview in *Spurs 'n Sparkin'*, Ali had no way of knowing when any of these photos had been taken. They could predate her initial meeting with Joe.

Stuffing the untouched sandwich in her bag, Ali escaped to the sanctuary of her car. *Darn it*, she couldn't let Joe and his snooty family keep ruining her life. She was going on this hiking trip, and she was sure as hell going to enjoy it.

Despite her vow, Ali cried the entire drive to Bellingham. The popular audiobook she'd chosen to entertain her might as well have been a scientific treatise.

At dinner, Ali's devastating news earned her the expected outrage and sympathy, but no surprise. Her friends were tired of the Joe saga and wished she'd move on. The next day, when the weather took a turn for the worse, she wondered if her mood had conjured the storm clouds. Try as she might, she wasn't good company. She lagged behind Becca and Jean-Louis, who gave her the space she needed to mourn.

AUGUST HAD BEEN TYPICALLY GLORIOUS, enough to make most people forget the other ten months oppressed by reams of fluffy gray ice crystals floating in the sky—late July and early September also being reliably clear and warm. But constant sunlight and balmy breezes did little to lift Ali's spirits.

It was well-nigh impossible to keep the faith when multiple tabloids confirmed that Joe was going to marry Rina. Catholic guilt, Ali surmised. The guilt stayed with you long after you stopped observing the rituals. Rina had probably gotten pregnant on purpose to snare him. On the other hand, like countless abandoned women before her, Ali couldn't help but nurse the remote possibility that it was all a lie. That somehow, somewhere, Joe was, to quote The Four Seasons, "working his way back" to her "with a burning love inside."

It being Saturday, Ali was at home, moping, but also listening to an audiobook and cleaning the bathroom. The distraction strategy was an epic failure. She was miserably obsessed with Joe, and her resolve not to vent to Becca, Jean-Louis, or her dad just made it worse. She needed confirmation from the horse's mouth. Or the horse's sister's mouth, anyway. Teresa would tell her the truth without rubbing it in her face. The calling card from Carrie's fundraiser … what had Ali done with it?

She rummaged through her drawers until she found her black leather clutch. There it was—the elegant calling card with Teresa's name and phone number. Surely Joe's sister wouldn't have given Ali the card if she hadn't expected her to use it. On the other hand, she'd been dating Jake at the time, and what if Teresa sided with him? So what? Even if—*especially* if—Teresa refused to see her, Teresa would tell her the truth about Joe.

"Hello, Teresa," Ali said to the answering machine after the beep, "this is Ali. Um, the woman who was dating your brother, Jake. Briefly. This isn't about Jake, it's about Joe. I'm not sure how much you know … not that there's anything to know. Other than the song, of course. 'Babe—' " The machine cut her off.

Yikes. Talk about awkward. Stop that, she told herself. Inane prattle or no, if Teresa thought it was worthwhile to speak with her, she would call back. Except that Ali hadn't left her phone number. *Sheesh.* She called again and repeated the number twice.

Afterward, she sat by the phone with her sketchpad and drew a robin in its nest, then a ladybug, then a doe and its fawn. They all looked pissed off, as if she'd violated their privacy. How had she managed that? What would she do if Teresa never called her back? An agonizing two hours passed before the phone finally rang.

It was Teresa's breathy voice. "Ali! I'm so glad you called."

Ali was amazed. "You are?" The barstool at the kitchen counter almost scooted out from under her.

Teresa didn't comment on the deafening clatter. "Of course! Joe hoped you would."

"Why didn't *he* call *me*?" Ali asked, staggered. "I have no way of reaching him."

"He's an idiot," Teresa said, as if that were a valid excuse. "Plus, he's on vocal rest again. We're all so worried about Joe."

Teresa paused. Though the silence was uncomfortable, Ali waited for her to continue.

"The baby isn't his."

"He knows that for sure?"

"Yes. There's no way in hell. He suspects Rina's been boffing one of the roadies. She can't admit that, and she doesn't believe in abortion, so she's trying to pin it on Joe."

"Then why—"

"Why isn't Joe issuing denials? Because Rina knows about that second time you visited him in the woods."

Ali was speechless.

"I know," Teresa went on, "how the hell did she find out? She's threatening to tell the press, to put a bad spin on the whole thing. She'll say Joe stole you away from his brother and seduced you, even though he was engaged to Rina and left her pregnant. He's afraid it would ruin your life. Afraid—"

It was Ali's turn to interrupt. "Ridiculous! Even if Rina splashed my name all over the press and accused me of being the devious other woman, my boss wouldn't fire me."

"Of course not, but the tabloid press would hound you. You have no idea. Your boss wouldn't *want* to fire you, but the hullabaloo might force them to cut you off just so they could get back to business. Joe wants to avoid that if he possibly can."

"So he's going to marry Rina?" Ali couldn't keep the despair out of her voice.

"When hell freezes over," was Teresa's reply.

Ali searched for something to break but settled on crumpling up the evil robin drawing and throwing it across the room. "Rina sounds like a terrible person," she said. "Didn't *she* break up with *him*?"

Teresa sighed. "Yes and no. He allowed her to save face by saying it was her idea. And she's not really a terrible person. Just self-absorbed. And desperate."

The doorbell rang, and Ali looked out the peephole. "Uh, Teresa?"

"Yes."

"I think it's too late."

"What do you mean?"

"There are people in my yard. Some of them have cameras and microphones. An unmarked van."

"Jeez Louise!" Teresa exclaimed in a strangled voice. "Can you drive away?"

"I don't think so, not without running someone down. One of them is leaning on the driver's side door of my car." She peered outside again. "Maybe if I just sit tight, they'll go away."

"Only if you're prepared for a week-long siege. Hang on. You shouldn't have to face this alone. I'm on my way."

TERESA'S BABY-BLUE MIATA DROVE UP an hour later. Ali had shut herself in the bedroom with the curtains pulled just enough to monitor activity. No one had budged. A platinum-blonde in a white skirt suit was filing her nails as she talked to a tall, string-bean-thin older man holding a camera. A hefty guy in a baseball cap and full beard was tinkering with electrical equipment. Like a gang of meerkats, they came to wide-eyed, full attention as Teresa sashayed blithely by, dressed to kill in a pink pantsuit, her light-blonde hair caught up in a French twist. They were firing questions at her, and as she lifted her hand to knock, Ali pulled her in and locked the door.

Admiring Ali's designer jeans, knee-high boots, and used leather jacket, Teresa grinned. "You look *good*. As for them"—she whipped a beringed and manicured hand in the direction of the reporters—"pretend they're disembodied spirits. We'll breeze right by them. You ready?"

Ali slung her overnight bag over her shoulder. "Yes."

"Good." Teresa hooked her arm in Ali's and they set off for the car in a carefree stride as though embarking on a day of shopping.

"Teresa," the female reporter said, "did you know Ali was your brother's secret mistress?"

"I'm not—"

Teresa pressed a finger to her smiling lips. "Shh."

Once they were safely ensconced in the car, Ali felt the burden of the day slide from her shoulders. The group scrambled for their van, but Teresa floored it, and in no time they were hiding in a nearby driveway as the van whooshed by. Teresa thrummed her petal-pink nails on the steering wheel. "We can't go back to my place or Mom's. Hmm."

She pushed a few buttons on her cell phone. "Joe? I know you're supposed to keep quiet, so no need to call me back. I've got Ali with me. The press tracked her down. I'm dropping her off at a motel, not sure which one. The more nondescript, the better. I'll let you know." She hung up and turned to Ali. "Got his voicemail."

They waited for fifteen minutes. Ali worried that her neighbors would report the car lurking in their driveway to the police. Meanwhile Teresa had a friend check the Yellow Pages for motels. She wrote down an address and told Ali, "I'm taking you to the Sleep Tite Inn near the University Village." She pulled out into the street.

"Where's Joe?" Ali asked.

"In Seattle. He's been holed up with Mom. Her place is like a fortress. The police wouldn't let anyone camp out on *her* lawn." At the stoplight, she turned to Ali and said, "You may have noticed that that crew, although intrusive, was not exactly a mob. It's a specialized group, the tabloid press. This little scouting party was hoping for an exclusive. Once they publish their account, others will look for new angles. It will blow over. Question is, when? They'll all want pictures, of course. They got a few shots of us. I'm sorry you were caught up in the middle of this mess. Rina's the story more than Joe now. I believe they think he's finished as a singer. She's the rising star who stepped in the deep doo-doo. Her ultra-religious parents are not going to be crazy about their daughter having a baby out of wedlock. Neither are her many Southern Baptist fans."

"She could marry the roadie," Ali suggested.

"Hah! That's a good one. Rina should have thought things through before messing around with the road crew. I'm sure she thinks she's too good for any little ol' roadie."

"Meryl Streep married a normal guy," Ali said.

"That's arguable. He's a sculptor of some renown. And Meryl Streep's the Dalai Lama compared to Rina. It all changes when there's blood in the water."

"Maybe he's a roadie with talent in his own right?" Ali said.

Teresa slapped her thigh. "That's another howler. Wouldn't matter to Rina. He'd need to be a star. And not the shooting kind. One with staying power."

Once Teresa had checked Ali into the motel room and insisted on paying for one night, she left her alone, ostensibly to make calls on her cellphone. Twenty minutes later, she knocked on the door and called out, "Hey! You have a visitor."

CHAPTER 34

———•———

Now that Ali's wish had been granted and Joe stood before her, larger than life, she felt all fluttery, but more like a butterfly caught in a net than a girl whose dreams were about to come true. Joe's hair was trimmed short and his lower face was peppered with five o'clock shadow. Glasses with John Lennon-style circle-shaped rims, a baseball cap, a maroon hoodie, and jeans with frayed knees completed the disguise. Subtler than before, but a disguise, nonetheless.

Teresa backed out the door, waving. "Hey, you kids, I'm off. They're not after me. Ali, Joe's going to … keep you company for a bit."

Ali cut her eyes from Teresa to Joe.

"It's not pretty," he said in a raspy voice, "but I can talk."

How did he read her mind like that? With Liam off the air, was she on Joe's psychic wavelength now? Unlikely. If so, the misunderstandings of the past several months would never have happened.

Teresa lingered outside the door. "I can find you a whiteboard."

He waved her away. "This requires talking, not writing."

Ali finally found *her* voice. "Even if it means risking everything?"

Joe made a derisive sound. "*Everything*. What does that even mean? What I've lost, I've lost." Tossing his glasses carelessly onto the side table, Joe shut his eyes and rubbed his temples as if warding off a headache. Opening them again, he focused on Ali with unnerving intensity while waving backward over his shoulder at Teresa. "Bye, Sis."

"Toodle-loo." She sidestepped around the corner and was gone.

Elbowing the door shut, Joe pointed to the chair next to his. "Sit, please. You're hovering."

Ali obeyed. He hadn't touched her, and his impatience didn't bode well. What if his sole reason for being here was to keep her from talking to the press?

As if noticing her anxiety for the first time, Joe flashed a grin that worked like a tonic. "Ali, *love*, I'm not here to confirm your worst fears."

If she'd had a tail, it would be wagging. He'd called her *love*.

Joe swept her out of the chair and into his arms for a full-body hug that flooded her with warmth and the irresistible aura of Joe-ness. How did he manage to smell like the forest even in the city?

"Rina and I are colleagues. Nothing more. According to Linc, she's going to marry Lester Phillips, her latest touring partner."

"Why would he do that? Doesn't he think the baby's yours?"

Joe scrubbed a hand through his hair. "A paternity test would prove otherwise. He's young, barely twenty-one. I imagine she dazzled him the way she did me. Linc says he's a good Christian boy, which would make him easy prey for a sophisticated woman like her. You gotta feel sorry for him."

* * *

GOD, HOW HE'D MISSED HER. On the earthly plane where Ali dwelled, Joe's problems melted away like hail on hot pavement. With the right woman, a life without industry awards and hordes of adoring fans could be a happy one, the happiest. He counted on that one simple truth to sustain him in the difficult days to come.

After his stay at the Waldron Island hideaway, Joe had rejoined the tour fully refreshed. The hard-won peace was short-lived. Soon he was dodging Rina at every turn. Her charm offensive quickly devolved into harassment, a head-scratching turn of events until the sound engineer relayed the rumor that she was pregnant. *Ah-ha.* By the time the rumors made their way to the press, Rina had gone totally berserk, insisting to all and sundry that she and Joe were engaged.

All the while, Joe had noticed the dogged devotion of Lester Phillips. Of course the sweet young man had finally stepped up to rescue Rina. Joe would have pitied him if Lester hadn't seen the need to give him a public tongue lashing. He'd refused to listen when Joe swore the child wasn't his.

Joe had been the one who convinced Rina to sign with Linc. His manager had the most to lose if Joe went ballistic on his touring partner. "I know Rina's way out of line," Linc had reasoned with him. "But *please*, give her time to make this right and save face in a way that works for all of us. Don't lose sight of the fact that your duets with her are on that album you're promoting. You don't want it to fail 'cause you got fingered as the one who kicked her to the curb. And if you set the record straight with Ali, you risk getting her sucked into this mess too."

When Ali was sucked in anyway, Joe was relieved. Finally he could tell her he was all in.

As for his vocal issues, Joe had finished the tour with few the wiser, but he'd paid a heavy price. His voice was now a permanent rasp. *Move over, Tom Waits*.

Fast forward to this incredible moment when he, at long last, could be with the woman who was never far from his mind. Ali wasn't pulling away— far from it. Time to take a chance. His next move would be over the top, but what the hell …. He went down on one knee. "Ali, I've dreamed of you ever since you collapsed in the doorway of Linc's cabin." He held out the small velvet box. "Marry me, please."

Dazed, Ali opened the box and stared at the platinum ring encrusted with small diamonds.

"It was my grandmother's," he explained. "If you want something flashier …."

She clutched the box as if it might sprout wings and fly away. "Joe, how can I marry you? We hardly know each other."

Not what he'd expected. She wasn't really going to turn him down, was she?

"I know enough," he said, rising to his feet. "With all that vocal rest, I've had plenty of time to think. I won't lie to you. Being married to me will be no picnic. Until the tabloids get what they want or the public loses interest, they'll hound us to kingdom come." He cleared his throat, wishing that for once he could speak freely. This was like trying to pour your heart out from a payphone with only one quarter. "I need water." He fetched a paper cup from the bathroom.

"Joe, I don't think you should be—"

He cupped her cheek, wishing this part wasn't necessary. The part where he had to find the words to convince her. Touching her would sure beat speaking. "Shh, love, don't worry so much. One conversation won't break me. Which begs the question, could you stand being married to a has-been?"

Ali uttered a little *humph* of disdain. "What makes you think fame matters to me at all?" She frowned. "Do you still think I'm a lost waif?"

"What?"

"Something your mother said. That you were attracted to the lost waif, not the strong survivor. Which is what I actually am."

He laughed, a painful sound, and coughed. "My mother … what a character. Are you kidding? I love your strength."

"But Joe … about Rina. I know she's history, but in the future … how can I compete with women like that? You must have been crazy about her once. Perhaps you'll get tired of me too."

It was a fair question. He pictured Rina in all her glory. Lust at first sight. She'd introduced herself at a bar, and he'd embarrassed himself in a painfully comic pratfall—so goggle-eyed that he fell off the stool and bruised his tailbone. He kept pinching himself for about two months before he woke up to the fact that she was too hot to handle. Women like her were big trouble. The craving was like a drug with nasty side effects. He no longer needed or wanted her brand of poison. "Rina …" he said aloud, the name like acid in his mouth. "Rina is a spoiled child. Nothing bad ever happened to her on the way up. Always beautiful, no ugly-duckling phase. At seventeen, she was plucked out of a talent show in some Podunk town in Georgia where her family owned the mansion on the hill. And voilà! Instant stardom. Maybe having a baby will give her the kick in the pants she needs to fill that empty cavity where a heart should be. Or she will just farm the kid out to nannies. I'm done with women like that." He hoped she believed him. He was running out of voice.

"How about some tea?" Ali was already heading to the Mr. Coffee machine. After filling it with water and flipping the switch, she held up a teabag. "Chamomile?" He nodded. She walked back over and patted his knee like he was her grandson. "I just have a few more questions."

Needing physical reassurance, Joe pulled her onto his lap. "Is this okay?" She didn't resist, but her discomfort told him her surrender was conditional. "What if I do this?" He brushed a tendril of hair off her face. "Or this?" A light kiss on her neck. Another on her cheek. Finally he zeroed in on her soft lips, sweet breath, and eager tongue. Satisfied that he'd turned her to jelly, he nuzzled her hair and whispered, "You haven't answered me."

What she did next surprised the hell out of him. She laid her hands on his chest and gave him a firm shove that broke their contact. When he moved to reclaim her, she wagged a finger at him. "Joe, we both know the effect you have on me." He winced at this reminder of all the mixed signals he'd given her. "I have one main worry: I don't fit into *your* life any more than I do Jake's."

Ah, she was looking for guarantees. *I'll prove it to you*, he wanted to say.

Give me time. Still, if it was more verbal reassurance she wanted, he needed that tea. He went over to the Mr. Coffee, poured hot water over the teabag, and let it steep in silence. Blowing on it, he took a few sips, and his cords cleared a smidgeon. "Okay, shoot."

"What?"

Holding the mug in both hands, he leaned against the dresser, facing her. "Ask me questions. I swear to tell the whole truth and nothing but." That wasn't strictly speaking true. Joe needed to win this round.

"Just like that?" Her panicked expression—as if she'd blanked on her lyrics during a concert—made him smile. She knew so little about the real Joe that he had no idea where to start. Maybe getting ahead of her questions was the best strategy.

He crouched down so that they were eye to eye, close enough to touch without touching. "First, tell me exactly who belongs in my country-music-star life? It isn't real. Besides, I'm an outcast now. As for my family, we aren't close. Not since Da's death. He was our anchor. And he was just a regular-guy engineer who scored some profitable patents and timely investments. He used that money to found Big Paul's Outfitters. A down-to-earth Irishman, cracking off-color jokes up till the end, when he died of lung cancer because he preferred cigarette smoke to—" His voice was cutting out. He coughed, then finished the sentence, "to fresh air."

Eyes wide with alarm, Ali reached out to touch his hand—a quick touch meant to quiet him, not start anything. "Drink your tea. I'll take a turn. Do you want to hear about *my* father?"

Joe sipped gratefully, playing dumb. "Your father?"

"You know already, don't you?" Her startling eyes seemed to pierce right through him.

"Only the barest of details."

Ali circled around the couch to put a barrier between them. He stood too but gave her the space she needed.

"On Halloween, after you left me, I got a call from Jean-Louis. A man who looked much like Liam had come to the restaurant, asking questions. Duncan—his name is Duncan Walsh—had seen the photo accompanying the review of La Fête Sauvage in the *Seattle Times* and thought I looked exactly like my mother, who he slept with nine months before Liam and I were born. Anyway, my father is a retired commercial diver. We kept in touch with phone calls and emails, and now he has a little place in Fremont. Becca likes to call him 'the coolest dad, ever.' "

"I can't wait to meet him." Joe took a step toward her.

Her open palm told him, *not so fast*. "He wears an earring. Your mother would probably make him use the servants' entrance."

Joe tried to joke, "There is no servants' entrance. And Mom might surprise you."

Her raised eyebrows told him she wasn't buying it. "You have brothers I haven't met. I know next to nothing about them. I don't even know how old you are. Somewhere around thirty would be my guess."

He held up a finger and took several more swallows of tea. "I'm thirty-one. Then there's the priest in Philly. Edward. Thirty-five. We seldom hear from him. We are too, uh, worldly. My family ... we're Christmas-slash-Easter Catholics at this point. Dad was the religious one. We attended services to please him. After he died, Teresa, David, Jake, and I stopped going to Mass, and although Mom still throws gobs of money at the Church, she's mostly a no-show too. No one's gone to confession since they started having anything juicy to confess." He ticked off his fingers. "David, who's thirty-three, is a physician traveling in Africa with Doctors for Humankind. Great guy. Jake, well ... you know about him. Teresa's the baby. I believe she's your age. Twenty-six?"

The "baby" remark didn't land well. Ali's reply sounded defensive. "Almost twenty-seven."

Joe gave her arm a squeeze. "When's your birthday?"

"September twelfth. I'm a Virgo. Worried that our horoscopes are a bad fit?"

"I'm a Scorpio. Everyone's supposed to steer clear of us. Especially Virgos, I imagine. My birthday is November eleventh."

Hearing what sounded like a gunshot, Joe rushed over to the window to peer through the curtains.

Ali paled at his reaction. "What was that?"

"Just a car backfiring." The Ford Taurus SHO backfired again as it drove away.

"Anyone lurking?"

"I think we're safe ... for now. Teresa's the only one who knows our whereabouts. Unless I was recognized on my way in."

"Where did you go to school?" Ali asked. "You told me it was in Boston, but you never gave me the name."

"Huh?" He'd hoped they could move on to communicating with their bodies.

"I've wondered how you got into the country music scene, with your background."

My elite *background, you mean*, he thought. "Berklee College of Music. My mother would have preferred Juilliard. I started out playing classical guitar, then I was a session musician—you know, recorded with bands and sometimes toured with them, though not as an official member. One night, Linc saw me perform a few of my own songs at a Nashville bar. It was the usual random chain of events. A lot of luck involved." He looked at his watch. "It's almost seven. Hungry?"

"Do we dare go out?"

He shrugged. "How do you feel about living dangerously?"

"Your danger, not mine."

"I'm afraid you're a target now too." He paused. "What about *my* question?"

Her brow furrowed.

"Will you marry me?" He got back down on one knee.

She pulled him up. "Yes! How could you ever doubt it? No more kneeling at my feet. It makes me nervous."

Joe had to restrain himself from lifting Ali into his arms and carrying her over to the bed. First things first. He slipped the ring on her finger, kissed it reverently, and planted a long, lingering kiss on her lips. Then he gathered her in his arms, every nerve ending on fire for her, until the last of her tension melted away.

He couldn't believe they'd finally gotten to this point. With all his heart, he wanted the sex between them to be good for her. He drew back, staring at her lips, so soft and sweetly parted, then into her fathomless mountain-lake-blue eyes.

Disoriented, she said, "Joe? Is something wrong?"

The hell with it. He backed her up until she fell onto the couch and started pulling off her boots. After he tossed them aside, his palms slid over her jeans along her slender legs until his fingers reached the zipper.

"Joe …." It was almost a moan.

He remained focused on his task. "What?"

"Show me what you want. You gave me so much. Let me do the same for you."

Cradling her like a child against his shoulder, he said, "There'll be lots of time for that. Last time was so …"—*frantic and clumsy*, he thought with chagrin—"uh, rushed." He carried her over to the bed and carefully laid her down. "We have a real mattress this time. We're gonna make full use of it."

Part of her appeal for him at their first meeting had been her complete lack of artifice and vanity. And yet, it was nice to see her in flattering clothing.

As he pulled down her jeans and skimmed off her tank top to reveal her sweet curves, he thought, *Baby, you're never going to fret over a price tag again.* She was the first woman who had never asked him for anything but how to please him.

All that remained was her lacy lingerie. Her skin had taken on a rosy glow. Was he scaring her? He whispered, "Ali, are you okay? Should I slow down? I want it to be good for you this time."

"It's always been good," she whispered back, tugging at his hoodie. "It's just that … I don't want to be the only naked one. I feel too exposed—like I'm posing for a life drawing class."

Someday he would tell her how much she looked like Goya's *Naked Maja*. His chuckle sounded lecherous even to him as he stood to quickly shuck off his clothing, tossing it to the floor. "Better? Now I'm the naked one."

Her eyes fixed on his cock. "I don't remember it being that big."

He glanced down at the enthusiastic antics of Joe Junior, inflated to his full glory, and covered himself with both hands. The fluorescent lighting was better suited to an examining room. "Too scary?" he asked. He wished he'd paid more attention to atmosphere.

"Maybe a little."

A lot, he thought, judging from her saucer eyes.

Temporarily stymied, he considered his next move. Real physical intimacy took time. To give her a breather, he switched off the lights.

"Not all of them," she said in the darkness. He pulled the chain on a reading light. She was resting on her side now, buck naked, having removed her bra and panties herself.

Maybe he wasn't going to have to wait until they'd downed a few glasses of wine. He was still covering his eager hard-on, weirdly self-conscious for the first time in a long, long while.

"Don't," she giggled. "I want to see it." She reached for him. "Come here."

The pink shade of the reading light cast the room in a rosy glow. *Better,* he thought. He climbed back on the bed.

* * *

Fighting embarrassment, Ali closed her eyes as Joe's tongue worked its magic. *Hell's bells*, he was good at this …. In spite of herself, she started to buck against his mouth and make weird little animalistic mewls and moans.

"You taste like honey," he whispered, saying what she needed to hear. "So sweet, so soft, so eager for me."

She gave in totally then, panting and squirming. "Oh God, oh God," she heard herself say. "Oh, oh, oh …." The pleasure gripped her in a blinding rush and she spasmed against his mouth.

SURRENDERING TO THE LANGUOR THAT had crept over her, Ali sank back onto the mattress, only gradually becoming aware of Joe's eyes on her. Her cheeks were on fire. "Joe …" she began but stopped herself. She should apologize. What about *his* pleasure? She was a horrible lover.

"Yeeesss?" He didn't sound disappointed. He sounded … amused.

Was he mocking her? She was going to drive him wild with desire if it killed her. Tugging at his hair, she urged him upward. She knew he was still hard because his cock dragged along her legs as he shimmied up her body.

"Is this okay?" he asked, serious again.

What? Oh. He meant, was it okay to enter her. "Yes, please."

He'd already rolled on a condom. As he began to slide inside her, the feeling of fullness she experienced was utterly glorious. She let loose an extravagant sigh of pleasure. It sounded ridiculous to her own ears, but he didn't laugh. She quivered with excitement as he began to move inside her, finding a rhythm that quickly grew more urgent. Now, eyes open, she reveled in what *she* had done to *him*—his flushed face, parted lips, and frantic breathing—the way his ridiculously long lashes fluttered against his cheeks. He groaned and grunted as his body convulsed inside her.

Whoever guessed it could be like this? she marveled. She felt his eyes on her again and noted his sly grin.

"We're gonna have a blast, sweetheart."

And …? Tell me you love me, she pleaded silently.

"God, how I love you," he said, planting a soft kiss on her lips.

Hmm, she thought. *Maybe he can read my mind.*

CHAPTER 35

—————

ALI HAD EXPECTED TO ENDURE a big Catholic wedding, but Joe delighted her by suggesting a venue that was small and discreet, a half-day's drive from Seattle and available for a last-minute booking. The century-old Tokeland Hotel. He'd remembered her mentioning, during that first visit to the cabin in the woods, how Becca had treated her to a stay there for her birthday.

The tiny town of Tokeland was located on Washington's southwest Pacific coast. Joe chose the third weekend in October when he could reserve the entire place—not that it was all that large. The guest list would have fit on a Post-it Note: Becca would be Ali's matron of honor with Teresa as her only bridesmaid. Jean-Louis would officiate, Carrie O'Connell, of course, Duncan and his new girlfriend Laurie, and Linc—Joe's manager and best man.

A month ago, Ali had moved in with Becca and Jean-Louis at the chef's home in North Bend after the Himmels' rental house had been overrun by the press. Nice as Teresa was, on such short acquaintance Ali wouldn't hear of inconveniencing her by staying at her Madison Park townhome until the wedding. And no way in hell would she agree to join Joe at Carrie's place on his brief visits to Seattle. Joe had many loose ends to wrap up before their wedding, giving them precious little quality time together. Also, the doctors had warned him to baby what little voice he had or resign himself to sounding like Joe Cocker on a bad day for the rest of his life.

They exchanged daily emails, and during their in-person visits, he kept a whiteboard handy to help him conserve what voice he had. When Becca and Jean-Louis questioned the rush to marriage, Ali had pointed out that Becca's own plunge into wedded bliss might be considered reckless. She believed in

Joe's innate goodness and their rightness as a couple as surely as she believed Liam was still alive.

Her fiancé didn't act like any celebrity she'd read about and barely resembled his own carefully constructed public image. For instance, Joe's car wasn't the Lamborghini or Ferrari you'd expect of a rich celebrity, nor was it the truck he'd declared his love for in "Babe in the Woods." Just a reliable Subaru Outback. Like her, he read the newspaper comic section every day. They both liked *The Simpsons* and *Seinfeld*, and Joe was always up for Turner Classic Movies, even the ones in a foreign language. He was educating her about country music's current stars, and she couldn't get enough of Shania Twain, Tim McGraw, and Garth Brooks.

Armed with Joe's credit card and instructed to go crazy with a new wardrobe, Ali still steered clear of Barneys and Boutique Luigi Zorro. When she argued that the high-fashion stuff didn't suit her, Joe insisted he was fine with her other choices: Frye boots, 7 For All Mankind jeans, and Gap T-shirts. He liked to see her in nice things, defining "nice" as quality clothing she felt comfortable in. Teresa and Becca were both delighted to accompany her as consultants.

"Mom tried to insist on a Church wedding," Joe explained on a rare weekend visit to North Bend after floating the Tokeland idea. His voice was still croaky. He claimed not to care if he ever sang again, but Ali knew better. "Catholics don't believe you're really married unless you say your vows in front of a priest. However, to do that, you'd need a dispensation from the Bishop. That's just for starters. The process can drag on for months. Besides, I told her we'd already finalized our plans. Typical Mom, she dug in her heels—as if she had the final decision."

Ali pressed her throbbing temples and squeezed her eyes shut. "If I were a priest, I wouldn't be so keen on marrying a nonbeliever and a lapsed Catholic. Still, I hate to disappoint your mother and Edward."

Joe wrapped her in his strong arms and rubbed her back, a move guaranteed to make her melt like butter. "I don't need my brother's blessing, and my mother will come around. It's not as if she goes to Mass regularly herself. She's a product of her generation and social standing, I'm afraid. It's all about appearances."

IT WAS SATURDAY, OCTOBER TWENTY-FIFTH, and Joe and Ali were on their way to Tokeland after taking the exit from I-5 South just past Olympia toward 101 North. It was a relief to leave the heavy traffic behind. Ali stared out the window at the passing trees, worrying about the subjects they still hadn't addressed.

Ever the mind reader, Joe said, "In the woods that first time, why didn't you tell me *your* last name?"

I'd already told you too much, she almost replied, *and you were giving me nothing in return.* Reluctant to be so forthright, she said, "I now get why *you* were undercover. How often do you meet people who don't know who you are?"

He gave a small huff of laughter. "Depends on where I am. In Nashville, rarely. But even where country music isn't everyone's obsession, most people have seen my photo. They might not be able to place me, but they think I might be *someone.* I get a lot of 'Do I know you?' or 'Are you famous?' I am invariably humble and polite." He blew out an exasperated breath. "It's exhausting."

Ali touched the sleeve of his crisp, blue button-down dress shirt. Freshly shaven, with his naturally curly hair tamed by a longish buzz cut, Joe looked nothing like the rumpled woodsman she'd fallen for. "That's because you're so devastatingly handsome," she said. *Not to mention charming and charismatic,* she added silently. "Anyhow, you didn't show me yours, so I didn't show you mine. You might have been another Ted Bundy."

"Withholding your last name wouldn't deter a serial killer."

"Yeah, I didn't think that one through." Ali paused. "Do you still have the police artist sketch of me?"

"You thought I'd toss it?" Stopped at a construction zone, they watched several classic cars zip by. "They must be having a meet-up. The car owners, I mean." He took her hand in both of his and looked deep into her eyes. "Most of my search was by phone. When I finally hit pay dirt, I couldn't get your manager to divulge any details, so I stopped by. In the end, she did give me your full name and address. Both were dead ends."

Ali wanted to kick herself for what might have been. "I left that job soon after meeting you. I was hired by a small catering company to take on a number of tasks. The events were in the evenings and on weekends, so they worked better with school. And the pay was great."

Joe let go of her hand as the flagman waved them on. "At least then I knew your last name, although there are even more Ryans in Seattle than independent coffee shops."

Ali shook her head. "The White Pages have me listed as M.A. Ryan."

He swore under his breath. "*Son of a bitch.* I assumed you were unlisted. I was in Seattle to record an album, and when it was done, I had no choice but to admit defeat. I might as well have been Ponce de Léon searching for the Fountain of Youth. When the song crossed over onto the pop charts, I hoped it might bring you to me. Eventually I decided you didn't want to be found."

They drove on for a while before Joe confessed, "The sketch doesn't really look like you."

Ah. She should have known. He'd idealized her too. Her own sketches looked way more like Jake. Fortunately she'd never shown them to Joe.

"I saw your sketches of me," Joe confessed.

Ali tensed. *Uh-oh.* "When?"

"That first time I came by the North Bend house. You were drying your hair. I flipped through the sketchbook." His sidelong glance read her alarm correctly. "It's okay. I'll admit it: at first I was jealous of Jake."

"You didn't need to be."

"I know that … now."

As long as they were clearing the air …. "Joe, in the cabin that first time … if we'd made love, would you still have searched for me?" She averted her eyes for fear of what she might see in his.

With no hesitation, he replied, "Absolutely. I was a goner from the moment I saw you approach the cabin. I hope you get why I couldn't make love to you then. No gentleman would take advantage under those circumstances and"—a rueful laugh—"no condoms. If you'd pushed me hard enough, I wouldn't have said no. But I'm glad you didn't, aren't you? Can you imagine if you'd gotten pregnant? Hell of a way to start a relationship. Our path was bound to be full of snags no matter what we did or didn't do. The timing was terrible."

"And fantasy is a powerful force," Ali said, unable to help herself.

Joe gave her a startled look. "Yes, I suppose," he admitted.

She told herself to buck up. Would the prince still have loved Rapunzel if she hadn't been trapped in a tower, in need of rescue? Come to think of it, what did they do together once he'd climbed her hair? She doubted they'd discussed religion or played Gin Rummy.

Was Ali clearing the air or raising a stink? Whatever it was, she couldn't stop now. "When you came to my house that time …." She waited for him to take the cue.

"I'd hoped to get a reality check—to prove to myself you really weren't that different from the others. I was totally kidding myself. I was way past the point of no return. If we'd made love, I would have wanted more."

"When we finally, uh, had sex …. I know you took precautions, but still …. I might have gotten pregnant."

"By then I kind of hoped you would." The answer pleased her, though he had the grace to look embarrassed. "It would have forced my hand, and I wouldn't have had so much time to overthink it. If you had gotten pregnant, you'd have let me know, right? Not tried to brave it alone." When she didn't answer immediately, he gave her a concerned glance. "Linc told me he gave you his card."

"Yes," she said, grimacing as she imagined Carrie's reaction.

He went on, "I believed I had no choice but to concentrate on getting my head straight, surviving the tour with the least collateral damage. When you came to me in the woods that second time, I was blown away by your courage. After we parted ways, I know your hands were tied—I tied them by telling you to wait. God, how I wanted to talk to you after everything blew up in my face. I needed to know you still believed in me … in us."

She gave her head a frustrated shake. "Wow. You ask a lot of a girl. Because you have to know, *everyone* thought I should give up on you. Becca, Jean-Louis, my dad. But you told me to trust you, at least I think you meant to say that. I'm not much of a lip reader. I wasn't going to give up unless I had proof you were done with me."

"Teresa told me I was an idiot. I know I put you through the wringer. I can't apologize enough. If I could do it again …." His words trailed off as the car slowed to round another bend.

They didn't speak for a while. The towns had become few and far between. Ali sighed. "There's still so much we haven't worked out. Like, where are we going to live?"

"How about Paris?"

"Are you serious?" He did enjoy being flippant.

"Why not? I'm not sure you and I can settle here and be normal. They won't let us. The tabloids, I mean. Not for a while, anyway. We'd always be looking over our shoulders. I'm sorry about the job."

Ali was on unpaid leave. After the tabloids started hounding her employer and haunting the lobby of her building, she'd had to work out of the Seattle office. The tabloids quickly caught on. Joe was right about leaving normal life behind. Ali hadn't really enjoyed working in an office. She *had* enjoyed earning her own keep.

Joe went on, "I'm not asking you to stop working, get pregnant, and become a hausfrau. Why not be your own boss? Become a professional illustrator. Like I suggested earlier, with those drawings you have the makings of a fabulous children's book. Design websites. You're great at it. You can start with mine."

She gave him a dubious glance. "A children's book needs a story. But really? *Your* website?"

"Bear with me on this. My current home page is all about my image as a performer. I need something that shifts the focus to songwriter over singer. I'm going to assume the singer part is history."

She had to protest. "Joe—"

He stopped her with a karate chop. "Happiness is all about expectations. If I assume that phase of my life is over, I'll be happier. If that's not true, I'll be pleasantly surprised. The road is not paradise, believe me. I loved being on stage, but the rest of it—the travel time, the squabbles between the back-up musicians and the roadies, the drunken groupies, the hotel rooms, the lack of exercise, the unhealthy diet … yuck. It's better to burn out than fade away, right? Or so they say."

"I thought that only applied to rock 'n' roll," Ali tried to joke.

Joe snorted. "I'm a crossover artist, right? At least I won't end up performing in plunge-pool joints like in *This is Spinal Tap*. I'm not in any hurry to subject my vocal cords to another Baler Tavern-type smokehouse gig."

"Plunge-pool joints?" Ali repeated.

"Places you land when you're washed up. Smaller and smaller venues. Playing empty houses is worse. The last thing you want is to see your audience reduced to a few diehards."

Ali couldn't imagine Joe regaining enough voice to outlast his popularity. She wouldn't say that aloud, of course. How did he manage to stay so upbeat about the future after his performing career had been cut off at the knees?

"I like the idea of designing websites, only, I'm starting to feel guilty. All this good fortune. I think of other foster children, what happens when they age out. I'd like to help."

Joe gave her a thoughtful look. "We can find ways to do that. Let's both mull it over for a while."

Ten miles later, Ali said, "Not much civilization out here."

"Yeah," Joe said, as they passed a boarded-up general store. "The residents in that last town have gotta be remarkably self-sufficient. Or make frequent trips to Raymond for supplies." He reached over to caress her hair, sending tingles of delight down her spine. "Could you live in the boonies? Imagine a big, comfortable house on a decent stretch of waterfront land surrounded by tall trees, with lots of fresh seafood and neighbors who keep to themselves. Well away from any good-sized city. So far removed from other targets, the photographers would be way less likely to stage a siege."

His smile was almost beatific as the movie spooled in his head.

Ali didn't know how to respond. They'd just passed through Raymond, and calling it a town was a stretch. Any smaller than that, and they'd be reliving that Fred MacMurray-Claudette Colbert movie, *The Egg and I*. Joe continued to surprise the hell out of her. That first time in the woods—she'd assumed he was open and friendly, but now she understood that in his social life, as on stage, he put on a good show. In truth, his need for solitude made Ali look like a social butterfly. Two introverts sequestered in a small town. Hardly a recipe for connubial bliss.

Was the Joe in her current sightline as illusory as the simple backwoodsman?

Her fiancé broke into her bleak thoughts. "Eventually, I suppose, I'd—excuse me, *we*—would long for civilization. Speaking of civilization"—the look he stole was full of mischief—"we're going to Paris for our honeymoon."

All premonitions of future hardship—including visions of Ma and Pa Kettle invading their kitchen—were erased as if Joe had wiped them from a whiteboard. Ali bounced up and down as much as her seatbelt would permit. "No … really, truly? You're not joking?" She had to restrain herself from throwing her arms around his neck and causing an accident.

He chuckled. "You might like Paris enough to stay awhile. A year, maybe two …. We'll play it by ear. Then there's New York. Or London. Big international cities are a good place to hide in plain sight. People recognize you, but they are too cool to ask for autographs. Usually. Tourists are a different story. We'll alter our appearances a bit. I was thinking a Fu Manchu mustache and a Van Dyke beard. How do you feel about going blonde?"

Her laughter was forced. "Funny guy. I'm guessing it's a bad match for my skin tone. You'd get awfully tired of inquiries into my health." She added in a creaky old person's voice, "Your wife is mighty sallow, Mr. O'Connell. Is she feeling poorly?"

He chuckled. "Sallow? No way. You're pale gold. And anyway, they say there's a blonde for every skin tone."

Ali shuddered at the vision that passed before her eyes. Natalie Wood had dyed her hair blonde at one point. Gorgeous as that actress was, it had not been a good look for her.

"Don't panic, sweetie," he said a moment later, as though her thoughts were displayed on a billboard. "I'm kidding, of course. Your hair is perfect as it is. You could style it differently, maybe, for the sake of disguise. Short hair works great with oval faces—the gamine look. Like Jean Seberg."

"She met a bad end," Ali tried to joke, aware of the serious undercurrent in Joe's teasing banter. Joe hated being recognized enough to go to any lengths to prevent it. Was he going to expect her to do the Lon Chaney thing too?

"Not *exactly* like Jean Seberg. Okay, then … Audrey Hepburn. She wasn't a blonde."

"Better. But listen, I think a Van Dyke beard requires its own mustache. And a Fu Manchu mustache—"

"So, Paris …" he broke in. "You've never had a chance to live anywhere but in Washington State. I want to show you the world. There's an upside to my vocal issues—freedom. I can write songs anywhere."

"What if you're not inspired?"

"How's that?"

"Aren't country songs about suffering?"

"Not all of 'em." He waggled his eyebrows. "I have some dark memories stored up for a sunny day." In his raspy voice, he sang, " 'Nothing but blue skies from now on.' "

A moment later, his mood changed again.

"Speaking of dark memories, are you still having those dreams?"

"Not as often."

He lapsed into silence.

"Why do you ask?"

"It's just that I've been thinking … about Liam. What if there was a really good reason for his over-protectiveness?"

"Huh?"

"Those years you only vaguely remember. The phantom by your bed that won't quite materialize …."

"Yes, I know. It's occurred to me. If the face ever comes into focus, it won't help. It was definitely a man, and Frida had a revolving door of male visitors. None of them stands out in my memory. I could try hypnosis, I suppose. What would that accomplish? Does it help our mental health to recover memories? Or does it just make the pain fresh? Only Liam knows the truth."

Joe turned onto the road that hugged the coast. "You've got a point. If you did manage to unmask the guy, I'd just want to kill him, and you'd be traumatized all over again. I'm looking forward to meeting Liam. In a way, he brought us together."

CHAPTER 36

———•———

THE TOWN OF TOKELAND WOULD never rival Westport. It was basically a short stretch of rocky coast facing Willapa Bay and a lot of boggy land on the other side of Kindred Avenue—the main coastal road. Paradise for crabbers, cranberry farmers, and water fowl—not so much for tourists, though in season, you could dig for razor clams nearby.

Built in 1885, the Tokeland Hotel was conceived as a luxury retreat for ferried-in San Franciscans who wanted to shoot guns and play golf while gorging on crab, mussels, razor clams, and venison. Now it appeared faded and scuffed but as charming as Ali remembered. The majestic building was constructed from local lumber—three-storied, gable-roofed, and wood-framed.

Becca was throwing a ball to a poky, gray-muzzled Golden Retriever when they arrived. "Wait till you see the lobby," she gushed as Joe unloaded the luggage. "It's under new management, and they've totally spiffed it up."

Joe winked at Ali and sang in a soft, raspy voice, "Over the river and through the woods ...."

She frowned. "You shouldn't be singing."

"Get used to it, sweetie. You're marrying a singer. I always have a song in my head. Usually something really obnoxious."

You're marrying a singer. His words cut her to the quick. *A singer who can no longer sing.* She couldn't think about that now.

Carrie hovered close by as they checked in. "Your father would have adored this place," she said, surveying the sprawling lobby with pursed lips.

"An antique furniture warehouse must have been having a fire sale." Carrie's comfort zone did not include actual comfort.

Admittedly, few of the tables or chairs were from the same set and represented a variety of periods, woods, and finishes. The couches' upholstery didn't match, either. Faded Oriental carpets and runners thinned by decades of heavy foot traffic were scattered in an apparently haphazard fashion. The owner had to have a keen eye. Somehow all the disparate elements combined into a cohesive whole.

The reception desk, parlor, and dining room formed one spacious open-concept area, and rows of the original wooden sash windows overlooked the former golf course, now a vast expanse of green and brown marshland. Swallows swooped for bugs, and a gaggle of Canada geese congregated near the firepit.

Ali heard Linc's booming voice say, "This couch is comfortable," as he shifted about experimentally. "And will ya look at those rough-sawn-cedar walls! That stuff costs the earth now."

Joe flopped down beside him. "Looks like the original fir floors too. A few sparks and the whole place would go up like a torch."

"It's amazing that it hasn't burned down already," Linc agreed.

Carrie regarded them in growing horror.

"It's only for one night, Mom," Joe reassured her. "There's a strict no-smoking policy. Besides, you know I'm kidding."

Carrie did not look amused.

Jean-Louis, wearing an apron, emerged from the kitchen. Ali was surprised the hotel's chef had allowed him to lend a hand.

Linc said, "Hey, Jean-Louis, they've got you beat as far as taxidermy goes. I'm surprised there are any game animals left on the Southwest Pacific Coast."

"*Bof*. They did not kill all the deer," Jean-Louis said, pointing to the herd roaming around the badminton court. He sank heavily into the adjacent couch where Becca had settled in. "I do not hunt," he declared, "so I do not like things that appear too dead. Like that." He pointed at two mounted pheasant plumages and shuddered theatrically. "In my new restaurant, all the horns and heads are not only fake but not terribly realistic."

"You're not against *hunting* though." Linc sounded mildly aggrieved.

Jean-Louis gave a careless shrug. "*Évidemment non*. I don't kill wild game myself, and I don't butcher them. I don't want to see their heads and claws. *C'est sketch*! If I could, I would cook vegetarian, but I am a carni*vore* to my *core*." He chuckled at his little rhyme. "*Là là*. At least the animals we serve wandered free while they lived. To the best of my knowledge."

Becca jumped in, "He's not as into taxidermy as you might think. When La Fête Sauvage was under construction, Jean-Louis visited friends in Tucson and drove through Quartzsite on his way home. That place is one giant flea market, emphasis on the fleas. He went a little crazy. Was forced to rent a U-Haul. Everything had to be fumigated. The gilding makes them look less, uh, realistic."

Teresa, her timing excellent, burst into the room and gave Ali and Joe each a big hug. "I love this place," she gushed. "Other than my bed. It could use a new mattress. It's just as well I'm not sharing it with anyone."

Carrie scowled. "Teresa!"

Ignoring her mother, Teresa asked, "Who will officiate?"

"Jean-Louis," Becca said, as if the answer was obvious.

Jean-Louis pointed to a massive elk head. "This is my kind of chapel. The Temple of Cernunnos, the Celtic god of wild things."

"Excuse me," Carrie said, jutting her aristocratic jaw at Jean-Louis, "but I assume he jests. He is a minister of *what* church?"

"The Universal Life Church," Becca replied without a hint of apology.

As if unaware that Carrie was building up a head of steam, Jean-Louis saluted them. "A fine institution, or at least a convenient one. I send in my fee, *et voilà*, I am ordained. They believe in complete freedom of religion. 'Do what's right,' is all they ask."

"That sounds binding," Carrie said, her tartness impossible to overlook. Jean-Louis gulped, having finally understood that the queen was not amused.

Carrie bristled even more as Joe patted on the back. "Mom, I have the marriage license. All nice and legal, if not in the eyes of the Church. We might do the Catholic thing when I figure it out. That's up to Ali. This is the wedding we wanted. God won't mind, even if He *is* paying attention."

Carrie pointed to the garment bag. "Is that your wedding dress?"

Ali tried not to sound defensive. "Teresa helped me pick it out. It's nice."

"I take it it's not from Boutique Luigi Zorro," Carrie sniffed.

Ali's breath caught in her throat. Did her soon-to-be mother-in-law mean to remind her of the clothing gifts from Jake? Carrie hadn't known the origin of the cashmere dress, had she?

Wanting to smooth her mother's ruffled feathers, Teresa rushed to say, "What does it matter where it came from as long as it's what Ali wants? She would look fabulous in a burlap bag."

Ali and Teresa had found the dress at Nordstrom in the department that sold designer clothing. Wouldn't that be good enough? Apparently not.

"Is everyone here?" Ali asked, eager to change the subject.

"I think so." Teresa pointed at the ceiling. "Your dad and his girlfriend Laurie are upstairs unpacking. David really wanted to attend, but he can't just hop a plane from the Congo. Jake is, uh, busy with, uh … the new office, and Edward says he will be present for the Catholic wedding."

Seeing Ali squirm, Joe mouthed, *Don't worry.* "What about Paul?" he asked Teresa.

"On a business trip," was his sister's clipped reply. *Isn't he her fiancé?* Ali wondered. *She doesn't seem to mind his absence.* "Anyone else?" Teresa asked Ali. "Work colleagues?"

Ali had no choice but to explain. "I didn't tell them I was getting married. They are sick to death of having their business disrupted. I'm on leave. I suspect I've already been replaced, and they are trying to figure out how to break it to me."

Teresa lowered her voice. "Oh, Ali. I'm so sorry."

Ali mustered up a big smile that felt like a rictus. "Hey, it's okay. It was an entry-level position, not a dream job." She shot a glance at Joe. "I'll figure out something."

Teresa looked at her watch. "Wedding's at six, right? It's already five. Shouldn't you be getting ready?"

It took a minute for Ali to realize what Teresa had in mind. "You mean hair and makeup? Becca's going to help out, but we'll keep it simple."

It was then she noticed that Carrie appeared on the verge of a total meltdown. Her skin was ashy gray, and a furrow marred the normally taut area between her brows. "Really," she huffed, "someone should have considered these things. It's a wedding, for Christ's sake! Did you even hire a photographer?"

"We bought a bunch of disposable cameras," Joe said after a moment of abashed silence.

Teresa started to laugh, and the sound was so infectious, everyone joined in.

"Hey!" Ali's father called out as he entered the room and gave his daughter a giant hug. "What are we missing? Sounds like a good time." Laurie was wearing a red velvet pantsuit and frilly blouse, and on her, the outfit worked. It looked very psychedelic '60s. She and Duncan held hands as if unaware they were doing it.

Carrie was shaking her head. "This is going to be a real country-music wedding. You all *so* owe me. Mind you, the Catholic ceremony is going to be the event of the season. It's getting more elaborate in my head with every passing minute."

Joe kissed Ali's hand. "Sweetheart, I'm afraid this is the price of our self-indulgence."

"I can take it," she said with mock bravery.

He whispered in her ear, "It will *never* happen." Louder, he added, "I have something for you. Can we grab a moment alone? Let's check out the honeymoon suite."

Teresa gave Joe's arm a shake. "I heard that. By all means, get a room, you two."

Joe towed Ali toward the staircase. "I don't need any more encouragement than that. Let's go."

Ali endured the snickering, even knowing Joe had something else in mind. Not that she didn't want to make love to him every second of every day.

"Uh, when should I come up?" Becca asked quietly when the ribbing died down. "I'm gonna do your hair and makeup, right?"

"Give us fifteen minutes," Joe said. "You won't be interrupting anything … uh … like that."

Their room was situated at the top of the creaky stairs. Gauzy curtains framed windows overlooking the former golf course and side yard. The cozy space was dominated by the queen-sized bed—its towering headboard elaborately carved with dozens of little scrolls. The bed was topped by a white chenille coverlet and the obligatory pile of embroidered throw pillows. One cherrywood bedstand bore a vase overflowing with exotic flowers; the other, a bottle of champagne on ice and two crystal flutes. Other than that, there was space for only a rocking chair and an armoire. One wall was decorated with a simple mural of a waterfall. On the other walls, a few small oil paintings depicting birds and flowers.

The honeymoon suite was *not* a suite, and it was the size of a modest entryway. It had to be humbler than the least of the rooms Joe lived in while on tour. The bathrooms were down the hall, for God's sake. Her fiancé had chosen this venue to please her. Were Linc, Teresa, and Carrie secretly appalled by Ali's plebeian tastes? Again, how was this marriage going to work? City upbringing or no, Ali was a hick from the sticks.

Joe drew her in for a close, comforting embrace. "Sweetie, you're thinking too much again. *Relax*."

She peered up into his sympathetic face. "Why are you looking at me like that?"

"Like what?"

Like I'm an object of pity, she thought. "How am I ever going to work in your world? You can still back out, you know."

Joe appeared bewildered. "Huh? Why would I do that?"

She indicated the room with an impatient flourish. "This all must seem awfully … *quaint* to your family and friends."

Joe startled her with a burst of merry laughter. "Do you think I'd rather be staying at some five-star monstrosity in Saint-Jean-Cap-Ferrat on my wedding night? I love that you get so much joy out of simple beauty. You forget that my family didn't grow up eating caviar and lounging in castle hotels."

You couldn't forget what you didn't know, and Ali knew only the sketchiest details of Joe's past.

Be careful what you wish for, she thought. *You already know an uncomfortable amount about his romantic past.*

Questions about his childhood would have to wait. From his suitcase, Joe had pulled out a blue velvet box with a gold ribbon and opened it to reveal a single strand of pearls. He draped them around her neck and fastened the clasp, then turned her toward the mirror, his gentle hands on her shoulders instantly soothing her frayed nerves.

The necklace fairly glowed against the flush of embarrassment that suffused her skin.

He caressed her cheek. "Sweetie, what's wrong?"

"Nothing," she blurted out. "I love them. You must have known all along mine were fakes."

He shook his head. "They *looked* real enough. However, you could hardly afford your own, and your foster parents wouldn't have bought them for you." He ran his fingertips between the pearls and her clavicle, making her quiver. "They're already getting warm. I love that about pearls. It's like they're alive."

A tear rolled down her cheek. "I've never owned anything so beautiful."

"Oh, darlin', your kind of beauty doesn't require embellishments. When I first saw you, I thought you must be a water sprite. Even soaked to the skin, you were radiant." He kissed the tear away. "We should have hired a professional photographer, if only to please Mom."

She snuggled against him. "Too much of a risk, right? You don't have any photographer friends, and anyone else might have sold the photos to the tabloids."

"There is that."

A knock on the door. "That must be Becca," Ali said.

Joe walked over to let her in. "Good! She can join us for a champagne toast."

Becca gasped at the sight of the pearls and clapped a hand over her mouth. "Omigod!"

Joe handed her a plastic cup filled with champagne. "Sorry. Only two flutes."

AT SIX SHARP, JOE AND Ali exchanged their simple vows. She wore a cream-colored chiffon sheath with a plunging neckline that provided the perfect setting for the pearls. Joe took Ali's breath away in charcoal-gray slacks with a matching sports coat and white dress shirt open at the collar. No bolo tie or Stetson, but he did wear his cowboy boots.

LATER THAT NIGHT, THEY LAY entwined in the center of the big bed, the moon shining, huge and orange, outside the window. "A harvest moon," Joe said. "I ordered it special, just for us."

Ali couldn't stop smiling. "I wouldn't expect anything less."

Other than ecstatic murmurs and more whispered declarations of love, they didn't speak again.

After her husband's slow breathing told her he was asleep, Ali lay on her back, staring into the darkness. What if Joe hadn't attended that fundraiser? Whether or not he'd truly wanted her, Jake would have pushed for sex, and the strong resemblance to Joe plus his role as her rescuer might have convinced her it was the right move. What then? Nothing good. Ali hoped the brothers would reconcile at some point. Or did she? How weird would it be to see Jake at family gatherings? She stashed that worry away. Joe had turned up in time. It was fate, that's all.

What about Liam's fate? The more time passed, the more she worried he might really be dead.

Come on, Alf, get a grip. You know I'm alive. It was definitely Liam's voice.

Then prove it, she told him silently. *Come home.*

"Ali?" A hoarse, sleepy voice said. "What's up?" Joe's laugh was low and sexy. "Other than me. Are you okay?" He brushed a lock of hair from her eyes. "Are you thinking again?"

"I still know so little about you," she whispered. "And why hasn't Liam come home? What happens if Jake starts showing up at family gatherings?"

"If it helps," Joe said, soothing her with his gentle touch, "I'm not worried about any of those things. They'll sort themselves out." He planted a soft, lingering kiss on her lips. "Mm, you always taste so sweet," he whispered. "Even if Jake bursts into our house during Christmas dinner and announces that he's going to marry Rina Bakersfield, I will take it in stride. And Liam is bound to resurface soon. I can feel it in my bones." He kissed her forehead. "Can you sleep now?"

She touched his erection. "Can you?"

Joe's hand wandered downward. "Will it help you sleep?"

Ali laughed. "It might."

Eventually she drifted off into a deep, dreamless slumber.

EPILOGUE

———•———

EPHRAIM HAD NO TROUBLE ZEROING in on the object of his search, who was sitting in front of an empty espresso cup and reading a newspaper. The man calling himself Sagiv Zaslow supposedly breakfasted here every morning before work. Sagiv cut a formidable figure, even here in Jerusalem, a city teeming with rugged men trained for the military. The security guard's uniform appeared to be tailored to his muscular body. So, the man was a bit of a dandy. It amused the detective to observe how this Sagiv acted impervious to the ardent stares and giddy giggles of several of Café Rafa's female diners. Was he aware of his fan club?

Deciding that Sagiv would respond better to a straightforward approach, Ephraim simply walked over and stood next to his table until the man was forced to acknowledge his presence. *Ma Pitom*, he thought when Sagiv looked up. He had the most compelling blue eyes Ephraim had ever seen. Also the face of an angel and soft ebony-colored hair like a blackbird's feathers. His smooth skin, the color of honey, was marked on one cheek by faint shrapnel scars. More like stamps of quality on silver than flaws.

"Yes?" the man said in Hebrew, eyes narrowing. The smile was mildly amused but there was steel behind those startlingly blue eyes.

"Sagiv Zaslow?" Ephraim said.

He folded his newspaper in half. It was the *Jerusalem Post*, an English-language publication. "Who wants to know?" he asked in Hebrew.

Ephraim continued on in Hebrew as if Sagiv's American accent hadn't given him away. "Working on your English?"

His friendly smile received a frown in return. Ephraim swallowed hard. Time to defuse the air of menace that surrounded this man.

"I'm looking for Liam Ryan," he said in English, gratified to see a flash of recognition.

Still no answer. Sagiv scanned the café terrace with slitted eyes, as if bracing for an ambush.

"His family wants to know," Ephraim persisted. "His sister Ali and her husband."

The silence grew less menacing, more thoughtful.

"Here is my card," Ephraim said. "You fit the description of this man, an American who has been missing for some time."

Sagiv took the card and tucked it into the pocket of his shirt.

* * *

JOE WAS SERENADING HIS BEAUTIFUL wife on the guitar with Albeniz's *Asturias* while she lounged on the couch of their Paris apartment. Jarred by an unfamiliar sound, he stopped abruptly. The telephone in the other room was ringing. "That's odd," he told Ali.

They exchanged looks of alarm. It was nine at night—too late for casual calls. Joe ran to pick up the receiver.

"Hello?"

"Mr. O'Connell," an accented voice said, "this is Ephraim Haddad, the detective you hired in Jerusalem."

Joe's heart began to race. "Yes?"

"I met with the man Sagiv Zaslow—the one we believe is Liam."

"That's fantastic!" Joe broke in, then noticed Ali standing in the doorway, eyes wide, unusually pale. She appeared to be holding her breath.

"Not so fast," the man said. "He does not admit to being Liam. I gave him my business card and told him you and your wife are looking for him. He works as a bank guard and has a reputation for being very tough, for keeping to himself. It's possible he doesn't know his true identity. You must prepare your wife for this."

Joe glanced over at Ali, now breathing hard. Pregnant with twins, she was dealing with worse than average morning sickness. She was in no shape to embark on a stressful quest.

"Mr. O'Connell, are you still there?" Ephraim said.

"Yes, I'm here."

"This Sagiv Zaslow breakfasts every morning at Café Rafa near the *shuk*—I refer to the Mahane Yehuda market. Perhaps a family member could approach him?"

"That sounds like the best plan, yes," Joe said. "I'll be in touch. Thank you."

After he hung up, Joe asked Ali, "What if Liam were alive but didn't know who he was?"

In a tense voice, Ali said, "We know for sure it's him?"

Joe shook his head. "Sounds really promising, though. Teresa has been wanting to go to Jerusalem. Let's see if she's up for an adventure." Seeing the tears streaming down his wife's cheeks, he gathered her in his arms. "I told you," he whispered into her hair. "I feel it in my bones. Liam is alive, and he's coming home to us."

Coming in August, 2023:

Book 2 in the Olympic Peninsula Series
The Guardsman

AUTHOR'S NOTE

———·———

THIS NOVEL BEGAN AS A dream that combined two news stories. In the first, forest rangers came upon a primitive tree house in the Mount Baker Snoqualmie Forest that had existed undetected for decades, though in this instance it housed a child pornographer. In the second, a woman mourning her dead husband wandered into the Olympic National Park with her dog to scatter her husband's ashes and lost her way, both surviving on bugs and plants until they were found. My dream had me lost in the forest and finding a cabin with a gorgeous, silent man. I didn't want it to end.

Joe's struggle with hoarseness is one I can relate to, having received bad vocal training early on and also having to teach singing and perform through many respiratory illnesses.

I went back and forth on giving the Tokeland Hotel a fictional name. I've taken liberties with my version—for instance, inserting a transitional owner between Catherine and the founders of the Wandering Goose. In the Catherine days, my sister-in-law Wanda once booked the entire hotel for an amazingly reasonable price to celebrate her birthday. Funky as it was and is, the Tokeland Hotel is a magical place. The newest owners have done wonders to freshen it up, including new mattresses and mouth-watering menu options. Shoring up the 1885 building is a labor of love with many challenges ahead, and I and my friends and family are so glad they decided to take it on. If you are a fan of historic hotels, be sure to put this one on your bucket list. We visit as often as we can.

Many thanks to my wonderful sister Laura and my great friend Karin for their priceless feedback as I shared my many drafts with them. My dear friends Tina and Anna also provided support and ideas. Thanks also to Jennifer, my friend and former colleague at Coffeetown Press, who offered some key suggestions after reading an early draft. A big shout-out to the Spun Yarn Beta Readers, who I found at a crucial point in the editing process. Their critiques were invaluable.

There are five books in this series, and I hope you'll join me as all the O'Connells get their stories.

If you've enjoyed this book, please help spread the word on social media. To find the links, go to www.CatTreadgold.com.

Photo by Claudia Meyer-Newman

Cat Treadgold has been a publisher and editor, a classical singer, an Equity actress, a coordinator in Newsweek's External Relations Department, a secretary at Siemens AG, a voice teacher at Shoreline Community College, a receptionist at a major recording studio, a cater-waiter with Glorious Foods, a restaurant hostess, and a coat-check girl at a fancy New York nightclub.

Cat has an AB *cum laude* in German Literature from Princeton University, a Master of Music in Vocal Performance from the University of Washington, and a certificate in Technical Writing and Editing from the University of Washington.

She was once semi-fluent in French, German, and Italian and occasionally attempts to revive those languages.

Thank goodness she's good with computers (for a digital immigrant) and learned to touch type in high school.

Two of her unpublished novels, including this one, made it to the finals in their categories (mystery and romance) in the Pacific Northwest Writers Association Annual Contest.

Three of her one-hour adaptations of operas (original translations and dialogue) were performed by Shoreline students while she was a teacher there.

She and her husband Jeff reside in Washington during its drier months and Arizona during its cooler ones.

Cat loves to hike and walk, ride her bike, hula hoop, play golf, listen to audiobooks, cook dishes with lots of leftovers, play piano (she used to be good at it), and play accordion (she will never be good at it). She sings in the occasional concert with Ladies Musical Club, but never in the shower. Her favorite classical composers are Ravel, Debussy, and Brahms. She prefers pop music from the '60s and '70s, particularly Steely Dan and the Rolling Stones.

One hot, humid summer in Ohio, while playing a Shawnee Indian in an outdoor drama during the week and Anne in the musical *Shenandoah* on the weekends, she became certified in stage fighting. That skill later helped her win the role of a broadsword-wielding Maid Marion in a Theater for Young Audiences musical titled *Maid Marion (and Robin Too)*. She always wanted to sing the role of Carmen, but only did it in Seattle Opera previews. She has played Edwin Drood in *The Mystery of Edwin Drood*, Maria in *The Sound of Music*, Julie Jordan in *Carousel*, Cherubino in *The Marriage of Figaro*, Prince Orlofsky in *Die Fledermaus*, Maddalena in *Rigoletto*, Julius Caesar in Handel's *Julius Caesar in Egypt*, and Rosina in *The Barber of Seville*. Along with other fun gigs (including a few at Port Townsend's UpStage), her opera quartet (The Operatic Four Players) performed regularly on Friday nights for about a year at an Italian restaurant. For three years, she toured with NOISE (Northwest Opera in Schools Etcetera).

Videos of her vocal performances can be found on the Cattread channel (www.youtube.com/@cattread),

For more information, go to www.CatTreadgold.com.

CPSIA information can be obtained
at www.ICGtesting.com
Printed in the USA
LVHW040713200623
750165LV00003B/20